IN THE GRAY

B.B. REID

In the Gray by B.B. Reid

ISBN: 979-8-9885233-0-7

Chief Editor: Rogena Mitchell-Jones of RMJ Manuscript Service LLC
Co-editor: Colleen Snibson of Colleen Snibson Editing

Cover Design by Amanda Simpson of Pixel Mischief Design
Interior Design/Formatting by Champagne Book Design

That's why I called my thing The Marathon
Because I, I'm not gon' lie and portray, um, this ultimate poise
Like I been had it figured out
Nah, I just didn't quit
That's the only distinguishing quality
From me and probably whoever else is goin' through this
Or went through this, or is gonna go through this
Is that I ain't quit
I went through every emotion
I went through every emotion with tryna pursue
what I'm doing
You know what I mean?
And I think that what, what's gon' separate whoever's gon' try
to go for something is that you ain't gon' quit

—Nipsey Hussle

ALSO BY B.B. REID

Broken Love Series

Fear Me

Fear You

Fear Us

Breaking Love

Fearless

Stolen Duet

The Bandit

The Knight

When Rivals Play Series

The Peer and the Puppet

The Moth and the Flame

Evermore (novella)

The Punk and the Plaything

The Prince and the Pawn

Standalone

Lilac

The Wrong Blue Eyes (novella)

In the Gray

PLAYLIST

Mr. Untouchable—Nipsey Hussle
Ginuwine—In Those Jeans
Sure Thing—Miguel
Grinding All My Life—Nipsey Hussle
Family Affair—Mary J. Blige
Bounce Back—Big Sean
Throwed—Lil Wayne ft. Gudda Gudda
Girls Need Love Remix—Drake & Summer Walker
Hush—LL Cool J ft. 7 Aurelius
My Little Secret—Xscape
ICU—Coco Jones
Wetter—Twista ft. Erika Shevon
Nights Like This—Kehlani ft. Ty Dolla $ign
Official Girl—Cassie ft. Lil Wayne
More & More—Joe
Still Not a Player—Big Punisher
On Chill—Wale Ft. Jeremih
What It Is (Block Boy)—Doechii ft. Kodak Black

FOREWORD

Dear Reider,

In the Gray contains themes that some may find upsetting—including but not limited to—strong language, graphic sex, violence, suicide ideation, drug use, morally gray characters, an aggressively dominant hero, an emotionally traumatized heroine, taboo relationships, and various kinks.

If you are concerned about your mental health, please check my website prior to reading for details or scan the QR code below.

Happy Reading!

IN THE GRAY

ONE

Atlas

IT WAS STILL THERE.

The old factory across the street.

The red brick building loomed three stories high, dominating this tiny low-income corner of Idlewild. I'd been lingering on the sidewalk on the opposite side of Temperance Street, watching the locals come and go. The cold rain had soaked through my hair and clothes, but at least it had hidden my tears.

Relieved that I hadn't made this trip in vain, my guard lowered for a *second*, enough time to embrace the kernel of hope blooming in my chest at finding this once-derelict edifice still standing.

A second was all it took for my mind to drift.

And for the still-healing wound to rip open again and bleed my grief all over the pavement.

Don't.

Lowering my gaze, I studied the faded photo in my hand once more. It was the only clue that I was at the right place.

There were differences, of course.

According to the date artfully written on the back in a feminine script, it had been twenty years since the photo was taken. The arched windows were no longer broken, the dead grass had been restored and shorn, the crumbling brick refortified, and the missing parts of the roof had been replaced.

But it was the massive basalt statue on the front lawn that had caught my attention and confirmed I'd found it—*them*.

Lions.

Four of them.

One roaring, one hunting, one searching, and one still.

Carved in the black rock were three words that sent a chill down my spine.

Pride of Kings.

I shivered and reminded myself that it was winter, and even Mississippi was cold in January. This had to be the coldest winter I could remember in a long time.

I ignored the warning creeping down my spine as I surveyed the building, searching for a way in.

Of course, I could just walk through the front doors and pretend I needed my car repaired, but that wouldn't get me close to the Kings. It probably wouldn't even get me in the same room as them, and it wasn't as if I could walk right up and say, "Hey, we need to talk."

Their reputation preceded them even hundreds of miles away, where their names were mentioned with the same reverence as a platinum-selling rapper or professional athlete. Except they weren't. The Kings were four ordinary men working ordinary blue-collar jobs—or would have been if not for their outlandish moniker.

My limited funds also meant paying for repairs I didn't need wasn't an option.

How much it had cost the Kings to gut and modernize the old factory to make room for the thriving mechanic shop? The outside still maintained some of its rugged appearances, blending in with the rest of the neighborhood as if the new owners hadn't dared be caught gentrifying.

A woman dressed in business attire left the building, and the sign on the door caught my eye as it swung closed behind her.

It should have bothered me that I barely considered what I'd do if I actually succeeded before darting across the two-lane street, but it didn't. This was the least reckless thing I'd done since I got that photo a week ago. It was just after noon, so the lunch-time traffic rush made not getting run over a task, but I somehow made it safely across, barreling through the front doors and into the waiting room before I could reconsider.

It wasn't as if I had anything left to lose.

The circulating heat slapped me in the face, and a few seconds later, I could feel the stabbing tingling in my toes and fingers as my frozen limbs began to thaw.

I took a wary look around.

The shop seemed even larger inside, with its tall ceilings and mostly open space. There was a wall of glass, interrupted only by a blue metal door marked Employees Only, behind the U-shaped reception desk. The window separated the waiting room from the workshop, where I could see the mechanics hard at work.

Facing the reception desk was another set of double doors leading out to the side of the building and drop-off area. Waiting on the other side, with only heat lamps and thick winter coats bearing the Pride of Kings logo to warm them, were the two young valet boys I'd glimpsed during my hour-long recon.

I spotted more chairs and tables where customers who'd chosen to wait for their repairs lounged comfortably. A few were perusing the well-stocked coffee and snack bar on the far side of the room. Adjacent, on either side, was a storage closet and bathrooms.

"Hello. Welcome to Pride of Kings. How can I help you?"

I followed the high-pitched sound and spotted a petite white girl with inviting blue eyes and blonde braided pigtails behind the receptionist's desk. Her peach-painted lips moved at a pace too fast for me to keep up, and I just stared until it got weird fast.

My first thought was that she was pretty. Young too. She couldn't have been older than her late-twenties.

My heart finally slowed enough for the receptionist's voice

to penetrate, but I still didn't respond. The words seemed stuck in my throat, and the longer it took to un-fuck myself, the deeper the furrow in her brows became until she was shifting on her feet and subtly looking around for help.

Shit.

"Sorry, um, hi," I greeted awkwardly. The receptionist's wary smile returned, so I took that as an invitation and approached the counter. "I saw that you're hiring." I thumbed over my shoulder toward the sign on the door. "Is the position still open?"

"That depends. Can I ask your name?"

"Atlas Beck," I offered. "Call me Atlas."

"Hi, Atlas. I'm Tuesday. We do have a position that just opened up. We need a part-time technician with at least one year's experience." *Fuck.* My shoulders deflated as I thanked her and backed away. As I pivoted on my heel, already considering plan B, she called out, "We're also looking for a full-time receptionist!" I looked over my shoulder in time to see Tuesday sliding an application toward me with a gentle smile. "No experience needed."

I rushed back to the counter and snatched the paper and pen she'd set on top. "Thanks." I gave her a close-lipped smile before leaving as quickly as I came. Instead of filling it out, I folded and slipped the application inside my pocket before resuming my watch from across the street.

The twelve-foot windows made it easy to scope out the activity inside. Beyond the waiting room, I spotted an old-school Camaro with burnt-orange paint and white stripes hovering above the ground in one of the stations closest to the waiting room. A brooding man in gray overalls tinkered under the carriage, and while his focus was on the car, I cataloged every magnificent detail.

Brown dreads were piled on top of his head while the top of his gray overalls hung from his waist. Sweat and oil had stained the once-white T-shirt clinging to his muscles like glue. I didn't know if the sun had chosen him personally as a spotlight or if the high-yellow undertones in his light brown skin were just that vibrant. The mystifying glow seemed to take over his complexion like a full-body halo.

Right now, his thick brows were bunched in frustration while the slight scowl on his wide mouth made him look anything but angelic.

Sinful was more like it.

Even from this distance, I could tell he was fine.

The traffic, the buildings, and the people rushing around me faded away as I studied him without his knowledge. I felt myself getting sucked in, so I forced myself to look away and took the photo from my pocket as if it were the key to what I was supposed to do next.

The edges were wrinkled, and the image faded, but I could still almost make out every nuance of the smiles on the five teenagers frozen in time. They were posing and dressed in their best—Sean Jean, Rocawear, and FUBU—as a party raged in the decrepit factory behind them.

None of them looked a day over sixteen.

I focused on the boy on the far left, who possessed the same aura as the man in the window, except he was smiling shyly instead of frowning. In the photo, he had short curly hair instead of dreads, and a strong jaw and facial hair replaced his baby face. But the most obvious evidence that twenty years had passed was how well he now filled out his shirt. The muscles in his arms bulged against the white cotton—unlike how the red material he wore in the photo dwarfed him.

At that moment, I knew I'd found one of the Kings.

The brooding mechanic before me was the same shy teenager in the photo, much older now, but I was sure of it.

For some reason, the knowledge only brought me sadness and regret rather than triumph. I had a pretty good guess why as I traced the curves of his once-innocent face.

Not the same after all.

His crown of light wasn't as bright now as it had been twenty years ago. Someone or something had dimmed it.

My mournful sigh billowed in the cold air before disappearing in the wind as I pocketed the photo without looking at the others. There was no need. I'd been staring at their faces every night since I received the photo.

I knew exactly which King I'd found.

The squeal of brakes announcing a city bus's arrival nearly made me jump out of my skin as it rolled to a stop in front of me. One shake of my head at the driver, and he pressed the gas to keep going. The moment the bus no longer blocked my view, my gaze traveled back to the window—to the man inside it.

I sucked in a breath as my stomach dipped and the ground felt like it had slipped from underneath me.

The mechanic was watching *me* now.

Judging by his comfortable perch—his shoulder pressed against one of the many window panes—it looked like he had been aware of me all along and had waited for the moment my guard was down.

I didn't breathe. I didn't blink. I just stood there like an dummy with a death wish as he openly waited for what I would do now that I'd been caught. There was nothing in his expression to guide me either. No hostility, paranoia, or curiosity. Just impassive patience for me to make a move.

So I did.

With more grace and nonchalance than I possessed, I turned and walked away.

There wasn't much left on Temperance Street. The pandemic had hit the economy hard, forcing most businesses to close. We were finally past the worst of it, returning to some semblance of normality. For this tiny street on the outskirts of Midtown, only Pride of Kings, a Caribbean café, seafood restaurant, hair salon, liquor store, convenience store, and car wash, remained. The other buildings were bleakly vacant.

I entered the mostly empty café, and the hostess seated me immediately. When the waitress, who introduced herself as Tanisha, arrived and tried to hand me a menu, I declined and asked for a glass of water instead. She paused, probably realizing I had no money, before rolling her eyes and leaving to get my water.

Once alone, I exhaled and stared at the hideous brown tabletop before praying to God that I hadn't screwed up my chance.

You've been lied to.

Find the Pride of Kings.

"Here you go." The waitress slammed my water down, making most of it spill on the table. Before I could check the bitch, the bell above the door chimed, and we both became distracted as we watched two of the finest men I'd ever seen swagger in like they owned the place.

Oh shit.

Immediately recognizing one of them, I slid further down in the booth.

My waitress had the opposite, and probably normal, reaction. Tanisha began to primp.

Of course, the one leading the pack was Mr. Dread Head himself.

Golden Boisseau.

"Hey, Golden! Hey, Roc!" the friendly hostess greeted as she rushed up to them. It was pretty comical since she couldn't have been taller than five-three, and both men were well over six feet. The sight reminded me of a small dog jumping, yipping, and running around your feet for attention when you came home.

"What's up, Desi." Only the man I now knew was Roc bothered to speak back.

The hostess didn't seem surprised, though. She just grabbed two menus from behind the stand and batted her fake lashes. "You want your usual table?"

"Thanks, baby," Roc cockily answered for them both once again.

Golden didn't so much as nod. His wide lips remained flat as his gaze surreptitiously swept the diner.

Somehow, I knew he was searching for me.

I slid down a little lower until my chin touched my heaving

chest, but in the end, it only made me look like a fool. Golden spotted me anyway and wasted no time starting my way with Roc on his heels.

Fuck, fuck, fuck!

"Um...so you have to leave," Tanisha informed me.

Caught off guard, I tore my gaze away from the duo to look up at her. "What?"

"Leave!" I barely registered her commend before she snatched my glass from the table and hurriedly wiped up the mess she'd made.

I blinked. "Why?"

"Because this is their table. That's why!"

I looked around at the other four or five empty tables before returning my stare to the waitress. "I'm not going anywhere," I snapped, even though that was exactly what I wanted to do. "And I'd like another water."

Golden and Roc could just sit somewhere else.

"No. If you're not going to order food, you need to leave. I know your broke ass don't have any money." Tanisha smirked while holding my glass of water out of reach.

I parted my lips to curse her out when the glass was snatched from her hand by none other than the sexy mute himself. The three of us watched in stunned silence as he gently set the glass back on the table before me. Thanks to Tanisha, it was only half full now, but thirst was the least of my problems.

"I—thank you." I waited for a reply or even a nod of acknowledgment, but Golden just stared at me.

Oh, boy.

"The fuck you over here plexing on little girls for, Tanya?" Roc snapped while remaining completely unaware of the tension between his boy and me. As if it was the worst thing Roc could do to me, irritation surged at him calling me a little girl. I had no idea how old they were, but my guess was mid-thirties.

"It's *Tanisha*," the waitress corrected.

"It could be Tina fucking Turner, and you'd still be out of

line. It's a damn table, girl. It's not that serious. Go get us our usual and hurry the fuck up."

Mouth agape, I watched Tanisha scurry off to do as she was told. *It couldn't be me.*

I was so caught up in watching everyone scattering like roaches when you hit the lights that I didn't notice the cause of it all sliding into my booth until it was too late.

"Uhh…" I wrinkled my nose at the sight of Roc and Golden, now sitting across from me. "What are you doing?"

"Sitting down. Having lunch," Roc answered while holding my gaze. There was a slight dip in his brows, and I could tell he was trying to place where he might know me from. Golden must have told Roc he'd caught me staking out their business.

Meanwhile, I was stuck on how unbelievably gorgeous they both were.

Roc had rich brown skin, long lashes, chestnut eyes, a thick patch of hair adorning his chin, a thin mustache and beauty mark above his thick lips, and enough waves in his close-cut hair to make you seasick.

And from what I glimpsed underneath his white ribbed tank and open long-sleeve uniform shirt, his chest, shoulders, and arms were a mosaic of colorful tattoos. One of them was a child's hand gripping the forefinger of a much larger one with a date under the wreath of sunflowers adorning the child's wrist. Written across his chest in Old English were the words, "Only Halo Can Judge Me," which I found odd but decided against asking about it.

I'd known the moment Desi called his name that I'd found another one of the Kings.

Like Golden, Roc was taller and bigger than his younger self, with the same mischievous glint from the photo. Each time my gaze fell on his image, I couldn't help returning his infectious grin and feeling the same pull growing in my chest now.

My gaze traveled to Golden, who was staring out the window like we weren't even here—like he hadn't followed me to this diner.

I flicked my fingers at them dismissively. "Well, go sit somewhere else."

Roc blinked his surprise that I dared to order them, and I could have sworn that was a smirk playing at the sensual curves of Golden's lips.

They both stayed put.

"Why would we do that?" Roc returned. "This is our table. *You* leave."

But you just said...

Roc was grinning now, his almond-shaped eyes practically glimmering, and I decided not to give him the satisfaction of going off. Rolling my eyes, I tore the wrapper from my straw and dropped it in my glass before taking a long sip to gather my thoughts.

"Aye, you look familiar. Who yo people?"

Choking on the cold water, I coughed for several seconds while they stared me down like I was a weirdo. I guess my reaction had been pretty weird. "You don't know them," I rasped.

"You don't know who I know. Answer the question."

"No."

Dumb for my cause, necessary for my ego.

I wasn't lining up to be stepped on by men who already had too much power. It didn't matter that I'd thrown away the opening I needed just to prove a point. I'd find another way in. One that wouldn't make me another bowing and preening subject.

My mama had always said my stubbornness would be my downfall.

I hadn't spoken to her since I left home. I never even told her where I was going or for how long. I knew she wouldn't care. She was trapped in a fog of grief so thick I knew it would be weeks before she noticed I was gone.

Just like I knew Dad would be disappointed that I'd run away.

Guilt ate away at the carcass of my soul, so I took another sip of water to wash down the bitter taste.

"Okay," Tanisha announced her return. "Oxtails, mac and

cheese, yams, and lemonade." She set down the first steaming plate in front of Golden, and my mouth watered. "And rice with peas, jerk shrimp, cabbage, and Coke." Roc stole a plantain from the plate before she could even finish setting it down. "Is there anything else I can get you?"

"Yeah," he spoke with his mouth full. I cringed as he regarded the waitress. "Get her whatever she wants." He nodded to me while staring her down. "It's on the house too."

Tanisha paused like she wanted to object, but when Roc simply looked away to answer his ringing phone, she sighed and turned to me. "What would you like?"

Feeling my stomach growl, I decided not to let my pride get in the way of a free meal. "I'd like the jerk chicken sandwich and fries, please."

"Coming right up," she said before flashing a fake smile at the same time Roc finished his call. "So, what are you doing la—"

"Aye, we good," he cut her off while typing on his cell. "We don't need nothing else."

Tanisha resembled a dying fish, but Roc didn't notice as he gave his phone his complete focus. The waitress stood there for a second longer before slowly walking away. As soon as she did, Golden leaned over to whisper in Roc's ear.

So he does talk.

I was almost fascinated as I watched his lips move. His mouth was downright sinful, which was a shame since he didn't seem to use it much.

Or maybe he found better ways to put it to use.

Before I could decide if the turn my thoughts took were weird or not, Roc started cracking up. "You're probably right, bruh." I frowned. Why had Roc been staring at me when he said that? Oh, fuck. They were talking about me, weren't they? "My boy said you might not want to eat that food when it comes. Tanya probably spit in it."

"Tanisha."

"What?" Roc's brows dipped in confusion.

"The waitress's name. It's Tanisha."

He waved me off. "It's whatever the fuck I say it is. So where you from?"

I blinked at how quickly he switched topics before responding with a question of my own. "Why?"

"Aye, you rude as fuck, you know that?" He was scowling now, all trace of humor and goodwill gone as he stared me down. "I want to know because Golden said he saw you scoping our place of business like you the Feds or something."

A moment later, I froze when I felt something cold and hard press against my knee.

"And in case you're wondering, that shit isn't rhetorical. I'll blow your fucking kneecap off if I don't like your answer."

I cleared my throat, forcing the tremble from my voice before I allowed myself to speak. "I'm supposed to believe you'll shoot me in front of all these people?"

"Why not? They get paid not to see shit, and I've been itching to use that meat grinder they got in the back."

The hard look in his eyes made it clear he wasn't fucking around.

"Where I'm from is irrelevant since I'm never going back. And for your information..." I glared at Golden, who was picking at his food as if he'd already lost interest. "I wasn't watching you," I lied. "I needed a job, and I saw you were hiring." I paused, waiting for some indication that he believed me. When none came, I said, "I can prove it."

I reached into my back pocket and snatched free my proof without regard for the gun Roc had pointed at me. Then, unfolding the application, I slammed the paper onto the table before pushing it toward him.

Roc merely glanced at it before meeting my gaze again. "It's not filled out."

I waved at the table and the restaurant in answer. "I was about to when you two followed me here like paranoid creeps."

The next few moments were the longest of my life as I waited for Roc to decide whether or not to shoot me and grind me into little pieces. Or maybe he'd be cruel and turn me into ground meat while I was still alive. I wasn't sure I'd make an amazing stew.

"Oh, aight," he said, shocking me before sitting back and putting his gun back in his waist like it was nothing.

I'd barely processed the news that he wasn't going to kill or maim me before the waitress showed up with my food.

I took one look at the suspicious-looking meat sandwiched between the brioche bun and pushed the plate away. Roc cackled when he saw my nose turned up and was back to grinning and looking partially sane.

"It's chicken, baby girl, I promise you. And I was kidding about Tanya spitting in your food. She got rocks for brains, but she ain't suicidal."

With a commanding look, he pushed the plate back toward me. After a second of deliberation, I picked up the sandwich and sniffed it before taking a reluctant bite.

The moment the greasy morsel touched my taste buds, I began scarfing the sandwich down.

I felt Roc and Golden watching me, but I didn't care about my table manners. I couldn't remember the last time I'd eaten. The only thing that had mattered was getting to Idlewild, finding whoever had sent me the photos, and forgetting why I'd left home in the first place.

"You said you're never going back to wherever the fuck you came from," Roc said after a few moments of watching me eat. "Why is that?"

"Does it matter?" I questioned after swallowing my mouthful.

Leaning forward, Roc braced his tatted forearms lined with thick veins on the table. I gulped down my food under the intensity of his gaze but didn't allow myself to look away. "You said you needed a job, right? Then it matters, so consider this an interview. And, baby girl?" At the answering rise of my brows, he said, "You better impress me because you won't get another."

My gaze darted to Golden, staring at me as he silently waited to hear my story.

I sat back and turned toward the window when I felt that familiar wave of anguish wash over me. I didn't need Roc or Golden to see it and feel sorry for me. I didn't need their pity. I needed answers.

I needed to know why some invisible hand had pointed me in their direction at the worst time of my life.

If I looked hard enough, I could see the reflections of my life—my *lie*—playing out in the finger-smudged glass. For the first time in weeks, I didn't push away thoughts of my father. He'd been the best dad a girl could ask for, and I didn't realize it until it was too late to tell him so. Because of my parents' lies, I didn't know just how lucky I'd been.

"I'm never going back because there is nothing left for me in Ossella." Turning away from the window, I met both of their gazes' head-on. "My dad died."

TWO

Rowdy

"WHO LET THIS BITCH IN HERE?"

I was screwing the oil cap back on a customer's blue Acura when I looked up and saw the last person I expected to see standing next to me.

Nipsey's "Mr. Untouchable" blasted from the workshop's speakers, but my voice still carried over the music. I watched the technicians—Tony, Shawn, Isaac, and Will—look at each other before gaping at me. They already knew what time I was on.

"Really, Rowdy?" Stiletto heels clacked the pavement as the bitch I'd been fucking on a semi-regular basis came to pose in front of me. Savannah was this semi-famous biracial Instagram model with good pussy and even better head. That was about as much as I cared to know about her. "I need to talk to you," she said. She'd been messaging me that bullshit all week. "You can't avoid me forever."

I didn't bother responding since Isaac and Shawn were now pointing at Tony.

It *had* to be the new guy.

Hudson was already on my back about employee retention after I put Tony's predecessor in a coma. I knew I'd hear his mouth once it reached his ears that he'd have to find yet another technician.

Now ask me if I gave a damn.

It was hard to find good help these days. Having employees was like having kids without the pleasure of busting a nut first. They wanted you to hold their hands for every little fucking thing, so I treated them accordingly.

Seven years ago, Roc, Golden, Joren, and I had pooled our ill-gotten funds together to buy and restore this old factory, and Pride of Kings was born. Going legit had its ups and downs, but it beat being carried by six or judged by twelve.

"Can you read?" I asked the moment I stood so close to Tony I could smell the coffee on his breath. He raised his hand, but only after realizing he'd already been snitched on.

The new guy was a good size, but he didn't come close to my six-foot-six, and unlike most guys my height, I wasn't all skin and bones. I had muscle. It was rare I came across someone bigger or stronger, but even if I were five-foot-three and a hundred pounds soaking wet, it wouldn't make a difference. I'd been born with the heart of a lion.

"C-can I—"

"Can you read?" I snapped since he seemed to be deaf too.

"Yes, boss. I can read."

Without breaking eye contact, I pointed to the blue metal door separating us from the lobby and waiting room. The lounge was super lux, thanks to Hudson, the general manager we hired since none of us cared for the business responsibilities that came with owning the shop. The couches were plush, the Wi-Fi was free, and we even had a minibar stocked with free snacks and drinks. "What does the sign on the door say?"

"The door, boss?"

"I hate repeating myself, Tony."

"Oh. Sorry. It, uhh, um… Well, it says… Employees Only."

"Does she look like an employee, Tony?"

"N-no, b-but she said she was your girlfriend."

My eyebrows rose at that. Oh, Savannah was a bold one.

I'd never had a girlfriend—ever. I definitely wasn't claiming someone who had my dick down her throat within five minutes of meeting me. It wasn't even how fast Savannah let me use her body that turned me off. I didn't play games, so I admired a confident woman who went for what she wanted. It was how little respect she'd been willing to accept from me in return.

I'd met Savannah on one of the rare nights I had time to kick back and actually enjoy my life. The Instagram model had walked right up to me and introduced herself. I liked what I saw, so I told her that her name wasn't as important as how fast she could make me come. Two minutes later, she was on her knees for me in one of the bathrooms. One subpar nut later, I had her bent over the sink. She'd been blowing me up like she was my bitch ever since.

"Oh, did she?"

Tony eagerly nodded. He probably thought throwing a helpless female under the bus would take the heat off him, but it just made me want to beat his ass that much more.

"So, when in the three days you've known me did you become an expert about my personal life, Tony?"

I appeared calm, but I was one wrong syllable away from blowing his head open. I had a lot of enemies, so I needed people around me whose heads were more than empty buckets, people who possessed critical thinking skills that should have developed in the third grade. It was the reason I'd never make a bobblehead like Savannah Goode my girl.

"I'm not. I just didn't think—"

The back of my hand flying across his face cut off the rest of his sentence. I slapped him three more times before his spit could even finish hitting the ground. Feeling no remorse whatsoever, I watched Tony stumble and cup his face. "That's right, Tony," I said coldly. "You didn't think."

"I'm sorry!" he cried out like a bitch.

"Are you yelling at me, Tony?"

Still cupping his cheek, he quickly shook his head while backing away so I wouldn't hit him again.

I turned my attention to a giggling Savannah and studied her with a blank expression before shaking my head and grabbing her arm. "Come on."

Thinking we were going somewhere private to talk or fuck like she wanted, Savannah happily followed. The other mechanics had already returned to work like it was just another day. Sadly, it was since I had to slap, fuck up, or fire at least two of them once a week.

It was like I said before. Good help was hard to find.

I led Savannah through the pedestrian door next to the loading doors, where we drove the cars in and out.

The gates on either side of the building were locked and controlled by electronic key fobs given to the employees or remotely from the app that only Joren, Roc, Golden, and I could access.

I led her through the gate that overlooked the street, and the moment we reached the sidewalk, I let her go and left her stewing on the curb like yesterday's trash.

I had no problem slapping grown men around like bitches, but violence against women was a hard fucking pass for me.

"Rowdy, you can't keep treating me like this!" Savannah screamed at my retreating back. "You have to talk to me!"

"No, the fuck I don't. Take your ass on, Sav."

Walking back inside, I pulled my phone from my work pants to check the time. Roc had actually taken some initiative for once and hired a new receptionist three days ago. She was supposed to be starting today—four minutes ago, in fact—but hadn't shown her face yet.

I searched my memory for her name but came up short and decided I didn't care. I wanted to greet her as soon as she arrived so I could get her ass to work immediately and warn her not to piss me off.

Golden had already given me the four-one-one on her, so I

was keeping my eyes open and a bullet with her name on it if she turned out to be the opps.

Returning to my station, I folded all six-foot-six of me inside the tiny Acura before driving it around the block for a test drive. I then dropped the keys and car off with one of the valet boys.

Dre was a seventeen-year-old dropout from my old neighborhood who had been in serious need of a positive role model when I hired him a year ago. He wasn't going to find it in me, but I gave him a job anyway, hoping I could at least save him from a worse fate. I knew firsthand what happened to young black boys when left with no other options.

Once repairs were completed, Tommy—our other valet—and Dre would take the car next door to Master Bubbles for a complimentary wash before handing over the keys to reception to settle the bill and return the vehicle to the customer.

I disliked dealing with the customers myself because even though my work ethic was solid, my customer service needed work. I was blunt and impatient in all aspects of my life and didn't give a fuck who was on the receiving end. It was the reason my boys and I hired Hudson since that bow-tie-wearing square could barely change a tire. That old fucker had a business degree, wisdom, and patience, which made him the perfect face for our business. I just liked fixing cars and making money. I had no interest in being anyone's poster boy.

Checking the time again and realizing our new hire was now twenty minutes late, I wandered over to reception, where Tuesday was manning the desk, to see if she'd at least called.

"Morning, boss," Tuesday absently greeted as she hung up the phone and started typing something into the computer.

Tuesday was one of the first people we'd hired after our business took off and one the few people whose ass I never had to get in since she possessed two of my favorite Ps—proficiency and proactiveness. Some might say she took her job a little too seriously, but I appreciated that shit. I made sure to show it, too, with a fat bonus at the end of every year.

"Sup. That new hire here yet?" I looked around the waiting room but didn't see anyone that fit the bill. Roc had mentioned she was young as fuck but hadn't specified how young.

"No," Tuesday answered with a grimace, already knowing how I was, "but she called and said she'd be a few more minutes." She tried to give me a reassuring smile, but it wobbled a little.

I ignored Tuesday's feeble attempt to calm me and ran my tongue over my teeth with an audible "tch." "Aight."

I nodded and turned on my heel.

I couldn't promise I wouldn't fire this new receptionist as soon as she walked her unpunctual through the door.

I returned to the workshop and started up the stairs to the second floor, where Hudson and the four of us had our own offices overlooking the workshop floor. Mine was the biggest and the only one with a full bathroom since none of them had been willing to fight my ass for it.

Noticing the light underneath Joren's door, I prowled down the concrete platform that was more like a balcony than a hallway with its metal balustrade facing the front windows overlooking the street. I then barged inside Joren's office without knocking.

With his bald head in his hands, Joren sat behind his desk, looking like his dog had died.

"The fuck wrong with you?" I barked.

Slowly raising his head, I realized what was up the moment I saw Joren's bloodshot eyes.

His dumb ass was hungover again.

Joren was the oldest of the crew, beating me by five days, but no one would ever guess that since he was still immature as fuck.

"Fuck you, O. I'm tired. I didn't get any sleep last night."

"Maybe you should take your ass to bed at a decent hour instead of partying and fucking bitches every night like you don't have a wife at home." I shrugged and checked my phone's notifications. Joren was my best friend, but I wasn't about to listen to him whine about bullshit. If he needed a shoulder to cry on, he was going to have to call up a bitch or maybe Golden or Roc.

Golden's ass never talked anyway, so he was the perfect person to vent to.

Joren and I had become friends when we were nine. He'd found me getting jumped by some older kids from Unity Garden and helped me fuck them up. There had been no questions asked when he came to my aid, and we've been best friends—brothers—ever since.

We were the closest out of the crew, our bond cemented by something more permanent than blood. It was an invisible pull that felt like an extension of myself, a phantom limb that could never be severed.

Before my parents decided the hood wasn't a good environment to raise a child and moved us to the suburbs, Joren and I had grown up in Third Ward together. It didn't matter, though. The low-rent district had always been home and was the reason I'd chosen this old factory at the heart of it to set up our shop.

Roc had grown up in Unity Garden to the north and Golden in Hooker's Cove to the east. Together, we cut down anyone in our path, taking power, wealth, and whatever the fuck we wanted until the city had no choice but to bow.

Our unlikely bond had even earned a tenuous ceasefire between the three feuding territories, and to honor it Third Ward became known as King's Cross.

I heard a knock at Joren's door and looked over my shoulder just as Hudson walked in with his exasperated gaze zeroing in on me. I grinned at him, already guessing why he'd tracked me down. "Rowdy, please tell me you did not assault another employee."

"All right." I shrugged. "I won't tell you that." Crossing my arms, I leaned against Joren's desk, who promptly closed his eyes and rested his head against the desk. Unlike Hudson, he already knew reasoning with me was pointless.

Hudson might run the show, but my boys and I ruled it all. This was our kingdom, our pride, and Hudson, wise as he was, was just another subject.

"Rowdy…" he tried again with a sigh.

Showing all thirty-two of my pearly whites, I sat on Joren's desk and rested my forearms on my thighs before speaking. "First, tell me who you heard it from so I can fuck them up too."

"This isn't a laughing matter," he fussed. "Do you want another lawsuit? Or maybe an assault charge this time? I swear I'll stand as a witness this time if Tony does press charges. Actions have consequences, and despite what you believe, young man, you aren't untouchable. You're a businessman, not some aimless street hooligan. It's time you behaved like a grown-up."

Brows raised, I looked over my shoulder at Joren, who silently shook his head, forehead rubbing against the wooden surface of his desk. He already knew Hudson's words had gone in one ear and out the other.

With a quiet chuckle, I stood and clapped our business manager on the shoulder, making sure to tighten my grip just long enough for him to remember who the fuck I was before leaving Joren's office without a word spoken.

Yeah, Hudson had book smarts, but streetwise, he was as green as they came. It was the only explanation for why he thought he and his bow tie could check me and get away with it.

Feeling my stomach growl and remembering I'd skipped breakfast and was still hours away from eating lunch, I headed to the lobby to grab a snack from the mini bar.

And to see if that new receptionist had shown her fucking face yet.

"Sir, I'm sorry you aren't happy with your service," Tuesday said as soon as I stepped foot in the lobby, "but you're still required to pay your bill to retrieve your car."

Looming at the counter was this Mannie Fresh lookalike who, judging by the girth of his stomach, must have eaten grown men whole for breakfast, lunch, and dinner.

I gritted my teeth and forced my feet in the direction of the snackbar.

Contrary to what Hudson thought, I wasn't some unhinged lunatic. I was perfectly aware that a room full of paying customers meant I wasn't the best person to step in and handle the situation. Tuesday could usually hold her own, so I would merely observe for now and step in only if—

"Bitch, I don't care if you're sorry!" he roared while pounding his meaty fists on the counter and making Tuesday's pale when she jumped. "I want my car! I'm not paying for shit!"

Upon hearing that, I swiftly changed directions and made a beeline for the reception desk.

"Sir, if you can't calm down, I'm going to have to ask you to leave."

"I'm not going anywhere without my whip," Mannie Fresh threatened.

"Then I'll have to call the cops."

"Put that down," I told Tuesday when she reached and lifted the phone receiver.

I could see the relief in her blue eyes when she saw me approaching. Obediently, she replaced the phone on the hook. The last thing I needed was IPD swarming my place of business.

Mannie, the killer whale, was looking me up and down now as I accepted his paperwork from Tuesday.

"Who is you?" he spat, violence brewing from underneath all that blubber.

"One of the owners," I absently replied, eyes still glued to his paperwork. Only once I was done reading it over did I give Mr. Desmond Miller my full attention. "What's the problem?" I asked civilly.

All right, so maybe Hudson's words had penetrated a *little*.

"Like I told her," Miller spat, "my car was supposed to be ready a week ago, and since it wasn't, I feel like I shouldn't have to pay. *Feel me*?"

Hearing the subtle threat, I slowly smiled. "Yeah, I feel you."

Mr. Miller had conveniently left out *why* his repairs were finished late.

He didn't have insurance.

Per our policy, he needed to pay twenty percent of the repair costs up front. It had taken three weeks and several phone calls before we finally received only *half* of the required deposit.

I remembered it distinctly because it had been my call to give a fellow Black man a break and had given Kane, the only other experienced mechanic besides myself and my partners, the okay to start his repairs anyway.

Miller looked pretty smug when I handed the file back to Tuesday without argument. I discretely looked around, noticed all the curious eyes pointed in our direction, and tapped Miller on his titty. "Walk with me," I said, nodding toward the door. "We'll discuss this outside."

Shrugging, he followed me outside with confidence in every step, and I could feel why. The ground literally shook with every step the mammoth took.

Slipping my hands inside the pockets of my long-sleeved overalls, I led him down the short paved path toward the side of the building and through the pedestrian gate. Adjacent to the building were a handful of parking spaces designated for cars ready to be picked up, and a dumpster, which sat closer to the back of the building where the employee parking lot was.

"Oh, shit…" I held my fist to my mouth and grinned when I spotted the glossy candy-red slab—which meant a car that was slow, loud, and banging. It even had chrome swangas that were cone-like twenty-inch rims that stuck out like an elbow. "This you?" I looked over my shoulder in time to see Woolly Mammoth grin.

"Yeah, that's me," he boasted proudly. "That's my baby."

I nodded in silent approval as I walked around the heavily modified Buick. "She's real nasty!" I praised it after I had finished checking it out. Whirling around, I finally let my smile drop. "It's too bad you didn't pay your bill, though."

"Why's that?"

"Because you ain't never getting your bitch back."

"Well, like I said—" The blow I sent to his gut cut him off mid-sentence.

"What was that?" I taunted as I pulled my nine from my ankle holster and proceeded to pistol-whip his ass. "Huh? I can't hear you, big homie. Can you repeat that? You not gone pay *who*?"

Blood spurted from his mouth and wounds, splattering my uniform and skin. He was easily twice my size, and still, I kicked his ass all over the pavement. I wasn't even close to being winded or getting my point across when it happened.

The wind shifted, bringing the intoxicating scent of oranges and vanilla. It cut through the chemicals polluting the city, the copper smell of blood leaking from Miller, and the motor oil and exhaust clinging to my clothes and skin.

Everything slowed and I stopped suddenly, feeling the hair on my nape and arms rise.

But not just that, no.

I could have sworn a gentle voice whispered in my ear.

As real as the phantom fingers gripping my chin and guiding my gaze away from the bloodied lump to where the girl with waist-length dreads and some kind of gold head chain resting on her neat locks and forehead like a crown stood outside the gates watching me. Our gazes locked, and only one word came to mind in the space of the breath that followed.

Queen.

My entire body seemed to tremble as adrenaline coursed through me, and my body's temperature plunged to terrifying depths, making my skin tighten and bumps appear along my arms. It took me a moment longer to realize that was a first-ever chill creeping down my fucking spine.

I glared at the girl who caused it all.

Her delicate brown fingers were wrapped around the metal bars of the gate as her attention returned once more to the man lying at my feet. I waited for her to flinch, scream, and run away from the gory scene I'd created.

She didn't.

Her head cocked to the side curiously, and suddenly, I was

contemplating some *wild* shit—like asking for her name and number.

Savannah didn't even have that luxury, and I'd been fucking her for years. Her only way of contacting me was by blowing up my DMs.

My reaction to *this* girl was something I could honestly say I'd never experienced before. I couldn't put a name on it, which made me trust the feeling even less.

She looked young—too fucking young—even from this distance.

Her jet-black dreads framed the sides of her diamond-shaped face and hugged her breasts while sweeping her lower back. Even her deep brown skin had a baby-soft glow to it, and I licked my lips as I imagined sucking and fucking and abusing every one of her holes.

I couldn't make out the rest of her features from this far away, but my dick had already decided it liked what it saw. Even now, my anger ebbed as an uncharacteristic calm washed over me like a wave. I wanted to snatch her nosy ass up before she realized she was staring down the mouth of a lion and disappeared forever.

The fuck?

"Nah," I whispered to myself aloud. I didn't like what this weirdo and her staring problem were doing to me. I knew Black didn't crack, but she couldn't be older than sixteen if she were a day.

She had to go.

"Ah! Help! Ahhh!" Miller suddenly screamed. I'd forgotten about his ass.

"Shut the fuck up." I sent one last blow to his temple, knocking him out cold.

Straightening, I slowly ate up the distance between this strange girl, who still hadn't moved, and me. I waited for her to show some sign of fear, but none came—not even when I was close enough to make out the small milky white patches of skin that looked like it had lost its pigment. The star-shaped patches traveled from the right side of her lower jaw, across her small nose, and stopped just above her left brow in a pattern that gave me pause before I shook it off as a coincidence.

I didn't know if she was frozen in terror or just weird as fuck, but I was only two strides away when I could no longer hold back.

I *had* to speak to her.

If only to satisfy this fierce and vicious need to hear her voice.

Even though that phantom voice from before warned me this moment was crucial, I only spared a second to think about what I would say to her, what my first words to this unknown girl who had provoked such a visceral reaction from me would be before I let them free.

"What the *fuck* are you looking at?"

THREE

Atlas

TWO KINGS FOUND, TWO MORE TO HUNT.

That was my last coherent thought before I saw *him*.

My brain told me to run, but my feet wouldn't move. Maybe some intrinsic part of me knew what was happening. He stepped out of the shadows that the cluster of clouds looming above had made as if it had known he was moments away from committing murder and sought to shield him from prying eyes.

Late for my first day at my new job, I'd been rushing down the sidewalk when I heard the pain whimpers and followed them without thought to this moment…to him.

His breathtaking features—medium-brown skin, unusually bright eyes, thick eyebrows with a diagonal line purposely cut in each, full lips framed by a short-boxed beard, neat and intricate cornrows pulled back and secured at his crown while the sides and back of his fine grade hair were shaved into a hide fade—became distinct with each step that brought him closer until there was no doubt in my mind about who he was.

Rowdy Wray.

The third King.

The one who'd ignited my blood every time I studied that

photo taken twenty years ago. Every time, I gave into the pull and let my eyes wander to him posing and brimming with arrogance.

I wasn't brave enough to reach for it now, but I knew his face by now like I knew my own.

Tall.

He'd been the tallest of them even then.

Taller than he should have been at fifteen or sixteen.

Unlike the others, he'd already filled out the white and red Chicago Bulls jersey he'd worn that night. His style had been simple yet, somehow, outshone them all. I told myself it was his height that fascinated me so, but how did that explain the trance I fell into every time?

He hadn't been smiling so much as smirking. Could it be that even twenty years in the past and frozen in time, he was aware of my unhealthy fascination?

Of course not.

Maybe.

Fuck me, I hope not.

There was no question that this man would ruin me if I let him.

I opened my mouth to say something, *anything*, but no words came. It didn't matter, though. He beat me to it.

"What the fuck are you looking at?" It would have been less jarring if he'd slapped me. "You deaf?" he barked when I remained silent. "The fuck you looking at, little girl?"

So that was how it was going to be then.

"Not sure." I squinted my eyes like I was trying to take a closer look. "The new bitch in cell block *D*?"

Rowdy gave me a blank look, so I rolled my eyes and turned before taking a few steps away so I could watch the street and put some distance between us.

A moment later, I heard the creak of the pedestrian gate opening and slamming closed behind me.

Roc had given me explicit instructions to wait for him outside for whatever reason. I wanted to make a good impression on my first day, so I agreed to his strange request.

Unfortunately, it was cold, and my jacket was thin, so I said fuck it after only a few seconds and spun on my heel to go inside the warm building to wait.

What was the worst that could happen?

The answer came when I collided with a wall made of hot flesh and hard muscle and smelled like mouthwatering cologne mixed with motor oil.

I blinked. "Oh, my God." I groaned when I saw it was Rowdy. "You're still here?" Standing this close, I had to tilt my head back until my skull damn near touched my spine. I wasn't even short. He was just that tall.

"Aye, you're rude as fuck." His slashed brows bunched as he frowned down at me.

"*Me*?" I pointed at my chest as my lips parted at his audacity. He had some nerve when he was still trying to intimidate me.

"Yeah." He stepped closer. "You." Somehow, we ended up in a staring contest that ended when he sighed. "Look, if you're not here to get your car fixed, then you need to move on. This is a place of business, and loiterers will be shot on sight."

I followed his blood and oil-stained finger to the bright yellow sign with actual bullet holes in it that read exactly that. I pursed my lips. "I'm pretty sure that's illegal."

"Does it look like I give a fuck?"

"Funny. I was about to ask you the same." I gave him my back again.

"You got a lot of mouth, little girl." I'd lost my virginity years ago, but I was still too slow to recognize the sensuous drop in his tone before it was too late, before he grabbed my hips in a punishing grip and yanked me to him. "I might just stick my dick in it."

I felt my nipples harden just before I tore myself away and turned to face him.

All that got me was my chest pressed against his abs when he grabbed me again and forced me right back against his body.

This time, I stayed put and wondered if his cologne also worked as some kind of sedative. He smelled *divine*. At least, I assumed it had to be his cologne since I didn't think a body wash existed that could overpower the smell of motor oil and exhaust fumes.

"Let me go, please."

I was annoyed with myself for even asking when he deserved nothing less than to have his shit rocked. I was also aware that Rowdy was now my boss, and despite how wrong our first meeting had gone, losing this job or quitting wasn't an option.

"How old are you?"

"Why?"

Instead of answering right away, his strong hands slid from my hips to my ass, massaging and memorizing the shape and curve of it through my jeans. He wasn't gentle either. I didn't understand how his touch could be so rough, the deep massage driving me to the tips of my toes until I had no choice but to cling to him for support, yet feel better than any sensation I'd ever felt. He was thorough too.

Before I could stop my reaction, my eyes fluttered close, and this time, I let my answering moan free.

"Because I want to fuck you," Rowdy eventually confessed. His deep voice dripped sex instead of malice now. "Today. Now. Five fucking minutes ago if you hadn't distracted me with your fucking mouth." I could feel his lips grazing my neck softly before he lifted his head to meet my gaze. "Why else?"

I ignored my throbbing pussy and the arousal ruining my panties and said, "We just met, and I don't even like you."

"And?"

"You're only supposed to have sex with people you like." I wanted to wipe the condescending smirk from his face. Instead, I tried once again to get away from him.

"Hate me all you want, beautiful. I'll still make you come." There was no trace of arrogance in his claim, only a simple statement of facts, which might have been the reason I found myself believing him. Staring at him while he distractedly searched the area, I realized his eyes weren't hazel as I'd originally guessed but green. "Come on."

Before I could tell him no, he grabbed my hand and pulled me through the gate where the man he'd beaten unconscious was still bleeding and lying unconscious on the ground.

My new boss, who was clearly not to be fucked with, stepped over his limp body like he was nothing, forcing me to do the same.

And now he was leading the only witness to his crime to some undisclosed location that was probably dark and known only to him.

"Where are we going?"

Rowdy's expression gave nothing away when he glanced over his shoulder. "To fuck. Where else?"

My next breath punched out of me, and I suddenly dug my feet into the pavement while trying to pull my hand free. It didn't deter him one fucking bit. He just tightened his grip and kept walking as if my consent was optional.

"You don't even know me!" I screamed at his back.

He cackled loudly and obnoxiously, making me double down on my efforts to get away from him. "I don't need to." He glanced at me again. "What else you got?"

"How about no? N-O, asshole. Heard of it?" I snapped.

When Rowdy didn't answer or slow his pace, I panicked. It was the only explanation for why I lifted our hands and savagely dug my teeth into the skin around his wrist until I tasted blood.

"Yoooo!" Finally, Rowdy stopped walking and turned to face me with wide eyes.

Holding his bewildered gaze, I turned my head to the side and spat out his blood coating my tongue before baring my bloodied teeth at him. "I said *no*."

Rowdy didn't reply as he looked down at his bleeding wrist and my teeth marks now deeply embedded in his skin. Slowly, his gaze rose, pausing at the sight of his blood on my lips and then meeting mine.

A moment later, I yelped when he shoved me against the

building's wall. My back smarted from the impact, and then all I knew was the heat of his strong body inflaming my skin and melting my brain when he used it to hold me in place.

His body…and his hand holding mine. Rowdy still hadn't let it go—as if our tenuous connection had been worth the pain and bloodshed.

Rowdy pinned our hands against the brick wall, and I screamed again when he lowered his head and sunk his teeth into my wrist. A whimper tore out of me when I felt the skin break, and then warm liquid trailed down my arm. Only then did Rowdy lift his head.

And then he rudely spat my blood on my clean white sneakers.

The rest had stained his lips red, but he didn't seem to care as his cold gaze met mine.

Neither of us spoke.

We merely existed for the intense stretch of a moment that passed afterward.

Rowdy seemed to read every one of my thoughts. His green eyes—a delightful compliment to his peanut butter complexion—tracked every heave of my chest, my tongue nervously flicking over my dry lips, and even the sweat that pooled between my breasts despite the forty-degree temperature outside.

"If you want me to believe you don't want to be fucked," he told me in a tone that promised sex, "you're going to have to lie better than that."

I had two warring reactions to that. My skin turned cold with dread, but my pussy…

It opened like a flower that answered only to him.

And then Rowdy was forcing me away from the wall and toward whatever dark and private place he'd been luring me to.

Nope.

This was not happening.

Fucking my new boss on my first day, or any day, was not an option, no matter how tempted I was to give in like he seemed so sure I would. If the Kings found out why I was really here, I was pretty sure they'd kill me, and the lion of Idlewild would be first in line.

I had to stop this.

So I did the only thing I could think of. I took his advice.

"Fourteen."

Rowdy was frowning now when he glanced over his shoulder again. We were almost to the dumpster, the spot he was aiming for, I realized too late. Apparently, he thought it was as good as any place to fuck me. Disgust mingled with the metallic taste of his blood as I tried and failed not to be utterly and irrevocably fucking offended.

"What?"

"You asked my age before." I lifted my chin. "I'm fourteen."

Rowdy hissed, swore, and then snatched his hand away from mine like it was covered in whatever was causing that god-awful smell from the dumpster. I could tell he was about to curse me out for not speaking up sooner when the sound of the gate sliding open, followed by the soft purr of a sleek red Mercedes racing toward us, saved him the trouble.

The four-door coupe with a rear spoiler stopped behind us, and a frantic Roc hopped out from the driver's seat. He was dressed for work in an open gray short-sleeve button-up with a white thermal underneath and dark blue jeans that looked too expensive to be sensible.

"Aye, Atlas, you good?" Roc's gaze darted between his psycho friend, who now refused to look my way, and me.

"Yup." I just barely managed to swallow my laugh at the disturbed look on Rowdy's face.

I started to ask Roc what the hell took him so long, but he beat me to it. "Sorry, I'm late," he apologized. "I had an emergency this morning and completely forgot you were starting today."

"That's okay," I offered quietly. Rowdy's head had snapped in our direction, and now his confused gaze was darting between

Roc and me. I simply hugged my waist and waited for the other shoe to drop.

Something told me that Rowdy wouldn't be pleased when Roc told him the good news—an important detail I'd failed to mention before he tried to fuck me behind the dumpster.

I hadn't started working for the Kings yet and was already questioning whether I could handle it.

"How the fuck do you know her?" my green-eyed monster and secret obsession snapped.

Roc sighed like he already knew what his friend's reaction would be and mumbled, "This is Atlas. The girl I told you about? She's our new receptionist."

It then occurred to me that Rowdy had never bothered to learn my name.

FOUR

Rowdy

"ATLAS, MEET ROWDY," ROC INTRODUCED. HE WAS BLISSFULLY unaware of how well acquainted Atlas and I had been moments away from becoming. I hadn't believed for a second that her pussy wasn't dripping for me. "He's one of the owners."

"No."

Roc's gaze snapped to me. "No?" he echoed. "What do you mean no?"

"I mean, *no,* she can't work here."

Roc gaped at me for a moment before the muscle in his jaw began ticking. "I'm not doing this with you, O. I already hired her."

"Word?" Unfazed, I turned my attention to Miss Twenty-Five-to-Life. "You're fired."

"What?" Atlas's lips fell open, delicate nostrils flared, and then her bewildered gaze flew to Roc for help.

I still wanted to fucking kiss her.

It was a first for me, to say the least. And disturbing as fuck if she'd been telling the truth about her age.

I hadn't put my lips on a broad since I was sixteen.

Kissing, for whatever reason, had always felt more intimate

than fucking. The latter could be done for the sole purpose of busting a nut or making a baby. Kissing, however, was completely fucking unnecessary.

It always felt like I was sending a message I didn't mean or making promises I didn't intend to keep. So, yeah, kissing was out. It was too affectionate, too personal, and most of the women I've encountered had never measured up.

"You're trippin'," Roc argued halfheartedly. "You can't fire this girl for whatever slight pissed you off this time." He already knew there was no use in trying to change my mind unless he was willing to throw down for her. Roc knew the rules. If he could best me in a fight, he could keep her, but I knew my brother. It wouldn't be worth the effort for some random he wasn't even fucking.

"Fuck you for one," I returned sarcastically. "Two, she was late as fuck. Almost an hour. That alone is a fireable offense. Three, did you even do a background check? She's not even old enough to drive a car. This ain't no goddamn sweatshop. Tell her ass to go find some brats to babysit and get the fuck."

Eyes wide open now, Roc's head swung toward Atlas's snake-ass, letting me know I was right, at least, about the background check. "How old are you?"

"Nineteen," she grumbled while purposely avoiding my gaze.

"You's a goddamn lie. You told me you were fourteen."

"Because you were trying to fuck me behind a dumpster, you psycho! I told you I didn't want to, but that didn't seem to matter to you, so I lied, okay?"

"No, motherfucker. Not okay. How do we know you aren't lying now?"

Huffing, she reached inside the little purse I hadn't noticed her carrying and pulled out her driver's license. "See? I was born November ninth, two thousand and one."

"Let me see this shit." I snatched the license from her hand, ignoring the feeling of being punched in the gut when our fingers touched. I could feel her attention on me as I read the proof that she was legal with my own eyes.

Beck, Atlas Ilana
908 W Indes Drive
Ossella, Mississipi, 39156
Sex: F
Ht: 5-07
Wt: 140
Eyes: BRO
Hair: BLK
DOB: 11/09/2001

I mentally stored the rest of the information she'd unwittingly offered for later and handed her license back without so much as a glance her way.

"She still got to go," I told Roc. He opened his mouth to argue, but I bucked my eyes at him, silently communicating that my reasons were deeper than I could admit in front of Miss Atlas Ilana Beck.

Roc sucked his teeth and then turned to Atlas to do what the fuck I asked. "Look, I'm sorry, but uh—"

"Please don't fire me," Atlas begged before he could finish. And just like a fucking simp, Roc fell for her doe-eyed bullshit. He cut his gaze my way, silently begging me to reconsider so he didn't have to crush her little feelings.

Realizing her employment here now rested solely in the palm of my hand, Atlas reluctantly turned to me. "Look, I'm sorry for lying to you," she lied again. I could see it in her eyes. She wasn't sorry at all. "I promise I won't be any more trouble."

Another lie.

I truly hoped humbling herself for my benefit felt like swallowing a bucket of rusty nails. My hostile demeanor, however, crumbled like dried leaves under her heel when she placed her small hands on my forearm in a grip I could easily break but didn't.

I cast a pointed glance at her hands on my arm and then at her, but she didn't let go. Atlas tightened her grip.

Interesting.

"I really need this job," she pleaded. "I'll do anything. Just don't let me go."

Very interesting.

Her hands were soft as shit. I'd known that from holding them earlier, but having her touch me willingly was a different kind of pleasure. I wondered what they'd feel like wrapped around my dick...stroking.

Gently covering her hand with mine, I felt her tense for only a second before she relaxed and kept her earnest gaze open for my scrutiny. "Take your hands off me before I break 'em," I coldly ordered.

Sliding my hand down to her dainty wrist like I was about to do just that, she quickly snatched them away from me. Now that I had her attention, I hooked my finger under her chin and made her meet my gaze. "You want this job? Fine. You're hired. But I won't be held responsible for what happens if you stay."

"I—" She started but stopped just as abruptly. The confused dip of her brows made it clear she struggled to decipher what I meant.

I truly hoped she wasn't a virgin.

I shifted my hold on her face until her chin was trapped between my forefinger and thumb, and then I let her see every filthy thought playing like a movie in my head.

It means I'll be balls-deep in that pussy by the end of the week if you don't get away from me now.

"Okay," she agreed with an eager nod.

I chuckled and let her go. I don't know if Atlas was desperate, dumb, reckless, or all of the above, but I decided it wasn't my problem as I walked away without a word. I'd warned her, didn't I?

Whatever happened next wouldn't be on me.

I was heading toward the bathroom to clean Miller's blood off my hands and the taste of Atlas's from my mouth when I was waylaid by none other than fucking Tony. He needed me to hold his hand through a head gasket leak, so I walked him through it, and after he swore he understood, I threatened to beat his ass again if he fucked it up.

That took fifteen minutes, and after I'd returned from the bathroom, I noticed that Jail Bait was still hanging around. She was with Roc and Tuesday at the reception and actually smiling, which I realized was my first time seeing her do so.

I found myself stuck as I drank in the sight of her through the panoramic window separating the workshop from the lobby until she noticed me staring, and her smile dropped.

Playing it off, I turned away and busied my hands by setting all my tools back in their place so they'd be easy to find for the next repair.

I should have known Atlas was young and not just another baby face as I'd hoped. Yeah, she was legal, but the sixteen-year age gap was still a huge turnoff. Personally, I preferred my women a little more seasoned. I had enough clinging to my dick as it was, and most of them were twice her age with twice the experience.

I still heard her words from earlier, spinning like a record in my head, about only having sex with people you liked. The last thing I needed was to get the new receptionist addicted to my dick and then be caught in the middle of some fatal attraction soap opera. It was out of the question.

I just had to stop picturing her naked first.

I didn't do missionary, but Atlas had me considering slow-stroking her pussy while I stared deep into her eyes on some sucker-for-love shit.

I'd barely known her an hour, and already I was at war with myself. Instead of starting on the Ford now parked at my station, I was sitting in the driver's seat, trying to picture the kind of man Atlas *did* like.

Probably someone square and lame, who let her walk around with his balls in her purse because he didn't even know what to do that pussy.

Fuck this.

Pushing thoughts of Atlas away, I shook off my thoughts and plugged the OBD2 scanner into the white port under the steering wheel. It wasn't like I would force myself into a skin that didn't fit just to fuck one girl. There were too many willing pussies out there for me to bother with a fickle one.

I hadn't figured out what brought Atlas here, but I didn't need her life story to know she was sheltered. If I touched her, I'd ruin her. There was no doubt about it.

An hour later, I was finished with the Ford and still thinking about that damn girl, so I left my station and headed upstairs to Joren's office. He was at his desk pouring over the new tickets that had come in.

Along with being a partial owner, he was the shop foreman, and since his pretty ass didn't like to get his hands dirty that often, there was no conflict of interest.

"I need a job," I told him without preamble. "Give me the hardest one in the stack."

"Um..."

I impatiently waited as he flipped through the stack.

"A possible engine replacement just came through, but I already promised it to Jerry. He needs the practice."

"Fuck Jerry. Give him the commission; just let me do the repairs."

Joren paused at that since I never passed on money, but I needed the distraction before I finished what I'd started earlier and dragged our new receptionist into the nearest dark corner.

Now that the frenzy had lifted and I was thinking clearly, I knew that under no circumstances could that happen. Atlas worked for me now, and fucking employees went against the code that Joren, Roc, Golden, and I had unanimously agreed on when we first started the business.

It was a rule that had never come close to being broken before.

In a single morning, one naive nineteen-year-old girl rendered me incapable of rational thought. Atlas had thrown me into completely uncharted territory, and damn if it hadn't intrigued me more. I couldn't get the image of my blood around her pretty mouth and her feral gaze staring me down out of my head.

"Cool," Joren agreed before handing me the paperwork.

I could tell he wanted to ask questions, but I snatched the folder and keys from him and left his office before he could. I returned to the workshop, and thankfully, Atlas was nowhere to be found. Roc was behind the reception desk, flirting with one of the customers waiting to be checked in, which meant Tuesday must have been giving Atlas the tour.

Pride of Kings had four levels, including the basement—where we kept inventory. The workshop was on the ground floor, the offices on the second, and the entire third floor was one big room we used for formal meetings and the occasional party.

I guess, in some ways, we hadn't completely let go of our past.

Outside, I noticed Miller must have either come to or someone had scrapped his ass off the ground, so I called the towing company we kept on call to put a boot on his car in case the ass whooping hadn't knocked enough sense into him.

I located the Kia Forte I'd be working on and towed it inside. Once I had it backed into my station, I called Jerry over and ignored the envious looks from the others.

Getting the chance to shadow and learn from me was rare. More often than not, I turned down their requests because patience was a virtue I lacked, and I couldn't promise I wouldn't snap their necks if I ran out.

Let them dick-ride Joren or Roc.

Golden was just as bad, except he flat-out refused to talk if he didn't know or like you. He had what professionals would call selective mutism. Since only a handful of humanity had made the cut, it was far easier to explain that he was simply mute.

A shadow fell over me as I sat in the driver's seat of the car, and when I looked up, I found Golden hovering near the passenger door. Jerry took his cue and wandered off to give us privacy.

Sighing, I ignored my partner and stuck the key in the ignition, turning it until the car reluctantly sputtered to life. "Not now, G."

"You don't see it, do you?" he whispered, voice raspy from disuse.

"See what?" I still didn't meet his gaze as I plugged the handheld scanner into the car to read the Kia's multiple systems. There wasn't a man alive I feared, but sometimes, I wondered if Golden's mutism allowed him to see more than most—more than you wanted him to.

It certainly seemed that way when he answered, "Atlas." Her name finally drew my gaze to him, and for once, I didn't find his usual impassiveness. No, this motherfucker looked like he'd just seen a ghost. "She's back."

I looked over and through the panoramic window at the reception desk, where she stood again with Tuesday, who was showing Atlas something on her computer. Since the desk was U-shaped—one of the two longest sides facing the waiting room and double doors leading to the valets and the other facing the window overlooking the workshop—it allowed them to have their own workspace.

Right now, Atlas was on Tuesday's side facing the double doors, so I had an unobstructed view of her ass. It was round, fat, and bounced when she walked, just how I liked it.

My dick jumped in my pants, and if Golden and his third eye weren't standing next to me and scrutinizing my every move, I would have squeezed it into submission.

When Atlas was done with her training, she'd be facing the workshop where I could look at her pretty face all goddamn day. My station was at the end of the middle aisle closest to the window, so there would be nothing to block my view of her and vice versa.

Just what the fuck I didn't need.

"Okay, so she's back." I feigned nonchalance even while still admiring the curve of Atlas's ass. I wanted to sink my teeth into it. Ginuwine's "In Those Jeans" started playing in my head, and I licked my lips like a fucking creep. "What about it?"

I forced my gaze away from Atlas to look at Golden, but he had left as quietly as he'd arrived.

Sucking my teeth in annoyance, I put stingy Atlas and her stuck-up pussy and cryptic Golden and his endless weirdness out of my mind to focus on a task I could actually conquer.

FIVE

Atlas

It was nothing short of a miracle when I ended my first shift in one piece, which was the best I could have hoped for after this morning. I was counting my wins and absorbing my losses. I now had money coming in, and I'd met all the Kings except one.

Joren.

He'd barked that he was busy from the other side of his locked office door during my tour with Tuesday, so I missed out on meeting him.

After barely surviving Rowdy, I was more than okay with that.

I'd even managed to avoid Rowdy for the rest of the day. At times, I swore I could feel him watching me through the window, but whenever I'd been brave enough to try to catch him, I only ever found him focused on his work.

I wouldn't entertain the thought that it had been wishful thinking.

I'd been curious when Rowdy was just a stranger in a photo. A piece to a puzzle I hadn't finished putting together. Now that I'd met him, that constant itch under my skin to be near him was skirting dangerously close to obsession. I'd be alarmed, except I'd known for a long time that I was wired to self-destruct.

In the past, my mom would silently fret over what might

send me over the edge next. I used to hate her constant worrying. Now all I wanted was for her to care even a fraction as much as she used to.

Each time I tried to excuse her sudden detachment as grief, I'd remember our last fight. Her last words echoed among the rubble of everything I'd known.

I know you are, Atlas, and that's the problem. I thought it would be enough.

It had taken until a letter came with no return address and the offer for a new start for me to accept that my mom had died too. The only difference was that her heart kept beating—no matter how often I'd overhear her begging it to stop.

"Good job today, Atlas," Tuesday praised. "See you tomorrow."

I waved at Tuesday and Will—one of the technicians walking alongside her—as they headed to the employee parking lot behind the building.

I headed in the opposite direction toward the street where I was parked. I was scheduled to work tomorrow bright and early, but luckily the shop was only open from nine to noon on Saturday, so it would be a blissfully short shift.

A neon-green flyer and a pink parking ticket were both waiting for me on my windshield when I reached my car. Balling up the ticket, I tossed it away, knowing I'd find another there tomorrow. I needed to keep a low profile for now, so parking at the shop was out of the question.

I grabbed the flyer, ready to toss it away as well, when I paused at the mention of a party on the other side of town. Was it wise to risk flying solo in a city where I had no one to call if I got in trouble?

It sounded like a terrible idea.

But…

It was better than going back to my crummy motel in Hooker's Cove with nothing but thoughts of my dead father and grieving mother to keep me company. I also didn't feel like dodging the pimps and prostitutes that lurked around Hooker's Cove, so I hopped in my car, plugged the address into my GPS, and drove off into the unknown.

The unknown turned out to be a massive hangover.

I'd gone to the party last night, which turned out to be a homecoming for some guys who must have been a big deal before they skipped town years ago.

The house had been so crowded I never even got a glimpse of the motley crew holding court in the packed living room.

And then I got so drunk I didn't care.

How had I even gotten back to the motel last night?

I didn't remember calling an Uber…or leaving the party. The room started spinning before I could figure it out, and I decided I didn't care how or when I'd made it back. I could tell it was morning by the subtle burning of my eyelids, so I turned away from the window and the sun streaming through and hugged the pillow under my head with a sigh as I settled on my stomach.

I was beginning to drift off again when I felt the bed shift… and a leg brush against my own. My eyes flew open, and my nausea returned tenfold when I realized not only was I not alone, this wasn't even *my* bed.

This wasn't my room, and I wasn't in Hooker's Cove.

The person lying next to me turned over while I was still trying to make sense of how I got here, and I paused at the face that greeted me.

Light brown skin.

Long lashes.

Smirking lips even while unconscious.

Smudged black eyeliner.

And a spiked silver hoop piercing the septum.

Slowly, my bedmate's eyes opened, drawing my attention to the words *bad news* tattooed in angry black letters high on their right cheek just underneath the eye. I felt my stomach turn because that couldn't be a good sign, right?

I was still figuring out what to say when she spoke first, her voice like a siren's song, even when tinged with sleep. "You forgot my name, didn't you?"

"Uhhh…"

She pouted. "I'm crushed."

"Sorry," I croaked.

"It's okay." She giggled a little cruelly. "I forgot yours, too, so I guess we're even." There was an awkward pause as we both questioned if we wanted to exchange names. "Ruen," she eventually offered.

"Atlas." And then… "How did I get here?"

"I invited you," she answered easily. A wicked smile curved her lips. "You seemed eager to come."

Subtle.

I groaned and hid my face in the pillow. There was no way she only meant her place. I felt Ruen watching me, so I peeked at her through one eye. "And do you always bring nameless strangers home?"

"Only when they're as pretty as you." Ruen winked. Speechless, I watched her stretch her lithe body and yawn before sliding out of bed. My gaze was drawn straight to her pierced nipples and perky tits before she turned and headed to the floor-length mirror in the corner.

She only wore a thong, her round ass jiggling with every step.

The thong was green like the skunk stripe on the right side of her black wig that was cut into a chin-length bob. The left side was dyed purple. It suited her high cheekbones, sharp eyes, and diamond-shaped face.

At some point, I decided what the hell and burrowed deeper under the warm covers, my nipples turning hard when they brushed against the soft cotton sheets.

Oh…*no.*

I shot up into a sitting position and clutched the sheet to my chest when I realized my clothes were gone, and I was even more naked than she was.

"Where are my—Did we—Um...did we, uhh..." I pressed my forehead into my palm when I couldn't even finish the sentence.

"Last night?" Ruen gleefully finished while twisting to face me. "Oh, yeah, you were an amazing fuck. Best I ever had."

Now I knew that couldn't be true.

I'd only had one sexual partner, and Sutton, my ex, had been a dick in every sense of the word. I'd like to think sex with another girl would be easier than pleasing a man since I'd had unrestricted access to the equipment all my life, but it still took me a while to learn my own rhythm, so...unlikely.

"Sure."

It was all I could think to say before she lost her composure and started laughing at my expense. I narrowed my gaze at her and just barely kept my hands from balling into fists. Her keen gaze seemed to catch on that I wasn't amused, and her lips quirked in a challenge.

"Chill, Twinks. I like pussy—love it, actually—but sobbing hysterically while sloppy drunk doesn't do it for me, you know?"

No. No, I don't know.

Wait, what? "I was crying?"

"Yeah." I caught Ruen's wince just before she gave me her back. Her tone was uncharacteristically somber and not at all cocky and teasing as she said, "You told me your father died. I'm sorry for your loss."

Oh, no.

What else had I said?

Had I mentioned the Kings?

Did I tell her about the letter and why I was here?

"Thanks," I forced out. "Um...did I...did I say anything else?"

"Nope." She peeked at me over her shoulder. "You should know we fooled around a bit, though. Above the clothes stuff, nothing heavy. Apparently, you turn into a raging lesbian when you're drunk, but don't worry. I realized you were boringly hetero before it got too far. I tucked you into bed, and you've been snoring like a grown man ever since."

I waited for Ruen to tell me she was joking again, but she was silent as she peeled off her wig and tossed it aside. Her brown hair was braided to her scalp in six neat rows and covered by a wig cap that she removed too.

That must have been how I ended up naked.

"I assume we met at the party?" I croaked as I searched the room for my clothes and phone.

Ruen turned from the mirror with a dip in her brows. "Yeah… how much did you drink last night?"

"Too much." I groaned again. The only thing I remembered was how much I needed to forget. I slowly stood from the bed, keeping the black sheet wrapped around me. I wasn't as comfortable with my nakedness around strangers as Ruen, who still hadn't bothered to put on clothes.

Her room was a *mess*.

There were clothes, shoes, makeup, half-empty *and* empty liquor bottles, records, manga, and video games everywhere. There was also an expensive-looking turntable in the corner next to purple over-the-ear headphones and a microphone. "You're a deejay," I reminisced out loud. "You were the deejay at the party."

"You catch on quick."

I rolled my eyes. "How did we—when did we…?"

Ruen caught on to the question I couldn't seem to ask and shrugged before turning back to the mirror. "You asked to come home with me, and since you're sexy as fuck, I obliged. Technically, we never left the party since I'm the one who hosted it."

That explained why I didn't remember leaving the party. I must have followed Ruen upstairs to have sex and chickened out. Or had I passed out? My throbbing head suggested the latter.

"Okay…so if we didn't do anything, where are my clothes?"

"No clue. You took them off after you threw up on them."

"Oh, God." I groaned. "Is there anything I *didn't* do last night?"

"Yup." She smirked. "Pray." There was a knock on the door a second later, and I clutched the sheet a little tighter while Ruen strode across the room on long, lithe legs and yanked it open without bothering to cover up. "Oh, hey, Rem. Yeah, she was just looking for these." I couldn't see who was on the other side, but I did notice Ruen motioning with her hands while she talked. There was a pause and then more gesturing with her hands. "Yeah, she's up. Bring 'em in."

Without any regard for my undressed state, Ruen suddenly stepped aside, revealing me to whoever waited on the other side. Thinking maybe I was still drunk, I slowly blinked in confusion at the sight of another girl wearing Ruen's face.

It only took a second longer for my drunk-addled brain to catch up.

Twins.

Ruen had a twin sister.

They were identical and yet like night and day. While Ruen was comfortable showing off her skin, her twin was covered from her neck to her toes in a modest white nightgown.

If it weren't for the hair, tattoo, and piercings, *no one* would ever be able to tell them apart.

"H-hey." I waved awkwardly.

"This is my sister Remedy," Ruen introduced. And then Ruen began gesturing with her hands again while speaking aloud. "Remedy, Atlas."

Once again, it took me a second to catch on. Ruen was signing.

My gaze flew to Remedy, who only smiled in greeting and held out the neatly folded clothes in her arms.

I slowly took them and realized they were mine.

She must have washed them for me.

Meeting her patient gaze, I gratefully returned her smile. "Thank you."

With hands now free, Remedy quickly signed her response,

so I looked to Ruen to translate, and she smirked at my helplessness. "She said you're welcome."

"I didn't see you at the party last night," I said to Remedy.

"That's because she wasn't," Ruen answered while signing something to her sister. "Not her scene."

"Oh."

Feeling awkward while they signed back and forth, I quietly excused myself, my brain recalling the tiny en suite where I sought refuge while Ruen filled her sister in.

On the way to the party last night, I'd detoured and stopped at the motel long enough to shower and change into the dress and heels I now quickly threw on.

The room was quiet when I left the bathroom.

Ruen and Remedy were nowhere to be found, but I could hear their voices drifting up from downstairs, so I took the opportunity to look around for my purse and phone.

I eventually found them both hiding underneath the bed. My phone screen lit up, and I blew out a breath at all the notifications waiting for me.

Three of them were missed calls from Pride of Kings, along with a voice message. I skipped listening to the voicemail and glanced at the time instead.

One thirteen in the afternoon.

Shit.

My stomach sank, and the next moment, I sprinted from Ruen's chaotic bedroom and down the stairs. I made it to the last step before I remembered the shop closed at noon on Saturdays.

"I'd tell you there's no rush for you to leave, but it looks like you just realized that all on your own."

I paused my panic to look over and found Ruen standing in the arched doorway that looked like it led into the kitchen. She was now dressed in a graphic tee with Snoop Dogg's face that reached the top of her brown thighs as she leaned a supple shoulder against the doorjamb and watched me with no expression.

"I missed my shift at work."

"Then there's no reason you can't say for breakfast." She smirked. "Rem made pancakes."

Blueberry pancakes from the delightful smell drifting from the kitchen. I loved blueberry pancakes. "I…" I swallowed down what I wanted to say and made the only responsible decision I'd managed in the last twenty-four hours. "I should go."

Ruen didn't reply as she pushed away from the wall and slowly crossed the small foyer. My body tensed, thinking she'd ambush me where I stood by the stairs, but at the last minute, she hooked a left and headed for the front door.

I released a breath, but then an image of Rowdy and how he would have tried to bully me into staying flashed before my eyes, and I was left even more confused when my skin flushed.

I followed Ruen to the open door and turned to say goodbye as soon I stepped onto the porch and was caught off guard when her lips crashed into mine, stealing the awkward goodbye I had all queued up.

Ruen's kiss was confident and demanding yet gentle enough to make it clear I could end it at anytime—not at all aggressive, filthy, or disrespectful like how I imagined Rowdy's would be.

The most confusing part was when I didn't want to admit, not even to myself, which method of seduction I preferred.

Ruen's tongue licked the seam of my lips, and I found myself answering her silent request with a noise I wasn't ready to define. At the first stroke of her tongue against mine, I fisted the front of her T-shirt to pull her closer. We were almost matched in height, with Ruen a little taller, so our bodies lined up perfectly, allowing me to feel her hardened nipples brushing against my own.

As if she knew I was ready to throw caution to the wind and let her take me back upstairs, Ruen broke the connection, and my eyes slowly drifted open to see her watching me with that cruel, cocky glint in her eye.

"Ummm…"

"Let me know if you're ever curious to see what else I can do with my mouth."

I blinked, and a moment later, the bitch stepped back and slammed the door in my face. I was left reeling from more than just that confusing kiss as I stumbled down the street to my car in a daze.

What were the odds that in the four days since I arrived in Idlewild, I'd managed to attract not one but two total alphaholes?

SIX

Atlas

I SNUCK INTO PRIDE OF KINGS A LITTLE EARLY MONDAY MORNING AS if thirty minutes could possibly make up for missing my entire shift on Saturday. I waved hello to Tuesday, who glared at me before I said fuck it and slipped inside the bathroom. I was only delaying the inevitable, but I needed a moment to collect myself.

It was only one shift.

My first offense.

It's fine.

I stared at my reflection in the mirror until the worry in my eyes changed into an emotion I could harness. My phone chimed, so I snatched it from the counter and smiled when I saw it was an email from Dr. Saunders, my psych professor.

Good morning, Atlas.

I was surprised not to see you in my class last week, and then I received notice this morning that you dropped my class.

Is everything okay?

I hope I didn't do anything to make you uncomfortable. Please know I'm here for you if you need to talk.

—SS

Dr. Saunders had become a mentor and big sister over the last few months, and in my darkest hour, she'd been the only constant in my corner. She wasn't stuffy like the other professors, so her classes were popular, even among non-psych majors.

After my dad died, she'd even given me her personal email, and though it violated multiple school policies, she assured me I could use it whenever I needed. That was just how cool she was.

Smiling still, I clicked reply.

Boom!

The bathroom door burst open and hit the wall.

Screaming, I dropped my phone in the sink, my professor's email forgotten as I watched the door bounce off the wall from the force of impact. From this angle, I couldn't see much through the mirror's reflection, but I saw clear as day the tattooed hand that caught it.

It was large and bore a familiar snarling lion.

No.

God, you sadistic fuck, I'll answer to any of them—Joren, Roc, Golden—anyone *else.*

Anyone but him.

"How the fuck you just started this damn job and you already missing shifts?"

I spun around to find Rowdy wearing the fiercest scowl I'd ever seen on anyone as he held open the door, which now had a large footprint on the paint.

This crazy fool must have kicked it in.

My legs wobbled, so I held onto the sink to keep me standing while my voice, thank fuck, kept up the ruse, sharpening into cold steel.

"Are you blind?" When he just stared at me, I added, "Did you not notice this was the women's bathroom?"

"Does it look like I give a fuck?"

No.

Rowdy looked like he wanted to strangle me.

"My office, Atlas. Now." He was gone as quickly as he had arrived, the door swinging ominously shut behind him.

I exhaled slowly and debated taking my time before rescuing my phone from the sink and leaving the bathroom. If I was going to be fired, there was no point in trying to get under his skin. I'd probably never see him again after today.

I ignored my stomach, which revolted at the thought as I trudged up the stairs like I was heading to my execution.

When I reached his office door, I politely knocked even though I knew he was expecting me. I could practically feel the toxic male dominance vibrating off him from here.

"Get your ass in here," he called from the other side.

I rolled my eyes to the ceiling, feeling my faux locs sweeping my ass as I let my head fall back. *God?* I silently prayed. *About what I said before...you know I was kidding, right?*

Opening the door, I slipped inside and immediately looked around.

I hated to admit it, even to myself, but I was impressed.

Rowdy's office was simple. Functional. It wasn't overly flashy, as if he had a point to prove. To be in his presence was to know who was in charge. He didn't decorate with a bunch of unnecessary trimmings. His office only had the necessities while being clean and smelling even better—much like the man himself.

Right now, my fuming boss was sitting at his desk, watching me look around and mean-mugging me from across the room. Behind him loomed a black wooden bookcase that had been built into the wall with an honest-to-God AK-47 mounted over the middle shelf. It was conveniently reachable among the framed photos, spare car parts, awards, rusted teal tackle box, and even a few worn books scattered along the other shelves.

"Close the door."

I did what he ordered before crossing the room and standing in front of his desk like a good little employee ready for correction.

If only my knees would get on board.

They were currently shaking like twigs in a category five

hurricane, and no mantra I recited would ease them. I'd seen firsthand how my boss handled those who crossed him, and I wanted no part of it.

I would have run my ass out of there if it weren't for the letter that told me to come here and find the Kings.

It meant I couldn't leave yet. That meant damage control.

"Listen, I'm really sorry about Saturday," I said before he could curse me out again. "I overslept, but I promise it won't happen again. It was a simple misstep on my part. Please don't fire me."

"*Please don't fire me*," he mocked in a high tone.

I balled my hands into fists, and even though I'd never had a problem using them when necessary, I wasn't that crazy. First impressions were hard to shake, and mine was of him beating a literal giant unconscious with his bare hands. I knew when to pick my battles.

Rowdy's impassive expression returned when he spoke again. "I thought you said you needed this job."

"I do."

"So give me one good reason why I shouldn't fire you."

My brows lowered. "I'm not sucking your dick if that's what you mean."

Rowdy chuckled at that before stroking his facial hair and looking me up and down like he saw all of me and found me lacking. "I'm not trippin', little girl. You look like all you'd do is lick the tip."

My jaw dropped, but he didn't notice as he yanked open his top desk drawer, searched it, slammed it close, and did the same with the others until he found what he was looking for. "Normally, I'd slap you around as a warning, but since I don't hit females," he informed me absently, "fill this out."

"Oh, my gosh! Thank you!"

"You're welcome."

I rolled my eyes, which he missed since he hadn't bothered to look up from the form. Of course, the insensitive jerk didn't understand sarcasm. *He* was always earnest in that psycho way of his.

My boss stood from his chair with all the grace of the lion tattooed into his deep brown skin and slid the form over to me. All of the Kings had a similar tattoo—each in a different place, wearing a different expression.

Well, I assumed all since I still hadn't met Joren.

I forced my attention to the paper in front of me because it felt like I was ogling Rowdy, and I read the bold writing at the top of the page.

"Are you serious?" I looked up from the employee misconduct form, my astonished gaze meeting his flat green one. "Is this really necessary?"

Rowdy's brows, which had a shaved gap in each to make his mean ass look even meaner, dipped low like he was genuinely confused. "You *want* me to slap you around?"

I gaped for a moment, but I didn't dignify that with a response. I snatched the pen he'd laid on top so I could fill the stupid form out.

In my gut, I knew he was just being petty, and it annoyed me more that it worked.

Rowdy disappeared through the open door of the bathroom just feet away from his desk. Moments later, my pen paused midstroke when I heard the unmistakable sound of his piss hitting the toilet water. The freakishly long stream was even louder than it should have been because that unbalanced asshole hadn't bothered to close the door.

And just like the form, I knew it was purposeful, so I calmly set the pen down before aimlessly looking around. Knowing I had only seconds until he returned, I grabbed the half-empty water jug responsible for his bladder and popped the top.

I considered spitting in it but quickly discarded the idea. I wanted Rowdy to know how much harder he'd have to work if he wanted to break me.

Grabbing the motor oil sitting at the edge of the desk, as if he'd unconsciously carried it up here with him, I started pouring until the mixture was half and half and replaced the top.

The running faucet as Rowdy washed his hands thankfully covered up the sound of me shaking the jug to mix the water and oil. I shook until my arms hurt, knowing it was hopeless—much like Rowdy and me sharing the same space.

In order to live in harmony, one of us would have to break.

Something told me Rowdy would fight just as hard to stay whole, forcing one of us to rise and the other to sink. It was just a matter of discovering which of us was oil, I guess.

Silence emerged from the other side of the bathroom, so I hurriedly popped the top on the jug and emptied the contents onto the wooden floor, each of my targets deliberate. Once that was done, I tiptoed back to the desk and quickly signed my name on the form before rolling it tightly and securing the top edge with a strip of Scotch tape.

I'd just put everything back where I'd found it when he appeared in the bathroom doorway.

Rowdy, unsurprisingly, seemed annoyed to find me still lingering in his office. I was standing where he'd left me but facing the bathroom instead of his desk with my arms dutifully folded behind me.

"Yo, if you're done, you can go," he barked. "The fuck you still—" His sentence was abruptly cut off when his feet—clad in the latest Jordans instead of his usual slip-resistant boots—were suddenly swept from under him.

I cursed his unnaturally quick reflexes when Rowdy quickly threw out his arms, catching the bathroom door with one hand and the jamb with the other to keep from falling. It was all I could do not to give myself away when laughter bubbled in my throat at the shock in his eyes. I had to contract my stomach muscles to the point of pain just to swallow the urge.

"What the fuck?" Righting himself, Rowdy took a cautious step forward, his accusatory gaze shooting directly to me. I knew my cover was blown when he bared his teeth. He started to speak, but one ill-thought angry step in my direction had him slipping again.

With nothing to hold onto this time, all six-foot-six of him went toppling backward. My mouth formed an *O* when Rowdy landed on his ass hard enough to make the impact of his muscled body hitting the unforgiving floor echo like thunder through the room.

"Oh, my gosh!" I shrieked to hide the laughter I couldn't hold back this time. "Boss, are you okay?" I was *almost* a perfect image of shock and concern as I took tentative steps around the trail of water and oil to reach him. A smile played on my lips as I silently celebrated my victory.

I knew once Rowdy regained his wits from falling, he would quickly figure out the spill was my doing and make me pay for it, so I bought myself some time to get away by leading the trail directly to me instead of his desk.

It was a gamble that had paid off.

I'd no sooner stopped where Rowdy was still sprawled on the floor than he reached out faster than a snake. His hand wrapped around my ankle was my only warning before he yanked me off my feet and sent me toppling with a yelp onto the ground next to him.

The air punched out of my chest while pain shot through my pelvic bone thanks to my ass, taking the brunt of the fall. I hadn't even hit my head, and I saw stars. I groaned and quickly gave up when I tried to move. There was nothing I could do but lay there and silently berate myself for not just taking my win and leaving.

I just had to gloat.

Movement next to me caught my eye, and my heart began racing, sensing the danger ahead. I desperately tried once again to rise, but my stupid muscles protested and refused, leaving me vulnerable to Rowdy's wrath as he slowly regained his feet.

A moment later, he stepped over my prone body and planted each foot on my fingers as he peered down at me. Rowdy didn't bear down, but the threat was clear.

Expression blank, he tipped his bearded chin up. "You got jokes, huh?"

"I think *prank* would be a more accurate description," my dumb ass just had to retort. He didn't say anything, so I just blew out a breath. "Look, you got me back, so let's just call it even, okay?"

"Even? Nah. Ain't no even." Before I could respond, his foot pressed down slightly on my trapped fingers, and I whimpered partly from the pain but mostly from the fear of having my fingers broken. "Your ass got two choices," he continued. "You can clean this shit up and apologize, or you can get the fuck out of my establishment and my city and make damn sure I never see your face again."

I sucked in a breath even as everything in me raged at the thought of letting him win. "How about I clean up my mess and keep the apology? We both know I won't mean it anyway, so is it really that important?" Rowdy's only answer was to press down harder on my fingers. "Stop!" I panicked and screamed.

"Apologize."

"The only thing you'll get from me is my ass to kiss," I gritted out. "I'm not sorry for shit, you boorish maniac. You deserved it!"

This time, it felt like Rowdy bore all his weight down, ripping a pained scream from me when the bones in my fingers began to give. My vision suddenly blurred as my back bowed off the floor, and I screamed again. A moment later, I felt the first tears slipping from the corner of my eyes and dripping onto the floor.

I still didn't apologize.

I wouldn't.

Rowdy would just have to break every bone in my body to get his pound of flesh.

A moment later, I heard him curse viciously, and then the pressure suddenly eased before disappearing entirely.

I didn't see him move away, and I couldn't remember how I got off the floor.

One moment, I was lying on the floor writhing in pain, and

the next, I was sitting on the couch, sniffling and staring at nothing while Rowdy crouched in front of me.

Neither of us spoke as he carefully inspected my fingers, the calluses on his own scraping against my skin as he tested each one by flexing the digits and cursing again whenever I winced.

"I don't think they're broken," he said when he was done, sounding almost as relieved as I felt.

"Okay."

Something cold touched my fingers, and I saw him holding a blue compress over them. I didn't take a single breath as I stared at the snarling lion, the scars marking his skin, the bruises around his knuckles, and the simple yet large black-faced Rolex around his wrist.

"You're stubborn as fuck, you know that?"

I inhaled deeply before slowly exhaling as I shook my head. "I'm not going to accept responsibility for what you did, Rowdy. I didn't ask you to hurt me." There was no venom or anger in my tone, just bone-deep exhaustion.

"Did *I*?" he shot back. "That wasn't a mattress I fell on, Atlas, or are you one of those females who ignore double standards? That could have gone all the way left. What would you have done if I had fallen wrong and cracked my head open? Did you think about that?"

My stomach twisted, leaving behind the first twinge of regret.

No.

I hadn't thought at all. I just...reacted.

And recklessly threatened his life.

Some might argue Rowdy wanting to make me submit had been mild considering his reputation.

I finally allowed myself to meet his gaze, letting him see my sincerity as I said, "I'm sorry."

Freeing my hands from the ice packs, he stared at them for a long moment, some indecision in his eyes that melted away a second before his head lowered, and he kissed my cold fingers. Warmth pooled in my belly and pussy as I gaped at him.

"Me too," he whispered. He carefully tucked my trembling hands back under the ice before meeting my gaze.

I was still searching for a response to *that* when the fire alarm began blaring. The office became bathed in red when the emergency lights lashed. Frowning, Rowdy stood and was halfway to the door to see what was happening when it flew open.

Roc barreled through it, looking like he was seconds from losing his shit, only to pause when his gaze landed on me. The breath he released at finding me sitting on the sofa in one piece was audible, and I would have found it funny if I hadn't come so close to it not being so.

"Why the fuck are you busting in my office like you IPD?"

"Are you crazy?" Roc roared at his partner. "The whole shop heard Atlas in here screaming. I thought you were up here murdering that girl. I had Golden pull the fire alarm to get everyone out of the building."

I thought it was a little dramatic until his reason dawned on me. Roc had done it just in case they had to get rid of a body without being seen.

My body.

I glared at Roc, and he gave me a perplexed look right back.

"Well, as you can see, she's not dead," Rowdy said sarcastically. I was grateful he hadn't said I was fine because I wasn't. "Anything else you want to cry about?"

Roc noticed the ice packs on my fingers but didn't remark on it as he turned on his heel and stormed back out of the room. Rowdy went to shut the door behind him when I shot to my feet, letting the ice packs fall to the floor. The last thing I wanted was to be alone with him a moment longer.

"I should get back to work."

"How are your hands?" he asked, turning to face me while blocking my path to the door.

"Fine. See?" I held up my hands and wiggled them, fighting my wince at the ache in my bones, and forced a smile. He'd been right. My fingers weren't broken, but they hurt like hell. "I'm good to go, boss."

I could see the tick in his jaw that told me he wasn't ready to let me leave but had no reason to make me stay. Rowdy nodded and put distance between us as he strolled behind his desk and took a seat.

"Hey, Atlas," he called out once I reached the door.

My hands were trembling now as I turned to face him. "Yes, Rowdy?"

"You were fortunate it wasn't me here on Saturday. The next time you don't show up for work, whether I'm here or not, it *will* be me who shows up on your doorstep. Am I clear?"

I wondered if he could hear the knot of fear I forced down my throat. "We're clear."

His beautiful green eyes dared me to try him as he braced his strong forearms on the desk and leaned forward. "Yes, what, Atlas?"

I should have known he wouldn't let me leave without getting what he'd been after from the moment he ordered me up here.

My submission.

I tested out a few responses I knew he wouldn't like in my head, but each time I tried to let them rip, my injured fingers spasmed in a reminder of what would happen if I defied him again. Besides, I wasn't done with my first act of defiance, so I guess there was no harm in letting him think he'd won.

"Yes, sir."

Shame on him if he believed the lie.

Rowdy's face gave nothing away, so I quickly left before he discovered the rest of my prank.

Downstairs the customers and other employees were slowly trickling back inside the building. Hudson was speaking to the fire marshal, who didn't seem pleased to learn he'd made the trip for nothing. I wondered what excuse Hudson had given him for setting the alarm off.

When I returned to reception, Tuesday was nowhere to be

found, so I headed over to my side of the desk to hold down the fort.

I stopped short when I spotted a familiar red envelope waiting for me with my name on it. Like the first time, there was no other writing, making it clear this letter had been hand-delivered.

My skin turned cold as I looked for the faceless, nameless person who'd left it. I wasn't sure what I was expecting since whoever my anonymous pen pal was had gone to great lengths to keep their identity a secret.

Slowly, like I was defusing a bomb, I freed the letter from the envelope, held my breath, unfolded the intricate stationery, and read the neatly written message.

Atlas,

I'm so pleased you've found your way home. The stars have truly aligned. It's up to you now to unravel the lies. I wasn't brave enough to expose them, but I know you won't let me down. Whatever you do, remember...it's your head in the lion's mouth, so I'd think twice about betraying me. The Kings will not show mercy.

Love,

Unrequited

Whatever the fuck that meant.

SEVEN

Rowdy

ATLAS HAD ALREADY LEFT THE ROOM WHEN I NOTICED MY TAMPERED water jug sitting exactly where I'd left it. It must have been where she'd gotten the water from, so I grabbed it to throw away when something inside caught my eye.

Scowling, I popped the top and upended the jug to fish out the unidentified object that turned out to be a tightly rolled piece of paper. I tore off the tape and felt a smile playing at my lips when it unfurled, and I realized it was her misconduct form.

I couldn't help reading her responses even though my gut told me they would only piss me off.

Description of Incident(s) or Behavior(s): I missed my shift, so my boss and his fragile ego followed me into the bathroom to yell at me like an entitled pervert.

Reported by: My boss with the fragile ego.

Other potential witnesses: Anyone with eyes and a spine.

Supporting Documentation: This form he made me fill out to stroke his fragile ego.

Supporting Evidence: Everything he's said and done since the moment we met.

Employee's Comments: I need a raise.

Corrective Action Plan: Avoid him at all costs.

Do you regret your actions? Unlikely.

Next Action Step if Problem Continues: Kick him in his big lion balls?

Employee Signature: *Atlas FUCK YOU Beck*

Employer Signature:

I plucked a pen from the tin can that used to hold soup and signed my name before opening the top drawer of my desk and placing it inside for my eyes only instead of in her official file.

Sitting back, I closed my eyes to regain control of myself. As soon as I did, though, I heard her soft voice calling me sir, and I palmed my hard dick through my work pants.

Each battle with Atlas made it harder to care about the rules or her age. I'd heard disobedient bitches had the best pussy around, and I needed hers in the worst way.

I shot up from my chair and proceeded to clean up the mess she'd made. Once that was done, I grabbed another water from underneath the sideboard, chugged a quarter of it down, and then headed downstairs to start my day.

Atlas was standing behind the reception desk with Tuesday, so I made sure to wait until I was in her view, and she was discreetly watching me from the corner of her eye before I uncapped my water and took a nice long drink.

While the untampered water poured down my throat, I watched her chew on her lip before turning away when she could no longer stomach the guilt.

Satisfaction bloomed in my chest, knowing I would always win every battle in this war between us. Because Atlas had a conscience, and I did not.

"O."

Hearing my name, I spun around and found Roc standing behind me. "Sup?"

"Atlas told me she missed her shift Saturday, so I'm guessing that was the reason for all the screaming I heard?"

The four of us worked the clock every day of the week, with alternating Saturdays while the shop was closed on Sundays. This past Saturday was actually supposed to be my shift, but luckily for Atlas, I had Golden cover for me because I had shit to do.

During the week, Golden and I both started our days at seven, an hour before the shop opened in the morning, while Roc and Joren came in at ten for the closing shifts, which ended at seven.

As they said, the early bird catches the worm, so yeah…I'd checked her little ass before Roc had the chance to coddle her.

"Yup." I started toward my station with him on my heels.

"And everything's good?" he asked, staring at me like he expected the opposite.

"Fuck you think? She's still here, isn't she?" Annoyed, I yanked open my tool chest to start my daily checks. Believe it or not, my slight OCD and paranoia helped keep my temper in check.

Sometimes.

"Can you blame me for checking, though? It's not like you have the best track record dealing with employees, and you and baby girl already got off on the wrong foot."

"That's because her stuck-up ass wouldn't let me fuck," I responded with an indignant sniff. I was serious as a heart attack too. I was used to females who fell to their knees and begged to suck my dick. With Atlas, I felt like I was in high school again, having to work for the pussy with professions of love and flowers.

All right, I'm bullshitting.

I never had to work this hard, even then.

I looked over to see Roc giving me the side-eye. "She's a little young, isn't she?"

"Didn't know that at the time," I defended, even though I wasn't sure I cared anymore. "I was hoping she was older. Black don't crack, know what I mean?"

"And now?"

All I could do was shrug as I moved some tools around. I'd never felt the need to lie before, and I wasn't going to start now. "She's an employee." It was all the assurance I could offer that

I wouldn't touch her. "Why do you care so much anyway? I've never seen you go this hard for Tuesday."

"I don't know," he said in a tone that suggested the opposite. I gave him a look, and the seal on his lips broke a second later. "All right, but you better not say shit to her." I promised no such thing, but his gossiping ass didn't even notice as he glanced over his shoulder to make sure we wouldn't be overheard. "She told me her father died, and from the state that I found her in, I'm guessing it was recently."

My gaze flew to the reception desk where Atlas was helping a customer. She was smiling, and I stared long and hard as if I could peel back the layers and see the grief she was hiding underneath her soft exterior. I wanted to penetrate that young bitch in the worst way, and I was beginning to suspect not just her body.

"What state was that?" I asked without taking my gaze from Atlas.

Her smile was strained now, as if she could feel my attention and was forcing herself not to look my way.

"I don't know…sad?" Roc answered unhelpfully. "On the low, it sounded like she ran away from home and had nowhere else to go."

"It's why you hired her," I mused aloud. I forced myself to turn away from the window.

Suddenly, it all made sense, the reason Roc had brought her into the fold with barely an interview and felt the need to grill me about every interaction I had with her. Having a daughter himself, it was all he saw when he looked at Atlas.

A lost little girl without her father.

"Yeah, I guess. It's something about her too. I can't put my finger on it. Seems like I…know her." His voice had trailed off, and now he was squinting as he stared at Atlas through the window. "O…sh-she don't look familiar to you?"

All I'd allowed myself was a quick glance over my shoulder. "Not really. Where would we know her from? She's young as fuck and not from around here." Her license had read Ossella, which was clear on the other side of Mississippi.

"I don't know—just a feeling, I guess. You talked to Golden? He's been acting distant lately." I gave him a flat look. "I mean more than usual," he amended.

"Yeah, I talked to him," I reluctantly admitted. I didn't want to give credence to this paranoid delusion slowly eating away at our inner circle. "He pretty much said the same as you. He thinks we know her."

He'd also been avoiding her too.

Roc was staring off in the distance for a while, and then he mumbled, "Maybe we do," before walking off.

I frowned, my gaze following him all the way to his station next to Golden's, which overlooked Temperance.

I went back to organizing my tools.

Golden was a drama queen, and Roc was an enabler. I wasn't about to entertain either one of their bullshit today.

Still, when the lunch hour arrived, I took a break, which I rarely did. I was usually the first one here and the last to leave, even though my shift ended at four. I was a bit of a workaholic, but it kept me away from people and out of trouble.

I washed up in the employee's bathroom inside the workshop and then headed into the lobby to grab a snack. I was leaning against the bar, doing my usual scans to make sure the customers were happy and business was running smoothly, when some guy I knew from around the way approached me.

"Man, I was hoping to run into you!" Donny's dick-riding ass greeted me with a grin. "I asked the new girl if I could run back there and talk to you, but she said you were busy."

That's my baby, I thought with a smirk before I could catch myself.

I knew Atlas had only refused to avoid having to speak to me, but I still felt something akin to pride bloom in my chest. At the end of the day, she got me, and that was all any man could ask of the woman he wanted to fuck—more than once.

And I would definitely need more than one round with little Miss Atlas Beck.

Donny held out his hand, which I ignored.

He thought I forgot that time in the third grade when I caught him leaving the bathroom after taking a piss and not washing his hands. His smile wavered at my pointed stare before he awkwardly dropped his hand.

"I brought my car in for an oil change," he said as if that would make me change my mind about shaking those dick-beaters.

"Cool. That's what's up."

Grabbing a honey bun and water, I sat at the bar on the side facing reception and watched as Atlas checked in a customer. Tuesday must have been on her lunch break because she was nowhere to be found. I was a little irked since it was too soon to leave Atlas on her own, but surprisingly, she seemed to have a handle on things.

"So anyway," Donny continued. "I saw the custom work you did to Nate's car and wanted to know if you'd be willing to hook mine up."

My gaze didn't stray from Atlas as I answered him. "I don't really got the time, Donny."

"I know, I know, but you could take all the time you needed. I can always carpool with my wife until it's ready. I'll even pay double what you charged Nate."

Unfortunately, that got my attention, so I reluctantly looked away from Atlas to regard Donny's thirsty ass.

"You got cash? I don't accept checks, favors, food stamps, or IOUs."

"Yeah, look." Like a dummy, he pulled out a large wad and counted out twice the cash I'd made from Nate. Ten years ago, I would have just knocked Donny over the head and confiscated the whole stack, but that wasn't me anymore, so I only took what he offered and let his bitch-ass pocket the rest.

"All right, fuck it, I'll do it. But listen carefully, Donny. I will only say this *once*. Pride of King's official business is my *first* priority. Your car won't even be my second or third, and I don't rush my work for anyone. It's ready when I'm ready. With that understood, let me make something clear. You've got one time to ask me when your car will be done, and I won't even sell it for parts. I'll fuck you up first and then make you watch while I feed that bitch to a car crusher." His eyes damn near bulged out of their sockets, and I could tell he was already regretting hiring me. It was too bad he'd already paid me because I didn't give refunds either. I placed my hand on his shoulder, my grip just tight enough to let him know I was serious as I looked him dead in the eye. "*One time*, Donny."

"O-okay."

"Cool." I stood up, cleared my trash, and started to walk away when I spun back around on my heel. "Oh, yeah. Appreciate the business, cuz." I offered him a rare smile, but that seemed to only scare him more, so I let it drop.

"You're welcome," he said before promising to email me ASAP, listing the work he wanted to be done. And then he fled the shop like his ass was on fire.

I started to head outside to get some fresh air when I felt a gentle tap on my shoulder. I turned to see none other than Atlas's pretty ass standing there with a vulnerable look in her eyes.

I ignored her silent plea not to upset or hurt her and let my gaze peruse her face and body. I'd been too angry earlier to notice her appearance, but I found myself obsessively tracking the star-shaped vitiligo on her face like some kind of coping mechanism. I wanted nothing more than to trace the pattern with my finger, so I slipped my hands into my pockets to quell the urge.

Today, she'd chosen to wear the black collared uniform shirt with our logo on the breast pocket and had paired it with a black pleated skirt and knee-high black socks that made her look like some kind of school girl instead of a receptionist.

Just like that, my dick was hard again, and I tried and failed not to be aggravated by it *and* her, so it was no surprise when I barked, "Fuck you want?"

If Atlas was bothered or shocked by my cruelty, she didn't let it show. "Sorry to bother you, but Tommy wants to know where they should take the cars to be washed before pickup?"

"What do you mean where? They take them next door as per fucking usual."

Atlas's expression was gratingly blank, her tone equally flat when she responded, "They're closed."

I was frowning even harder when I left her standing there without an answer and started for the double doors.

Every cell in my body screamed to go back, pull her close, and promise to take care of everything. The car wash situation, the grief I knew she was hiding, and whatever else she needed. I wanted to be at her complete disposal.

But I didn't go back.

I kept walking even though my feet felt heavy, as if the J's she'd ruined were filled with lead. I kept walking for her own good—one last desperate attempt to save this innocent little girl from me.

Master Bubbles Car Wash was a short walk away at the west end of Temperance Street, so I reached it in time to see Harry's ancient ass wrapping a thick chain around the door handles and securing it with a padlock.

For some reason, my heart dropped, and I quickened my steps. "Aye! Harry! Aye, Harry!"

The man in question turned to face me with a somber look in his eyes. "Hey, Rowdy. How ya doing, son? I was just getting ready to come see you."

"What's up, old timer?" I quickly closed the distance with my arms thrown open in disbelief. "Why did you close early? Bingo ain't for a few more hours. Them geriatric thotties can wait."

I chuckled to lighten the mood, but I could tell my joke didn't land when Harry simply shook his head instead of flaying my ass open with one of his infamous insults.

I'd learned all my shit-talking from Harry. He was one of the few people besides my boys, my parents, Hudson—and now

Atlas, I guess—who wasn't afraid to give me a taste of my own medicine. They usually got away with it too.

Right now, Harry's sad gaze was on the ground, his shoulders bowed in defeat, and I fucking hated the sight of it.

"What's up, Harry? Talk to me."

He sighed. "This is for real, son. I'm closing the wash. I appreciate all the business you boys sent this old man over the years, but it's not enough anymore. The well's dried up. I can't afford to keep this place open a day longer."

"If money's the issue, I can talk to the others, and maybe we can front you the cash. How much do you need—" Harry's proud ass waved me off before I could even finish.

"It's more than that, son. I'm tired. I don't have it in me to fight anymore. This corona-whatever was the last straw." Sighing, Harry bent and lifted a manila folder from his briefcase on the ground and handed it to me. Before I could ask what it was, he said, "I watched as you knuckleheads terrorized these streets for years and dared to call yourselves kings while destroying your own community. But I never lost faith in you, Rowdy Wray. I never stopped waiting for the day the four of you stopped being boys and became men. I'm happy to say you didn't disappoint." A wistful smile briefly broke his somber expression. "I guess the rumors are true." Harry reached out a gnarled finger and poked my chest. "A lion's heart indeed." He nodded. "I know you'll make me proud."

Harry patted my arm and ambled off before I could find a fucking vowel.

I stood in front of the car wash, watching him go, the silence on the other side haunting me like a weary ghost.

I didn't feel the winter breeze chilling my blood as I flipped open the folder to find the deed to Harry's car wash along with the title to his business signed over to me and a contract already bearing his signature and a note.

Don't make the same mistakes I did.

EIGHT

Atlas

SOMETHING WAS WRONG.

I could feel it as indubitably as the winter air that breezed in through the shop's door when Rowdy returned from next door. I had this vision of him terrorizing innocent bystanders in his wake like a radioactive monster with an aversion to people.

Rowdy was silent and holding a folder as he prowled through the lobby, oblivious to all the lustful stares from the horny housewives and desperate singles who insisted on waiting hours for their vehicle repairs to be completed.

Even worse, I'd thrown myself within their ranks.

Rowdy didn't look at me once, but that didn't stop me from watching him stalk past reception. He didn't speak a word to anyone as he headed upstairs to shut himself in his office.

I'd just lost the battle against following him and making him tell me what was wrong when a shadow fell over my side of the desk.

"I guess the stars have finally aligned."

Startled, I jerked my gaze away from the window and followed the voice that was deep like a chasm yet smooth like silk and richer than cashmere to see *him*.

The elusive fourth King.

The final lion of the pride.

Joren.

My first thought was that he wasn't as tall as Rowdy. It was a weird comparison, considering it wouldn't have mattered if the man before me was three feet tall or thirty. No one would ever have noticed anything beyond his looks.

To say that Joren Dorsey was handsome would be underselling it by a *mile.*

He was downright beautiful.

Arguably, the best looking of all of the Kings with his Adonis physique, deep dark skin, raven eyes, straight white teeth, deep dimples, bow-shaped lips, and bald head that I knew had once been covered by a silky grade of jet-black hair much like my own.

He was shorter, yes, but packed more muscle than Rowdy. The platinum Cuban link he wore rested against the white tank underneath the overalls. He stroked the full beard framing his lips and jaw as those shark-like eyes pinned me in place and waited for my response. Where Rowdy was sexy in that rough-around-the-edges way, Joren was a pretty boy through and through, and I could tell he knew it.

Each of the Kings had their weapons.

Rowdy's was brute force, Roc's was duplicity, and Golden's was silence.

Seduction was Joren's.

The evidence was there in his stance and his smile, in how he leaned forward to give me a whiff of his cologne and a peek at the muscles underneath his uniform. It was in how his smile would have been genuine if not for the arrogant tilt that kept it from reaching his eyes. And if that didn't work, I bet he thought the bust down—the diamond-encrusted watch on his wrist—would dazzle me into submission.

Instantly, I was annoyed at yet another domineering male attempting to handle me, so I turned to face my fourth boss fully.

I wondered if his beauty was a lie, and he secretly hid scabs and boils underneath that beard he couldn't stop stroking.

"So, I hear you're our new receptionist."

"Yup." I moved across the small space created by the U-shaped desk until I was standing directly in front of him. I couldn't have him thinking I was intimidated by his attention. "Is that a problem?"

Joren dropped the act and was squinting now as he attempted to read me. I couldn't decide if he was baffled by my immunity or just feeling plain ole sore about it. "Only if you make it one."

I guess Roc and Golden had put the word out to keep an eye on me. Clearly, I was not cut out for a career in espionage.

"Well, then. Glad that's settled. Consider me thoroughly threatened." I flashed him a saccharine smile before giving him my black ass to kiss. "It was nice meeting you, boss."

The phone rang before Joren had the chance to realize that a low-level employee had dismissed him, so I quickly answered it. I could still feel him lurking, though—watching and assessing… probably wanting to strangle me.

Eventually, he fucked off, and I focused on the screaming customer in my ear.

I'd successfully pushed Joren from my mind by the time Tuesday returned from lunch. He'd gotten under my skin way too easily, and no amount of pondering could unearth the reason why. Rowdy had, too, just not nearly in the same way. I'd come way too close to letting him degrade me behind a dumpster our first meeting.

Joren, I'd just wanted to stab in the eye.

"How did it go?" Tuesday eagerly asked as soon as I was done booking the customer's appointment. "Not too bad, right?"

"No, it was fine." I quickly filled her in on the car washing situation—since I never did get an answer from Rowdy—before the phone rang, and Tuesday snatched it up as if her life depended on it.

"Pride of Kings Mechanics, how may I—Oh, hey, boss."

My stomach dipped. It was weird, right? I had four bosses. Technically, five if I counted Hudson, whose role as General Manager consisted mostly of being the Kings' sounding board—and conscience on occasion. It could have been any one of them on the other end of the line, but somehow, I knew it was him.

"Sure," Tuesday agreed, chipper as ever. "Do you want your usual? Okay, I'll go right now. Oh…No, she's still here. Yeah, I'll let her know. Okay. Bye."

Tuesday placed the receiver down, and I pretended I hadn't been eavesdropping as she quickly wrote something down on the notepad bearing the Pride of Kings logo. "So, you can take your break now," she announced, "but on your way back, Rowdy wants you to pick up his lunch from Fred's."

"He…what?"

Of course, Tuesday was oblivious to my change in mood as she read over whatever she'd written before adding a few more things, then ripping the sheet off the pad and handing it to me. One glance at what was written, and I just barely stopped myself from tossing it in the trash where it belonged.

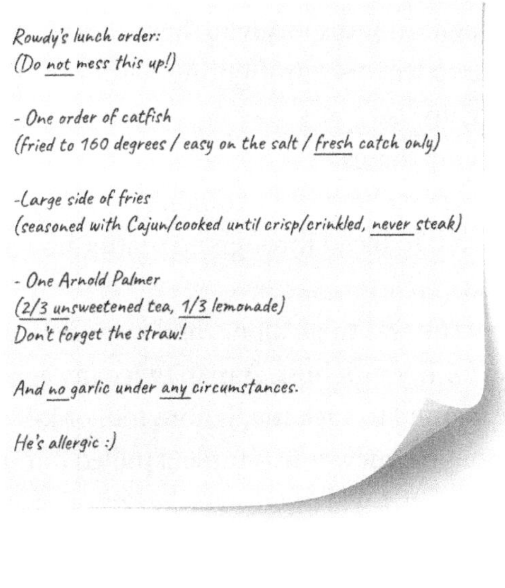
Rowdy's lunch order:
(Do not mess this up!)

- One order of catfish
(fried to 160 degrees / easy on the salt / fresh catch only)

-Large side of fries
(seasoned with Cajun/cooked until crisp/crinkled, never steak)

- One Arnold Palmer
(2/3 unsweetened tea, 1/3 lemonade)
Don't forget the straw!

And no garlic under any circumstances.

He's allergic :)

As soon as I finished reading, I met Tuesday's blue gaze. She was holding a stack of new tickets, but the look in her eyes said she already knew what I was thinking, so I swallowed my response. "He would also like you to know that if his food is tampered with in any way, you will be sorry." Tuesday walked away as if this was all normal.

I guess it was when you worked for a psycho.

Grabbing my purse and jacket, I stuffed the note inside and headed out. The cold air slapped me in the face as soon as I stepped outside, so I zipped up my jacket to ward against the chill. February was only a week away, and it was getting colder.

I thought about how I couldn't wait for spring.

And then I thought about my dad and how he died before he could see another. Spring had been his favorite time of the year because of the flirty dresses mom would wear to show off her legs just for him. Mom said winter was her favorite time of year because Dad would always hold her just a little bit tighter to keep her warm through the night.

God. Mom. She'd taken his death so hard. The part of me that loved her too much and remembered what a great mom she'd been up until she'd lost her soul mate wanted to forgive her for the things she'd said.

But I'd spent months forgiving her.

For lying to me, for not fighting harder to get out of bed, and for giving up.

For so many things.

I kept forgiving her until I couldn't do it anymore. Until resentment started to bleed through no matter how hard I pressed on the wound.

And now she was there alone, and I was here alone—taking lunch orders for my new boss. A man twice my age who couldn't decide if he wanted to fuck me, ignore me, or kill me.

Even though I knew it was futile, I pulled out my phone and dialed my mom as I walked down the street. It rang and rang until the voicemail picked up, so I ended the call without leaving a message. She never returned my calls anyway. I guess we'd said all we needed to.

I passed Fred's, an alley big enough for a car to drive through to the small parking lot at the rear, and then a vacant building before coming across the hair salon at the end of the street. I'd spotted it before during my surveillance of the Kings. The salon had been my backup plan in case I couldn't get a position at POK.

On the other side of the street was a liquor and corner store with a few hardheads hanging around. Instinct sent me fleeing inside the salon the moment their watchful eyes landed on me. I could feel them wondering if I was a potential customer or potential mark.

"Welcome to Bossin' Up Hair Studio."

I was greeted by a short, curvaceous beauty with dark-brown skin, a round face, and deep dimples. She was older than me but still young. I guessed her age to be around the late twenties or early thirties.

"Hi." I waved, looked around the empty salon while she finished sweeping up the hair on the floor, and searched for an excuse for wandering in here. I was still grappling for a reason when she approached the front counter where I was standing.

"Do you have an appointment?"

"I—no, sorry. I was walking by, and I saw your salon. I just started working over at Pride of Kings."

"Oh." I could see the hairdresser's surprise as her gaze flicked to the door in the direction of the shop and back to me. "You're a mechanic?"

"God, no. I can't even change a tire. My dad tried to show me once so that I wouldn't be totally helpless in a bind, but it never stuck. No, I work reception."

"So you know Tuesday then." She cocked her head to the side. "How do you like working with her?"

"She's cool. Helpful. Energetic. Knows her shit." I thought about the note in my pocket. "Takes her job a little seriously, though."

The hairdresser lifted her flawless brows at that. "Oh, I don't blame her. You just started working there, so I don't want to scare you, but you should know the Kings are not to be fucked with."

I kept my face blank even as a chill worked down my spine. "Rowdy's crazy for sure, but the others don't seem so bad."

"Good. That means you haven't gotten on their bad side." I felt the hair on my nape stand up because I knew that was where I'd eventually land when they found out I not only came to Idlewild to find them but that I was carrying around a picture of them from twenty years ago. "Rowdy's different," the hairdresser continued. "He basically wakes up on the wrong side of the bed every day. He's got a thorn in his paw, and everyone's too scared to rip it out."

"And he just doesn't give a fuck." It made him more dangerous than the others.

"Nope," the hairdresser agreed with a pop of her glossy lips. "God definitely lost a screw or two when He made that one." Her eyes widened in mock horror, making me chuckle. When she smiled, her deep dimples became even more prominent. "So here's the thing," she said while handing me a white slip of paper. It was a new client intake form. "I don't do walk-ins, but I've got fifteen minutes until my next client arrives. I can do a free consultation to assess your hair's needs, and then we can book an appointment if you'd like."

"Sounds good."

"Great! Oh, I didn't catch your name?"

"Atlas," I offered.

"Nice to meet you, Atlas. I'm Demetria, but everyone calls me Demi. Follow me."

Even though my hair was the least of my worries, I followed her. Demi had a sincerity that I desperately needed, so I found myself wanting to spend more time in the hairdresser's company. Besides my coworkers and the twins, who I hadn't seen or talked to since I fled their house Saturday morning, I didn't know anyone in Idlewild. Loneliness was the most silent killer of all.

I also wasn't ready to go back to the shop if it meant Rowdy wasn't done with me today. Sending me to get his lunch was just another form of torture, and I was going to crawl, not run toward it.

I followed Demi to her chair and let her appraise the faux locs I'd gotten a month ago. On top of being kind, she had gentle hands and seemed knowledgeable, so I booked an appointment for Saturday to have the outer rim re-twisted. Demi had an opening sooner, but my funds were funny, and I wouldn't receive my first paycheck until the end of the week.

My stomach growled as I left, so I caved to the inevitable and walked over to Fred's two buildings over. The bell above the door chimed as I entered the restaurant. The inside was small, with only a handful of tables, a drink station, and one of those bubble gum machines in the dining area. The black and white checkered floor was dingy but clean according to the Wet Floor sign by the door, and the strong Pine-Sol smell wafting from the peeling tile.

I could hear "Family Affair" by Mary J. Blige playing faintly from the speakers as I approached the empty counter and rang the silver bell resting on top.

A moment later, a tall, lanky black man in his fifties wearing a hair net appeared.

"Welcome to Fred's, young lady. What can I get you?"

I wordlessly pulled Rowdy's lunch order from my pocket and stared at it for half a beat before handing it over. I figured it was better to hand over Tuesday's directions than to repeat Rowdy's neurosis aloud and offend a perfect stranger.

To my surprise, the cook didn't seem surprised at all. He read it over, and then I could feel him sizing me up as he handed it back to me. "You must be the new receptionist." He chuckled when I gaped. "I'm Fred. Cook and owner."

Fred held out his hand, so I shook it. "Atlas."

"Take a load off, Atlas, and I'll have Rowdy's order right out."

I offered him a grateful smile that was small but felt genuine. "Thanks."

"You don't have any stops to make after this, do you?" When I frowned, he held up his hands and added, "Rowdy likes his food piping hot. Don't want to have to make it over when he sends you back." He leaned forward. "And trust me, girl…he will."

Cracking up, Fred slapped his leg when my lips parted in disbelief. *Wow.*

"Nope. This is it," I assured him.

"All righty. Should be ready in ten minutes."

I popped a squat while Fred disappeared inside the kitchen. There was a narrow opening in the wall with a ledge, which allowed me to see his head and shoulders as he moved around. Moments later, the sound of oil crackling drifted into the dining area.

The phone rang off the hook, but Fred never stopped preparing Rowdy's food, even once, to answer. I cringed, wondering if he was missing potential orders.

I shook my head before pulling out the photo that had gotten me into this mess. This time, however, I don't fixate on the four teenage boys who had grown into men—into kings.

I was focused on *her*.

The gorgeous girl posing between them.

She had "It Girl" written all over her with her curly reddish-brown hair and pink velour tracksuit from Baby Phat. The jacket was cropped, exposing her silver belly chain and flat stomach, while the matching shorts showed off her long golden legs. She was smiling at the camera like it was the happiest night of her life.

Maybe it had been.

I still didn't know who she was or what had become of her. Flipping the photo over, I read the words on the back for the thousandth time.

Golden, Roc, Joren, and Rowdy with Jada at the V-Day bash.

Could Jada have been the one who'd sent the letter and photo?

"Okay, pretty girl. Order's up."

I quickly stuffed the photo back in my purse and walked to

the counter to pay. "How much is it?" I asked when Fred simply handed me the bag without giving me a total. *Rowdy better at least pay me back.*

If not, I'd find some way to take his balls as restitution.

"It's taken care of," Fred announced while handing me an empty styrofoam cup. "Hope you like fish. I threw a little something in there for you as well." He disappeared again before I could thank him, whistling a tune I didn't recognize.

Grabbing the bag, I moved over to the drink station to fill the cup half full with sweetened tea and the other half with lemonade.

One Arnold Palmer coming right up.

I checked the time and darted out the door after realizing my lunch break had ended ten minutes ago. Crossing Temperance was fairly easy since it was the middle of the day, and most businesses on this street had been forced to vacate. I planned to talk Tuesday into delivering Rowdy's food, but the reception desk was empty when I walked through the front door.

Grumbling, I headed into the workshop, hoping to find him there—around witnesses—but his station at the end of the middle row was also empty. I truly must have been desperate because my gaze darted to Joren's station next, then Roc's, and Golden's, before accepting that I was going to have to be an adult about this.

Fine.

I started up the stairs, feeling the bottom of the bag as I climbed to make sure Rowdy's food remained hot while I hunted him down. I wouldn't put it past him to be hiding on purpose so that he'd have a reason to punish me or send me back.

Music spilled from underneath his closed office door, so I knocked and waited.

I caught the sound a moment too late, the quiet chatter of multiple voices speaking low on the other side, and the sudden hush that told me it was too late. They'd heard my knock.

The door was snatched open before I could leave the food and run.

I was met by brown eyes so dark the pupils were barely

noticeable, and then Joren wordlessly stepped back to let me inside when I tried to hand him the bag.

Asshole.

I slowly entered the room, the thick cloud of smoke stinging my eyes and the smell of weed assaulting my nose. The smoke was so heavy I could barely see three feet in front of me. Or the three other figures huddled in the dark.

"'Bout fucking time," Rowdy griped. I didn't notice him standing beside me until he rudely snatched the bag from my hand. "This shit better be hot too, or your ass is going back."

The smart response on my tongue was cut short by the distinct sound of the door slamming closed, shutting me *inside* with them. Joren walked past me and returned to his seat in front of the desk while I swallowed nervously at the rustling sound of the paper bag filling the otherwise pointed silence.

"Ay—what the—I ain't order this."

My eyes had adjusted to the dark enough now to see Rowdy frowning down at the open takeout tray with distaste. For a paranoid moment, I panicked, thinking Fred had set me up before I remembered his kind offer.

"What is it?" A voice I recognized as Roc's spoke through the smoke and dark. Relief at having at least one ally in the room almost overcame my anxiety. Almost. I wasn't naive enough to think Roc's loyalty wasn't first and foremost to his partners.

"A swordfish sandwich."

"Shit, I'll take it."

My lunch was tossed across the room, and before I could tell him it was mine, Roc tore away the foil, eating half the sandwich in one bite.

Huffing a breath, I noticed Golden sitting still on the sofa next to him. He tensed a little when he noticed my attention, and then I watched, fascinated, as the panic slowly left his eyes, and he forced himself to relax before turning his head and ignoring me.

It almost seemed like he was…pouting. At me for being in his presence or himself for showing a moment of weakness?

Rowdy popped open the second tray containing his food and promptly sat to begin stuffing his face without even a thank you. "Where's my drink?" he demanded without looking up.

It was only then I realized I was still holding it.

I walked the two steps over to his desk and set it down.

"Thanks," he surprised me by saying. I exhaled when I spotted the steam still curling from his fried catfish and turned to leave. "Hold the fuck up."

Fuck. Are you kidding me? I'd been so close.

I gripped the door knob a little tighter. Could I get away with pretending I hadn't heard him?

Probably not.

Left with no other choice, I sucked it up and faced the room. "Yes?"

"Come here."

I pursed my lips before obeying. I hated him and myself for every step that brought me closer. Once I was standing in front of his desk again, I watched Rowdy take a testing sip of the Arnold Palmer and then another before calmly holding it out to me. "Does this taste like what I asked for?"

"How should I know? It's your drink."

"*Taste it.*"

I could feel all four sets of eyes on me as I debated my next move.

No one was less surprised than me when I slowly reached for the cup. A private thrill chased down my spine at the thought of my lips touching where his had been. My gaze was firmly fixed on the styrofoam as I took the cup from him, but the moment our fingers brushed, my eyes locked with his green ones, and my pussy begged me for just a taste.

Rowdy licked his lips as if he knew, but for once, he didn't say anything. Was it because we weren't alone? He had fuck boy written all over him, but I could have sworn that was a territorial gleam I glimpsed in his eyes.

"Uh...do you two want us to leave?" Roc nosily blurted.

"Now, Atlas," Rowdy ordered while ignoring his friend.

I brought the straw to my lips and sipped.

The sweetness of the tea and the slight tang of lemonade flooded my taste buds, and I almost cringed at what tasted like nothing but sugar.

It was then I remembered.

Rowdy had asked for *unsweetened* tea and I'd given him sweetened. I was pretty sure I'd gotten the measurements wrong too, but it was partially his fault for being so fussy in the first place.

I slowly set the cup down but said nothing.

"Now, either you can't follow simple directions," he snapped, "or Tuesday fucked up, in which case, her day is about to go to hell. Which is it, Atlas?"

I recalled Demi's warning not to get on the Kings' bad side, but that didn't mean I was ruthless enough to throw Tuesday under the bus to save my own ass.

"I fucked up," I admitted to the quiet room.

"Apparently, our talk this morning wasn't enough for you to shape the fuck up, so tell me, Atlas…what will it take?" I just barely stopped my lips from curling as Rowdy sat back in his chair, looking smug. "What should I do about your inability to do what I tell you?"

I almost did it.

I almost turned to beseech Roc for help—maybe even turn them on each other—but Roc and Rowdy had been friends longer than I'd been alive. My plan could backfire, and then it would be four against one instead of me and Rowdy at each other's throats in this private war of ours.

I was on my own.

"I don't know what you *should* do," I said to Rowdy, "but you *could* act like a grown-up and get over it."

From the corner of my eye, I could have sworn I saw Joren wince.

The room was silent for one long, tense moment, and then, *"Fuck."*

The sound drew my attention behind me in time to see Roc staring at the floor like he wanted to be anywhere else but here. Even Golden's usual impassivity was gone as he stared at me like he was seeing me for the first time. Or maybe he was just getting one last look since he'd probably never see me again.

I'd done it again. I'd reacted without thinking.

"Get out." Hoping he'd meant me, I immediately started for the door. Of course, I wasn't that lucky. "Bring your ass back here, Atlas."

Damn it.

The chair next to me scraped across the floor, and then Joren unfolded his muscular frame from the seat. Ignoring me, he headed for the door and left without a backward glance. Hearing movement behind me, I turned completely, stupidly giving Rowdy my back as Roc and Golden followed suit.

"Wait..."

Surprisingly, it was Golden who stopped.

Roc's bitch-ass pretended he didn't hear me as he headed straight for the door, leaving me on my own. Once he was gone, Golden walked past me and around the desk to whisper something in Rowdy's ear.

His expression remained aloof even as he said, "Golden said to tell him who you really are and why you're here, and he'll take you with him."

"What?"

Rowdy ignored me. "I don't even know why you're wasting your time, G. This little bitch been suspect since the beginning."

My heart skipped a beat, but I said anyway, "Kind of like four grown men sitting in the dark behind a locked door?"

"Door wasn't locked," Rowdy returned with an indignant sniff.

Golden just stared at me, waiting for me to fess up. I started to do so many times I lost count.

"I'm sorry, Golden. I don't know what you mean."

The air in the room was thick with my lie, and I could see the disappointment in Golden's eyes just before he whispered something else to Rowdy, who nodded. "Appreciate it, bruh."

Golden didn't look at me as he strode straight for the door.

A moment later, I was alone with Rowdy for the second time today.

NINE

Rowdy

ATLAS WAS DOING A TERRIBLE JOB PRETENDING SHE WASN'T ABOUT to lose it.

"Did you know corporal punishment in the workplace used to be legal?" I bullshitted. I had no idea if that was true, but I enjoyed watching her pause, her nervous gaze shifting toward the door.

Atlas must have realized she'd never reach it in time because she said, "Touch me, and you'll lose a hand."

"I doubt it." I stood up and walked around the desk until I was standing close enough to force her head back to hold my gaze—the stubborn little thing. "You can try, though," I offered seriously.

Just to show her and satisfy my own curiosity, I ran my hand over her hip.

I could tell Atlas was torn between begging me to shift my hand a few inches to the left and making good on her threat. A moment later, she settled for blindly fumbling behind her to grip the edge of the desk.

"Stop touching me."

"You didn't ask nicely."

"Please stop touching me. Fuck you. Thanks."

I grinned. "Keep it up. I just might."

Atlas shook her head, looking a little forlorn. "I can't fuck you, Rowdy. You're my boss, and I need this job."

"I won't be for long if you fuck up again," I told her honestly. I might want her pussy, but that didn't entitle her to special treatment. It wouldn't matter if I fired her anyway. She'd still let me hit.

"People make mistakes, Rowdy. You can't kick everyone out of your life who isn't perfect."

Without warning, I grabbed her hips and lifted her onto the desk before forcing my way between her legs. "Yes, I can." My hands palmed her calves now as my thumbs teased the soft skin above her tall black socks that stopped just beneath her knees. Naughty schoolgirl, indeed.

"I doubt your friends are perfect."

"They're the exception, not the rule. I'm stuck with their asses, and they couldn't get rid of me if they died."

"I think you mean tried," she corrected.

"You heard what I said." Testing her boundaries, I slid my hands further up, my fingers skimming the side of her legs while my thumbs continued to tease her thighs. Her muscles tensed as if she would push me away and then relaxed a moment later.

"Do you feel that way about your girlfriend too?"

"I don't have a girlfriend," I told her fishing ass. My hands disappeared underneath her skirt. When she didn't tense up this time, I kept going, enjoying her quiet, horny sigh. "I don't want one either."

Atlas's hand suddenly reached for my wrist, stopping my exploration just as my fingers grazed the edge of her panties. "I'm not really the sex-without-commitment type," she announced with an attitude. "Sorry."

I broke her hold and kissed her jaw. "That's because you've never had sex with me."

"Arrogance isn't attractive." She hissed when my finger flicked her fat lips through her panties.

"Then why is your pussy wet, Atlas?"

"Oh, *boss*…" She gave me a mocking pout. "Is that what you call wet?"

"Yeah?" I didn't give her a chance to respond before I hooked my finger in the seat of her *drenched* panties, pulled them as far away from her pussy as the cheap lace would allow, and then let them go.

Atlas yelped when the material hit her pussy with a wet slap that had her jerking away from the sting and shifting her hips on my desk to chase the ache happening much deeper.

"Look at me." Her guilty gaze darted up to mine. "I don't know if I made this clear, but I want you, and I'm not a patient man. I'll give you a few more days to reconcile with the fact that we're fucking. Tell yourself whatever you like. Lie that I really want more and just don't know it yet if you have to. But when that day comes…" She made another sound when I adjusted my hand until I was palming her hot cunt. "This pussy will only weep for *me*."

"You're saying a lot of things." She gasped when I hooked my middle finger and pressed against her entrance. "And I hear you. You want me? Well, words are pretty, but talk is cheap, old man."

Just as her pussy greedily swallowed the tip of my finger, Atlas put her hand around my wrist again. This time, she dug her nails in. Right over the still-healing bite mark she'd left the first time I touched her without her permission.

I'd jerked off so many times to the memory and feeling of her sinking her teeth deep. She didn't stop until she tasted blood, and it was the moment I knew her wide-eyed innocence was a ruse and that this young doe could handle a beast like me.

"I value actions above all else, and you've done nothing to show me you want me. All you've done since we met is try to scare and hurt me. Am I tempted? *Yes.* You're fine as hell, and I haven't been fucked in a while. You seem like you're good for a nut… if nothing else. If hell somehow freezes over and I let you fuck me, I promise not to get my feelings involved. I know I'm much younger than you're used to, but I don't just fall for any man who shows me a little bit of attention. *You* don't really seem worth the effort of falling in love. You're a fuck boy, Rowdy Wray, and my mama always told me to take men like you with a grain of salt."

She was glaring at me now like she expected me to be upset and hurt her again. Little did Atlas know, she'd only carved my obsession in stone.

The receptionist wanted me to romance her?

Fine.

I was a lion, a predator. We were built to chase our food.

I was staring at her lips, unaware that I'd leaned forward until her eyes drifted closed and her lips parted with a sigh. I stopped just short of brushing her mouth with mine before pulling back with a smile. "Something on your mind, Atlas?"

Her eyes snapped open, and I saw the moment she realized I had no intention of kissing her. I wanted to, and *that* should have been enough to make me reconsider fucking her. I'd never been tempted before.

"Yes," she hissed. Despite her little speech, Atlas didn't like being played. "I'm thinking that you're crazy, and I want nothing to do with you." Placing her small hands on my chest, she tried to shove me away, but I might as well have been a wall to her.

I locked her wrists in my grip and forced them down by her sides as I pressed my forehead against hers. "Oh, I'm mental, baby, and rule number one is never give us crazy ones any pussy." I lifted my head just enough to meet the fire in her gaze. "Unfortunately for you, beautiful, you lost that privilege."

I yanked her off my desk with the gentleness of a bull in a china shop and dragged her across the room before throwing her insubordinate ass out of my office.

The commotion drew the gazes of everyone in the workshop below, but they all wisely pretended they didn't see the new receptionist lying on the floor and me standing over her and promptly got back to work.

I waited on the threshold of my office as Atlas struggled to her feet. Her chest was heaving as she glared at me with murder in her eyes, but all it did was make my dick harder.

"Get back to work, beautiful. I'm not paying you to stand around flirting with me."

With a growl, she flew at me with her fist cocked, so I stepped back and slammed the door in her face.

"I hate you!" she screamed from the other side. The door thumped once from her pounding her fist.

"I hate that pussy too!" I yelled back with a smile. "That's why I'm going to beat it up." I leaned against my desk and watched her shadow underneath the door. Atlas didn't move until a full minute later.

And she called me a psycho.

In my thirty-five years, I'd never courted a female before. As first attempts go, I have to say that it went fucking splendidly.

TEN

Atlas

I'D DONE IT.

I'd made it a whole week at Pride of Kings.

There had even been a pool going on whether or not I'd make it a measly seven days. By the end of the week, the bet had reached a whopping five hundred bucks, which Tuesday had won. She'd been the only one who believed I'd make it to the end of the day after Rowdy ripped me a new one earlier for messing up his lunch order again.

It was Friday evening, and everyone had been buzzing with excitement for the party tonight. Apparently, a POK party was legendary, and even though it was technically a company party, the guest list wasn't employee exclusive. I had no intentions of attending, so I didn't share in the hysteria.

I was currently helping Tuesday set up on the third floor after Hudson closed the shop early so we could prepare. The other mechanics—Kane, Jerry, and Norman—had all been given the day off and would return later for the party while the technicians remained on the clock to do all the grunt work. Pretty much whatever Tuesday and I deemed too heavy to lift.

The Kings were still here, though.

The four of them were downstairs in the workshop helping

Rowdy with some custom work he was doing on the side to an old-school Caddy.

Despite all his possessive male rah-rah bullshit, Rowdy had kept every interaction between us professional, which was when he wasn't avoiding me completely.

Fine with me.

"Did you grow up in Idlewild?" I asked Tuesday out of the blue.

I couldn't take the silence anymore. My thoughts were never good company. I also felt guilty that I hadn't tried to get to know her when we worked so closely together every day. After Sutton and Sienna betrayed me and then finding out my parents…

Ugh. Whatever.

I just wasn't ready to dive headfirst into trusting anyone any time soon.

Even Ruen had taken to trolling me online when she realized I was ducking her.

I thought being a receptionist would be easy, but I was starting to question how Tuesday had done it on her own for so long. The hours were long, the customers were *horrible*, and our bosses were demanding. At least the pay was good. The Kings had been surprisingly generous with my salary considering I had zero work experience. My parents had wanted me to focus on school and had promised to cover my expenses while at college despite my father's medical bills piling up.

Tuesday paused in the middle of shelving a bottle of rum in the bar at the far end of the room and looked over at me. "No, actually. I moved here four years ago from Oklahoma. I needed a change, and Idlewild was just one of many stops on my way to nowhere."

Kind of like me. "What made you stay?"

Tuesday grimaced as she struggled to crack open a case of wine with a crowbar. Once she had it open, she wiped the sweat from her brow before looking at me. "Honestly? This place. It's more than just a job. It's home. We're kind of like family if you can get used to...Rowdy." I snorted at that since I didn't believe it was possible. At least for me. "I was around before the shop became what it is now. When the Kings were just four mechanics taking any job they could get. I've had the chance to be a part of its growth, and that's not easy to walk away from. Plus, the benefits are great." She began removing the bottles of wine from the case.

I laughed and finished blowing up the black and silver confetti balloons with the helium tank, then moved over to help her. "You can find great benefits anywhere, T."

"Not like these. Remember that change I mentioned?" Sobering, I nodded, peeping the haunted look in her eyes. I knew whatever she was about to tell me couldn't be good. Tuesday looked like her mind was a million miles away as she stared at nothing. "It was actually my ex I needed to get away from."

My voice was quiet—somber—when I asked, "Why?"

Tuesday inhaled deeply, and I wished I could snatch the question back if only to erase the pain in her eyes. "After I lost our baby...after he beat me so badly I miscarried for the third time in a year, I just couldn't...I couldn't stay anymore." Tuesday chuckled bitterly. "The first two weren't so bad, I guess. Can't say the same for the last one." She glanced at me. "I was in my third trimester."

Oh.

"I'm sorry." In the wake of all she had revealed, those two words seemed so inadequate but were all I could think to say.

Tuesday shrugged like it was no big deal when I could see her in sad blue eyes that it still was. "Anyway, Rex tracked me down six months later and showed up while I was working one Saturday to drag me back home."

"What happened?"

There was an evil smirk on her face now as she accepted the bottle of wine I handed her. "Nothing. I told him I didn't love him anymore. He accepted that it was over and returned to Oklahoma."

I paused, and not just because Tuesday had produced a corkscrew from some hidden place, popped the top on the bottle of wine, and chugged about a fifth of it in one go. I wasn't an expert on abusive relationships and the victims who survived them, but I smelled a big fat lie.

When she burped and passed it back to me, I hesitated since I was underage and technically still at work before taking it and doing the same—sans burp.

"Oh, that's good stuff," I said when I immediately felt a buzz. Just as I began to imagine Tuesday murdering her abusive baby daddy and burying the body somewhere, something she'd said tugged at my memory. "You said he showed up on a Saturday?"

Her focus was back on stocking the bar, so she hadn't noticed my shift in mood. "Yeah, why?"

"Who was working that day? Which King?" I clarified when she looked up at me in confusion.

"Oh." She shrugged and turned away again. "It was Rowdy, I think."

I exhaled slowly and started stacking the glasses so that I had something to do with my hands.

Bad idea.

I must have been more upset than I realized because I dropped one and it shattered. To make my reaction even more embarrassing, I stupidly crouched to pick up the shards with my bare hands and sliced my palm open.

Blood dripped onto the floor, and I fell into a trance as I watched it puddle on the concrete. The floor up here wasn't smooth like the lower levels, so it would probably even stain.

Troublesome blood.

Mine wasn't even particularly special. It wasn't worth its weight in gold, wondrously rare, giving, or receptive.

But it had led me to the truth of who I was—and who I wasn't.

"Oh, my God! Atlas!"

Hearing Tuesday's shout, I snapped out of my stupor and dispassionately watched as she bent, grabbed my hand, and inspected my palm before pressing the dish towel I'd been using to dry the glasses against the wound. I then let her lead me downstairs even though I didn't know what for.

I still didn't catch on to her intention until we entered the workshop. I opened my mouth to object, but it was too late.

"We need help," Tuesday's dramatic ass announced. "Atlas is hurt."

All four heads of the Kings swiveled our way.

"It's not that bad." I waved her off with my free hand.

Unfortunately, she chose that moment to hold up the injured one, bringing their attention to the blood already soaking through the cloth.

To my utter horror, it was Rowdy who was first to act.

He had been sitting in the driver's seat of the Cadillac, one foot planted on the ground and the other revving the engine, but then he was out of the car quicker than a man his size should be allowed to move. He shoved his friends aside to gently take my hand from Tuesday. "What happened, T?"

I rolled my eyes at him asking her about *my* injury just to avoid speaking to me. "Not sure, boss. Atlas was cleaning the glasses when she dropped one and must have cut herself cleaning it up."

Rowdy said nothing as he pulled the towel back and revealed the jagged cut along my palm.

"Shit," Joren cursed as his nosy ass peered around Rowdy. "She should probably go to the hospital. That looks deep."

"No." I snatched my hand from Rowdy and backed away a step while they all looked at me like I was crazy.

If I went to the hospital, they'd send the bill to my mom since I couldn't very well have them send it to the motel or...here. My mom, if she was even lucid, would find out I wasn't at school.

Then again, maybe she'd finally be my mom again when she inevitably tried to force me to come home. But I couldn't go home—not yet.

"I'll be fine." I was sure it looked worse than it actually was because of all the blood.

"That must be common sense you're dripping all over my floor instead of blood," Rowdy snapped. "You're not fine."

"Give me a first aid kit, and I will be. Do you have one?"

Rowdy just stared at me for a long moment before nodding. "Yeah, come on."

"Just tell me where it is. I don't need your help. I can take care of it my—" My rant was cut off when Rowdy grabbed my nape in a punishing grip and forced me forward. I fought him all the way up the stairs, but I was no match for him with *two* hands. It was useless with only one. All I managed to do was irritate him more, so much so that his control eventually slipped, and he spanked my ass hard enough to make me gasp.

"Now, are you going to behave?" he questioned menacingly. "Or do I have to light your ass on fire to make you hear me?" When I wisely kept my mouth shut, he steered me to his office and into his private bathroom, which was minimally decorated and clean to the point of OCD.

"Sit down." He punctuated his command by shoving me down onto the closed toilet lid.

"Rowdy—"

"Shut your fucking mouth, Atlas. You've said enough." I watched him yank open the medicine cabinet and pull out a first aid kit. "Give me your hand." This time, I didn't bother to argue and just held out my arm. He moved to stand over me, his legs straddling mine, and pressed a wadded strip of gauze to my wound. "Tell me what happened," he demanded while we waited for the bleeding to stop. He didn't sound angry, though. He sounded concerned. It was hard to reconcile the Rowdy I'd met only a week ago with the one before me now.

"What do you mean?"

"Why did you cut yourself?"

I frowned even as I kept my gaze on our hands. "It was an accident." When he didn't respond, I chanced looking up. I didn't like that he was staring at me like he didn't believe me. Did he think I'd hurt myself on purpose?

Once the bleeding stopped, Rowdy started to clean my wound. And unlike moments ago when he dragged me up here, he was gentle. "It's not deep," he announced after a long and rather stilted silence.

"I told you that," I said with a hiss. When he gave me a warning look, I shrank and adjusted my tone. "It looks worse than it is."

"Mmmh." Rowdy was silent, too focused on his task as he used some type of glue to seal my wound.

Once it was dry, he tightly secured my cut with more gauze. I winced from the pressure on my wound and then could have sworn I felt the soothing brush of his finger. It happened so quickly that I wondered if I'd imagined it.

"It won't scar," he told me once he was done.

I didn't respond since I kind of hoped it did. It would serve as a reminder of what kind of man he was. I didn't believe for a second that Tuesday's ex had simply cut his losses after hunting her down.

It was more likely that Rowdy had scared him away, but why? He didn't strike me as the type that strapped on a cape and flew around saving women for the hell of it.

"Thanks." I stood from the toilet as he cleaned up the mess and repacked the first aid kit. "I think I'll go home now."

"No."

I blinked while wondering if I'd misheard him. "We're pretty much done setting up, and I won't be much help to Tuesday with one hand anyway. She can handle the rest." *And if not, I'm sure you can give her a hand since you're soooo helpful.* I rolled my eyes while his back was turned.

"You're Pride of King's newest employee," he told me as he placed the kit back in the cabinet. "This party is for *you*, so no, Atlas. You can't go home."

I thought it was an uncharacteristically sweet gesture until another thought occurred to me. "Wait...you made me decorate my own welcome party?"

"Somebody had to do it." Rowdy shrugged before leaning

against the sink and placing his hand on my hip to pull me into him. I was wearing jeans today, thankfully, but that didn't stop him from roughly groping my ass in his large hands. "I can't wait to see you throwing all this ass on my dick," he told me as he nestled his face in my neck and inhaled. "The way it's sitting in these jeans, I'll be giving you back shots all night."

Oh, God. I didn't have to question if it was true. Somehow, I knew sex with Rowdy would be rough, dirty, and a little disrespectful. "You're talking like it's a done deal," I said a little breathlessly.

"It is."

Rowdy pressed an open mouth kiss against my throat, and I sighed when I felt an invisible force pulling me toward the inevitable. "I don't even know your real name."

I thought Rowdy was his real name until I'd heard the other Kings call him *O*. I hadn't been brave enough to ask and show too much interest in him.

I'd also had zero luck finding out who'd sent me those anonymous notes. I hadn't received another since the second mysteriously arrived here of all places, and I couldn't decide if that was a good thing or not.

Rowdy was biting and sucking on my neck when I felt his lips forming a name against my skin.

"Owen."

Owen, I echoed in my head. My belly dipped, and I smiled despite myself. The name fit somehow. It was soft and unassuming, while he was hard and turbulent.

Balance.

"What's your middle name?"

"It's Rashaad, nosy. Anything else?"

"Um...your favorite color?" I yelped, surprised when he nipped my collarbone.

"Blue and green."

His answer made my heart skip a beat, and I found myself smiling goofily at the ceiling. "Mine too," I confessed.

Rowdy lifted his head and smirked. "Yeah, right, Atlas. You just wanted to copy me."

"No, I don't!" I giggled when he pinched my butt. I tried to swat him away, but he only pulled me closer. My knees buckled a little when I felt his dick growing against my stomach.

All thoughts of names and colors went poof as I quickly became alarmed. Rowdy alone was intimidating enough. The sheer size of the monster waking up terrified me.

"Um...how big are you?" I blurted.

Rowdy's green eyes gleamed as he bit his bottom lip. "You'll find out soon enough."

"Maybe I should just ask Tuesday."

I was pleased to have wiped the smugness from his face for all of two seconds before his expression turned savage. "What the fuck are you talking about, Atlas?"

"Are you telling me you've never fucked her?"

He stared at me for a long, long while. "Why does it matter?"

"Because I need to know if you go around fucking all of your employees or just me."

Rowdy exhaled through his nose and dropped his head back to stare at the ceiling. "Where is this coming from, Atlas?"

I parted my lips, but no words came. It dawned on me that Rowdy may not even know about Tuesday's past. What if she had told me about Rex in confidence? What if I destroyed that trust she'd shown me by blabbing out of a misplaced sense of jealousy?

Rowdy wasn't even mine.

When I said nothing, he pushed me away from him none too gently and left the bathroom.

My heart pounded out of control as I followed him into his office.

He was at the sideboard now, pouring himself a glass of Hennessy, and then he plopped down in the cushioned armchair with a sigh and made himself comfortable. Still feeling reckless, raw, and pissed off, I ignored the major "keep away" energy coming from him and stood between his long legs with my arms crossed.

Rowdy simply took a sip of his drink while staring up at me like I was something to entertain him.

"So you're really not going to answer me?"

"Nah."

"Why not?"

"Because you're talking stupid right now, and I'm liable to choke you. I want to fuck you, beautiful, not hurt you."

I prided myself on keeping my expression blank. "I have a right to know."

"Do you? You're not my girl," Rowdy reminded me. "I haven't even fucked you yet."

"And you think I'd let you, knowing you go around sticking your dick in everyone?"

"You can think whatever you please, but I already told you, we're fucking. There's no ifs, ands, or buts about it."

I felt my nipples pebble against my shirt. "How about no? Do you understand that word?"

"You won't say no."

"I seem to recall saying it once or twice before. Try me." I didn't wait for his response as I turned and stormed away before he could see the depth of my hurt.

I'd already reached the door before I heard him say, "I never fucked Tuesday, you fucking crybaby. Come here."

"No." I refused to turn around and let him see that he was right. I wanted to cry. "I don't believe you." I hurriedly checked my cheeks for wayward tears when I heard him set his glass down, stand, and cross the room. Once he was standing close enough, he grabbed my arms and spun me around to face him before pushing my back against the door.

"Are those tears for me, bad girl?"

I huffed and looked away. "In your dreams," I blustered.

"I definitely dream about you," he confessed. "But you're only crying when my dick is inside you, and you're begging me to go deeper."

"God, you're a pig." Baffled, I shook my head.

A fresh wave of tears came, and this time, I didn't have the fortitude with Rowdy so close to hold them back. He made me feel like I could withstand anything while breaking down my walls at the same time. As if he sensed my internal struggle, he kissed them away, his lips peppering every inch of my face, even my eyelids and forehead, which were free of tears. He kissed everywhere…except my lips.

"Why haven't you kissed me yet?" I asked him.

He smirked. "You were just telling me I'd never hit, and now you're begging me to kiss you?"

"Begging? Boy, please. I was just wondering."

"Hmm."

I could feel him scrutinizing me, so I changed the subject. "So you and Tuesday…"

He released a frustrated exhale. "I already told you. I never fucked her, Atlas."

I stared at him for a long while, and he let me until I was satisfied he was telling the truth. "Just checking."

"She sucked my dick, though." Rowdy barked a laugh when I shoved him. "I'm playing, mean ass! Damn. I've never touched her, but I did fuck up her boyfriend or whatever after he came to my place of business with his chest out," he said, making my heart drop. "I couldn't let the disrespect ride, but keeping it real, I would have done it anyway."

My stomach twisted as I fought to keep my voice level. "Why?"

He shrugged, but for the first time, he actually looked uncomfortable. "All right, don't tell her I told you this, but I could tell Tuesday had been getting her ass kicked by him."

"Oh."

"And before you say anything, no, I didn't fuck him up because I wanted her for myself. Tuesday is good people and a good employee. I'm not a perfect man, Atlas. I've done things a lot worse, but it still didn't sit right with me how afraid she was of him."

"It's okay," I said quietly but honestly. "I'm not mad." How could I be, knowing what Tuesday had gone through and that Rowdy had been perceptive enough to sense it and help her instead of turning a blind eye?

I guess...*maybe*...I was wrong about him a tiny, little bit.

"Better not be," he returned gruffly. I was deep in thought while Rowdy rubbed his hand up and down my sides and kissed my cheek over and over.

"Well, I don't think you have to worry about him anymore. Tuesday said he went back to Oklahoma, but I...I don't know if that's true."

Rowdy furrowed his brows. "Why would she lie?"

"Because she killed him?"

Rowdy lifted his head, and our wide-eyed gazes locked for a long moment before we both burst into laughter. "Yo, can you imagine happy-ass Tuesday actually murking someone?"

I shrugged, not as willing to underestimate her after hearing her terrible story. "People do crazy things when backed into a corner."

I should know.

"I guess," Rowdy said, his voice trailing when someone started pounding on the door behind me. He pulled me away and tucked me behind him before opening it to reveal a frustrated Roc. "What did I tell you about banging on my door like you IPD?"

"Fuck is y'all doing up here?" Roc barked back. "I've been texting and calling you for twenty minutes!"

"Clearly, I was busy, motherfucker. What do you want?"

"The deejay backed out, and everyone we know is booked. We don't have anyone to do the music."

"Fuck."

Roc and Rowdy stared at each other, silently considering their options, before a crazy one popped into my head.

"Um..." I slowly raised my hand. "I may know one."

ELEVEN

Atlas

"THANKS AGAIN FOR COMING." I HUGGED RUEN AS SOON AS SHE strolled through the doors of the shop like she owned the place. The only thing that gave her away was her looking around like she was seeing it all for the first time. "I know it's last minute."

It was also probably a little too soon to be asking favors, but in my defense, Ruen *had* been asking to see me again. At least this way, I could solve two problems with one equation.

"No problem. I'm glad you called. Rem's been asking about you."

I was too floored to bother hiding my surprise as I took her warm hand and squeezed. "She has?"

"Yup. I told her you were new in town and all alone," Ruen said absently, if not a little cruelly. She was still looking around the shop. "Idlewild can be cutthroat if you're not careful. Rem worries."

That was…nice of her. "Where is Remedy?" I looked behind Ruen through the glass door she'd come through. "Did you bring her?" There was a car I didn't recognize parked just outside, and I could see what looked like four figures sitting inside behind the dark tint.

Ruen shook her head, her silver drop earrings dangling with

the movement. I seriously hoped those diamonds were fake, but the way they caught and owned the light, I doubted it. They had to be worth a fortune and were totally at odds with the cheap purple leather jacket she wore over her black dress, worn combat books, and sheer tights that had more holes than material. "She wanted to stay home and work on a new cake recipe."

"I didn't know she baked."

Ruen pursed her lips, her full attention returning to me now. "You didn't stick around long enough to find out."

Mmmh...yeah, okay. So we were going there already.

Before I could apologize for ducking her, Rowdy, Golden, Roc, and Joren prowled through the employee's door that separated the lobby from the workshop. My focus immediately zeroed in on Rowdy, but he wasn't looking at me.

He was watching Ruen.

Jealousy struck a hot chord through me, and it was all I could do not to slap the shit out of him. I bet he liked what he saw. Why wouldn't he?

Ruen was fucking *gorgeous*.

It wasn't just her looks, though. Ruen oozed sex and confidence and had "bad bitch" written all over her—something that probably appealed to a savage like Rowdy. He was too used to walking all over women, though. He probably couldn't even handle someone like Ruen. There was no question whether *she* could handle *him*.

I could almost picture them together, running the streets, taking what they wanted, and not caring about the destruction they left in their wake.

Ruen even had a few years on me, which meant Rowdy wouldn't have to feel like a dirty pervert if he chose to pursue her instead.

It didn't help that she looked amazing in her skintight dress while I looked frumpy in my work uniform. I hadn't bothered to bring a change of clothes with me for the party since I'd had no intentions of going.

It had been four days since Rowdy declared war on my vagina, and so far, his idea of romance had been to watch me like a hawk, nitpick over everything I did, and torture me with increasingly menial tasks.

Yesterday, he had me organize his files.

When I pointed out that *he had no files* since Hudson handled all the paperwork, he told me to find some and shut the fuck up.

Rowdy reached us first since he was leading the pack, and I braced myself for what he would do or say. I already knew he wouldn't care if he hurt my feelings. To be honest, I was more worried about what *I* would do if he hit on another girl in front of me.

I eyed the box cutter sitting on the counter a few feet away. I'd used it earlier to open up the new shipment of business cards that had been delivered today.

I watched Rowdy's focus move from her face, and my heart dropped at the same time his gaze did. I felt the back of my eyes burn and inhaled to keep the hurt from spilling, but then my breath caught in my throat when his gaze completely skipped her body, torpedoing in on where our hands were still linked.

Before I could think to drop Ruen's hand, Rowdy—in full view of the other Kings—curved his finger around one of my belt loops and dragged me away from her.

Alarmed, I instinctively braced my hands against his chest to push him away, but the warning in his eyes had me dropping them just as quickly.

As if the space he'd forced between us wasn't enough, Rowdy tucked me behind him, inserting himself fully between Ruen and me and hiding my new friend from sight.

"Who is you?" his ignorant ass rudely demanded.

I couldn't see Ruen's face to gauge her reaction, but knowing Rowdy all too well, I jumped to rescue her anyway. "Can you chill? She's the deejay I told you about, crazy. She's here to do the party."

There was an uncomfortably long pause, and then, "How do you know her?" he asked too calmly. His attention was still firmly fixed on Ruen but I knew the question was meant for me.

I blew out a frustrated breath. "I met her at a party, Rowdy." And then I hesitated the span of a single nervous breath. "She's my friend."

"Hmm."

It dawned on me then that Rowdy was…jealous. It sounded awfully like he was staking his claim.

And I'd foolishly thrown two apex predators in the same cage.

Fearing a blow out, I pushed between them. "Okay, enough," I snapped at Rowdy before turning to Ruen. "Ignore him. Are you okay?"

I don't know why I felt the need to ask.

Ruen didn't look scared. Instead, she looked amused, her usual smirk plastered on her face. "Oh, I'm just great."

The other Kings, sensing the tension, walked over. I quickly gave the introductions and was glad they at least had better manners than Rowdy and actually thanked Ruen for coming.

Well, Joren and Roc did. Golden just politely dipped his head.

"Oh, Atlas," Ruen said at the first lull in the conversation. "Almost forgot. I have something for you." Ruen's expression gave nothing away as she dug into her jacket pocket and pulled something free.

I frowned when she held out her hand and slowly uncurled her fingers, revealing a balled-up scrap of royal blue material with tiny red hearts.

My heart skipped a beat when I immediately recognized the item.

Mistaking my shock for confusion, Ruen let my panties from last Friday hang from her finger while the Kings looked on. "You left these in my bed. I thought you might want them back."

I still didn't move or speak. Neither did the Kings. I just let the agony of humiliation swallow me whole.

Rowdy, of course, was the first to speak. "Friend, huh?"

I didn't need to turn around to see that he was *pissed*. I could hear the storm brewing behind the quiet calm. "So, that's why you've been acting like you don't want this dick," he mused aloud, adding to my embarrassment. "You prefer your own equipment, huh?"

Fuck my life. "Really, Ruen?"

"What?" she returned innocently. Her brows even shot up to her forehead, but I wasn't fooled.

Rowdy had marked his territory, but Ruen had let it be known that she'd gotten there first.

"Wow, Atlas," Roc drawled. His amused gaze was practically sparkling as it bounced between me and the panties Ruen still held out for everyone to see. "I'm learning so many things about you right now."

Huffing, I snatched my panties from Ruen, only for Rowdy to snatch them from *me* and crudely sniff them before stuffing them in his pocket. He then wrapped a possessive arm around my shoulder and pulled me close until there was no space left between us. "Thanks, Rude," he said, intentionally messing up her name. "You didn't have to do that. Daddy would have just bought her a new pair."

My skin grew hot, and suddenly, I understood why these two would never make sense. They were *too* alike. Both of them were alphas in their own right, looking for someone to rule, ruin, and possess until there was nothing left.

I could hear Roc, Joren, and even Golden snickering, and I shook my head. In some ways, the four of them were still the teenagers in the photo I carried around.

"Hey, uh...Ruen," Joren spoke up. Of all of them, I had the most trouble meeting his gaze, so I stared straight ahead. "Do you need help taking your equipment upstairs?"

"Nope, but thanks." She backed up a couple of steps, opened the door, and placed her fingers between her lips before releasing an impressively loud whistle.

On cue, the sound of several car doors opening simultaneously and slamming shut followed. Moments later, the shop door opened, and the testosterone in this place suddenly doubled when four guys filed in.

Their muscular arms were bulging as they carried speakers, a mixer, several turntables, and other equipment I couldn't see inside the black gear bags.

My gaze flicked between them, hoping to make sense of the motley crew.

Two of them were White—the only commonality I could find in the group—but even they looked like they'd both wandered into the wrong circle and couldn't find their way out. The third guy was Black, and the fourth was of some Asian descent that I hesitated to put my finger on. Korean, maybe?

The front runner had dirty-blond hair partially shielded by his hood, with somber brown eyes and a golden tan that made it clear he spent his time outdoors. The gray sleeveless hoodie he wore unzipped showed off his sculpted abs and huge arms with thick veins running the length that really rounded out his All-American look—a total beefcake.

The second guy looked like some kind of mix between a sexy vampire and a tortured rock god. I really couldn't decide. His platinum hair made his pale skin look almost transparent, while the heavy black eyeliner did nothing to make his fair blue eyes less piercing. He was taller than the rest—almost as tall as Rowdy—but leaner like he'd never seen a gym, or the sun, in his life. It was obvious he was strong, though, as he quietly held one of the large speakers without complaint.

"What the hell did we say about whistling at us like we're your pet bitches, Buns?" Mr. All-American griped. He also carried a speaker in his huge arms and sported the most vicious scowl I'd ever seen. He looked like he'd never been happy a day in his life.

"Aw, give it up, Christian," Ruen said as she gave his sculpted cheek an affectionate pat. "We all know crawling around on your knees for me is your favorite kink."

"Yeah, yeah, that's all fine and fuck you," the third guy complained. He stepped forward into view, and my first thought was that he looked like a model with those impossibly high cheekbones. Rowdy tensed beside me, and I glanced up, seeing something akin to recognition in his eyes. Guy number three was the definition of tall, dark, and handsome as he rocked a high fade like Rowdy's but wore his shoulder-length hair in plaits that fell over his forehead and hazel eyes. Even I had to admit that there was something familiar about him. I just couldn't put my finger on it. "This shit is heavy, girl. Where should we put it?"

Before Ruen could answer, Roc stepped forward. "Malik?"

Tall, dark, and handsome's head swiveled, as did the other three, so it was hard to pinpoint who Roc was actually speaking to until the third guy's eyes bulged. "Uncle Roc?" My boss's only response was to rush forward, wrap his nephew in a bear hug, and lift him off his feet in an impressive show of strength. "Unc! Unc! Unc!" Malik panicked and screamed a little dramatically when he almost lost his grip on Ruen's expensive-looking equipment.

"My bad," Roc said before setting him on his feet. The look in Malik's eyes was almost comical when his uncle popped him on the back of the head a moment later. "When did you get back in town, and why didn't your mama tell me?"

A shadow fell over Malik's eyes before he looked away. "Probably because she doesn't know," he grumbled.

Roc scowled as he regarded his nephew, who was looking anywhere and everywhere now except for at his uncle. "We'll talk about this later," I heard Roc say.

Malik didn't respond.

I wasn't psychic, but something told me that conversation wouldn't be taking place.

The familial resemblance between the two was uncanny. Rowdy must have recognized him too.

"Wait, so you're really his uncle?" I couldn't help but ask. "How old *are you*?"

Based on when the photo was taken, I'd guessed the Kings were in their mid to late thirties, but maybe I'd been way off. Roc couldn't have been more than a decade older than Malik.

"I have an older sister," Roc explained without looking my

way. His mood had visibly gone to shit and there was now a troubled dip in his brow. "She had Malik when I was like nine or ten."

Oh.

I was about to ask another question when Rowdy suddenly tensed again. "Aye, homeboy," he barked aggressively. "There's no smoking in here."

My alarmed gaze traveled among the group until it landed on the silent fourth leaning against the door.

Ruen's bag was now resting at his feet while he lit up, the casual bad-boy demeanor at odds with the tailored black suit he wore. I could see a hint of the colorful artwork that traveled from his long neck and disappeared underneath his crisp white shirt. His black hair was tousled, strands falling over his dark eyes, the longest one almost reaching his small nose. However, the two tiny hoops he wore in each ear were what I liked the most about his style.

My admiration lasted until he opened his mouth.

"Really, homeboy?" Fourth toked on his cigarette. "I don't see a sign." He blew out a puff of smoke, and before I could blink, Rowdy's arm left my shoulders. One moment he was next to me, and the next, he was pinning Fourth to the door by his throat.

"How about I cut you open and use your intestines to make a sign?" Rowdy suggested.

I didn't like the gleam in Fourth's eye when he smiled.

"Ky, chill, man!" Malik yelled at his friend. "This is not going to go how you think it will. Rowdy doesn't make idle threats."

"Neither do we," the sexy vamp responded darkly. He'd been so quiet and still up until now. My heart seized in my chest at the gun now pressed against Rowdy's temple. I hadn't even noticed him move. "Let him the fuck go."

I looked around for someone to diffuse this situation, but everyone around me was either at or holding someone else at gunpoint. The only ones who seemed uncertain were Malik and Roc, but still, they were both locked and loaded, obviously willing to live with the consequences if this went left.

Even Ruen had a silver gun with a long barrel and some kind of beaded charm tied around the trigger housing pointed at the back of Rowdy's thick skull.

Where the hell had she even hidden that thing?

Glimpsing movement in my peripheral, I looked away in time to see Tuesday slowly step off the stairs, pause, and then with a straight face, turn and haul her scary ass back upstairs like she hadn't seen a thing.

If the situation wasn't so dire, I might have laughed.

A choking sound forced my focus back into the fray, and I saw Ky was no longer smiling. He was slowly turning an awful shade of blue as Rowdy suffocated him with the weight of his arm.

"You might as well kill me," Rowdy warned. "Either way, I'm taking this disrespectful bitch with me."

Hearing the sincerity in Rowdy's tone, Ruen moved her finger from the barrel to the trigger.

"Nooo!" Before I could register the screaming voice as my own, I had once again thrown myself between Ruen and Rowdy. "Ruen, please," I begged from the end of her crosshairs. "You have to stop this."

"Sorry, Twinks. I like you and all, but they're family." I thought I'd seen Ruen look cruel before, but that was nothing compared to the coldness in her eyes now. There was no warmth or humor when she spoke either.

"What about Remedy?" I asked out of pure chance and desperation. "Your sister. Your twin. Would *she* want you to do this? Do you really want to leave her all alone? You said it yourself. Idlewild can be ruthless if you aren't careful."

The shift in Ruen's eyes was minute, but it was enough. I'd reminded her of her *real* Achilles heel.

"All right, Atlas," she said, her tone sweet but dripping venom as she slowly lowered her gun. "Since you're so persuasive, I'll give you fifteen seconds to convince your boyfriend to let my friend go. A second more, and I pull the trigger."

Shit.

Whatever it was that I had with Rowdy was still new and resting on a foundation that teetered with the wind. It was impossible to think I had that kind of pull with him yet.

One look around at all the grave faces, and I knew I had no choice.

I had to try.

They all still had their guns aimed.

I gave Ruen one last pleading look, but she only raised her brow and mouthed, "Tick tock."

Double shit.

Okay.

I inhaled a deep breath.

My hand trembled when I reached out and placed it gently on his shoulder. To my utter horror, Rowdy didn't react. He gave no indication that he even remembered I was standing here—moments away from watching him die.

"Owen."

I felt it then.

The subtle tensing of his shoulder beneath my palm. The recognition of this moment. *Our* moment.

It was my first time uttering his name and his first time hearing me say it. It was an irrevocable turning point in our toxic love affair, and right now, it was unfolding for the world to see.

Tilting his head, he didn't dare look away from Ky, but with that small gesture, he let me know that he was listening.

"You promised me a party," I reminded him gently. "I made it a whole week without running away from you. Don't let me lose you now."

Everything slowed, even my heartbeat, as we all waited to see which would win Rowdy over—his need for violence or…me.

I could feel the deadly intent thickening the air in the room. Joren, Roc, and Golden were willing to die for their brother just as Ruen and her crew were willing to die for theirs.

And then it happened.

The desperate sound of air being pulled into Ky's lungs as Rowdy released him and took a reluctant step back.

Me? I did the opposite. I released the breath I'd been holding, only to have it stolen again when Rowdy whirled around, grabbed a fist full of my faux locs in a punishing grip and kissed me.

For the first time.

In front of prying eyes and enemies.

His lips were hungry and demanding as they forced mine open, not waiting for my consent or the implication of what was happening between us to sink in.

The first stroke of his tongue against mine had me fisting his shirt in my hands to keep from melting into a puddle. I didn't care that we weren't alone or had been so close to death. He tasted too good. He felt too right. I never wanted our connection to end, and I wasn't just talking about the kiss. Rowdy already had a hold on me that should have scared me but didn't. Instead, I finally felt like I was where I was always meant to be.

His *kiss* made me more and more certain with each press of his lips.

Rowdy was never going to let me go.

And I didn't want him to.

I was ninety-nine percent certain that if I disappeared tomorrow, he'd hunt me down. The question was, could I walk away?

I was too caught up in that world-altering revelation to notice him leading me past reception, the waiting room, and the snack bar. A few more steps, and I was vaguely aware of him fumbling for something behind me.

I heard a knob turn, followed by a door pushing open, and then Rowdy finally broke the kiss by shoving me backward into darkness. I was only allowed a second of clarity before he stepped inside the storage closet with me and slowly closed the door behind him.

I backed away, suddenly realizing I was trapped.

Trapped in a cage with a very hungry lion.

TWELVE

Rowdy

"ROWDY, WAIT," SHE WHISPERED, BUT MY HAND AROUND HER delicate throat cut her off.

"No." I found her mouth in the dark again and slipped my tongue inside. One hit of her, and I was already addicted. Atlas must have felt the same because it wasn't long before she kissed me back. "Say my name," I demanded against her lips. "I want to fucking hear it."

She didn't even hesitate. "Owen."

I pressed her into the stocked shelves and shoved my hands underneath her uniform shirt to feel the warmth of her skin. This girl made me feel so fucking alive—so goddamn mortal after being only seconds away from death. The only reason I was still breathing was because Atlas had glimpsed something in me worth saving.

A shuddered breath left me at the thought.

Atlas had risked herself for me, and though I wanted to worship at her feet for riding for me, I didn't like that shit one bit.

She couldn't see me in the dark, but I'd make her fucking feel me.

"Don't ever do that again, Atlas."

"Do what?"

"Put yourself between me and a bullet."

She was silent, and I knew what her stubborn ass would say before she even spoke. "What else was I supposed to do?"

"Keep yourself safe, and let me answer for my bullshit."

"No." I couldn't see her, but I could picture the stubborn pout on her pretty face clear as day. "If you don't want me to follow you into fire, then *don't run into fire*."

I was lowering my head to kiss her again when her words penetrated. Reaching up, I yanked the cord hanging from the ceiling, making light flood the closet and startling her when she saw my scowl. "Your fraud-ass stole that from *Frozen*!"

"What? No, I didn't." Now that the closet was lit, I could see Atlas shaking her head in denial while looking guilty as fuck. When I just stared at her, she shifted on her feet, sighed, and then rolled her eyes. "How do you even know that?"

"Roc has a four-year-old daughter. She makes me watch that damn movie every time I chill at his spot."

"Oh." Atlas snickered before chewing on her lip and trying her best to look sincere. "Well, you should know I really mean it."

"Shut yo' fake ass up." I punctuated my order by kissing her again until my dick was hard as a brick. "I want to eat your pussy so bad," I admitted hoarsely. The sound she released had me ready to fall to my knees and do just that.

But I didn't.

The first time I tasted Atlas, I wanted her laid out and ass naked so I could take my time. I was going to get her addicted to my dick and then drop her troublesome ass like a bad habit.

Atlas whimpered in pain, and I loosened my grip. I was slow to realize what I'd done. Something deep inside of me must have rebelled at the idea of letting her go, and I'd tightened my hold on her as a reflex.

Choosing to ignore that, I shoved my hand up her work shirt and under her bra until I had Atlas in the palm of my hand. My thumb worked her nipple as I deepened the kiss, keeping her distracted while I pulled the tab on her jeans free.

A shuddering breath left her, and she jerked slightly at the feel of my fingers skimming her lower belly before diving into her panties and zeroing in on her engorged clit.

"Owen," she moaned the moment I began to tease her.

"You've been keeping it tight for me?"

My baby eagerly nodded. "Yes."

"Yeah? Let me see." I slipped my hand down past her fat lips until my fingers found her opening already dripping. "Why is this pussy so wet, Atlas?"

Her eyes drifted open just a bit. "You know why."

"Do I?" I carefully pushed one, then two of my fingers inside her and felt her slick walls immediately grip me. *Fuck, yes.* "I'm starting to think who you really want is that little weird bitch out there. You been giving her my pussy?"

Atlas shook her head, but I wasn't sure I believed her. In the end, it wouldn't matter once I got inside her. I'd ruin her for all.

Detached, I played in her pussy, watching the emotions play out on her beautiful face as I fucked my fingers deep. The sheer ecstasy in her expression was the only thing keeping me from going out there and putting two in her little "friend."

I was an only child, and even if I wasn't, I did not fucking share.

"Owen. Oooh…fuck!" Atlas cried out after I stabbed her pussy harder, the heel of my palm smacking against her clit. It was violent. Ruthless. Dirty. And she loved every second of it. If not her moans, then the wet squelch of my fingers tunneling in and out of her pussy made that a fact.

My dick pushed against my pants curiously at how much she was leaking around my hand.

But then…a foreign emotion suspiciously close to insecurity filled me as I wondered if Ruen was the reason. Was she thinking about her right now?

The moment the question formed in my head, my free hand flew from the shelf where it was resting above her head and closed around her throat. "Look at me."

Her eyes slowly opened at my command, and the way she looked at me—like I was the sun after a storm—nearly persuaded me from my course, but in the end, my jealousy won out. All it had taken was me picturing her looking at someone else that way—giving them what should have been mine.

"If I find out you're lying to me," I warned. "If I found out she touched you, I'll kill you both. I'll snuff that bitch for taking what's mine, and I'll make you watch. I'll fuck you while she bleeds out."

"Oh, Owen," she said again, this time softer and less desperate. Sure. Steady. Her hand rose and settled on my chest, right over my heart. It suddenly lurched in my chest as if reaching for her too. "There's only you."

A wave of calm rippled over me, and I leaned down to kiss her. I'd never been jealous before, so I didn't know a healthy way of handling it. At that moment, I was going for what I knew, what felt natural. This, making Atlas feel good and showing that pussy who it answered to, was as raw and real as it could possibly get.

Somehow, though—when she kissed me back like this—it felt like she was the one who owned me.

Wanting to exorcise those thoughts, I paused to push a third finger inside her. She whined and rose onto the tip of her toes to escape the impossible invasion I was forcing on her tight little pussy.

"Shhh," I hushed against her lips when she whined again. "You're too tight, baby. Gotta stretch you if you're ever going to take my dick."

As soon as her pussy swallowed my third knuckle, though, she was coming, her walls spasming around my fingers, her lashes fluttering, and her lips parting on a silent scream.

Once her orgasm subsided, she sank against the shelf, and I pulled my hand free. I stared at her closed lids as I brought my fingers to my lips and licked them clean.

Fuck.

My dick jumped in my jeans at the first taste, and I just barely stopped myself from throwing her against those shelves and fucking that pussy open until it curved for me.

I rested my forehead against hers, closed my eyes, and sighed. "What the hell are we doing?" I rhetorically asked aloud. I felt her irritating ass give a tired shrug anyway. "You got my dick hard as a rock." I lifted my head and stared down at her. "What are you going to do about it, Atlas?"

She gulped while blinking up at me through deceitfully innocent eyes. I wasn't sure how much experience she had, but I'd bet every dime I had she wasn't a virgin. She'd let some little boy get in my pussy, and it was all I could do not to make her give me his name and address.

"What do you want me to do?"

I inhaled deeply before saying fuck it and dropping my hand to my belt as I stepped back. "Get on your knees." I could see the indecision in her eyes seconds before she sank to the floor. Slowly, I undid my belt and jeans giving her time to say no if she wanted to. Her nervous gaze dropped to my crotch once I was done, but she didn't say a word. "Take it out."

This time, she didn't hesitate.

My stomach dipped violently, and I bit back a curse when she slipped her hand inside my boxers. Her skin was so fucking soft and warm it made me that much more eager to feel the rest of her.

For now, I'd settle for her mouth.

Atlas's hand slowly slid though my coarse pubes before curling around my dick. I watched with the attentiveness of a magnifying glass as the timid curiosity in her expression slowly shifted to shock and then horror when she realized she couldn't close her hand.

The terrified gasp that escaped her was my only warning before she snatched her hand back and let it rest in her lap. I only just managed to keep my irritation down as I brushed her bottom lip with my thumb. "What's the matter?" I questioned gently. "You change your mind?"

I could see her internal war to prove herself before common sense kicked in, and she gave a wordless nod.

"That's cool." I zipped my jeans back up and buckled my belt before helping her to her feet.

"Are you mad?" she questioned worriedly.

"I'm a grown man, Atlas. No, baby, I'm not mad."

With one text, I could have another bitch kneeling in this exact same spot within minutes, but I chose to leave out that part since I knew her ass would only cry about it.

Truthfully, Atlas's reaction had come as no surprise. I'd fucked inexperienced girls before when I was just a kid myself, and this happened more often than not. Females always claimed they wanted a big dick to ride, only to run scared as soon as they found one. I never really gave them a second thought nor a chance to waste my time again, but I'd be lying if I said I wasn't tempted to make an exception for Atlas.

"Go finish helping Tuesday set up. I'll get at you later," I told her as I pulled my phone out and opened the Instagram app to type a private message.

My dick is hard

I could feel Atlas's gaze on me as I read the response that came seconds later.

Savvy G: where r u

I messaged my location, and Savannah's reply came before I could close the app.

Savvy G: Omw can we talk after

I pocketed my phone without responding and finally allowed myself to meet Atlas's gaze. I didn't like the hurt I saw there, but it wasn't my problem. I was as single as four quarters. I owed her nothing.

As if she could read my thoughts as easily as I'd read hers, she shoved past me and ran from the closet.

Alone, I leaned against the shelf with my head back and my eyes closed, and that was where I stayed until I was sure I wouldn't chase after her. I then climbed the stairs to my office, where I used the same hand still sticky with Atlas's juices and a wad of spit for extra lube to make myself come.

Afterward, I used a Kleenex to clean up the evidence and cracked open a new bottle of Hennessy.

Two glasses later, I checked my phone.

Savvy G: hey im here

Savvy G: im waiting for u big daddy

Savvy G: where r u

Savvy G: hello?

Ignoring Savannah's attempts to reach me, I lit up a blunt and did some sleuthing to find Atlas's Instagram. I didn't have time for social media, but luckily, I'd made a profile years ago when the shop first opened to help promote it.

Now I guess it's main use would be for stalking Atlas's complicated ass.

Savannah kept messaging me, but I ignored every one. If my hesitation to hurt Atlas's feelings wasn't reason enough to leave her alone, I didn't know what was.

THIRTEEN

Atlas

MEN, I REALIZED, WERE EASILY PACIFIED.

All it took was one half-assed apology, an offer of beer, and all was forgiven. Or, in Rowdy's case, a Ziplock bag full of Grandaddy.

Women were way more cutthroat. When the beef was up, it was stuck, and it didn't matter how petty. Until death do us part, bitches and cunts!

I pursed my lips as I watched the bloodthirsty vamp who had held a gun to Rowdy's head, whose name I'd learned was Britain, approach Rowdy now as he lounged on the couch surrounded by his subjects—six or seven hoes wearing next to absolutely nothing and all hoping to be chosen.

I noticed the men all kept a safe distance from Rowdy and gravitated to the other Kings instead. Well, except for Golden, who was also surrounded by women hoping to fix him. I rolled my eyes.

The worst part was watching Rowdy flirt back. At the moment, he had his hand on the thigh of some woman draped all over him. I knew it was for my benefit. I knew he wanted me to see it and hate him with every fiber of my being. Well, it worked.

Even from this distance, I could tell she was a ten, suspiciously resembling the Instagram model Savvy G.

I felt so stupid. After what I'd allowed Rowdy to do to me downstairs in the storage closet, I'd expected, I don't know, respect? Friendship? Genuine interest that lasted more than five minutes before he decided to ignore me again? The whiplash was real.

Every muscle in my body was strung tight as I watched Rowdy notice Britain. His expression was unreadable, but I knew that keen mind was silently sharpening as he tracked Britain's approach.

Ruen's friend, who it had taken me no time at all to learn was in charge of this ragtag group, uttered something I couldn't hear over the music. I sucked in a breath and inched closer in case I needed to intervene. Although, I didn't know why I'd bother. After the way I'd turned my back on my father before he died and then my mother after he was gone, I didn't know what I deserved anymore, but I knew one thing was for certain.

No one deserved a selfish ass like Rowdy Wray.

I was halfway across the room, barreling down anyone in my path when Rowdy took me by surprise for the umpteenth time tonight.

He nodded to whatever Britain had said to him and then silently held out his hand to shake.

It seemed like a small gesture, but if one were fluent in the language of Rowdy Wray, one would know it was the highest level of respect he would ever bestow on another person.

"Aye. Move your thirsty ass over," he snapped at the woman he'd been feeling up a moment ago. "You see this man needs a seat." In typical asshole fashion, Rowdy allowed his voice to carry over the music for others to hear.

The poor girl scooted over on the couch, allowing Britain to take her seat, and then the soft-spoken vamp reached into his backpack and handed over a gallon-sized Ziplock bag full of Indica.

My stomach dipped at the sight.

That much weed casually proffered as a truce could only mean one thing.

Britain wasn't just a smoker. He was a distributor too.

Rowdy's smile was small, but his green eyes were practically glowing as he took in Britain's peace offering. "'Preciate it," he said, cool as a cucumber as he accepted Britain's gift.

The party had been in full swing for a couple of hours now. Ruen had agreed to stay and deejay, but her crew had made it clear she wouldn't be staying without them, so the Kings invited them to the party. Ruen had been clearly annoyed but didn't argue. I guess she knew it would be pointless. Ruen might be a gun-toting badass, but she'd surrounded herself with other gun-toting badasses who didn't care that she could handle herself. Protecting one another came with the territory.

Reassured that the furniture wouldn't be violently rearranged anytime soon, I worked the room before heading over to Ruen to see if she needed anything.

"I'm good!" she yelled over the music before lifting a drink from the small table next to a plate of food. The only thing the party had been missing was servers, but someone must have brought her the refreshments since she hadn't once left her booth for a break.

My money was on one of the doting boys in her crew hovering nearby. Britain, Christian, Ky, and Malik never seemed to be far away, their heads on a swivel, constantly clocking who came and went before eventually finding their focus lingering on Ruen once more.

Their dynamic was…interesting.

I left Ruen to do her thing and moved over to the buffet Fred had catered just as she switched the song to "Bounce Back" by Big Sean.

"You know Ruen's pissed at you, right?" I overheard someone say. Intrigued, I looked up from my perusal of the lobster tails in search of the voice. "Diamond earrings won't get you out of the dog house this time."

There.

I found them skulking in the shadows by the windows as Mr. All-American scoffed like buying a girl jewelry was a ridiculous notion when really he sounded…jealous, almost like he resented Ky for being the one to drape Ruen in diamonds.

I guess those earrings were real, after all. A priceless trinket you only wore during special occasions—like tea with the Queen. Meanwhile, Ruen was casually wearing them with an outfit that looked like it came straight out of Forever 21. She hadn't even bothered to remove them before placing the oversized headphones on her head.

"Let me worry about that," Ky murmured, head down as he broodily stared out the fogged window with his hands stuffed in the pockets of his suit pants.

"Seriously, what were you thinking? We just got back, and you're already trying to start a war with the Kings?"

"We needed to know how big of a threat they posed, didn't we? Now we know." He looked up, and I could swear his gaze found mine in the window's reflection. "We know their weaknesses too."

My gaze darted back down to the lobster tails.

No way he was talking about me. He *couldn't* have meant me. I was nothing to the Kings. Also, it sounded like Ky had purposely provoked the Kings. If Rowdy, Roc, Golden, and Joren found out, this party would turn into a bloodbath that would probably end with them killing the witnesses, too, so I made the decision right then to keep my mouth shut. I owed the Kings nothing. Sure, they took me in—sort of—and gave me a job, but I was earning my keep, and they made sure I regretted it every day. Not exactly a recipe for inspiring loyalty.

"That's great, Ky," Christian said, sounding anything but impressed, "except we need them as *allies*, not enemies."

Ky turned and openly watched me now as he sat on the window sill and whispered something in Korean. "결국 다 똑같습니다."

Whatever it meant, it made Christian abandon his attempts to reason with him and storm away.

"You're wasting your time," I told Ky after a long moment of contemplation. It was pointless pretending I hadn't been listening. "Whatever you want from them, I can't help you get it. Rowdy doesn't care about me; he only wants to fuck me. I'm just an employee to the rest of the Kings and not a very good one."

"Has he?"

I frowned at his question. "Has he what?"

Ky pushed away from the window and came to stand next to me, facing the opposite direction. He was so close I could smell his soap and had to tilt my head back to meet his black gaze hooded by monolids. "Has he fucked you?"

One sweep of his tattooed finger down my arm, and I took a step back. "I don't think that's any of your business."

I tightened my grip on my fork in case I needed to stab him, but after a few seconds of waiting for him to pounce, I realized I was no longer his focus. Instead, he was staring over my head, amusement playing on his small but pouty mouth.

"Apologies if I made you uncomfortable, Miss Beck. It might please you to know how wrong you are, though." He didn't bother to clarify before he strolled away. I'd only just loosened my hold on the fork when a familiar cologne invaded my senses, and I tightened my grip again.

"Atlas."

Sucking in a breath, I spun around to face him. Rowdy had been clear across the room a moment ago, and now he was standing in front of me. "What do you want?"

His lips parted to answer, but I grabbed my food and walked off. I wasn't interested in what he had to say.

A part of me expected him to come after me, but he didn't. Of course, he didn't. Because despite what Ky thought, I wasn't wrong.

Rowdy didn't give a damn about me.

The party lasted a few more hours, and by the end, the last

of the stragglers were either too drunk to drive or had already passed out.

It didn't matter to Rowdy, though.

He'd disappeared from the party for a while after I'd snubbed him and had returned just in time to order everyone to go home. When the grumbling started, and everyone stayed put, Rowdy pulled out the shotgun he'd hidden behind the bar, cocked it, and yelled for them to get the hell out or get blasted.

Sobered, the guests scattered like roaches, pushing and shoving to get through the door because not one of them had to question if Rowdy was crazy enough to start shooting.

There was a frustrated dip in his brow when our gazes met across the room, but he looked away just as quickly and ignored me.

Tuesday and I helped everyone who needed it arrange safe transportation home, and then we started to clean up with the help of the Kings. Ruen gave me a quick hug goodbye once Roc paid her, and then she and her crew left quieter than they'd arrived.

Tuesday was next to go once her ride arrived. She'd gotten tipsy and had spent the last hour of the party making out with Malik in the corner. Weird that he still ended up going home with Ruen.

I finished up, waved goodbye to the Kings—Rowdy still refused to look my way—and headed to my car behind the building.

I'd finally started parking in the employee lot after leaving my shift one day and finding a boot on my car instead of the usual ticket. It had cost me the last of my money to get it removed, but at least I'd gotten paid today.

I was halfway to my car when I noticed it seemed to be favoring one side. As I got closer, I realized the tires on the driver's side were completely flat, and I was unequivocally screwed. I'd only been working at the shop for a week. My paycheck wasn't enough to cover two new tires, food, and my room at the motel for another two weeks.

Frustrated tears pricked the back of my eyes, but then footsteps behind me had me holding them back.

"What are you still doing here?" Joren drunkenly inquired. I turned and found him with his arm tossed around some woman who was not his wife. Although, I'd never met the woman, so I couldn't be sure.

Behind them, Golden was silently helping an equally drunk Roc to his car. He helped him into the passenger seat before hopping in the driver's seat and racing out of the lot without looking our way even once.

"My tires are flat."

Joren slipped his arm free from his companion's shoulders and stumbled over to inspect them himself. He blinked, then blinked again to clear his vision. "Yeah," he slurred while rubbing a hand over his bald head. "Someone stabbed them motherfuckers."

I blinked. "What?"

The door to the shop flew open, and out swaggered Rowdy. He now wore a navy-blue pullover with the words *Idlewild's Finest* written in bold white letters and his hood tossed over his head, shielding his braids.

Strutting in high heels beside him was none other than the model who'd been all over him at the party. Even after he humiliated her, she was still going home with him. I curled my lip at them both, but then my head began to swim. Bile rose in my throat, so I quickly inhaled to draw fresh air into my lungs.

"O! Yo, O!" Joren's drunk ass called out when Rowdy walked right past us and toward his gorgeous Hellcat in B5 blue.

"What?" Rowdy snapped back a little aggressively.

Joren seemed oblivious as he waved him over. "Come here."

Rowdy hesitated only a second before unlocking his car and telling his fuck buddy to get in. I rolled my eyes when she wasted no time obeying him. "What's up?" he asked after walking over.

"Someone flattened Atlas's tires."

Rowdy's green gaze immediately strayed to me instead of my car. "Yeah? That's too bad. She must have pissed someone off."

I crossed my arms instead of rising to Rowdy's bait and hitting him like I wanted to. I'd already figured out who was responsible for the mutilation of my car the moment Joren said someone had stabbed my tires. "I'm sure they were more than deserving," I returned.

Rowdy released a pissed-off chuckle before nodding. "All right. See ya." He spun around and started toward his car again.

"What the—Yo!" Joren called out while throwing his arms out wide. "She needs a ride home."

"Then take her," Rowdy tossed over his shoulder.

It was so easy for him, wasn't it? To inject chaos into my life and then leave me to clean up the mess. There was absolutely no way I was getting in the car with Joren. He could barely stand, and his date didn't look any better off.

Joren's head swiveled my way, but I was already shaking mine. "That's okay," I declined politely. "I'll take the bus."

I pulled up the GPS on my phone to search for routes and saw that the closest bus was a half a mile walk away, so I waved goodbye to Joren and his date and started toward the street before hooking a right on Temperance and beginning the trek home.

I must have been walking for all of three minutes before I heard the roar of Rowdy's Challenger and looked up just as he sped by me before disappearing down Fourth Street.

Asshole.

I didn't see Savannah in the car, but I knew she was with him.

Pride of Kings was located in the heart of Idlewild, which meant walking down seedy streets at three in the morning. Still, it was better than dying in a fiery car crash or begging for Rowdy's help. That had probably been his plan all along when he slit my tires.

Fifteen minutes later, I was beyond the business district and cutting through a rundown neighborhood when a sound like a glass bottle rolling over concrete had me glancing over my shoulder.

I searched the shadows, waiting to see if any of them moved, but when nothing jumped out at me, I forced myself to keep going. I was already halfway to the bus stop, so I quickened my steps, only glancing at my phone when necessary since I didn't know Idlewild well enough to navigate without it.

My heart was racing, and the pounding beat overpowered the late-night sounds of my surroundings until there was only its erratic rhythm and my panting breaths.

Maybe that was why I didn't hear it until it was too late.

The sound of glass crunched under an otherwise silent foot right before a sack was shoved over my head and all I saw was darkness. It muffled my startled scream and the increasingly hysterical ones that followed as I was lifted off the ground, my feet and legs kicking and flailing as I was carried away.

FOURTEEN

Atlas

WE DIDN'T GO FAR.

My hands were quickly tied, and I was tossed inside a trunk, the door slamming shut behind me before I could leap free. The sack was too thick to see through, so I focused on freeing my hands. I fought against the knots of the rope until my muscles burned and my skin was rubbed raw. Eventually, I gave up and started screaming again, hoping someone heard me.

My abductor did.

The music volume steadily rose until it drowned my screams for help, and in a flash, the car raced forward. I was tossed around the trunk for the next few minutes as my abductor drove like a bat out of hell.

At some point, I began hyperventilating as I tried to piece together who my kidnapper could be. The car made another sharp turn, and I was thrown to the other side of the trunk, my spine colliding with the wheel well just as the answer hit me like a sledgehammer to the chest.

Unrequited.

It had only been a week, but they must have grown tired of waiting for me to figure out my connection to the Kings. But why kidnap me if they already knew everything? Clearly, this was a person who didn't mind waiting if their plan had been for me to uncover everything on my own. It didn't make sense.

The car finally reduced its speed just as the answer tugged at my memory.

"We needed to know how big of a threat they posed..."

"We know their weaknesses too."

"It might please you to know how wrong you are."

The car suddenly stopped, the engine died, a door slammed close, and then heavy footsteps carried my abductor closer as I quickly ran through my options. Scream? Fight? Beg for my life?

I remembered the ruthlessness of Ruen's crew and knew that nothing I did would make a difference, but I wasn't going down without a fight.

The trunk opened before I could form a plan of attack, and red and yellow neon lights nearby penetrated the black bag over my head. Two hands closed around me, and now that I knew who they belonged to—what they wanted from me—I fought even harder to escape.

I kicked and screamed short bursts of broken sounds until I was on the verge of losing my voice altogether.

My abductors must have been frustrated because the one trying to grab me stopped and ripped the bag off my bed instead.

Tears clouded my vision, and I filled my lungs with the fresh night air as I blinked them free until the tall blurry figure standing over me became clear, and I was staring into the familiar face of my would-be murderer.

It wasn't Ky or his crew.

It was Rowdy.

"You want to get out, or you want to stay in there?" he casually inquired like I wasn't tied up in his trunk—as if it wasn't him who'd *put* me there. "I don't have all night, beautiful."

As soon as he was done speaking, the invisible chains fell away, and I was freed from my stunned silence. "Are you kidding me?" I questioned hoarsely, pushing my ravaged throat past its limits.

Rowdy didn't respond.

He tried once again to help me out, but I kicked out at him, catching him in his chest and making him grunt before he finally got the hint and backed off. I climbed out of his trunk—awkwardly since my hands were still bound—and ended up tumbling over the side and hitting the ground *hard*.

The fall hurt like a bitch, but Rowdy was smart and didn't try to help me again. With gritted teeth, I pushed to my feet and warily looked around.

My belly sank as I took in the dimly lit parking lot and run-down motel a few feet away.

Hooker's Cove.

Rowdy had driven me home.

I whipped around to face him again. A sneer on my lips. "You couldn't have just offered me a ride like a normal fucking person?"

My voice and all of the commotion must have carried.

The curtains moved inside a few of the rooms, so I turned my head, silently beseeching the guests who were discreetly peeking out of their windows. Once they noticed me looking, the drapes quickly drew back, and the message became clear.

No one was going to come to my rescue if Rowdy decided to murder me.

I didn't think he would, but I'd been wrong about people before. Sutton. Sienna. My parents. Rowdy was particularly wishy-washy. It was like he couldn't decide if he wanted to hate me, ignore me, or...be with me.

Right now, there was no emotion on his face to guide me as he stared blankly down at me. "Would you have come if I had?"

No.

Not while he had *her* with him, riding shotgun and touching him while I silently languished in the back seat. There was no sign of Savannah in his car now, and I stopped myself from wondering where she'd gone...and if she was waiting in his bed for him while he dealt with me.

I was silent, so he arrogantly spat, "*Exactly*." His face was balled up like *I* was the cause of all our problems. "You like to do shit the hard way, Atlas, so this is me giving you what you want."

"I didn't ask to be kidnapped and tied up, Owen! I really thought—"

I'd thought I was going to die or be tortured for information I didn't have.

I didn't allow myself to finish that thought aloud—to let him see how vulnerable and helpless he'd made me feel. I already hated myself for allowing him to have so much of me when he'd done nothing to earn it.

"You thought what? You thought I'd hurt you?" He came toward me, but I backed away. "Atlas," he pleaded, sounding frustrated. "I would never do that. If it ever came to it, I'd walk away before I ever raised a hand to you."

"That's your problem, Owen. You think physical pain is the only hurt there is. It's not even the kind that cuts deepest. You'd know that if you knew how to care for anyone but yourself."

I returned the blank stare he'd given me moments ago. This time, he was the open book. I saw my words land and watched with a twisted satisfaction as they mutilated his overinflated ego.

"All right," he said lowly when the silence became too heavy. "I'll give you that, Atlas. Just let me help you."

"No. I don't want anything from you."

"Too bad. I'm not leaving you like this, and that's not up for fucking discussion. You think I'm bad? Look at where you are." All trace of the remorse he'd felt was gone as he basically demanded I let him clean up his mess.

Unfortunately, he was right.

As ruthless as Rowdy was, there were far worse creatures skulking around Hooker's Cove.

Fancy Mack, the gold-tooth, silk-wearing pimp who loved pastels and lorded over the treacherous territory, was the worst of them all. A couple of his girls had even tried to recruit me up until a few days ago, and now they avoided me at all costs, but I wasn't stupid enough to think that made me safe.

Hiding my sniffle, I nodded once before turning and granting him access to my hands bound tight against my spine. I stiffened at the cold press of metal against my skin, but with a flick of his hand, it was gone, and so was the rope. I rubbed at my sore wrists before silently turning to face him.

Rowdy tossed the rope and the knife in his trunk before handing me my purse, which still lay inside, and meeting my gaze. "I'm not good at this, Atlas. I can count on one hand how many times in my life I've apologized, but I can't let you walk away without knowing that I would never hurt you."

I visibly softened at his words and allowed him only a glimpse of my uncertainty before lowering my gaze to the ground. "You really mean it?" My voice was unguarded now. Hopeful. An open invitation.

It only took the span of a single breath before I saw his work boots—black Tims with blue laces—appear within my line of sight. His hands settled on my waist, drawing me in until there was no space left between our bodies. I could feel his heart beating wildly beneath my palms. It was the only thing that gave him away. That and, "Yes, pretty baby. I wouldn't say it if I didn't."

Somehow, I believed him, even after all the reasons he'd given me tonight not to.

"Good." I smiled softly at him, and his green eyes practically glowed with pleasure at the sight as my hands shifted from his strong pecs to his shoulders. "I really mean this too."

Rowdy was somewhat of a freak—a sexy, mouthwatering freak—but a freak nonetheless. His height was basically a physical anomaly, so it really took some power and determination to bring my knee up high enough to connect with his balls. My efforts were rewarded with a pained *whoosh* from Rowdy as he let me go and bent over slightly.

I was a little disappointed. I thought it would be like in the movies, and he'd fall to his knees, screaming in pain or maybe even pass out. In reality, it was all so anticlimactic.

Or maybe Rowdy truly did have the heart of a lion.

"Aaah!" My irritation quickly morphed into panic when Rowdy limped forward and tried to grab me. I retreated, but he only kept coming, albeit slowly. He was obviously in pain yet determined to get to me anyway. I could run, but I still wouldn't be quick enough.

And this time, it *would* end like the movies.

I'd run for safety just to be delayed by a locked door, and then I'd fumble to find my keys before the killer reached me, only to die on my doorstep anyway.

No.

That wouldn't be me.

Reaching inside my purse, I pulled out the welcome gift I'd gotten tonight from the Kings during the party and aimed it right between Rowdy's vengeful eyes.

His gaze slowly drifted to my weapon before dismissing it altogether and staring me down. "Come here, Atlas."

"No." I really shouldn't have been surprised that my show of force did nothing to deter him since he'd had *multiple* guns pointed at him only hours ago, and it hadn't fazed him.

"Atlas, bring your ass here!" he roared. He was standing up straight now, the pained dip in his brow now coupled with fury.

"Fuck you!" I shouted back.

Losing his patience, Rowdy grabbed for me, and I panicked, pressing down on the trigger with a squeal.

"Fuck!"

This time, he did go down, his hands instantly flying to his eyes to assuage the sting of the high-grade pepper spray. I waited for the sense of satisfaction to come at finally having bruised him as he'd bruised me.

I waited, but it was notably absent.

Rowdy released another pained groan, and guilt guided me forward to help him, but then I stopped, suddenly hearing a voice I never thought I'd hear again. As if the blood-pumping root of me could read my thoughts, it pulsed in answer to the question in my head.

"My father wasn't a religious man, but there was a scripture he'd heard once that stuck with him. *Above all else, guard your heart,*" I recited to Rowdy's bent head. I could have sworn he stiffened as if he knew what I'd say next. "*For everything you do flows from it.*"

I'd heard my dad say it to my mom all the time. The interpretation varied for each person, but for my dad, it was a reminder that every decision he made, everything he did, affected her. My mom was the center of his world, and he never did anything without putting her feelings and well-being first. I guess it stuck with me, too, but in a different way.

"You demand things from me I'm not ready to give, but you're so good at making me want them too—so much sometimes that nothing else matters. But then…then you make me feel like a fool for feeling that way, and I'm lost all over again. I know what I said before, but I lied, Owen. I don't think I can give you my body without giving you my heart too." Rowdy was still as if bracing himself for what I would say next. "But you said it yourself. You're not interested in that part of me, and I couldn't trust you with it even if you were."

Ignoring the pain of what I had to do, I walked away and left him kneeling alone on the pavement, injured and at the mercy of the other monsters lurking in Hooker's Cove.

FIFTEEN

Rowdy

MY EYES WERE STILL SORE WHEN I OPENED THEM THE NEXT MORNING. After calling Golden to come and get me from the motel last night, I ended up downing Benadryl to knock myself out since no amount of washing my eyes would stop them from burning.

I gripped the edges of my bathroom sink and stared at my reflection in the mirror, but I didn't see the mild swelling, redness, or the leftover capsaicin crystalized around my lids.

I saw the man Atlas had seen last night.

The man she'd taken a deeper look at and found lacking. The man she'd rightly decided wasn't good enough for her.

Turning away, I rushed through my morning routine since I was running a little late, and on my way out, I texted Tony to see if he'd taken care of that errand I'd requested moments before passing out last night.

Tony: All good, boss. New tires are on.

Tony: Also changed oil, checked brakes, and topped fluids.

Tony: Dropped off the car an hour ago.

I smirked my approval as I texted back. *Thanks, T.*

Hudson may not have agreed with my methods of leadership,

but not even he could deny that Tony's sudden competence wasn't a mere coincidence after I'd whooped his ass.

Hopping in my car, I sped to the shop. Today was my Saturday to oversee our small kingdom, and I didn't accept tardiness—not even from myself. When I arrived, I found Atlas already waiting. Her gaze flicked up to me as I walked passed, and then she pushed away from the door she was leaning against so I could unlock it. Tuesday had her own set of keys, but since we didn't trust Atlas yet, she was stuck waiting until further notice.

"Good morning," she greeted, surprising me. Her tone was pleasant enough, but I could hear the wariness sheltered underneath. I guess this was her armor—pretending nothing had happened and it was business as usual.

All right. I could play along.

I paused from turning the lock and glanced over my shoulder to see her chewing on her lip. "Sup?"

She shrugged her shoulders. "How are your eyes?"

It was then I remembered I was still wearing shades, so she couldn't gauge for herself the damage she'd done. Returning her gesture, I shrugged. "I'll live."

Out of pure curiosity, I waited to see if she felt any guilt, but she only nodded and jutted her chin in the air before looking away. Something akin to pride bloomed in my chest, but I pretended I didn't feel it as I debated asking how she was. I knew it wouldn't change a thing, but it fucked me up to think I might have broken her when a week ago, it was all I wanted.

Since my concern wouldn't be appreciated anyway, I pushed the urge aside and finished unlocking the door.

I entered the building and scanned the darkness for any threats lurking before flipping on all the lights and letting Atlas inside. For now, it was just the two of us since the shop didn't open for another hour.

Atlas's training was officially over, so today would be her first time flying solo. The shop would only be open until noon, which meant it would be a pretty chill day.

I was headed for the stairs so I could have a few moments alone in my office to get my shit together when I heard her quiet voice at my back.

"Owen."

"What?" I replied without slowing my stride or looking back. I couldn't let her see how much I liked hearing her same my name. Only my mom called me Owen, but Atlas took the cake for sure.

"How did you find me last night?"

"This is my city, Atlas. I knew only one bus was still running that late that would take you back to the motel."

"But how did you know I was staying at the motel?"

I paused and then mouthed, "Fuck." Against my will, I turned around to face her. This was not the time to reveal I'd been stalking her pretty ass every chance I got. Some nights I even slept in the room next to hers just to make sure no one fucked with her. "Allow me to repeat myself. This is my city," I stated arrogantly instead. "There's not much I don't know."

Atlas looked me up and down but didn't comment on my statement. "And Savannah?"

I sighed. "What about her, Atlas?" I found it interesting she was asking twenty-one questions about a bitch after she'd pretty much told me I didn't have a chance in hell with her last night.

"I didn't see her in the car when you dropped me off."

Several responses filed through my head before I decided Atlas couldn't have it both ways. She couldn't run me off and keep me on a leash at the same time. "What are you asking me?" I played dumb. "If I went home and fucked her after leaving you last night?"

"Yes," she immediately hissed.

My dick gave a curious twitch, hearing the jealousy in her tone, so I held her gaze as I brought my hand to my erection and squeezed it through my jeans. I was letting him know there was nothing happening.

Atlas had that pussy on lock.

It seemed only one of us remembered, though. I watched

as her gaze lowered and lingered on my dick growing against my thigh.

"Why?"

Her gaze shot back up to mine and she gave a guilty startle. "Huh?"

"Why does it matter?" I repeated. I sunk my teeth into my bottom lip and felt my lids lower as I leaned my shoulder against the wall and regarded her across the room. "You don't want me, remember?"

"Yes, I remember," she said a little too quickly. I watched her inhale deeply and then slowly exhale. "It matters because I know you still want to fuck me, and I'm not too proud to admit that I'm afraid you might succeed." She squared her shoulders to make herself appear taller and unyielding. "I can't be with you if you're with her."

I shook my head as I stared at her. "Little girl, why are you playing games with me?"

"I'm not," she denied defensively.

"You are."

It wasn't often I was reminded of her age, but right now was one of those times. She was nineteen to my thirty-five, and I was beginning to wonder if I was crazy for thinking I could throw away the rule book for her.

"I just need to know if I actually mattered to you or if I was just a challenge."

"You were starting to." My confession floated in the air between us before dangling over our heads like a sharp ax that would strike at the first wrong move. "I didn't fuck Savannah last night. She tried to give me head, but I wasn't feeling the situation, so I dropped her ass off on the curb and left her there to find you."

Like Atlas, I wasn't too proud to admit that I was holding my breath as I waited to see how much deeper a hole my honesty would land me in.

Her lips parted and closed a few times before settling on, "Oh."

I pushed away from the wall, ready to end this conversation since it was going nowhere. "Anything else, Atlas?"

She wrinkled her nose before giving me her back. "Nope. You can go."

I was tempted to choke her out for dismissing me like she was crazy, but I went upstairs to my office instead.

After giving myself a few days to think about it, I'd decided to accept Harry's offer and buy the car wash, but first, I wanted to do my due diligence, so I quickly typed an email to my lawyer and accountant and let them both know I needed to speak with their asses expeditiously. I'd call the contractor and inspector who helped us restore the old factory once Paris had a chance to look over the financials and give an okay.

My phone vibrated in my pocket, so I pulled it out and saw I had a new DM on Instagram. Since Atlas wasn't fucking with me, I clicked on the message out of spite and immediately regretted it as soon as I saw all the messages Savannah had sent me last night and this morning.

3:19 a.m.

Savvy G: did u rlly kick me out ov ur car chase after dat yung bitch

Savvy G: itty bitty titty ho look twelf n shes not even all dat pretty

Video call at 3:26 a.m.

Video call ended at 3:27 a.m.

Savvy G: I now u c me callin u

Savvy G: Rowdy

Savvy G: ROWDY!!!!!

Savvy G: u now wat find u sum1 else 2 fuck n duck I'm done

8:44 a.m.

Savvy G: I can fuck u better then she can…

I had to read over some of her messages twice because Sav refused to use punctuation and spelled like she'd quit school in the third grade to show her ass for the gram.

I was the last person to knock how the next chose to survive, but Savannah was a trust-fund baby from the suburbs with a doctor and a lawyer for parents. Everything she did was for the right look, including fucking me.

Females like Sav would call me toxic with one breath and throw their pussy at me in the next. Money used to be the most coveted currency in the world, but now, in the age of social media, it was clout. People would lie, cheat, and steal for something that wasn't even real or tangible. It would be there one day and gone the next.

When I first met Sav, I'd treated her well enough, but as time went on, what modicum of respect I had for her quickly disappeared. Talking to her felt like plucking the hair from my balls one by one because all she ever did was obsess over her appearance, brag about how many likes she got on a new photo, or mention what rapper or ball player was in her DMs this week in some sad attempt to make me jealous.

This wasn't even her first time claiming to be done with me.

The first time was after she'd realized I had her and three other fuck buddies in rotation. She said she couldn't live that way, and as I wasn't particularly attached, I respected it and left her in the dust. That lasted a few weeks before she realized I wasn't going to chase her, and she came crawling back.

Her second time being "done with me" only lasted a few days—same story, different girls.

Eventually, Savannah realized I wasn't going to commit to her or any other girl, so she stopped demanding one from me and settled for beating up or running off any female whose direction I even sneezed in.

Now that Atlas had entered the chat, Savannah was back to her old tricks, but this time, her newfound sense of worth had only lasted a few hours.

I closed the messages without responding because I never did unless I wanted some pussy and left my office to start my day.

Downstairs, some of the guys working today had already arrived and were in the workshop finishing up whatever repairs were scheduled to be completed today while Atlas was at the doors, unlocking them for the handful of customers already waiting outside.

Saturdays were by appointment only for same-day services since we were only open for three hours, so most of the people we'd see today would either be dropping off or picking up their car.

I currently had three open tickets and Donny's Caddy to finish customizing, but I still found myself in the lobby, leaning against the snack bar and not even bothering to pretend I wasn't watching Atlas.

This girl had me in a chokehold and the longer I went without air, the less I needed it. I only wanted to be near her, whatever it cost me.

The fact that her back was turned, but she still knew I was close by, made it all the sweeter. It was evident in the way she kept turning her head as if to look over her shoulder, only to remember she hated me and stopped herself.

She still hadn't thanked me for fixing her car, but I hadn't expected her to since I was the reason she'd needed new tires in the first place. I'd taken the keys out of her purse after I'd hogtied her ass and thrown her in my trunk. I'd already regretted slashing her tires even before she kicked my ass all over the motel parking lot.

Eventually, I got a little hungry watching Atlas, so I rounded the bar and was perusing my options when I felt her presence at my back a second before her body wash reached me.

Atlas always smelled like oranges and vanilla, making me want to pour some Patrón all over her body and get drunk off her ass. It didn't help that I'd already sampled her pussy and knew she tasted just as good as she smelled—like a fucking dream.

Without turning to confirm it was her, I said, "How can I help you, my little Dreamsicle?"

I turned around in time to see her pause before pursing her lips and pretending she hadn't heard my new pet name for her. "There's a customer here whose trunk won't close and would like it fixed today."

"Does she have an appointment?"

"No. I told her she'd have to come back on Monday, but she said her car was serviced here last week, and she believes the mechanic who performed the repairs damaged the latch. She doesn't want to wait."

I didn't respond, simply jerked my chin toward the lobby, where the fuming woman waited for her return. Atlas paused, and I could see her reconsidering her decision to ask for my help.

"Be nice," she ordered as if she were my boss instead of the other way around.

I chuckled under my breath while admiring the natural sway of Atlas's hips and the way her round ass bounced as I followed her back to reception like a dog sniffing after his favorite toy.

"This is Naomi Irving," Atlas introduced. "Ms. Irving, this is my boss, Rowdy. He's one of the owners."

"It's *Mrs*. Irving, sweetie." The customer looked Atlas up and down like she thought she was above her because some dumb fool who probably had a weak chin and a weaker stroke married her ass.

Atlas, the consummate professional, forced a smile. "My apologies, ma'am."

Coming to stand behind Atlas, I placed my hands on her shoulders and gave them a reassuring squeeze before speaking to the customer over her head. "How can we help you, Mrs. Irksome?"

"*Irving*." I just stared at her, waiting for her to tell me what her problem was before I lost my patience. She huffed when she realized I wasn't going to kiss her ass and said, "As I told your little secretary…" I felt Atlas tense underneath me when Irksome shot her another look of disdain. "I—

"Nah. Let me stop you right there. Whatever your issue is, Atlas didn't cause it. She's actually trying to help your rude ass, so before you utter another syllable, I need you to apologize right fucking now or get the fuck out of my establishment."

Irksome made a sound like a Chihuahua after you kicked it while literally clutching the string of pearls around her neck. I narrowed my gaze on the necklace, imagining Atlas wearing them and nothing else while I ate her pretty pussy until she creamed. "Is this how you treat your customers?"

"Only the annoying ones."

"Wow. Way to lose a customer. I'll be taking my business elsewhere from now on." She snatched her purse off the counter and stormed out of the door.

Once the door slammed shut behind her, I immediately pushed forward and flipped open Mrs. Irving's file lying on the counter in front of Atlas.

"Owen," Dream whined.

I had her body trapped between me and the counter, unable to escape while I took longer than necessary to read over Mrs. Irving's maintenance and repair history.

Kane, whose expertise I trusted explicitly, had been the one to replace the clutch and pressure plate in her Beamer, which meant he hadn't gone anywhere near her trunk.

Seeing all I needed to know, I closed the file and whipped out my phone while Atlas squirmed pointlessly to get away.

"Owen, there are customers right there, not to mention I don't like you anymore. Let me go."

"Shhh." I kissed the top of her pretty head to shut her up while scrolling through my contacts with one hand and rubbing her flat stomach under her shirt with the other. Once I found the name I was looking for, I typed out a quick text.

I know how you can repay that favor.

The bubbles appeared almost immediately, and then a response came shortly after.

Britain: How?

I texted him what I needed and where to find it before pocketing my phone and giving Atlas my full attention. She'd given up trying to dislodge me and was now clicking around on the computer. I squinted my gaze when I realized she was on fucking Facebook. I was about to rip into her for talking to her little bobblehead friends while on the clock when something more pressing caught my eye.

A new message had popped up at the bottom of the screen from someone named Sutton Hayes.

"Who the fuck is that?" I pointed at the screen right over the kissing emoji taunting me. It was all he'd sent, but it was enough to land him on my ever-growing hit list.

Atlas looked back at me over her shoulder with a frown. "My ex. Why?"

"Why is he messaging you?" Her ignorant ass shrugged while keeping her sexy mouth closed. "Oh, all right," I said simply while seething. "Block him."

"Did you block Savannah?"

I ignored that. "This shit is not up for discussion, Atlas."

She sighed while typing "cute" on some girl's picture. "On that, we can agree."

"You still fucking him?" I didn't wait for a response before I reached around her and clicked on his profile before she could stop me. Once his page loaded, I blew up his profile picture, committing his face to memory so that I could kill that lame if I ever ran into him.

"Absolutely not." She scoffed. "I'd fuck *you* before I ever let him touch me again." She shuddered in my arms.

"I'm going to ignore that." Atlas could pretend otherwise, but she wanted this dick. Resting my chin on her shoulder, I found myself breaking yet another one of my rules. "What happened?"

The last thing I wanted was to talk about her fucking ex, but I was also obsessed with knowing everything about her. To know your enemy was to conquer your enemy, and right now, my dick and her pussy were at war.

"Oh, nothing," she said easily. "I just found out he and my best friend were messing around at one of the worst times of my life."

I grimaced but said nothing. There was nothing I could say to make her feel better since I was no better. I'd fucked my fair share of friends, sisters, and cousins before. I'd even dipped off with a mom or two. The difference between her ex and me though was that none of the women I'd screwed over had been mine.

And none of them had been Atlas.

My nature was one of the reasons I avoided commitment in the first place. Why get into a relationship if I know I'm going to cheat? At least single, I owed no loyalty and could do whatever I wanted.

"Why was it the worst time of your life?" I asked her instead. I had a pretty good guess, but she didn't know I knew.

Atlas shook her head, telling me she didn't want to talk about it. I decided to respect her wishes for once since I really didn't want to get that deep in the middle of the shop's lobby.

Instead, I turned her around and stared into her soul-stealing eyes until I heard myself say, "I would never do that to you."

Even more shocking than my uttering such a promise was the bone-chilling knowledge that it was the truth. To conquer Atlas Beck was to conquer the universe. There'd be no need to search elsewhere.

Unable to hold back a moment longer, my head lowered.

I saw Atlas still, and just when I thought she'd reject me, she lifted her mouth for me to take. It was an offering that could only be described as tentative, the quick brush of her lips against mine ephemeral.

The connection was over as quickly as it had happened.

"Let me know if you have any more trouble," I told her quietly. And then, not so subtly, I squeezed her ass, earning a glare from her. "It doesn't matter how small; I want you to come and get me. It doesn't even need to be work-related. Anything you need, and Daddy will make it happen. And Atlas?" I gripped her chin when her stubborn ass looked away. "Only me."

"Thanks, but no thanks. I'd rather gouge out my own eyes with Rick Ross's toenails. I can take care of myself, Owen."

"You think after last night I don't know that?" She didn't respond, so I kissed her again, this time hard enough to force a startled moan from her, then pretended I didn't see her mouth chasing after mine when I pulled away and headed into the workshop to get some work done.

SIXTEEN

Atlas

Today was my appointment with Demi, so I headed straight over after the shop closed. I walked into the shop with a smile on my face that slowly fell when I found none other than Golden sitting in her chair.

Demi was animatedly talking as she re-twisted his locs, and to my utter shock and jealousy, Golden was actually speaking in low tones back to her. Of course, his sudden bout of chattiness ended as soon as I walked through the door. They were alone in the salon, and I suspected that might have been by design.

"Hey, girl," Demi greeted when she noticed me. "Take a seat at the bowl. I will be with you in just a sec."

"Cool." On my way to the sink, I stopped and smiled down at Golden, who was silently assessing me as he often did. I didn't think he was interested in me or anything, but I absolutely believed he didn't trust me for a second. "What's on your mind today, G?"

He raised his brow as if to say, that's the best you got?

I grinned and took a seat in the styling chair next to him. *Challenge accepted, my silent friend.*

"You know, I was thinking about our conversation the other day, and I decided you're right…you do look a little like J. Cole."

His expression dulled.

"Hey, don't get mad at me, dude." I raised my hands in mock surrender. "You're the one who said it." Golden took a sip of his drink a little too late to hide the subtle lift of his lips. "Anyway, bet you fifty bucks I can crush you in the quiet game."

He rolled his eyes.

"All right, I'll tell you a secret...but you have to promise not to tell anyone."

Golden gave a quiet snort, but seeing the triumph on my face, he rocked his hand in a so-so gesture that said I'd still have to do better than that.

I faked a sigh and stood. "Fine. Have it your way, boss."

"If you really want to get him talking," Demi cut in, "ask him if LeBron is better than Kobe. You won't be able to turn him off then."

I stared at Demi. "Kobe is obviously better than LeBron."

Demi tossed her head back and groaned, so I let my attention fall to Golden, who was watching me now with newfound appreciation in his gaze. "I should ban you both from my shop," Demi grumbled.

She finished with Golden, and they both walked to the front of the salon, where Golden whispered something to her, making her smile softly and blush a little before paying and leaving.

I watched through the window as he prowled to the same orange Camaro I'd seen him working on the day I'd arrived on their doorstep. He dropped into the driver's seat, and the engine roared to life before he slowly pulled away from the curb and disappeared from sight.

"Don't tell me you've got the hots for the Golden boy too."

I was alarmed when I looked up and realized Demi had caught me watching my silent boss leave. She was standing over me with her hands on her generous hips, waiting for an answer from me.

I barked an incredulous laugh. "No. You don't have to worry about that." I was too busy catching feelings for a man that would have sent my father to an early grave if he wasn't already dead.

Grief punched a volleyball-sized hole in my chest without warning so I said, "I'm pretty sure Golden hates me."

"Because he won't talk to you? I wouldn't take that personally. It took him two years before he would even say hi to me and then another two years before I got full sentences from him. We all have our ways of keeping the world at bay."

Great.

Except I didn't have two years. I needed answers now, and whoever had sent me those letters had gone silent.

"So Golden's is selective mutism?"

"I guess." She grabbed a clean black cape from the cabinet near the sink and secured it around my neck before arranging it to protect my clothes. "So, how's it going over there in the lion's den?" she asked as she checked my scalp.

I snickered at her name for the shop. "I took off my training wheels today, so that was...new."

"And the party last night? How was that?"

"It was okay," I said as she leaned me back and began to wash my hair. "You should have come."

Demi scoffed, the thin layer of scorn catching me off guard as she scrubbed my scalp. "Yeah, I'll pass, but thanks."

I frowned at her dry tone. "I'm sorry. Did I say something wrong?"

"No. No, no. Sorry, it's nothing you said. It's just there's some...history between me and one of the Kings that I'm not looking to revisit."

My belly sank as I wondered if she meant Rowdy. "Really?" I tried to keep my tone casual as I added, "Which one? If you don't mind me asking."

She paused for a heartbeat before she sighed loudly and grumbled, "Roc."

"Oh." I blinked my astonishment. "*Oh.*"

"Yeah."

There was a short pause before we both started laughing.

"No offense." I chortled. "But I just don't see it." Demi seemed way too sophisticated and sweet for immature-ass Roc.

"Yeah, well, that just means you're a lot smarter than me." She shut off the water and wrapped my faux locs in a towel to soak up the extra water.

"I'm not so sure about that," I murmured as I thought about Rowdy. He'd been all over me this morning, and I hadn't tried all that hard to stop him.

As if we'd conjured him up, a shadow suddenly darkened her door, and I recognized Roc immediately.

He was holding a little girl in his arms.

Roc pushed inside the salon with an irritated frown on his handsome mug as he listened to the caller on the other end of the phone plastered to his ear.

The little girl, who I assumed was the daughter Rowdy had mentioned, was babbling animatedly, oblivious to the fact that her father wasn't listening.

Suddenly, she quieted and began looking around before catching sight of Demi and squirming to get down. Roc set her on her feet but only after a cautious sweep of the shop with his eyes, and she immediately ran in our direction as fast as her little legs would take her.

"Demi," she squealed.

"Halo!" Demi swept Roc's daughter off her feet as soon as she reached her. "How's my best friend?"

"Goooood." Halo giggled, making her warm light brown complexion glow. "I asked my Daddy to buy me a Gucci purse, and um, he, um, he said he would."

"Miss thang, what do you know about Gucci?"

"A lot."

"Oh really?" Demi tickled her tiny tummy, making her giggle. "Well, make sure you get me one too."

"Okay!" Demi set her down, and then Halo's focus shifted to me. "Hi," she greeted shyly.

"Hello." I returned her wave with a smile. Halo was definitely a beautiful brown girl, but this close, I was able to detect the bisection of European features, too, making me wonder who her mother might be.

Feeling bolder, she asked, "What's your name?"

"Atlas. What's yours?" I inquired, even though I'd heard Demi shout it already. It seemed rude not to, and I didn't want to make her feel unwelcome.

"Halo."

"That's an awfully pretty name for an awfully pretty girl."

"Thank you! You know my daddy?"

"I sure do. I work for him."

"Oh. I like your hair. Is it yours?"

I snorted because this little girl was too grown. "No, it's not mine. Is this *your* hair?" I reached out and tugged one of her lopsided pigtails.

"Uh-huh! I grew it all by myself."

"Wow."

"My Daddy does it for me." Halo stepped a little closer to me and whispered—but not really—behind her hand, "He's really bad at it."

"But you know what?" I whispered back.

"What?"

"I bet no one will notice because you're so cool."

"Kacy doesn't think so," Halo told me with a deep frown. "She tells everyone at school I smell."

"Kacy sounds like a hater."

Halo nodded enthusiastically. "Uh-huh. She really is. And she's the one that smells. Not me."

"I bet."

Roc ended his phone call and sauntered over. "What's good, ladies?"

Demi wasted no time answering his question with one of her own. "Not your hearing, apparently. I thought I told you not to step foot in my shop again?"

Roc dismissed her question with a wave of his hand. "I'm not trying to hear that, Demetria. I came looking for Golden."

"Well, as you can see, he's not here, so bye."

"Anyway." Roc's gaze traveled to me sitting at the sink bowl with the towel still wrapped around my head, my hair forgotten. "What's up, Atlas? Fuck did you do to my boy last night?"

"Nothing he didn't deserve," I shot back. "But did he also tell you he tied me up and locked me in his trunk?"

Roc's brows shot to his hairline, telling me all I needed to know. Rowdy had conveniently left that part out.

"Stop playing games with that man, and maybe he won't have to act so crazy."

I shook my head at his ignorance. "Roc, you and I both know Owen was crazy before he met me. I am not responsible for his complete lack of respect for human decency."

"Oh, Owen, huh?" Roc said, completely ignoring everything else I'd said. "Yeah, okay. Sounds to me like he's not the only one playing crazy." He dismissed me and regarded Demi. "Did Golden say where he was going? He's not answering his phone."

"No, Roc. Contrary to what you must think, I do not keep your best friend or anything concerning you in my back pocket."

"Yeah, all right." He frowned as he lifted his phone and dialed Golden again with no answer. "Fuck, man," he spat as he hung up. "Come on, baby girl. We got to go."

"Noooo!" Halo, who had been silently playing with Demi's supplies, ran to hug her leg from behind. "I want to stay with Demi."

"Well, you can't, but if you come with Daddy, I'll get you some ice cream."

"No. I don't even like ice cream."

"Oh, word? So I should just throw out all those ice pops you made me buy when we get home, huh?"

Halo seemed to consider it for a moment before looking up at Demi. "Demi, you buy me ice cream?"

I chuckled under my breath. Halo had to be the most cunning four-year-old I'd ever met.

"Hmmm." Demi pretended to think. "How about this? You be a good girl and go with your father, and I'll fix your ponytails before you go."

"Umm… you buy me Starbees next time too?"

It took me a second longer to realize Halo meant Starbucks.

"Of course."

Demi's offer was apparently better than her father's because Halo yelled, "Yay!" before running to Demi's styling chair and trying unsuccessfully to climb on top. Her father saw her struggling and helped her into the chair before moving to stand next to her.

I was still watching them when I felt Demi gently touch my shoulder.

"You can sit under the dryer while I take care of her. You don't mind, do you?"

I shook my head and followed her to the overhead dryer.

Demi set the timer and then moved over to fix Halo's hair as she'd promised. I could see Roc's lips moving as she worked and Demi giving him short responses in return, but the dryer was too loud for me to hear what they were saying. Eventually, Roc gave up when he realized he wasn't getting anywhere with Demi and focused on his daughter, who was eating up the attention.

I'd already surmised Halo was spoiled rotten. I guess being the daughter of a King had its perks, and with uncles like Rowdy, Joren, and Golden at her beck and call, I almost felt a little envious.

The dryer shut off while Demi was putting the finishing touches on Halo's new hairstyle.

Halo now had nine plaits twisted halfway in rows of three, each decorated with blue butterfly clips with the untwisted ends secured inside the ponytail Demi had created with the back half of her hair.

"This should last her the rest of the weekend. And Roc, your daughter may be half White, but all of this—" Demi gestured to

Halo's gorgeous mane of hair—"came from you, so stop letting her go to sleep without a scarf on her head."

I heard the unmistakable sound of Roc slapping her ass before he lustfully said, "Thanks, baby."

"I'm not your baby, and keep your hands off my booty, Rochendrix."

Rochendrix? I burst out laughing, interrupting their not-so-subtle flirting and drawing their gazes over to me. "I'm sorry, but what kind of ghetto-ass name is that?"

Roc retorted with a fake laugh of his own. "I don't know," he deadpanned. "Who names their kid after a map?"

Well, he had me there.

Roc reached into his jeans and pulled out a money clip before peeling off more than a few of the crisp hundred-dollar bills and trying to hand the stack to Demi.

"Roc, this is too much, and I've told you before I don't want your money."

"Take it," he insisted though it sounded like an order.

"No."

Without missing a beat, Roc looked down at his daughter. "Baby, remember what Daddy told you when you said you wanted to stay up late like a big girl?"

Halo nodded solemnly. "Yes, I 'member."

"Here you go, baby girl." Roc handed her the cash. "Now, what are you going to do with it?"

"Ummm..." Halo thought with her fingers in her mouth. "Put in my pocket?"

I tucked my lips to keep from laughing. Halo was just too much.

"No," Roc said before exhaling through his nose and leaning over to whisper something in her ear.

Whatever he said made Halo's eyes brighten with excitement before she climbed to her knees in the chair and thrust the fist full of cash toward Demi. "Here you go! I'm a big girl now, so I pay my own bills!"

Demi's pissed-off gaze slid to Roc a second before my astonished one did. "You dirty bastard."

Halo giggled. "What's a bastard?" she screamed, delighted at learning a new word. "Bastard! Bastard! Bastard Bastard!"

"It's something you shouldn't say," Roc scolded right before he turned it on Demi. "Aye, hate me all you want, but don't curse in front of my daughter."

"Then stop using your daughter to manipulate me!"

"Ain't nobody manipulating you!"

"Okay, Roc." I could see Demi widening the emotional and physical distance between them as she stepped back. "You can go now."

Before either of them could spew any more venom, Halo burst into tears, crying her little eyes out and raising the invisible white flag between Roc and Demi.

They both stopped fighting to console her.

"All right, Halo. Daddy's sorry. Come on," Roc pleaded. "Stop crying." He picked her up, and she immediately laid her head on his shoulder while Demi rubbed her back in soothing circles.

"I'm sorry for making you cry, best friend."

Halo lifted her head in response and wiped away her tears. "It's okay. My daddy said him going to marry you and make you my new mommy, so don't be mad, okay, Dem Dem?"

"All right," Roc grumbled while Demi surprisingly giggled. If I wasn't mistaken, there was even a blush creeping up her cheeks. "You doing too much," he continued to fuss. "What did I say about telling all of my business? Let's go." Now that Halo had exposed him, he couldn't get out of the door fast enough.

"But you did say that!" Halo whined just before the shop door slammed shut behind them.

SEVENTEEN

Atlas

"THIS IS SO STUPID." I HUFFED FOR THE THIRD TIME IN TEN minutes and tucked a loose loc back inside my top knot. I was sweating my ass off down here despite the cool draft circling the basement of Pride of Kings.

I'd been down here in the stockroom hauling boxes and supplies since the start of my shift.

Why?

Because I'd been six minutes late.

Rowdy had apparently woken up with a thorn in his paw and had been looking for an excuse to punish me.

To teach me a lesson in punctuality, he'd ordered me down to the basement to get started on a preliminary assessment of inventory to prep for the official count that would take place *months* from now.

After he'd walked away, I'd asked Tuesday what that even meant, but she'd only shook her head while avoiding my gaze, confirming what I'd already known.

It had been two weeks since the party, and just like when he made me sort his files, today's task was total bullshit.

I huffed again and wiped the sweat off my brow after hauling a particularly heavy box from one of the shelves over to the metal table to count whatever was inside for no apparent reason.

God, I hated that man.

I grabbed the huge fifty-ounce bottle of water I'd had the forethought to swipe from Rowdy's office and greedily guzzled down the last of the water.

Sure, I could have taken one from the snack bar in reception, but they were the cheap kind that was basically water from the tap with a bunch of chemicals thrown in to dilute the rotten smell and taste. Rowdy, on the other hand, had the good stuff. It was no wonder he drank it all day long. The water was cool, crisp, and, most importantly, no bad aftertaste.

I also may have wanted a little revenge from when I'd asked Rowdy for one yesterday after working through my lunch break to complete yet another useless task, and the asshole had told me no. I'd taken one then, too, when his back was turned, and now I was addicted to the taste.

I swallowed the last gulp with a gasp and set the bottle down to recycle later. As soon as I did, my bladder suddenly swelled, increasing the pressure in my lower pelvis until I was dancing on my feet. "Oooh, gotta pee. Gotta pee, gotta pee, gotta pee."

I hurried upstairs to empty my bladder and check on Tuesday. She waved off my concern and continued scrolling Facebook on the computer while looking bored out of her mind. It was a slow day today.

When I returned to the stockroom minutes later, I found Rowdy leaning against the work table with a greasy bag from Pluto's, a popular local burger spot whose line was always wrapped around the block, sitting next to him. He had the clipboard I'd been using to jot down my notes in his hand, and his gaze slowly lifted when I entered.

Rowdy was wearing a navy-blue Henley today instead of his usual work shirt and black cargos. I couldn't help drooling over how his arms and chest looked in the material.

The smell of the food reached my nose across the stockroom,

and my stomach gave an interested growl as I realized I'd worked through lunch again.

"How can I help you, Owen? And before you tell me what I did wrong or isn't to your satisfaction," I said while squaring my shoulders, "let me remind you that I still have until the end of the day to *not* meet your impossible expectations. I would also like to point out that you sent me down here with no real direction or goal, so it's impossible for me to anticipate your needs if the objective isn't made clear from the start."

He stared at me for so long that I began to question if he'd even heard a word I'd said until he spoke. "Are you done?"

I blew air out through my nose and reminded myself that hitting my boss was a fireable offense. "Yes," I chewed out.

"Good. I brought you lunch," he announced as if it were a normal thing for him to do. "I thought we could eat together and get some shit understood—"

"Oh," I said before he could finish. "That's…nice of you. I guess that would be ok—"

"Until I found this," he interrupted right back. I frowned my confusion until he picked up the empty water bottle I'd forgotten to take with me upstairs.

Shit.

The way I saw it, I had two choices—I could apologize and throw myself at his mercy, or I could play it cool and lie my ass off. "What about it?" I asked, choosing the latter.

"I don't appreciate being stolen from."

"I'd hardly call quenching a thirst theft. Besides, I bought that from the corner store down the street."

"That's cap, and you know it. One, they don't sell this brand in Lee's. Two…" He lifted the bottle, showing me the bottom and the *R* written on the clear plastic in black marker.

"You marked your water? Who the hell marks their food, you obsessive-compulsive jerk?"

Rowdy gave me another blank look. "I don't, but when you

got pissed off yesterday because I told your spoiled ass no, I put my initials on all of them to see what you would do."

My mouth fell open. "You set a trap for me."

"And you fell right into it." He tossed the clipboard and empty bottle back onto the table and straightened. "So let's get this over with. Take your pants and panties off and bend over the table."

My stomach dipped, and I shifted on my feet. "Um…what?"

"You heard what I said, Atlas." His hands fell to his belt, and he began to undo it. The sound of the buckle clinking barely registered over my pounding heart. "Get your ass over here."

"I'm not fucking you."

Rowdy gave a dry laugh. "You think that's what this is about?" He shook his head and stalked forward. "Nah. I don't stick my dick in disobedient pussy. I'm going to do what your father should have done a long time ago and saved me the fucking headache."

He yanked his belt free of the loops of his pants, making his intentions clear.

The stockroom faded away at his mention of my father, and suddenly, I was transported across time and space back to the hospital room where my father had died.

The last place I saw him alive.

My incorporeal form stood in the corner as I watched a past version of myself call him a liar and swore never to forgive him before storming out the room while he struggled for the strength to beg me not to go.

The memory faded and shifted to my parents' bedroom. My mom lying in bed, disheveled, gaunt, and haunted. And me, begging like my father had begged and then screaming because she'd chosen to give up.

My dad was dead.

Mom was fading away.

And I'd abandoned them both.

I deserved whatever punishment Rowdy wanted to give me.

The revelation caused my mind to snap back into my body, where I stood in the stockroom across from Rowdy. I blinked, and my vision cleared enough to see Rowdy pause and then swear as if he, too, had realized what he'd said.

But how?

He couldn't have known my father was dead unless Roc or Golden had told him. Rowdy looked like he was getting ready to speak until I beat him to the punch.

"Okay."

His shoulder's stiffened as he watched me warily. "Okay?"

"Punish me," I clarified and started forward, my hands undoing my jeans as I came to stand next to him. "Make it hurt." I could see a thousand emotions warring in his eyes when I shoved down my pants and stepped out of them. "I won't fight you."

"Atlas..."

"Please," I whispered, the pain lacing my voice too thick to conceal. I held his gaze until he nodded, and then my panties joined my jeans on the floor. I paused, and then for good measure, I lifted my shirt over my head for some reason but left my bra on.

Without another word, I bent over the table and placed my cheek on the cold metal surface, exposing my ass and pussy to the open door in full view of the table.

It dawned on me then that anyone could walk in and catch us.

I didn't care.

I closed my eyes and waited for the pain to come and absolve my guilt.

It wouldn't, but I could hope.

A soft experimental caress across my right flank was the only thing I felt a moment later.

"*Please,*" I begged again. I could already feel the mood shifting from angry to something...not. "You promised."

"I know what you're doing," Rowdy said as he came to stand behind me. I could feel his tall, muscular stature looming over me like a shield between me and the rest of the world—maybe even myself—and I felt my stiff muscles slowly start to relax. "I know what you want. You want to use me to punish yourself for whatever you think you did before you darkened my doorstep."

My breath shuddered out of me when I heard his belt falling to the floor. He leaned over me then, his groin now flush with my naked ass as he planted his hands next to my head and whispered in my ear. "But I won't let you," he said, making me whimper. "Let that guilt go, baby. Whatever wrong you think you committed, leave it in the past. It doesn't belong here. I won't let it take any time away from us."

"What if I can't?" I cried as tears streamed down my cheeks. "What if it's too late?"

"Then I'll help you," he said simply. I didn't know what he meant or how it was even possible until his hands lifted from the table and ran down my sides. I could feel him growing hard, his bulge nestling my ass cheeks, but Rowdy's focus seemed to be entirely on me as he continued to drive me crazy by grazing his rough palms all over my soft skin.

"Owen," I sighed before I recognized the urge.

"Yes, Atlas?"

"I..." I couldn't seem to put into words the need coursing through my blood and setting every drop on fire until there was a blazing inferno in my veins and warming my skin.

Rowdy seemed to know exactly what I needed. I felt his fingers undoing the clasp at the middle of my back, then my bra fell to the table beneath me, and I shoved it away. I didn't think my nipples could get any harder, but then he cupped both of my breasts, their size fitting perfectly in the palms of his hands.

"These fucking tits," he said, groaning as I pushed my ass back against him. He pushed back, and just like that, we were dry humping each other's brains out. He stood up straight, taking me with him as he tugged and plucked at my nipples, stretching them out impossibly far and delivering that taste of the pain I'd been looking for.

"Feels so good," I moaned.

"Yeah?" Rowdy thrust his hips upward, and I responded by circling my own, my eyes rolling back from the friction we created. I was distantly aware that I was completely nude while he remained fully clothed. I also wouldn't think about the fact that we were both at work, and the man currently humping me was my boss.

"Oh, fuck, yes," I cried as much to his question as I did to the idea of being left bare and completely under his control. I reached back and up, gripping his braids in my hand as I fought to get closer. It still wasn't enough. "More."

His lips abruptly left my neck where he'd been suckling and leaving his mark. "More? Use your big girl words, Atlas. What do you want?"

I paused and swallowed. "I want…I want to come."

I couldn't see his face with my back to him, but I could sense his smile just before he kissed my cheek. "Good girl. Lift your right leg on the table and bend over. Open that pussy for me, baby."

I bit my lip and did as he instructed, hooking my right leg until my knee and calf were resting on the cold surface.

"What are you going to do?" I asked when a little of my common returned. It wasn't enough to make me stop, but my legs gave a nervous tremble as he kissed down my spine.

"I'm going to get my water back," he answered between pecks. A bolt of alarm shot down my spine, but before I could ask him what he meant, I felt his hand between my legs, and I moaned when his fingers teased my wet pussy, playing with my arousal.

"Are you going to fuck me?" I asked quietly. I didn't know what I wanted his answer to be.

"No."

Something suspiciously like disappointment coursed through me, but then his fingers circled my clit, and I forgot all about it.

"Why are you always so fucking wet, Atlas?"

My hips began to move in time with his fingers, but his hand on one of them stopped me. "I can't help it. It's only when you're around."

Rowdy didn't respond, and the only sound that could be heard was his fingers stirring through my wetness.

I was fucking *soaked*.

Done teasing, he pushed two of his fingers inside me, and my lips parted as I moaned long and low as they sank to the last knuckle without stopping.

My walls gripped them greedily, but Rowdy paid them no heed as he pushed deeper—almost impossibly so—before pulling out and repeating the motion.

"Your pussy's fucking tight, baby. Gotta stretch you good before you take my dick."

"I haven't...I haven't been with anyone in a while." There had been opportunities, but I was starting to think I was waiting on him. Sutton and I had stopped screwing long before I caught him in bed with my best friend.

Rowdy's free hand suddenly threaded through my locs before closing around them in a punishing grip and yanking my head back toward him. "Keep it that way," he warned brutally. His mouth was so close I could feel his breath and the subtle scrape of his teeth against my jaw. "You understand me?"

"Yes." The way his fingers felt inside me, fucking and stretching me out, I would have agreed to anything. "No one else but you."

"Need to get deeper," he said hoarsely. It was his only warning before he yanked his fingers out of me. I started to panic, but then Rowdy lifted me, turned me around, and placed me on my back. His hands roughly spread my thighs as wide as they would go until my muscles strained from the stretch.

A moment later, I had his fingers back inside me.

"Oh," I gasped when his middle and ring fingers—his two longest digits—reached my G-spot while the heel of his palm brushed my clit. "Oh, Owen."

He held my gaze as he fucked my pussy open, abusing that fleshy spot deep inside me that turned my brain to mush and every word I tried to utter into incoherent babbling. After a while, his hooded gaze dropped to my pussy where his fingers tunneled in and out, slow and deep.

God, yes.

I rose onto my elbows to watch our union as well.

The sight, combined with the sound of my arousal and the table squeaking loudly from our movements, was almost too much to bear. My tits were bouncing in rhythm with our fucking, the muscles in my ass clenching and unclenching as I rocked my hips…

The pressure built and built in my lower belly, spreading to my pelvis and making the muscles deep inside tremble until I felt this incredible need to *bear down.*

Oh, God.

Oh, God, no.

"Wait," I managed to gasp. "Wait, we have to stop." He kept going. "Owen, *please.*" When his gaze finally lifted even while his fingers kept going, I whimpered, feeling utter humiliation wash over me. "I have to pee."

Damn me and all that water I had to drink. I'd already emptied my bladder, but fifty ounces consumed in under two hours…

"Come on, Owen, please," I begged again, even while my own hips kept rocking and chasing an orgasm that would never come. It would only be denied by a more pressing need. A need that Rowdy ignored as he continued to fuck me.

He shook his head, licking his lip as if dying of thirst, and said, "That's not pee, Atlas."

What?

Before I could beg to fucking differ, he curved his fingers inside me, applying even more pressure to my G-spot while he ground the heel of his palm down on my engorged clit, making my eyes flutter wildly. "Come on, baby. Let it go. Be a good little bitch and come for me."

"Uhhhhhhh!" I groaned when my pelvic floor muscles gave out. A stream—no, an erratic *spray* of clear liquid burst out of my urethra over and over, soaking the hem of Rowdy's Henley just before he dropped to his knees, gripped the back of my thighs, and wrapped his lips around my clit and the imperceptible opening just below it.

Horrified, I tried to back away, but he tightened his grip, keeping me in place while he…*drank*.

"Oh, *fuck*!" I screamed again, gripping his braids and holding him to me when I still kept coming. Or was it peeing? I didn't know.

My body spasmed out of control despite my reservations, and it felt like I'd never stop. Rowdy greedily and audibly gulped it all down like he'd been wandering the desert, and I was his only chance at salvation.

His words from before slowly penetrated the fog I was trapped in as I came and came and came.

"What are you going to do?"

"I'm going to get my water back."

"God, please," I begged for mercy when it seemed like I'd never stop coming. My legs shook wildly while my orgasm dribbled down his jaw and chin and spilled onto the table.

Finally, mercifully, whatever had built up inside me reached the end of its well, and Rowdy released me with a gasp like he'd just enjoyed a cool drink of water.

Through half-lidded eyes, I watched him stare at my pussy in awe just before his head bent, and he cleaned my soaked pussy from anus to clit with a long, slow, and *thorough* swipe of his flattened tongue. "Fucking delicious."

"You're going to make me come again," I whined and scooted away from him. I didn't get far since I could barely move. It was an effort just to keep my eyes open. And my body was still twitching.

Rowdy chuckled and rose to his feet. His wet palm skated over my knee soothingly. "Would that be so bad?"

"Yes." My stomach was already cramping, and I could feel a strange ache deep inside my pussy, even though he'd only penetrated me with his fingers. I could only guess that it came from how hard I'd strained my pelvic floor by first holding back and then bearing down. "What was that?" I asked him quietly after I mustered the courage. My cheeks felt warm, and I had a hard time meeting his eye. I'd never done that before. I never even knew that I could.

"First time?" he questioned with an assessing gaze. I wordlessly nodded, and he licked his lips like he wanted to do it again. "Some females can ejaculate like men. Not all, but some. The frequency and intensity vary, too." He paused. "Did you like it?"

"I don't know," I answered honestly. "It felt good, but it..." I grimaced. "It hurt a little too."

"That's because you were fighting it. Next time don't think so much."

"I *thought* I was going to pee on you," I reminded him. My words brought a spark to his eye that I didn't quite trust, so I quickly changed the subject. "So, this was fun, but I have to get back to work. My boss is a real jerk on the rare occasions he's nice and an insufferable ass when he's mean. I'd sooner not piss him off again today."

Rowdy snorted and helped me from the table. "I'm sure your boss will understand if you take the rest of the day off."

I stiffened at that while eyeing him warily, but he didn't notice as he crouched on his haunches and rifled through my discarded clothes before finding my ruined panties. I cringed, but when he held them open for me to step in, I obeyed and held onto his powerful shoulders for balance. My pants were next, and then he rose to help me into my shirt.

"Was this some kind of trick?" I finally asked once I was dressed again and felt more like we were on equal footing.

"What?"

"This." I waved around the room in answer. "Sending me down here. Setting the trap. What we just did. Was it some kind of trick to get rid of me?"

"Okay, first of all, I don't just go around putting my mouth on any female. Second, if I wanted you gone, you'd be gone. I don't beat around the bush because it takes too much time. I prefer to go for the jugular, so no, making you come wasn't some trick, Atlas."

I chewed on my lip before nodding. "Can I ask you another question?"

He sighed. "I guess."

"How did you know I'd do…that?" My orgasms, whenever Sutton could be bothered to care, had been subpar and *nothing* like that.

"Squirt?" Rowdy crudely clarified. "I didn't."

"Oh."

He helped me clean up the mess we'd made, and then we ate the cold lunch he'd bought in silence. Finishing first, Rowdy stood and gathered his trash. I watched him, biting my tongue whenever I caught myself wanting to ask him to stay.

"You finished?" he asked me when he was done. I glanced at my food and nodded before bawling up my sandwich wrapper and dusting the salt from the fries off my hands. "So let's go."

I looked up at him. "What?"

"I got shit to do, and I want you to come with me."

My mouth opened and closed several times before settling on, "Why?"

Rowdy fingered one of my locs while gazing down at me softly. I'd never seen that look in his eyes before. Lust, yes, but not…this. "I already told you why."

Because he wanted me to.

Did I want to?

I already knew the answer before I spoke. "Okay."

EIGHTEEN

Rowdy

As I turned off Temperance and onto Third, with Atlas riding shotgun in my Charger, I tried to remember a time I felt more relaxed than I did at that moment. She looked good at my side, almost like she belonged there.

Even if she did keep throwing me suspicious looks every time I turned down a new street.

"You smoke?" I asked her after she'd glanced my way for the umpteenth time. I thought about giving her some to relax, but I low-key wanted her to keep a clear head today. This was my first time vibing with her without work, sex, or anything else between us.

"No." Atlas shook her head, drawing my attention to her hair. It looked different. The same but…I don't know. Newer, I guess. I'd never paid this much attention to a female before to notice shit like that, so I was having trouble articulating what I saw. I knew she'd been getting her hair done at Demi's lately, so maybe that was it. "I mean…I've never tried it."

I threw her a weird look. "I thought you said you were in college." College students were the biggest dope fiends around.

"I was only there for one semester," she spoke to her lap like she was ashamed.

"What made you quit?"

"I didn't quit." She inhaled deeply before releasing it slowly. "I just needed a break."

Since I already knew she wouldn't answer, I skipped asking her why. "What were you studying?" I asked instead.

"I'm still undecided, but would it be totally cliché if I said I was considering pre-med?"

"Why would that be cliché?"

"Because my focus would be dermatology and—" She paused to gesture to her face and body and the vitiligo that had caused patches of her skin to lose pigment.

"Are you doing it because you want to help people or because you think it's what you should want to do?"

Atlas seemed to mull it over before she lifted her chin and met my gaze. "I want to help people. I spent years feeling uncomfortable in my own skin because of my skin. It took me a long time to understand that this disease wasn't my fault and that I shouldn't be ashamed of it. I may not be beautiful by traditional standards, but it's okay to think I'm beautiful by my own standards."

"Sounds like a good enough reason to me. And you shouldn't be too hard on yourself. I don't know too many teenage girls whose self-esteem didn't start in the toilet or who didn't wish they could wear someone else's skin. The fact that you caught on so soon and thought, 'fuck what anyone else thinks,' means you're already ahead of the curve." I paused, biting my lip to keep my next words down before saying fuck it. "After what you just told me, the last thing I want to do is make you think your journey needs validation, but I have to say it. I look at you, Atlas, and all I see is art. I don't think you're beautiful despite your condition or because of it. You just are. Period."

I watched a slow smile etch across her pretty face. "City Girls period?"

"You got me fucked up."

We burst out laughing and then fell into an easy silence that ended when she said, "Thank you."

I was thankful I'd stopped at a red light before I crashed my fucking car from staring at her pretty ass for so long. "Ain't shit."

The light turned green, so I focused on the road as I sped away.

"So, what about you?" she asked. "What made you want to be a mechanic?"

"Kind of fell into it, I guess. I bought my first whip out of an auction when I was sixteen, but I couldn't afford much, so it was basically a heap of junk that kept breaking down. My pops told me if I wanted to keep it, I had to pay for the repairs myself. Money was tight since he and my mom were both out of work, but on the real, it was his way of punishing me because he didn't approve of the way I'd gotten the money to buy the car in the first place.

"How did you get the money?" she asked me quietly.

"Whatever I had to," I answered cryptically. You never knew who could be listening. I glanced at her, and noticing my attention, she nodded her understanding, and I returned my focus to the road. "Anyway, he had been cussing my ass out for months about staying off the streets and becoming another black male stereotype, but I wasn't trying to listen, you feel me? People would take one look at me and assume I'd grown up in a broken home anyway, which couldn't have been further from the truth. My parents were solid. They loved each other, and they loved me. Life just got in the fucking way. We were already in the middle of another recession when motherfuckers started flying planes into buildings and shit. People were getting downsized left and right after the country literally took another hit, and neither of my parents was exempt. I'd just made sixteen, and in my head, I was pretty much a man, so I did what men are supposed to do. I stepped up. My pops was no square, but he still didn't want me throwing my future away by getting sent to the pen or dying, but I think it killed his pride too. His teenage son was providing when he couldn't, and there wasn't a damn thing he could do about it. After that, he barely had two words for me, and that lasted a few years until some shit went down with my mom."

I fell silent, lost in the bitter memories, until Atlas's soft voice gently guided me back to the now. "What happened?" I could hear the urgency in her request for me to continue.

I just shook my head, not quite ready to get that deep with her. "It doesn't matter. My pops still resented me and low-key blamed me too. It didn't matter that I'd proved him wrong. I'd graduated high school and wasn't in and out of jail like he'd predicted. Yeah, I was doing dirt and digging myself deeper into it every day, but I was smarter than most. I never took more risks than was necessary. I wasn't trying to become hood rich or famous. I just wanted to survive. I wanted to give my parents the security they'd sacrificed to give me all my life. It didn't matter to my father, though. Every time I came around, he would have some slick shit to say. We'd argue, and my mom would almost kill herself each and every time to stop it."

I found myself gulping as the memory of our last fight played in my head with crystal-fucking-clarity as if it had happened only yesterday.

"Eventually, my father got it into his head to disown me even though I'd already moved out and was taking care of myself. He knew that, so he called himself changing the locks on me and banning me from the house."

"What did you do?" Atlas whispered. The veiled horror in her voice told me she knew it wasn't anything good. I hadn't reacted well to being turned away *at all*.

I sighed and found myself hesitating—almost like I was ashamed of my actions for the very first time. "I kicked the fucking door in," I grumbled.

"Owen."

Strangling the steering wheel, I forced my grip to relax, only to clench my teeth, knowing that I hadn't told her the worst of it yet. "My father was there, and when he confronted me, he told me I wasn't welcome in their home as long as I was in the streets. I told him he could try to keep me out, but as long as my mom was there, he'd have to either deal with me or kill me."

I heard Atlas's sharp inhale. "What did your father say?"

I bucked my eyes as I glanced at her with a shit-eating grin. "He didn't say shit. He just laid my ass out."

A choked sound escaped Atlas. "He…what?"

"You heard me." I was cackling now despite the bittersweet memories. "I was standing in my parents' living room with my chest puffed out like I was the baddest thing walking when my pops started going across my shit."

It had been the first time I'd gotten a taste of my own medicine in a fight. Whenever I threw a punch one way, my pops was already coming at me from another direction. It was like fighting a rabid pitbull and a tornado at the same time. Impossible.

"He was throwing hammers left and right, and I was throwing them back, but I was green to the man my father really was and no match for him and four years' worth of aggression."

My father had been a professional boxer and was just shy of a heavyweight champion when he ended his short career mere months after I was born. I guess he'd decided that he'd rather see his son grow into a man than chase a title. Maybe he even hoped I'd follow in his footsteps when he taught me everything I knew.

He'd warned me once that no teacher was ever as good as experience. I'd taken those words to heart and made him regret ever uttering them after I provoked as many fights wherever I went as I could.

"Wow."

"Yeah," I said as I pulled into the parking lot of the auction site. It was here that I bought most of the cars I rebuilt in my spare time, most of which I flipped for a profit, while others, like the Hellcat and Jailbreak, I added to my personal fleet. "He fucked me up, but I made sure that was the last time I'd ever lost a fight."

"Is that why you fight like there are three of you?" she asked me.

I parked the car and glanced at her to see her brows raised as she shook her head.

Fucking beautiful.

"I still don't know how you were stomping that guy out and punching him at the same time. Isn't that like trying to pat your head while rubbing your stomach?"

"There's a lot of things I can do with my hands and other parts at the same time, Dream." I sank my teeth into my bottom lip as I imagined stroking her deep while using my hands and mouth to drive her crazy.

"Why do you keep calling me that? What does it even mean?"

"It means you smell and taste just like a Dreamsicle, so that's what I'll call you."

Her response was immediate. "No."

"Yes." I smirked at the flare of irritation in her gaze.

"It's the stupidest thing I've ever heard, Owen. Besides, you didn't even know that when you came up with it."

"You're right," I lied, remembering she hadn't seen me steal a taste of her after fingering her in the storage closet. I sat up and pretended to look around to make sure we were alone. "Let me eat your pussy real quick."

Her lips parted, but then she quickly looked away to hide her blush. She shifted in her seat a moment later, telling me just how deep my words had reached. "No thanks. I prefer not to make the same mistake twice in one day." I was leaning against my door now as I watched her look around the lot before focusing on the small white nondescript building a short walk away. "What is this place? What are we doing here?"

Declining to answer her, I ripped the key out of the ignition before climbing out of the car. I felt her heated gaze on me as I rounded the hood to her side and saw the shock on Atlas's face when I opened her door and held out my hand like the perfect gentleman. "Come on."

NINETEEN

Atlas

IT HAD TO BE THE EARTH-SHATTERING ORGASM.

That was the only logical explanation for why I placed my hand in his and let him pull me from his car. Just the memory had my legs shaking like jello, and I would have collapsed, furthering my humiliation if it weren't for Rowdy's quick reflexes. Once I was standing in front of him, he pulled my coat tighter around me before zipping it up and pressing his soft lips against mine.

I released this sound—part hungry and part scandalized—that later I'd fervently deny when I realized I could still taste myself on his lips. He'd brushed his teeth and changed his shirt before we left, but lingering in small traces with the cool mint was…me.

Smirking, Rowdy kissed me one last time before releasing me and declining to comment on how badly I obviously wanted him to fuck me right now.

My knees felt weak, and it wasn't just from me wishing I'd taken him up on his offer. I was quiet as he led me by the hand into the building.

There was a wide clearing with tire tracks in the middle of the building, with people standing on either side like they were waiting for something.

Higher up and overlooking the concrete floor was a smaller

room that looked like one of those press boxes you'd find at a stadium, complete with a microphone and window spanning the length of the room.

We'd barely made it ten feet inside the building before we were spotted. One after another, some of the people standing around came over to either shoot the shit, ask Rowdy's advice, or thank him for some past repairs. It took us twenty minutes to make it to the other side of the building, and Rowdy never let go of my hand the entire time. Even when he'd dap up someone he knew from around the way, he never let go.

"Who's that you got with you?" one of his bolder homies inquired. Teddy, I'd heard Rowdy call him, inched toward me while eyeing me up like I was on the menu and he wanted to sample me. "She's bad as hell." Before I could question my instinct to seek out Rowdy for refuge, I was glued to his side, watching Teddy lick his cracked lips while rubbing his ashy palms together. He wore blue jeans and a white tee three sizes too big for him like he was stuck in two thousand and seven and waiting for Crime Mob to make a comeback.

"She's my business," Rowdy warned, brows dipped murderously now like it hadn't been love between them moments ago. "And back your ass up. You standing too close to her."

"Oh, my fault." Teddy looked as confused as I felt, but he did what he was told, backing away from me, his eyes bouncing between us as he tried to decipher Rowdy's territorial pissing. I didn't have to question if this reaction from Rowdy was unusual. "I ain't mean no disrespect," Teddy added before scurrying away with his tail tucked between his legs.

Rowdy watched him go, and I could see the indecision in his eyes whether to follow him and fuck him up.

Curling my free palm around the back of the hand clutching mine, I caught his attention and offered him—for what might have been the first time—a smile that wasn't laced with barbed wire.

Slowly, I watched the violence fade from his eyes, but he

didn't return my gesture. Instead, his green gaze greedily roved all over my face as if he were committing the sight to memory.

"Come on," he whispered after the moment had stretched dangerously close to something meaningful.

I followed him through the garage opening large enough to fit a truck through and out into a second lot—this one much bigger and packed full of cars parked haphazardly. The ground was covered with gravel, and a few rows over, I spotted a forklift speeding by with a red convertible in its grip.

We paused just outside the door while Rowdy checked something on his phone. "This way."

I was silent as I obediently followed him through the maze of cars. Even with my long legs, I had to practically run to keep up with him as he strode through the crowded lot like he was on a mission. Rowdy's head was on a swivel, swinging left and right as he searched for something.

"Owen," I spoke up once I started to lose my breath. "Can we slow down?" Rowdy looked back at me as if only just remembering I was there before slowing his stride. "What is this place anyway?"

"Car auction." He didn't bother to explain further before bracing his weight on the trunks of two cars backed so close together there was no hope of squeezing through and lifting his body over them until he stood on the other side.

Since I wasn't feeling very acrobatic, I started to walk around when I felt his hands close around my waist. Without warning, he lifted me off the ground, ignoring my surprised yelp as he hauled me over the trunk of the blue sedan.

"Owen!" I had to admit my reaction was a bit dramatic, and I was sure anyone watching got a good kick out of seeing me flail in the air like a fish out of water.

"Chill out." He huffed his irritation as he tucked me against his hard body. My arms flew around his neck as I held on to him for dear life, even though the ground was only a few inches away. "I got you, Dream."

Of course, *having me* meant rewarding himself with two handfuls of my ass while he slowly slid me down his body until I was back on my feet again.

"Why did you bring me here?" I all but stomped my foot. Maybe if I acted bratty enough, he'd grow tired of me and take me home. It just wasn't possible for me to think clearly around him so soon after he ate my pussy like a demon.

I felt like I'd sold my soul to the devil.

"Killing two birds with one stone," he absently replied as he let me go and walked two rows over to check out this white Mercedes that still looked pretty new. "I had some business to conduct and wanted to spend time with you. Is that a problem?"

I wanted to say hell yes, but he made it clear he wasn't interested in my opinion when he turned away while reaching into his pocket and pulling out a pair of black disposable gloves. He slipped them on before rounding the car to the driver's side, and through the passenger window, I watched him turn the key tied to the steering wheel and listen as the car purred to life.

Now, I was no expert, but it sounded like the car was running fine. I couldn't understand why it was being auctioned until I followed Rowdy to the driver's side and saw the huge dent that had almost completely caved in the back door.

Rowdy paid me no mind as he sat with one foot planted on the ground and the other on the gas, revving the engine a few times as he fiddled with the A/C controls. He then drove the car forward a couple of feet and then reversed it to make sure the brakes were good.

I just stood there twiddling my thumbs and feeling like a pretty ornament until I grew tired of that. "Let me help."

Not a question.

A demand.

If he was going to force me to be here, I might as well be useful and distract myself from what happened in the stockroom. The dampness in my panties wouldn't let me forget anytime soon, though. He hadn't even penetrated me, and my pussy felt sore. I'd come that hard.

Rowdy's head whipped my way, and I could see him trying to figure me out before he gave up and wordlessly dug into his pocket for a small orange and blue device I'd seen the technicians and mechanics use around the shop.

"Know how to use this?" He wore a smirk I wanted to kiss off.

No! God! *Slap* off. I wanted to slap his face. *Pull your pussy lips together, Atlas Beck.* "Obviously not."

Rowdy bent and plugged the device into some white port under the steering well before popping the hood and rising from the car. I didn't have time to back away before he was standing close enough for me to smell my lingering pussy juices on his breath.

"Here," he said, handing me the device. "There's no check engine light, but that doesn't mean it hasn't been cleared to cover up any problems with the car. This scanner will read the engine and report any pending codes, stored codes, or incomplete monitors."

I frowned down at the cheap plastic device in my hand. "But clearing the light doesn't make the problem go away, so how can they cover it up?"

"Because you'd have to drive the car enough miles for the monitor to reset. If the car is still operable, the new owner won't know they've been fucked until it's too late."

"Oh."

"Should only take a few seconds to run through the cycle," he mumbled as he gently moved me aside and swaggered to the front of the car, where he opened the hood and disappeared from view. I puffed out a breath—my relief at the much-needed distance between us billowing in the cold air—and hit read.

I could hear Rowdy tinkering under the hood as I watched the asterisk dance across the tiny screen. A few seconds later, two words and an arrow appeared.

"It says there's a code!" I shouted in case he couldn't hear me over the running engine.

"Call it out."

My unsure gaze danced between the only two buttons on the pocket-sized device—read and erase—before hitting read again. This time, the actual code showed, and I read it out to him. "What does it mean?" I asked when I heard him curse.

"Suspension's fucked up," he mumbled as he slammed the hood closed and returned to the driver's side to inspect the damage to the rear door with a furrowed brow. "Shit must be in worse shape than I thought."

"Maybe I did it wrong," I suggested, even though I knew I hadn't. I couldn't explain this sudden and burning urge to ease his troubles—so much so that I had to stick my free hand in my coat pocket to keep from taking his. "Do you want to check for yourself? Make sure I did it right?" I tried to hand him the device back, but he absently shook his head as his green gaze scanned the lot.

"I trust you."

Unaware of what those three little words did to me—spoken as casually as if trusting me came naturally for him—he continued to search the sea of cars while I tried to calm the butterflies that had taken flight in my belly.

"Okay."

He must have heard the breathlessness in my tone. Giving up his search, Rowdy looked down at me, and whatever look he found in my eyes smoothed away the frustration darkening the sculpted lines and artful curves of his handsome face until an almost serene expression took over.

A heartbeat later, we were kissing.

It wasn't one of those spontaneous moments when I couldn't recall who had initiated this monumental mistake.

Owen had.

And I'd been eager to meet him halfway.

There'd been no hesitation whatsoever on my part when he bent to take what he wanted. In fact, I couldn't get there fast enough—already missing his kiss and wanting more when it hadn't even ended yet.

I wasn't aware of him turning us until I felt my back suddenly pressed against the Mercedes and his tall frame blocked the sun behind him.

"I want my dick in your mouth," he said without breaking the kiss.

"Okay." I was even more breathless than before as butterflies erupted in my stomach. It didn't matter that we were exposed, out in the open, where anyone could see. I was going to let Owen Rashaad Wray do whatever he wanted to me.

He gave me one last kiss and then shifted his hold to my jaw so I couldn't look away as he pinned me with those green eyes. "Are you gonna be a big girl, or are you going to back down again?"

I gave a vehement shake of my head. "I'll be good. I promise."

I was one-hundred-percent certain he could feel my thighs shaking, but he didn't seem to care as he placed an unforgiving hand on the top of my head and gently pushed me to my knees.

I didn't feel the rocks on the ground digging into my skin and bone. I only knew him and the spine-chilling look in his eyes as he ripped open his belt and jeans while holding my gaze.

He was already hard when I wrapped my hand around him. This time, I didn't need any encouragement when I rose up on my knees and licked the flared tip. That first salty taste of him burst on my tongue, and unlike before, I couldn't get him in my mouth fast enough. I swallowed half his length in one gulp, stretching my lips and jaw as far as it would go, making him hiss and his green eyes glow as he watched me.

"Mmmh…make that shit sloppy, baby."

I obediently pulled away, gathering all the moisture in my mouth before spitting it on his shaft and using my hand to spread it around. He nudged his hips forward, indicating he wanted my mouth again, and I slowly enveloped him while keeping eye contact.

"Fuck, Atlas," he groaned, throwing his head back as soon as the tip reached my throat. I was still only halfway.

I pulled back and did it again, needing to hear that sound again. Neither of us was disappointed. Together, we established a rhythm—me taking him deep and him chasing me whenever I retreated.

My spit and his pre-cum had gathered at the back of my throat, making a gargling sound as he fucked my mouth while the excess dribbled down my jaw and chin, creating a mess that only spurred us on.

Eventually, his hold on my hair shifted—tightened. It was my only warning before he took over completely, fucking my face and making me choke on his dick whenever I tried to catch my breath.

Tears leaked down my face, and I couldn't tell which was wetter from his brutal treatment—my eyes or pussy. I heard gravel crunch somewhere nearby, but before I could pull away to warn Rowdy, he was coming down my throat with a grunt that made me forget we were no longer alone. My pussy wanted to be abused by him next.

Rowdy pulled away, and I held his gaze as I swallowed his seed. His green eyes gleamed with pleasure a second before he mumbled, "I'm going to kill him."

I blinked. "Kill who?"

Rowdy's thumb lovingly stroked my bottom lip, smearing the cum there. I flicked out my tongue to get another taste. "The boy who taught you to suck dick this good."

"I—no one taught me unless you count porn. You were my first."

Rowdy was frowning deeply now. "You're a virgin?"

"No." I shook my head. "I just never did that with my ex. He asked all the time, but I…I never wanted to." *Before you* was what I didn't say. We both knew I didn't need to.

I could see the possessive glint in his eye as his lips parted to speak, but before he could, we both froze at the same time when he heard someone call his name. "Rowdy!"

I'd forgotten we weren't alone.

I quickly wiped the nut off my chin while Rowdy tucked himself away before helping me to my feet. Once his jeans were righted, he turned his head to glower at the portly Black man of average height bundled up in winter gear to escape the cold.

"Row-dy! Ha-ha!" the intruder called again. "My favorite customer. I thought that was you!" He came to stand in front of us while I searched his face for signs that he'd seen us.

Rowdy now leaned against the Mercedes next to me with his arm casually thrown around my shoulder as he regarded the much older man with a blank stare. "Earl."

I secretly tittered because I could tell he was in a fouler mood than usual despite the nut he just busted in my mouth.

"I see you found the Mercedes," Earl said, nodding as he looked the car over himself. Either he was oblivious to Rowdy's dark mood or used to it like me. "It's a beautiful ride, for sure. I can get one of my boys to pull it around if you're ready to bid on it?"

"Yeah, I'll take it, but I'm not bidding on shit. I can give you eighteen for it right now, and the papers better be clean."

Earl's confused gaze danced between Rowdy and me before settling on me for some reason. "I'm Earl, young lady, and you are?" He held out his hand while forcing a smile to his lips, and I hated myself for the asking glance I gave Rowdy. My self-loathing doubled when I saw that he was paying me no mind. His focus was now firmly fixed on the man he was attempting to bully into submission.

"Atlas," I reluctantly offered while accepting Earl's dry and callused palm.

"It's nice to meet you, Atlas." His smile was warm and genuine this time as he patted my hand gently before letting it drop. He then turned back to Rowdy with a sigh. "You know the rules, boy. Everyone bids."

Feeling Rowdy straighten next to me, I quickly wrapped my arms around his waist as if I could really stop him from fucking up Earl if he wanted to. With a sharp turn of his head, Rowdy turned his glare on me. I could see in his eyes that he was ready to cuss me out. Until the gentle smile I gave him made every ugly word poised to cut me down vanish into thin air. I placed a gentle kiss on his bicep as I wordlessly pleaded with him to spare the nice man.

Licking his thick lips, Rowdy turned toward Earl again and calmly said, "But not everyone knows that the suspension is fucked up and that one of those morons you hired tried to cover it up."

I closed my eyes in relief and laid my head on his arm. Even while being completely rigid and full of muscle, it was the best pillow I'd ever known. There was so much power in these arms. The kind you just knew could keep you safe through anything.

And, okay, yes, seeing him beat up a man twice his size helped with that assumption too.

When I opened my eyes again, I saw Earl shaking his head. "I'm sorry about that, son. I didn't know." For some reason, I believed him, and I could tell Rowdy did too. He also didn't seem surprised at hearing his employees were attempting to swindle his customers.

Interesting.

"I told your ass to fire them," Rowdy chided, even though Earl was old enough to be his father. "I know they came from your nuts and all, but family clearly don't mean shit to your sons if they're willing to sabotage your name and business."

I nodded at the truth in his words.

It was always "family this, family that" whenever your relatives needed a favor, but given half the chance, they're usually the first to screw you over. "No," in my opinion, was the most underutilized word in the dictionary.

"You're right, you're right," Earl conceded with a nod. "And I'll definitely talk to them because hiding faults from customers is not the way I do business."

"Just put your foot up their asses like you should have been doing, and you won't have to waste time with words. If you want, I can do it for you." Rowdy's smile was sharp enough to cut.

"No, no," Earl said with a nervous chuckle. "I don't think that will be necessary."

"Mmm," Rowdy hummed, making it clear he didn't agree.

Oh, boy. I held on to him a little tighter in case he felt strongly enough about it to hunt Earl's sons down.

"For the inconvenience, I can let the Benz go right now for twenty-two, but I can't go any lower than that. It's worth at least twenty-four—more once you rebuild it. Parts should only cost you two or three grand, and we both know you'll do the labor yourself."

"Except my time is valuable, and I take no shorts, least of all from myself. Eighteen is my final offer. If I wanted to haggle, I'd wait to bid on it."

"Listen, Rowdy—"

"I can hear, motherfucker. Clearly, it's you that has the hearing problem. It's eighteen or nothing, and by nothing, I mean I go find whichever one of your Blow Pop-head-shaped sons tried to stiff me and light their ass up."

And as if his words didn't paint a clear enough picture, Rowdy gently pushed me away before pulling the burner from his waist and flipping the safety off.

Even though it wasn't me at the end of the barrel of his gun, I still gulped. "Owen," I started cautiously.

His gaze stayed fixed on Earl. The only indication he'd heard me was the flaring of his nostrils. Feeling Earl's pleading gaze shift toward me, I sent him an apologetic one back and stayed quiet.

Rowdy's mind was made up. I wouldn't be able to save him like I had Ky.

"Eighteen," Earl reluctantly agreed after a long and silent deliberation that looked like it might end in bloodshed. Rowdy wasn't known for his patience. Earl held out his hand to seal the deal, which Rowdy ignored as he put his gun away.

"Hurry up and get the paperwork so I can get my girl out of the cold."

Awww.

Wait…

No.

I should be angry and embarrassed, not swooning.

"I'm not your girl," I denied as soon as Earl trudged away with his shoulders bowed. I felt bad for him, but there was nothing I could do. I was just as afraid of this psycho as everyone else. I just refused to let my fear win. "I don't date bullies."

Even though my knees weakened at the thought of being Owen Wray's girl, my arms crossed as if that alone could suppress my heart's desires.

"I didn't say we were dating." He shrugged as he pulled out his phone and started typing.

"You told Earl I was your girl."

He glanced up at me briefly before returning his gaze to his phone to finish texting. "I'm dating your pussy, Atlas. I'm not dating you."

What the fuck does that mean?

As calmly as I could, I asked him to explain.

"It means once I get up in it, it's mine," he told me without shame or remorse. "You won't be fucking anyone else."

"But you can fuck whoever you like?"

"Exactly."

I let out a slightly hysterical laugh. "Well, I have a problem with that, which means my pussy has a problem with that."

His ignorant ass smirked as if my words didn't mean shit to him and put his phone away. "Come on."

Since he was my ride, I reluctantly followed him through the maze of cars again, keeping some distance between us. Halfway across the lot, I decided I wouldn't speak to him *ever* again.

Back inside the warm building, the auction that Rowdy had bullied his way out of was already underway. People lingered inside the press box now as a man sat at the microphone calling out bids and descriptions of the cars being driven through the building.

Rowdy seemed perfectly content as he smoked a blunt and quietly scoped the scene as we waited for Earl to return. It was an almost obsessive habit of his that I'd noticed from my obsessive habit of watching him when he wasn't looking. He tried to offer me the blunt to "perk the fuck up"—his words—but I ignored him.

Thankfully, we only had to suffer the charged silence for a few minutes before Earl returned with the title and other paperwork for Rowdy to sign. If I'd expected him to be bitter at having a gun pulled on him, I was clearly mistaken. His big belly bounced as he laughed at something Rowdy said—no doubt rude—until the older man caught me staring in astonishment and chuckled.

"Young lady, this is Idlewild. This isn't the first time I've been held at gunpoint, and it certainly isn't Rowdy's first time pulling a gun out in my establishment. My wife works triage down at Sunnyside General. I keep her and a well-stocked first aid kit on standby just in case Rowdy decides to stop by."

Oh, wow.

"Just be glad you lived to tell the tale, old man. I can count on one hand and have four fingers left at how many can."

I rolled my eyes even though I knew it to be true. Rowdy didn't seem like the type to pull his gun out unless he meant it. He was lethal enough all on his own.

Once the papers were signed and hands were shaken, Rowdy escorted me from the building with a hand on my back, and I loathed how good it felt. When we reached his car, he opened my door for me and helped me in before hopping into the driver's seat and peeling off.

It was safe to say that this man perplexed me.

How could he be so brutal one moment and then tender the next? It didn't make any sense. Was he fighting a part of himself that wanted to treat me the way I deserved, or was I just searching for crumbs to justify my attraction?

As if my private thoughts were an open book, his voice broke the quiet chaos happening within me. "You mad?"

A scoff was my only answer.

Rowdy was many terrible things—reckless, violent, vicious—but dumb wasn't one of them. It was funny how none of his traits scared me as much as his intelligence—and just how much he saw through me.

I stared straight ahead, pretending not to flinch when his

hand traveled a little too close to my thigh. I died a little foolish death when all he did was grab his phone from the cupholder. I was expecting him to make a call and tune me out until the ride was over, but no.

Miguel's "Sure Thing" filled the car and I found myself blushing as I listened to lyrics I knew by heart. It was one of my favorite songs, and I'd sing it every day no matter where I was or who was around. I knew I'd sung them more than once around the shop—and probably within earshot of Rowdy.

I was caught even more off guard when Rowdy started singing the lyrics...to *me*.

"Stop!" I squealed when he stopped at the red light and pinched my cheek. I was grinning and blushing so hard now that I thought my face would break. When he grabbed my hand on cue, I was done for as Rowdy became animated and made a fool of himself...for me.

Miguel, he was not, but he could at least carry a tune.

"I didn't know you listened to him," I said as soon as the song ended.

"I don't. I heard you screeching this shit every day, so I finally downloaded it to hear how it actually went without the sound of dying sheep as backup."

My jaw dropped in silent outrage. "I do not *screech*." He sent me a look. "I sounded better than you!" His lips twisted as if to say, "Yeah, right," and I couldn't help but laugh. "Fuck you, Owen, okay?" I chuckled, and he did the same. "So, what's your favorite song?" I asked him as I admired his profile. He had the longest lashes and his lips...my *God*.

"The sound of you coming."

"I'm serious, Owen."

"So am I, Dream."

I decided to let it go since I had the feeling his answer wouldn't change. "Okay, so who's your favorite artist?"

"Nip."

Paying no mind to his one-word responses, I shouted, "I knew it!"

When he glanced at me and caught me grinning in victory, he shook his head and returned his attention to the road with his lips quirked. "You so damn corny."

"So." I was still smiling as I thought of another question to ask. "So, is your favorite color blue or green?"

"Green. The color of money."

I rolled my eyes at that. "What's your favorite thing to eat and please don't say my pussy."

"So what you ask me for?" he said as he mugged me. "You want me to lie to you?"

I sighed. "I want you to be realistic. There's only of one us you'll ever have again, and spoiler alert, it's not me."

"You should take your own advice," he said as he pulled into a busy parking lot and shut off the engine. I took a moment to look around and figure out where the hell he'd taken me now. It wasn't the shop or the motel. It was—

"Where are we?" I looked up at the white net that stretched toward the sky. It enclosed the fake green grass with huge glowing rings spaced apart to cover most of the field and kept the flying golf balls from escaping, landing either within the different colored rings or the grass instead.

"Top Golf."

"You play golf?" I uttered incredulously. Being a secret Miguel fanboy, I could see. This? No. Not in a million years.

"You so fucking rude," he had the nerve to say. I'd never met anyone more insensitive than Owen Wray. "I could wear them tight-ass booty shorts and play golf if I wanted to. Ever heard of Tiger Woods?" He was frowning now, making my heart skip a beat.

Thinking I might have offended him or hurt his feelings—however improbable—I rushed to apologize. "You're right. I'm sorry. You could do anything you set your mind to. I don't know why I said th—"

"I'm fucking with you, Dream. It's not that kind of golf." He cackled at the look on my face.

I swear I felt my eye twitch—my only warning before I lost my composure completely and cussed him out. He grinned throughout my entire tirade as if he thought my tantrum was cute—right up until I told him his mother should have swallowed him.

Losing the tenuous grip on his own cool and snatching me up by my neck, he brought our faces closer—his mean and mine terrified—before scolding me. "My mother is the only woman I'll kill for, and as bad as I want to fuck you, your fine ass is not exempt, so watch your fucking mouth, Atlas."

"Let me go."

He choked me a little harder as a cruel glint entered his eye. "Apologize first."

"You're hurting me!"

"Apologize!"

I swear even the windows shook under the force of his roar, making my fear heighten and a whimper slip free. "I'm sorry," I forced out around his hand on my throat.

He didn't release me immediately, holding me a second longer as his green gaze pierced my own, checking to make sure I meant it. I expected him to shove me away and take me home, but true to the psycho he was proving to be, he gently stole a kiss before releasing me. I coughed a little and rubbed my sore throat as he sat back and relaxed in his seat.

"As I was saying," he continued calmly, like he hadn't just choked me, "this is like mini golf, but way more fun. I'm too busy to come as much as I'd like, but Roc convinced me to make the time tonight. Joren and Golden are probably up there too," he mumbled.

I didn't respond as I checked my neck in the visor mirror for marks. Finding none, I sighed my relief and debated asking him to take me home. In the end, I was too terrified of what I'd do if he said no. And what he'd do when I tried to leave anyway.

He'd probably drag me, kicking and screaming, past hundreds

of spectators before letting me call an Uber, and frankly, I'd rather avoid the drama. As soon as his back was turned, I'd quietly slip away and be safe inside my motel room before he even noticed I was gone.

I could feel his perceptive gaze on me before he gave up on getting a response out of me and climbed out of the car. I waited as he rounded the green hood of the Jailbreak and helped me out. His hands were gentle, but I knew now it was a lie. Even now, I could feel my body wanting to put more space between us.

Rowdy had been mad and annoyed with me before, even threatened me a few times, but he'd never actually hurt me.

I felt even more discombobulated because he had shattered the illusion that I was safe with him, and I didn't know where to go from here.

I guess I only had myself to blame. Rowdy had never given me any real reason to think he'd never hurt me. It had only been my foolish hope that he never would.

I didn't fight him when he linked our fingers together or when he led me toward the building.

Because it still felt good.

It still felt *right*.

I despised him even more for the deceit.

Inside the building, there was barely any room left to breathe as people either waited in line to pay or crowded around the bar in the next room.

Through the glass window on the other side of the lobby, I spotted more patrons outside, huddled around the patio furniture in each section. They were either eating, cheering, arguing over scores, striking the balls—or *attempting* to strike the balls, I thought as I watched a girl swing and miss.

From every direction, above and below, the white golf balls went soaring, but I didn't get to see where any of them landed before Rowdy led me to the set of stairs on our right. As we headed up, Rowdy's phone rang, and my jealousy didn't seem to get the memo that I was done with him because my eyes flew to his screen to see who was calling.

My nostrils flared when I read the name Sissy. Rowdy's fake ass sucked his teeth and grumbled like it wasn't some bitch he was probably fucking while trying to call the shots with my pussy.

I snatched my hand away from him, and when he glanced back at me with a confused frown, I sneered at him. Shaking his head, he continued to lead the way. I guess he'd finally grown tired of fighting me, so I took that as a small victory and hoped that after tonight, he'd leave me the hell alone.

I followed him with my arms crossed until we reached one of the bays already packed, brimming with bodies and inebriated faces—some I recognized, most I didn't.

"About time," Roc grumbled as he swaggered over to meet us. "Started to think you weren't coming."

"You stay on my dick just like a ho," Rowdy playfully snapped as they clasped hands to dap each other up.

Boys and their secret handshakes.

"Anyway." Roc waved him off. "We reserved two bays since more of these fuckers showed up than we invited." His attention then shifted to me. "Hey, little girl," he teased.

"Hey."

"Damn, you dry. Fuck I do to you?" Unlike Rowdy, who was terrifying, Roc wasn't the least bit intimidating—at least to me—when he was upset. His confused gaze bounced between Rowdy and me before settling on his boy, and whatever Rowdy's look conveyed—his back was turned so I couldn't see—seemed to settle the issue. "Oh, aight. Little sis giving your ass the blues, huh?" Roc cackled as he turned on his heel and walked away.

Rowdy mumbled something about shooting him, but I ignored him as I followed Roc into our assigned bay, feeling Rowdy's gaze on me the whole way.

It was overwhelming being surrounded by so many unfamiliar faces. Luckily, I found an empty seat at the end of the L-shaped sectional next to Golden. Even sweeter, I wouldn't have to worry about making conversation since he, you know, *never* talked. He didn't even acknowledge my existence when I sat, which I was more than fine with me.

"Ya'll right on time," Roc said as he tapped the screen of what looked like a small TV with a larger one right above it. "We're about to start the next game. Jailbait, you in?"

I knew Roc was talking to me even before his humored gaze found mine, and now every assessing eye in the bay was on me.

"Sure...*Rochendrix*." His full name earned a few snickers as I knew it would.

"Good. We're playing teams, and you're on Golden's. He cheats, so you might actually have a chance of winning."

I didn't respond as I waited for Golden to deny the claim. I should have known better. Golden continued to eat his wings as if Roc hadn't spoken.

All right then. "Whatever you need to tell yourself to keep from crying on some poor girl's shoulder tonight, Rocky."

I heard a low and raspy chuckle, and—could my ears be deceiving me? I whipped my head in Golden's direction, searching his still visage for proof that the sound had come from him. He wordlessly picked up another lemon-pepper wing from his platter and tore into it, giving no indication that he had.

I sighed.

They said nothing worth having was ever easy.

I'd make Golden Boisseau speak to me.

"Just make sure ya'll broke asses pay up when you lose," Rowdy dictated as he muscled his way through the other eight or nine people gathered around the bay to study the golf clubs. "Or you'll be going home with a golf ball lodged in your cranium."

I noticed how most of the other players were female, and I didn't like how their gazes had lit up when he'd arrived. They followed him now, just waiting to be chosen as if he hadn't come with someone.

"And that's why we're not playing for money," Roc said as he snatched away the club that Rowdy had chosen.

"Why not?" Rowdy was frowning now as if the reason was truly a mystery to him.

"Because your ass is crazy, and ain't nobody trying to end up in ICU over a couple of hundred bucks."

Rowdy shrugged. "If they pay, they won't have shit to worry about it."

Some light-skinned bitch wearing a busted lace front and a cheap dress better fit for a nightclub giggled as she leaned forward, showing off her tits spilling out of the bodice. Even more annoying was that it worked. It caught Rowdy's attention.

And now he was gazing down at her as he toked on his blunt, like this whole building wasn't a non-smoking area. But like Golden, his face didn't betray his thoughts as he perused the smorgasbord in front of him.

"Aye, get your ass up," he told her. "My feet hurt."

"Oh...sorry." Her cheeks were red now, and I almost felt bad for her, but any sympathy I started to feel for her went right out the window when Rowdy took her place, then pulled her onto his fucking lap.

Rowdy gave her his undivided attention, and with each passing second, I became hyperaware of everything. I could hear my heart beating, feel my body flushing, and the hairs rising along my skin.

Somehow, I missed my hand darting out and curling around the handle of the dirty steak knife someone had carelessly left behind. I was oblivious to it until warm fingers wrapped around mine and gently wrestled the knife away from me, tossing it on the table out of my reach.

Golden.

He was staring at me now with his brow raised, and I could hear his silent question. *Is it really worth it?*

I guess that would depend on my intended target—Rowdy or the girl. Perhaps both. I couldn't say for sure. The girl didn't owe me a damn thing, and neither did Rowdy. He'd been nothing but honest about his intentions even when I didn't like the answer.

Still, Rowdy couldn't eat my pussy the way he did, let me suck his dick the way I did, and expect me not to get territorial. It wasn't even enough for him to hurt me once tonight. No, he had to cut deeper.

"Get that ho off your lap, or I'm leaving," I snapped.

"Uh? Excuse me? Who are you calling a ho?" the girl shot back.

A smile played at Rowdy's lips as we both ignored her. "Nah, she's good right here. Why? You jealous? There's room for both of you." He shifted the bitch on his lap and patted his other thigh.

The game had already begun while we went back and forth, so some girl chose that moment to walk by me for her turn. I shot to my feet, snatched the club out of her hand, and hopped onto the table without regard for the drinks and food cluttering he small surface. The smorgasbord was knocked to the ground as I lifted the club like a baseball bat.

The girl on Rowdy's lap had only a split second to dive out of the way before I swung.

Screams erupted as the blunt head of the club cut through the air. Before it could connect with Rowdy's temple, however, the club was snatched out of my hand with so much force it almost sent me toppling off the tabletop.

Suddenly, Joren, who must have arrived during all of the commotion was there. He stood between Rowdy and me now with a perplexed expression on his handsome face and my murder weapon in his hand. "What the fuck is going on?" he shouted.

No one answered him.

Everyone just stood there gaping at the scene I'd made. Rowdy still sat in his exact spot, not uttering a word. There was no anger, shock, amusement, or fear in his expression as he stared up at me.

He just…looked at me.

Slowly, the red haze I'd fallen in lifted at the same time I felt gentle hands guiding me off the table.

"Easy," a quiet, raspy voice soothed when I tried to snatch

away. My gaze followed the unfamiliar voice, and I froze when I saw who it belonged to.

Golden.

He'd *spoken* to me.

I stared at him, mostly from awe, but partly because I was too afraid to meet anyone else's gaze.

This time I let Golden help me down, and together, we left the bay. I thought he was taking me home until we stopped at the adjoining section. The group there was smaller, but they all gave me a wide berth, having seen my outburst.

It was just like the co-eds after I caught Sutton and Sienna together. I'd blacked out and let the dark thing lurking inside of me free. It had been there ever since my father started dying, slowly taking form and growing stronger as he became weaker.

Golden led me over to the couch, and surprised me again when he sat next to me instead of leaving me on my own. I wanted to beg him to take me home, but I didn't trust my own judgment after what I almost did, so I stayed silent.

Golden didn't speak to me again, and I wondered if I'd imagined it. By the time the current game finished, I was feeling normal again—if not a little embarrassed—and had even agreed to play when this cutie named Will, who was cool with Roc invited me.

It took me a while to get the hang of it even with Will's help, but once I did, I was addicted. Rowdy had been right, as reluctant as I was to admit it. This was fun.

Before long, I was on my fourth game with the third highest score, beaten out only by Will and Golden.

"Yes!" I cheered when I managed to sink the ball into the third farthest ring. The only ones who'd been able to reach the last ring so far had been the Kings. Even though I was now in a different section, the space was still open enough for me to see what was happening in their section and vice versa.

Rowdy was back to himself, talking shit, scaring everyone, and pretending nothing had happened, so I decided to do the same.

"See? I told you all you needed was the right form," Will told me as he crossed the red line meant to keep spectators at a safe distance and came to stand beside me.

Feeling a little too much of Will and Golden's drinks that I'd stolen sips from whenever they weren't looking, I threw my arms around Will's neck and grinned up at him. "And the right teacher," I flirted back. "Thank you, cutie."

The blinding grin he gave me was charming and adorable enough that I considered kissing him for a split moment. He was much closer to my age and a lot nicer too—completely my type before I ever came to Idlewild.

I didn't get beyond the thinking stage of my plan when Roc's voice broke through my drunken haze. "If you really want to thank him, Jailbait, I suggest you let him go. *Immediately.*"

I couldn't recall why my brain pushed me to listen, but I released Will anyway and pouted at Roc. "Booooo! Go back to your section, party pooper."

"Just trying to keep the man alive," I thought I heard him mumble as he strolled back to his side.

I rolled my eyes.

Will reclaimed his seat, and after looking around, I realized there weren't any left as I swayed on my feet. Stumbling over legs and feet, I made my way over to Will and stood between his legs with my hands on my hips. "It appears my seat was taken."

"Don't sweat it, beautiful. I have one for you right here." Will patted his lap, making me grin.

"My hero." I started to lower myself into his lap as seductively as I could when I was suddenly snatched away from Will. I stumbled and landed in a startled Golden's lap, making him spill his beer on his clean white shirt.

Whoops.

I blinked to clear the spinning room brought on by the sudden movement. As it all slowly came back into focus, I could hear screams from both near and far, shattering glass and food and drinks spilling everywhere. The unmistakable sound of chaos unleashing.

"O, you trippin'!"

Roc's panicked shout drew my gaze to the source of the destruction, and my stomach dipped in horror at the brutal beating unfolding before me.

Oh, my God...*no*.

Roc and Joren were attempting to pry Rowdy away from Will but weren't having much success. I looked away in horror only to see Will's friends staring at me accusingly. I was still sprawled across Golden's lap, too weak from shock and liquor to move.

This was all my fault.

I'd pushed Rowdy too far, knowing he wasn't all there.

And now Will was paying the price.

He'd long given up fighting back and was barely conscious when Rowdy pulled his piece, prepared to end his life.

Thankfully, Roc was quick to snatch his gun before he could fire, so Rowdy sent one last vicious punch to Will's temple, knocking him out cold.

Will had never even stood a chance.

Knowing I was next, I finally pulled myself up to my feet, stumbling a little, which caught Rowdy's attention.

He'd taken one step toward me before I bolted.

I darted around the toppled table and fled the bay, pushing aside anyone who got in my way.

"Atlas!" My heart skipped a beat, but I wisely kept going. "Bring your ho ass back here!"

Outrage had me turning on my heel to confront Rowdy's hypocrisy, but my lips parted in a soundless gasp at the sight of Rowdy being tackled to the ground. It took Joren, Roc, and Golden to take him down while Rowdy kept his furious green gaze on me. The same fury that had driven him to choke me in his car.

As I raced toward the exit and safety once more, I didn't look back or stop again.

TWENTY

Rowdy

"I'VE HAD A CHANCE TO READ OVER THE CONTRACT, AND THE TERMS are more than fair," Robert, my lawyer, told me through my car's speakers as I left the interstate and followed the directions on my GPS. "Mr. Henderson is practically *giving* you his business. He owns the property and land and doesn't appear to have any family from the information I've gathered, so there shouldn't be any pushback if you decide to accept his offer."

"All right." Hearing all I needed to, I disconnected the call.

I tried to focus on the drive, but my mind kept drifting back to Harry.

He'd put his blood, sweat, and tears into building a successful business and keeping it going until he was physically unable to. In the end, it was all for nothing.

It had taken me a couple of days to decipher his message and the mistakes he'd warned me away from making.

Harry should have retired years ago, but somewhere along the way, he'd forgotten to ask himself who he was doing it for. His only hope of keeping his legacy alive was now in the hands of...me.

I wasn't his son, but I was the closest thing to it, even though our relationship had been mostly business. I scratched his back, and he scratched mine. I was sure it would have meant more to him to leave the car wash in the hands of someone with whom he shared deeper ties.

I hadn't been able to stop thinking about it.

The future.

Once I set my mind on something, there was no changing it, and I'd decided a long time ago that marriage and baby carriages were not for me. Still, the thought of ending up like Harry made my stomach hurt.

I was stuck.

Atlas said I wasn't worth falling in love with, and even though it stung more than I let on, she'd seen more of me in three weeks than most of the people who'd known me my entire life.

I guess that was why I wasn't surprised when it was her face that I pictured the moment I began to even mildly entertain the idea of starting a family. The image of Atlas with my ring on her finger and a baby in her belly popped into my head with crystal-fucking-clarity.

It disappeared when I remembered she wasn't even old enough to drink yet.

I highly doubted she was ready for that kind of commitment when I was nearly twice her age and struggling with the concept myself.

I wasn't the type to half-ass things either.

It was the reason I'd hesitated pursuing her, knowing I'd develop tunnel vision, and nothing but an act of God could sway me. I was even starting to think that was what Atlas's sudden presence in my life represented.

An act of God.

It had been two days since my failed attempt to take her on a date.

She hadn't known my intentions, and I was grateful for it now. After the disaster of Friday night, I'd gone out of my way to avoid her, knowing I would only make things worse.

Initially, I'd only been trying to get her to bust it open for me, but then she tried to kill me and everything changed. I couldn't stop replaying how she looked standing on that table, full of jealous rage, and wielding a golf club meant to end me.

It was the moment that I knew claiming her body wouldn't be enough—would never be enough. I needed it all—her mind, heart, body…her fucking soul.

Fuck.

I was getting ahead of myself.

First, I had to figure out what she was up to before I did something irreversible like marry her immediately.

I was beginning to think Golden might have been on to something. Since I wasn't the type to sit on my ass, I made use of my day off to drive to the only place I could think of to get answers. It had taken a few hours but—

"Your destination is on the right," my GPS announced as I crept through the middle-class suburban neighborhood.

I turned it off and parked a few houses down before hopping out and pulling my ski mask over my head. It was just after midnight, so the street was quiet as I stuck to the shadows and ran to the modest blue and white house I'd spotted when I drove past.

It stuck out like a sore thumb among the other manicured lawns. The grass and small hedges separating the property lines were overgrown. The wilting flowers strategically planted to line the driveway on either side looked like someone might have loved them once, and the mailbox at the end of the drive overflowed with mail while more piled up on the front porch in front of the door.

I cut around the side of the house until I was in the backyard and tried the back door with no luck. Eventually, I found an unlocked window and hauled myself inside. Regaining my feet, I looked around and realized I was in the kitchen. A smaller stack of mail sat on the counter, so I crossed over to it and picked up the first envelope with my gloved hand.

It was an overdue hospital bill addressed to Kareena and Tyler Beck.

Atlas's parents.

I set the mail back down and tiptoed deeper into the quiet house. The air was stale, with a thick layer of dust coating the furniture and picture frames I found hanging in the hallway.

It was obvious the house hadn't been lived in for a while.

Nevertheless, I kept my steps light as I stopped in front of the first picture that caught my eye. It was Atlas. She had to be about six or seven and was beaming at the camera, showing off her missing tooth as she held up an award for perfect school attendance.

I moved around the house, studying every single picture I could find of her and watching her grow before my eyes into the young woman I'd met less than a month ago. Some of the memories were with her parents, but most of them were of Atlas solo.

It became clear to me by the last photo that she had been well-loved. Almost to the point of obsession—as if the Becks knew the precious gift they'd been given.

At some point, love stopped being enough, though.

It was evident in the most recent photo I found of her. She was wearing a burgundy and orange Ossella University T-shirt and standing by her car, hugging her mom. There were boxes in the back seat and a sad smile on her lips. Her father was noticeably missing from the photo, and judging by the angle of the shot, it was a selfie.

I moved my investigation upstairs, but not before swiping one of her high school graduation photos for myself and stuffing it inside my back pocket.

Finding Atlas's bedroom was easy enough.

It was the first room to the right of the stairs, the closed door bearing her name in sky-blue letters and a Keep Out sign. Not wanting to be caught slipping, I checked the bathroom and the other two bedrooms first.

The master bedroom at the end of the hall clearly belonged to her parents. The rumpled bed looked like it might have been slept in recently but was now as empty as the room.

"If you're here to rob the place, you won't find anything

valuable," a quiet voice spoke from behind me. I whirled around to find the small outline of a woman lurking in the shadows of the dark hallway. "Just old ghosts."

Light flooded the space between us a moment later, revealing a woman at least twenty years my senior, clutching a framed photo in her swollen hands. Her brown skin had a gray pallor, while her unruly hair framed her sunken cheeks. Kind brown eyes stared back at me. Behind her, the door to Atlas's bedroom was now cracked open.

"Kareena?" If Atlas's mom was surprised I knew her name, she didn't let on. She only nodded. "I'm Rowdy," I said foolishly. "Rowdy Wray."

"Hello, Rowdy Wray. How can I help you?"

"I—" I had no idea what to fucking say. I must have really been off my game to have been caught sneaking around. Although, in the past, whenever I'd broken into someone's house in the middle of the night, it wasn't to snoop. "I'm sorry to disturb you."

"Oh, that's all right." Atlas's mom waved me off. "As long as you forgive my appearance. I would have worn my best pajamas, but I didn't know I'd be having company." Kareena gave a weak smile, and I chuckled despite the awkward situation.

At least now I knew where Atlas had gotten her love for sarcasm.

"I know your daughter," I blurted nervously. My palms were sweating for some reason, and I was frozen to the spot.

I could see the surprise in Kareena's eyes at my announcement. And then her gaze narrowed suspiciously. "Forgive me, but..." Her head tilted curiously. "*How* do you know my daughter? Are you one of her professors?"

"No." I chuckled. "I'm her boss."

"Boss?" Kareena blinked. "I wasn't aware my daughter was working. What do you do?"

"I'm a mechanic. I own a shop in Idlewild. Your daughter is my receptionist."

"Idlewild," she echoed flatly.

"Yup."

"So my daughter isn't at school?"

"Nope."

"And you're her boss?"

"Correct."

I waited patiently while Kareena let the information sink in. There was a calm passivity in her tone when she finally spoke. "Well, if my daughter is there, what are you doing here, Rowdy Wray, the mechanic?"

"Background check," I answered plainly. It wasn't a lie since I was absolutely here to fill in some blanks.

"I see." Kareena's gaze turned shrewd. "Must be some mechanic shop."

Yeah, she was definitely Atlas's mom.

"I like to think so," I answered humbly.

"Hmmm. And did you find everything you needed to know?"

I shrugged and gave her a pointed look. "More questions than answers, honestly."

Kareena nodded sympathetically. "My daughter can be complicated."

"Your daughter is a pain in my ass if I can be honest, Kareena." I paused. "Excuse my language."

She waved me off again, but the gesture somehow caused her to sway on her feet, and I rushed across the short hallway to reach her before she could collapse.

"Shit," I cursed again under my breath before saying fuck it and carrying her inside the bedroom, where I laid her on Atlas's bed.

I only allowed myself a quick glance around at the teenaged frills decorating the room before refocusing on the woman in front of me. Kareena was close to my mother's age since my mom had me very young. She'd only been a few years older than Atlas was now. "Are you okay?"

"I'll be fine." Kareena gave me another weak smile. "Just a little dizziness. I must have skipped dinner."

I gaped at Atlas's mom when she trembled violently. I was no doctor, but I was pretty sure it wasn't hunger causing her body to convulse.

"You're sick," I accused, never one to beat around the bush. For the first time, Kareena avoided my gaze. I sucked in a breath. "Does Atlas know?"

Kareena sobbed suddenly and shook her head. "I didn't have the heart to tell her after her father died. She's already been through so much." I said nothing as I plucked a tissue from the box on the nightstand and handed it to her. Kareena wiped her eyes before saying, "Atlas spent a year watching her father die. I couldn't do that to her again." Kareena's body started trembling again, but I knew this time had nothing to do with whatever sickness was ravaging her body. "I was so cruel to her."

"You pushed her away."

Kareena looked at me, and the guilt in her eyes became a reflection of mine. I'd pushed Atlas away too. "I knew she'd never leave my side. It was the only way."

Yeah, that was the excuse I made too. I told myself that Atlas was better off if she hated me, but really, I was just afraid of what was happening between us. I'd never come this close to falling in love before.

And I'd done fuck all to show it.

"So...is my daughter happy? Is she safe?" Kareena inquired. She peered up at me from the bed like she knew my interest in her daughter exceeded that of a boss.

I cleared my throat. That nervous feeling crept down my spine again. "She's good. I haven't exactly been making things easy for her, but you should know your daughter can take care of herself."

Kareena searched my gaze, and then warm fingers weakly trailed down my cheek, and she smiled softly. "Something tells me she won't need to."

My heart skipped a beat as a thousand responses came to mind, none of which I was brave enough to voice.

Kareena's eyes drifted closed, and I watched her chest rise and fall until I was satisfied that she was only sleeping. The picture she'd been clutching earlier caught my eye, and I carefully freed it from her slack grip before looking at it.

It was a picture of Atlas when she was around eight or nine. She was jumping on a trampoline, and right there next to her was the man who must have been her father, jumping with her.

Tyler Beck was too far away for me to make out his features other than his average height, muscular frame, long dread locs, and light skin tone. Atlas was smiling hard at her dad like it was the best day of her life while her long black pigtails flew in the air around her.

Setting the photo on the white nightstand, I moved away from the bed to look around Atlas's room. It was as girly, soft, and feminine as I'd pictured in my head.

There were more pictures hanging in the mirror over her dresser, so I moved over to it only to suck my teeth when I saw most of them was of her hugged up with her ex.

I had a mind to pay him a visit while I was in town. Just in case Atlas ever thought about doubling back.

I didn't know if she was telling the truth or if she was still with him, but I didn't give a damn. Their situation was dead once I stuck my dick in her.

Grabbing all four pictures, I ripped them to shreds and let them rain over the dresser before moving to the chair by the window overlooking the bed and settling in for a long night.

TWENTY-ONE

Rowdy

I SOPPED UP THE SYRUP ON MY PLATE WITH THE LAST OF MY HOMEMADE pancakes before standing and rinsing my plate in the sink, then sticking it inside the loaded dishwasher. I then turned and faced the frail woman sipping herbal tea and staring out the window.

"Thank you again for breakfast. You sure you don't need anything before I go?"

Kareena waved me off. "It's the least I could do for keeping me company last night while I slept. You're very sweet, young man, but if I wanted someone fussing over me, I would have told my daughter the truth."

I snickered at Kareena calling me sweet. If only she knew her daughter wouldn't agree with her.

"It's nothing. You shouldn't be alone at a time like this." I hesitated before saying, "My mom…uhh…I went through something similar when I was Atlas's age, and even though it was my fault she shut me out, it killed me that I couldn't be there for her." It's been a minute since my mom's accident, and I still didn't like talking about it.

Kareena touched her throat with a shaking hand as she let my words penetrate. "My husband was sick for years before he passed, and my daughter spent her final year of high school visiting her father in the hospital every day instead of spending time with her friends and getting excited about college. I watched the light in her eyes dim every day, and I just…I can't do that to her again."

"Is it fatal?"

She looked at me and smiled sadly. "Very."

My next breath rushed out of me. "I'm sorry."

"It's okay. I've had my entire life to make peace with it." She paused, and then, "I have the same illness my husband had. We were both born with it. It's why we—" The teacup rattled in Kareena's hand. "It's why we never wanted to take for granted the gift God gave us. Atlas was the bright light in our darkest hour."

"It's genetic," I guessed aloud. And then I sucked in a breath, feeling like the floor had been swept right from under me. "Is Atlas—"

"No," Kareena said immediately. "She's perfectly healthy."

"How do you think she's going to feel if you die alone while she's hundreds of miles away with no idea that you were ever sick? She's going to carry that guilt around for the rest of her life, Kareena."

Atlas's mom only shook her head—just as stubborn as her bullheaded daughter. "It's my choice, and while I appreciate you, Rowdy, I know what's best for my child." She set her mug down and crossed the small space between us, clasping my hand between her much smaller ones. "Promise me you won't tell her."

"I—"

"Promise me, Rowdy. I can tell you care about my daughter, and while your age difference doesn't excite me, I can tell you're a good man. Even if you don't believe it yourself."

My eyes widened a little, and she gave me a knowing smile and patted my hand. "I wasn't a nun before I met Atlas's father. I've had my fair share of bad boys to know one when I see one, Rowdy Wray. You've got trouble written all over you."

I gulped. "And if I wanted to…date your daughter?" I forced out. It was my first time admitting aloud what I truly wanted from Atlas. And to her mother, of all people. "You're telling me you would be cool with that?"

"No," she answered honestly. "You're twice her age. No mother would be okay with that. And if her father was still alive, I couldn't promise he wouldn't shoot you on the spot."

I smirked at that because I'd do the same if it were my daughter. Regret settled deep in my chest, and I suddenly wished I could have met Tyler Beck.

"But I know my daughter," Kareena continued. "She's strong. Stubborn and a little impulsive, but she knows her own mind. If anyone is biting off more than they can chew, it's you, baby."

"I wouldn't have her any other way," I said with a wide grin.

"So, do we have a deal?" Kareena prodded, her eyes shrewd. "You don't tell her I'm dying, and I give you my *tentative* blessing to date my daughter?"

I gulped, already knowing this was a bad idea but feeling myself wanting to agree for my own selfish reasons. Kareena couldn't have been more wrong. I wasn't a good man. "Fuck." I huffed quietly. "All right. I'll agree on one condition."

"Yes?"

"You call someone to check on you every now and then, and you see a doctor." I could tell she hadn't been going, probably wishing to expedite her death rather than prolong her life.

Kareena's already weak shoulders deflated even more. "Rowdy, I'm afraid that list will be very short and sad. My husband and I both grew up in the system. And when he became sick, it didn't leave room for maintaining friendships." She smiled sadly. "I'm afraid there's no one to call."

I nodded and tightened my grip on her hands slightly when she started to pull away. "Then let me."

Kareena frowned, and I searched her features for signs of Atlas but found none. Atlas must have taken after her father. I tried to recall his face from the photos around the house, but then Kareena said, "Let you what?"

"Be there for you. I can give you my phone number. Anything you need, I'm just a phone call away."

"I don't know." She peered up at me skeptically. "Are you doing this just to have your way with my daughter?"

I smirked down at this sharp woman who raised Atlas. "I can't tell her you're sick, remember?"

Kareena sighed, and I knew I had her. "Then I suppose that will be okay."

"Cool." I gave her a quick hug before Atlas's mom took a step back as I dug my keys out of my jeans and started to leave.

"Maybe you could send me photos of her?" she called out when I had one foot out of the kitchen. "So I can see for myself that she's all right?"

I debated my next move for only a few moments before pulling out my phone. I quickly scrolled through it while I closed the distance between us again, and when I found what I was looking for, I didn't allow myself to think twice about it before handing my phone and the evidence of my obsession over to Kareena.

There were plenty, but I chose the least disturbing.

It was a photo of Atlas standing at reception, smiling at whatever the person on the other end of the phone she was holding had said. I remember feeling jealous because she had never smiled at me like that before pulling out my phone without thinking and capturing the moment for myself. I'd never admit how many times I caught myself staring at it while pretending that smile had been for me.

"This was taken a few days after she started."

Kareena's gaze seemed to drink in the sight of her daughter before saying, "She's lost weight."

I raised my brows at that because I had no idea. "She gets sad sometimes," I told Kareena. "She tries to hide it, but her eyes give her away."

"She was never good with expressing her emotions. She prefers to bottle them up—except love. Atlas was the best at making you feel important to her, and she loved her father very much," Kareena whispered mournfully.

"She loves you too," I reminded her.

Of course, Kareena chose to ignore that truth and simply wished me a safe drive back to Idlewild.

The shop was already closed, and everyone was gone by the time I returned to the city. I told myself it was better this way as I made my way up the stairs to Hudson's office, where I knew he'd still be pouring over paperwork. He was the only one with a work ethic that nearly matched mine. The only difference was that Hudson had a wife at home waiting on him, so I never understood why he spent all his time here.

I knocked on his door before opening it since it was cracked and found him sitting behind his desk, pouring over printed spreadsheets. He always complained that the fifteen-hundred-dollar computer the four of us had chipped in to buy his ass hurt his eyes.

"You still here, old man? Now, you know you got one more hour before Ms. Sheila drives up here to drag your ass home again."

"Yes, yes, I know." He waved me off as he peered over his glasses at the paper in his hand. I sat in the chair across from his desk and responded to some emails on my phone as I waited for him to finish. Ten minutes later, he finally set the paper aside and sighed as he removed the reading glasses from his eyes. "You ready to tell me what's bothering you, boy?"

I tucked my phone in my jeans before running my hand over my braids as I struggled to figure out how to voice the question I came to ask.

"When you met Ms. Sheila, did you…um…did you know you wanted her to be your girl?"

"Well…no. I was younger than you are now, so I had only

one thing on my mind, but my wife was hell on wheels, and she never let me forget it."

"So you struck out?"

"The opposite, actually. She gave me exactly what I wanted, and I walked around for a week thinking I was the baddest cat around. Every player from the Battery to Unity Garden wanted Sheila, but I was the only one to get her. I was so confident in my game that I went to call on her again, and she shut me down."

"What?" My eyes bucked, and I started cackling when Hudson somberly nodded like he was reliving the moment his ego was bruised. "Don't tell me your stroke was so weak that she wouldn't let you hit it again?"

"No, no. I assure you it wasn't that," he said with a reserved chuckle that made it clear he wasn't going to dishonor his wife by going into detail.

I respected it like a motherfucker, so I changed the subject. "All right, so what was it then?"

"It was my arrogance. We men make the mistake of assuming that when a woman catches our eye, it's solely by chance and not by design. My wife had chosen me long before I chose her, and I didn't know it until she sent my ass packing."

"Okay, I'm lost."

He gave me an impatient look. "Normally, I would say this is the problem with your generation, but I know you, Rowdy, and I know your parents. They're good people, and they raised you right. Because of them, you've never had an issue working hard for what you want. You don't sit around blaming the White man for your problems. Instead, you stood up and forced your way through them. It's one of the reasons I risked my wife's wrath coming out of retirement to work for you knuckleheads. I want to see you succeed in every way, and no man—no matter how talented and ambitious—makes it very far without a good woman by his side. *Your* problem is that you haven't met one until now. That's why you're pushing forty and sitting in my office seeking advice on how to court one." Hudson peered at me, and whatever he saw in my gaze made him chuckle. "Goddamn, it finally happened. You found her, didn't you?"

"Found who?"

"A woman who sees your potential and possesses the fortitude to help you reach it."

I scratched the back of my neck. "Something like that."

"I thought so." He nodded, and I could see a glimmer of amusement like he knew the hell I was in for and couldn't wait. "Well, I'm glad to hear it. It's about time." Hudson paused, and I could see the gears turning in his head as he stared me down. "Though I suppose *woman* might be a generous admission since Miss. Beck isn't even old enough to drink yet, and you're damn near old enough to be her father."

I could see the censure in his eyes, but I really didn't give a fuck. I was too far gone to care if it was right. "I don't know about all that. She's a little young, but I wouldn't say I'm old enough to be her father. I had to be like fifteen or sixteen when she was born."

"You were fucking at sixteen, weren't you?" he snapped.

I sighed and slouched a little in my seat, already seeing where he was going with this. "Yes, sir."

He grunted at my reluctant honesty. "Then you're old enough to be her father."

"Yo, you out of pocket for saying I'm pushing forty, though." I cackled, and he did the same. "I'm only thirty-five, old man. Don't put that monkey on my back just yet."

"Time comes for us all, son." His phone rang at that moment, and I knew it was his wife when he winced. "And it looks like I'm out of it." I snickered when he started throwing shit in his briefcase like Five-o was at the front door and he had enough drugs on him to put him away for life. Ms. Sheila really did have his ass trained. "Anything else you need to know?" he impatiently asked as he finished packing up and stood.

"Umm…yeah. Hypothetically, if I wanted to waste my time

romancing her with flowers and dinner just to fuck, where would I take her?"

Hudson's shoulders sagged with disappointment while his face said he was in disbelief. I impatiently tapped the face of my watch to remind him that his wife was waiting and to get his ass talking. "It's amazing how you've watched your father dote on your mother enough to make sugar taste bitter and yet have learned *absolutely nothing*." Hudson shook his head. "She's young, so she'll want something *lit*, as you youngsters say. Take her to Taste. It's classy, romantic, and expensive enough to impress her, I'm sure. My grandson is the head chef there. I'll call him and get you a last-minute reservation."

"'Preciate it."

I remained where I was as he rounded his desk to leave, so he stopped by my chair and placed his hand on my shoulder. "Remember what I said. Even if hell freezes over and she gives you her body, it doesn't mean you've won her. Not yet." Hudson patted my shoulder and left his office.

I sat there thinking about what he said before pulling out my phone to make a few phone calls. After that was taken care of, I headed downstairs to close down my station and the shop before driving home to prepare.

Hudson was wrong about one thing. I *had* paid attention to the way my pops treated my mom.

In particular, how he would bring her flowers just for wearing his favorite dress that day or making his favorite meal. So, after debating if I wanted to follow in his footsteps, I stopped by this boutique that was out of my way since Joren swore it got him out of hot water every time he didn't come home.

I walked out feeling like a fucking simp after spending three hundred dollars on roses. I didn't even know if Atlas liked flowers. I knew she had no choice but to like these or—

No.

There could be no "or." Not if I wanted an "after." I would just man the fuck up like she'd told me so many times and pray she liked them.

I strangled the flower stems as I told myself to chill, but all I did was try to picture her reaction, and my stomach ended up doing some weird shit that made me want to puke. *Fuck.* Why was it so fucking hot out here? I huffed and tugged my collar away from my neck despite it being the middle of winter.

I still had to convince Atlas to go out with me.

No.

Fuck that.

She would go on this date with me even if I had to knock her out to get her to the restaurant.

I spotted a hooded figure lingering near my car while he looked in the opposite direction, so I pulled my heat free as I snuck up on him and had the muzzle pressed to his temple before he even knew I was there. The figure froze, and while I couldn't see his face, I knew he contemplated making a move.

"You picked the right night to try me, or I'd have splattered your thoughts on the pavement and asked questions later. Lucky for you, it's date night. My girl won't appreciate it if I'm late, so I really don't have time to hide your body."

"I hope she's the same girl you had me lift these for." Taking advantage of my confusion, he used the moment to pull his hand from his hoodie pocket to dangle a familiar string of pearls from his pale tattooed fingers.

"Oh. My bad." I dropped my hand to tuck my gun away, and he turned around to face me, creeping me out with those blue eyes. His skin was so translucent I could see his veins through his skin, and his white hair made him look like he'd disappear at any moment. Motherfucker looked like a ghost. He even moved like he wasn't quite of this world. "What's up, B?"

Britain shrugged and scoped the scene before slipping me the stolen goods.

I had him take it from that rude bitch who came to the shop and talked down to Atlas like she was beneath her. *Mrs.* Naomi Irving had us both fucked up.

I couldn't really explain my need to punish anyone who crossed Dream, but I was going to defend her honor nonetheless. After meeting her mother, I knew Atlas believed she didn't have anyone left in her corner.

"Thanks," I told Britain as I slipped the pearls in my pocket. "I'll talk to the others and discuss if we're willing to sit down. You won't get much warning, so stay ready, be prompt, and don't bring me no bullshit."

Britain nodded, and I shook his cold hand before sending him on his way.

I watched him jog across the street and hop into the back of a Pontiac G8. The driver's window rolled down, and that Korean motherfucker's mug appeared a second before he flipped me off and attempted to drive away.

I guess he still felt some kind of way about me snatching his ass up. Too bad I didn't give a fuck.

For the second time tonight, I pulled my gun.

Pop! Pop! Pop! Pop!

With perfect aim, I shot out his windshield, both rear tires and the trunk, for good measure.

It would suck if they had someone in there.

Ky lost control of the G8, spinning several times before stopping in the middle of the street as the few people around this time of night screamed and ran for cover.

I got in my own whip, cranked it, and busted a bitch before pulling up alongside them with my fist over my mouth in mock surprise as the four of them gaped at me like I was crazy. I guess that little deejay bitch who'd been eyeing my girl a little too closely had sat this one out.

Ky gripped his hair and looked like he was seconds away from bursting into tears while the other two—Malik and the one who always looked like his dog died—had gotten out to inspect the damage. Britain was the only one calm as he spoke softly to Ky, who glared at me.

"Tell your bitch to come by the shop, and I'll give her a good deal to fix her car."

"This is my car, asshole!" Ky screamed at me.

"I wasn't talking to you."

Britain's gaze shifted to me, and he nodded to indicate he understood. Checking the time, I cursed and sped off to the sound of Ky switching back and forth between English and Korean as he cursed me out.

Britain and his crew wanted a meeting with the Kings, so the pearls had also served as a test to see if he was worth my time. Our approval was a requirement if anyone wanted to set up shop in Idlewild. It didn't matter what you were selling—ass, drugs, guns—no one ate unless we said so.

Word on the street was that Britain and his crew had returned to their old stomping grounds with every drug one could imagine and enough of it to land them an automatic RICO charge if caught. They had a product they needed to sell swiftly and a supplier they needed to pay even faster.

I'd meant it when I told Atlas I was legit now, but once you played this game, you were never truly free of it. I might not get my hands dirty anymore, but that didn't mean they were completely clean, either.

And neither was the mayor's, the police commissioner, half the force, and more than a few key judges for this district.

Joren, Roc, Golden, and I had the city on lock and possessed the power to make or break any crew.

I made it home in record time to shower and change before heading back out to pick up Atlas. Even though I didn't live far, I wasn't a fan of my girl staying at that motel alone. Each time the urge rose to demand she find somewhere else to stay, I talked myself out of it for fear of sending the wrong message.

Funny how getting Atlas to understand that she was mine was the only message I wanted to send now.

As I pulled into the parking lot of Montrose Inn, I caught the eye of Fancy Mack, who was walking to his car with two of his top hoes flanking him. He nodded in deference, which I ignored.

I hadn't forgotten our last meeting a few weeks ago.

The day after I'd met Atlas.

I'd shoved my gun in the pimp's corroded mouth and promised to make him eat every bullet in the clip if he so much as spoke to her. And then I paid every last one of his girls, including Lacy—his bottom bitch—to tell me if he did. They'd been easy to turn since the majority of his stable weren't there of their own free will.

Fancy Mack knew I didn't make threats, only guarantees, and my promise to kill him was the reason Atlas hadn't already been forced on the track. She was young, defenseless, and alone in his territory. She might as well have painted a target on her forehead when she unwittingly chose Hooker's Cove for shelter.

I was at her door in no time, but after ten minutes of knocking with no answer, even though the light was on and her car was parked outside, I turned on my heel and headed for the front office.

"Welcome to Montrose Inn. My name is Carl. How can I help you?" the clerk greeted me without taking his eyes off the TV.

"Give me the key to room two-two-eight."

"I'm sorry. That room is occupied, but I have other rooms if you—"

"I know it's occupied, motherfucker. That's why I want the key. My girlfriend rents it."

The clerk finally looked away from the TV and shook his head. "I'm sorry, sir. I can't do that."

"Aight." I walked away like I was leaving and then turned and kicked in the mini swinging door that separated his workspace from the lobby.

"Hey!" Carl shouted when I walked behind the desk.

"Shut the fuck up."

He stood up like he was planning to stop me, but one look had him stumbling back into his seat. I quickly found the spare key and walked out of the office and back to Atlas's room, where I quietly let myself in.

There were lit candles everywhere as if Atlas was trying to burn away the stale smell of the room. The purple bedding was definitely not the motel's and looked like some shit she'd gotten from Target. The room had a mini fridge, microwave, TV, and a small table with two chairs.

I could hear the shower running and music playing inside the bathroom as I crossed the room to the cheap armoire, where her clothes were neatly tucked away, and quickly found a suitable dress in my second favorite color and heels to match.

I thought about snooping some more before deciding that anything else I needed to know should come from her, so I laid the clothes on the bed and sat down in the armchair by the door to wait.

It was another ten minutes before she emerged with a towel wrapped around her sexy body. She had some extra-long shower cap covering her faux locs while water dripped onto the ugly stained carpet.

She hadn't noticed me yet, and I was in no rush for the moment to end as I watched her grab her toothbrush and begin brushing her teeth. It wasn't until she leaned down to spit out the paste that she caught my reflection in the mirror and screamed.

"Ahhh!" She looked so adorable, spinning around with one hand clutching her towel protectively and the other holding her toothbrush out like she was going to shank me with it.

"Calm your dramatic ass down. It's just me."

"What the hell, Owen?" she shouted at me. "How did you get in here?"

I held up the spare key and then slipped it into my pocket. "Get dressed, baby. We're going to be late."

"Late for what? I'm not going anywhere with you. Did you forget what happened the last time I was stupid enough to go anywhere with you?"

"Yes, you are. No, I didn't. And we're going on a date."

She shook her head. "No, we're not."

"Yes, we are."

"No."

"Yes."

"No!" She stomped her foot and pouted.

"You can get dressed or go like that, Dream. I really don't give a fuck, but I know you'll feel responsible and probably cry if I murk every man who looks at you in that towel."

I knew I'd won the moment her shoulders deflated, and she sighed. "Fine. You have one hour and not a minute more."

"You're so funny, baby. Look..." I gestured toward the clothes I'd laid out on the bed, a blue off-the-shoulder sweater dress with long sleeves that I knew would look dope as fuck against her pretty brown skin. "I already picked out something for you to wear."

She glanced at the clothes and then at me before rolling her eyes and turning back to the sink to finish her hygiene. I figured it would take her a while despite the time crunch we were on, so I grabbed the TV remote from her nightstand and sat back down to wait.

The room only had the local channels, which made me wonder how she passed the time whenever she wasn't at work since I knew she didn't know anyone in the city.

It only took me five minutes of channel surfing to get bored, so I stood up and crossed the room to where Atlas was carefully applying her makeup. I wanted to curse her ass out for wasting time with that shit, but I didn't want her to change her mind about going with me willingly.

Contrary to what she might think, I didn't relish the idea of forcing her hand. I wanted her to choose me, but if she *chose* to do shit the hard way instead, then so be it.

Our reservation was in an hour, and apparently, they were impossible to get, so I plucked her toothbrush from the holder and grabbed the jar of edge control sitting next to it. I didn't know what the fuck I was doing as I dipped her toothbrush in the gel and brought it to her hairline.

"Owen!" she screamed when I started brushing her baby hair. You'd think I'd slapped her the way her horrified gaze was staring at me through the mirror. "What the hell are you doing?"

"I'm trying to help you hurry the fuck up so we can go! Now, stay still." I tried to do that swoop shit that had black women in a chokehold, but she ducked and dodged me like I was trying to murder her ass.

"That's my toothbrush, crazy! That's nasty!"

I stared down at her to see if she was serious, and when I saw her holding back a laugh so she could stay mad, I sucked my teeth. "Cap. I've seen girls on the gram using this shit before."

"They use a *different* toothbrush, dummy, not the same one they brush their teeth with." She snatched her ruined toothbrush from me and threw it in the trash before reaching over and digging through her toiletry bag. She eventually found what she was looking for and pulled out a thin, hot-pink tool, holding it up to show me. "You can also use an edge brush, *which I have*." It looked and was the same size as her toothbrush but with a little comb attached to the bottom.

"Oh…my bad."

She shook her head, and I saw the dimples in her cheeks appear as she tried her hardest not to laugh. Eventually, she lost the fight, and we both lost our composure until there was only the sound of our laughter.

"I can't believe you did that." She went back to applying her makeup with one last chuckle.

"Your edges were looking rough, baby. I was just trying to look out."

"Whatever." She sprayed her face with some mist and then picked up her brush to finish what I'd started. "You're buying me a new toothbrush."

"I got you." Her phone was still playing music, so we both fell into a comfortable silence as "Girls Need Love" by Drake & Summer Walker came through her speakers. Halfway through the song, our gazes met and held in the mirror for the third time as the lyrics quickly shifted the mood from relaxed to sexual. "Where the hell did you get this shit from?" I asked to distract myself. I was close to saying fuck it and bending her ass over the sink, so I picked up her discarded shower cap to inspect it. "I didn't even know they made them this long. Shit looks like a used condom."

"Stop!" She chuckled. "It does not."

"If you say so," I mumbled. I set it back down and returned to the chair by the door to put some space between us.

Once she was finally done with her face and hair about ten minutes later, I watched her walk over to the bed and stare at the dress I'd picked out. I could tell she was contemplating whether or not it was worth fighting over when I tapped my watch, and she rolled her eyes before plucking it from the bed.

I'd been expecting her to take the dress into the bathroom to change, but she didn't. Atlas slipped the towel from her body and let it fall to the floor while watching me from the corner of her eye. I didn't notice the bottle of lotion she'd brought with her until she uncapped it, squirted some in her palm, and started to slowly spread it on the leg she had propped on the bed.

"Damn, Dream." I groaned under my breath after watching her for a while. My dick jumped in my slacks—yeah, I'd dressed up for her mean ass—but I knew by the small smile on her lips that she'd heard me. Her body was fucking incredible. Her tits were small, round, and perky with nipples like chocolate gumdrops, while her ass was just enough for me to grab, slap, and sink my teeth into the moment this date was over. "You know what you're doing," I told her. I fixed my accusing gaze on her as I watched her come to her senses and quickly slip on a thong and then the dress.

"No, I don't," she denied. "It fell off."

"Yeah, okay, Atlas. Keep playing with me."

She sat on the bed to put her heels on, and then I had to sit through her switching out her purse for one that matched her shoes. I was one more delay from pulling her ass out the door by her hair when she slung her purse over her shoulder and announced that she was ready.

"About fucking time," I grumbled under my breath.

I was standing to go when I caught her gaze darting from me to the roses I'd forgotten all about. Her dark eyes lingered there before guiltily returning to me, and I watched her bite her lip when she caught me watching her.

"Are those…are you those for me?"

I wordlessly nodded, and she hesitated for a moment before walking over to them. I watched her lift them to her nose and sniff before smiling.

"They're beautiful, Owen. Thank you."

Something inside of me sighed with relief. "You're welcome." I felt a little weird but happy as fuck that I'd made her smile. Remembering the other gift I had for her, I reached inside my pocket, and watched her eyes widen when I held up the necklace. "Turn around."

Atlas hesitated for only a second before doing as she was told. Silently, she gathered her hair in her hands and lifted them out the way, and I draped the pearls around her neck and fastened the clasp.

I kissed her nape when I was done and brought my lips to her ear. "This is all I want you wearing later when I eat your pussy."

Her breath rushed out of her like she wanted that too, but when she turned to face me, her gaze was stern. "That's not happening, Owen. It can't. I'm only agreeing to dinner."

When I bent and kissed her lips, she didn't fight me, but she didn't kiss me back either. "Come on. Let's go."

"Okay." She set the flowers back down and met me at the door, which I held open for her before following her out into the night, using my key to lock up. "How did you get a key to the room?"

"I took the shit. Fuck you mean?" I looked back in time to see her shaking her head as if I cared about her disapproval. Okay, maybe I did a little bit, but she was partly to blame for the crazy shit I did, making me chase her pretty ass.

"Do you not care at all that you might go to jail? You should be in jail," she mumbled after the fact.

"No." I took her hand and led her to the car, where I held the door open for her and helped her fine ass in. "Hey," I said as I dropped to my haunches so that we were at eye level.

She tucked a loc behind her ear and blushed. "Yes, Owen?"

"Thank you for having dinner with me. You look beautiful." Her lips parted in shock, and I grinned as I stood and closed her door.

Yeah, I'd paid more attention to my pops than I cared to admit. I also meant every word.

My heart was beating fast as fuck, but I felt excited and eager to get to the restaurant so we could eat and vibe. And then later, for dessert, I could finally make her mine.

TWENTY-TWO

Atlas

I DIDN'T LET ON HOW EXCITED I WAS WHEN WE WALKED THROUGH THE door of the restaurant hand in hand. Taste was a TikTok sensation, and I'd been dying to come here with no hope of ever doing so. I wondered how Rowdy had heard about it.

I somehow doubted that he'd found it on the app. He was a pretty busy man, so I couldn't imagine him sitting around wasting hours watching people dance—sometimes horribly—or do skits. It had been a godsend for me while stuck in that dingy motel room with only the local news and religious programs to keep me entertained.

Rowdy gave the hostess his last name. After confirming our reservation, we were shown to one of the cloth-covered tables tucked into the corner that allowed us to see the entire restaurant while offering privacy as well.

I blushed again when Rowdy pulled out my chair for me like the perfect gentleman before hiking up his slacks and seating himself next to me rather than across from me. It was a constant effort not to drool seeing him dressed in something other than his work uniform or usual jeans and hoodie. The only visual that could possibly top it would be seeing him in his birthday suit, and I wasn't sure I was ready for that.

The hostess left us alone with menus, but thanks to my internet sleuthing, I already knew what I wanted. I just wished I were old enough to order a drink. I'd heard they were amazing.

"Can I ask you a question?" I asked as soon as Rowdy was done perusing the menu.

He side-eyed me before saying, "Keep it brief."

I rolled my eyes. "I was just wondering how you knew about this place."

When he stared at me this time, it was an effort not to fidget under his assessing gaze. "Nah, be real with me, Atlas. That's not what you wanted to ask me. You wanted to know if I've brought other women here before."

"Have you?"

He seemed irritated when he looked away from me to glare at the laughing couple at the table in front of us.

They seemed to be having a great time. There was no tension between them. I was willing to bet my very limited funds that their night would even end with sex.

"No, Atlas, I haven't."

"Really?" I hated the insecurity in my voice. I hated how much I hoped it was true.

"Really. You're not just the first girl I've brought here. You're the first girl I've taken on a date. I don't even know what the hell I'm doing. This shit is new to me, but I was hoping we could have a chill night, get to know each other, and figure it out together. Is that cool with you?"

There was no arrogance in his tone. Only the same uncertainty mirrored in mine. It was all it took to knock down the last of my walls. I didn't allow myself to think twice before I framed his handsome face in my hands and pressed my lips against his soft ones. I still hadn't forgiven him for Friday night, but this was a start.

"I'd like that."

He grinned at me, and I let him kiss me again until his nasty ass tried to slip me some tongue.

"Hello. Welcome to Taste," greeted the cheerful voice belonging to our waitress. "My name is Felicia, and I'll be helping you with your dining experience today. Can I start you with something to drink?"

Rowdy ordered his usual—a glass of Hennessy—and to my utter shock, a Passion Sunrise while I begrudgingly asked for a boring glass of lemonade.

I was going to have some of his cocktail, and he would just have to get over sharing it. Felicia smiled politely and wrote our drinks down before disappearing.

Rowdy and I made small talk until she returned a few minutes later with our drinks. I wasn't sure what had happened in the space of time our waitress was gone, but she was extra friendly with Rowdy as she took his order while barely acknowledging me when I gave her mine.

Felicia was slower to leave this time with a lingering look at Rowdy like she hoped he'd be overcome with lust and bend her over the table.

I'd only ever seen him lose his composure like that with me.

Even while out of his comfort zone and not knowing how to behave on a date, Rowdy wisely pretended to be oblivious. I guess me trying to cave his skull in with a golf club taught him not to play with me.

"Now it's my turn to ask you something," he said after taking a sip of his drink.

"Keep it brief," I said, throwing his words back at him.

"Funny." He licked his lips, drawing my attention to them. "Why did you need a break from school?"

My heart stopped as he patiently waited for what he probably assumed was a simple answer but was secretly laced with pain. "What do you mean?"

"Most girls your age are in college chasing some bullshit degree, studying abroad, or partying with their little friends. Why aren't you?"

I stared at the clean white tablecloth so that he wouldn't see me mentally struggling to keep the lid on the box holding all the memories of my father and shrugged. "Just some stuff."

"Like what, baby?" I could tell it was an effort for him to remain patient while making it clear he wasn't letting me hide anymore. I'd unknowingly traded my secrets when I agreed to this date with him.

"Well, you already know I, um, I caught my best friend and boyfriend together."

Rowdy's gaze searched my face, and I could tell it wasn't what he expected me to say. My gut told me Roc had ratted me out to Rowdy. By now, I was sure all the Kings knew my father was dead. "They were fucking?"

A tear slipped free as I nodded, but I knew it wasn't for Sutton and Sienna. Their betrayal was just another reminder of how alone I'd been before Idlewild and the Kings.

"I was already living my worst nightmare when I walked in on them. They were all I had left, and they *knew it*, but they still—" I drew in a deep breath and slowly exhaled. "They still did that to me." I guess Sutton's and Sienna's feelings for each other were stronger than their care for me. "I couldn't handle seeing them around campus together, smiling, happy, and in love like they hadn't stepped all over me to get there, and I knew no one would miss me if I just disappeared, so that's what I did. I dropped my classes, hopped in my car, and drove…here."

It was the truth—if only part of it.

I didn't mention the letter that had led me straight into the heart of their den. I'd gotten it the same day my eyes were opened to Sutton and Sienna's betrayal. I'd rushed to the dorm I shared with Sienna to ask her advice and walked in on my best friend since third grade, moaning and bouncing all over my high school sweetheart's dick like there was no tomorrow. In all the years since Sutton had taken my virginity, I had never ridden his stubby little dick with that much enthusiasm.

I remembered standing there in disbelief as I watched them fuck each other in *my* bed but not much else.

One moment, I was standing in the doorway, that damn letter falling to the floor forgotten, and the next, I had a fist full of Sienna's quick weave as I yanked her off my bed and my man. I must have dragged her naked body out into the hall where I beat her ass in front of the entire co-ed dorm because that was where I was when the haze lifted, and I realized I'd been pinned to the wall by my RA and two other girls from my floor while my boyfriend of four years cradled Sienna's naked body protectively.

I remembered his lips moving as he yelled something at me, but not what he said. I remembered Sienna sobbing like she was the goddamn victim and everyone who had witnessed the fight eyeing me like I was crazy.

I didn't, however, remember being escorted to the associate director of housing conduct's office. I didn't remember the conversation that ended with me being banned from campus living for violating the school's no-nonsense policy on violence or having three days to pack my things before returning to the desolate husk that used to be my parents' home.

It was as if my rage and sorrow had me checking in and out to protect me from the parts that hurt too much to bear.

I guess I should have been grateful that I hadn't been expelled altogether, but I dropped all my classes anyway, so fuck your silver linings.

Sutton and Sienna could have each other.

Somehow, I knew Rowdy wouldn't judge me or look at me differently, so I laid it all out for him, every sordid detail, and when I was done, he didn't say a word. He just pulled me into his lap in front of the entire restaurant and kissed away my tears.

"Why was it the worst time of your life?"

I sniffled and absently traced the black and gold medusa on his expensive crew knit sweater. The top of a white button-up was peeking out the collar, making him look like the kind of guy you'd take home to meet your father. Except I never could. "Huh?"

"Before, you said you were already living your worst nightmare. Why?"

"Oh." I kept my gaze on his chest so the depth of my pain stayed locked inside where it couldn't destroy me. "My dad died." A little bitterly, I added, "But you already knew that, didn't you?"

"Dream." I shook my head, already knowing what he wanted. "Look at me."

"I can't." I sobbed before throwing my arms around his neck and hiding my face there. "I miss him so much."

I could feel Rowdy's steady pulse thrumming against my lips. It magically soothed the agony clawing its way out of my chest. My dad was dead, but Rowdy was still here. His arms were around me, keeping me safe. His hands rubbed my back so deeply that my eyes fluttered in pleasure. God, he smelled good. Dad had smelled good too.

"Fuck, I know, I know, but I need you to look at me," he pleaded gently. "Can you do that?" I nodded, but I still didn't lift my head. I stayed put where I knew I was safe from the world. "Come on, baby. Let me see those pretty brown eyes."

Reluctantly, I lifted my head to meet his gaze. He cradled my face with his hands and used his thumbs to brush away my tears. "I'd miss you," he told me. "And if you left, I'd follow you. There's nowhere else I'd rather be than on your bumper, Dream."

"What if I died?" I threw out jokingly to lighten the heavy mood.

Rowdy didn't crack a smile as he held my gaze. "Even then."

I sucked in a shocked breath as the fragmented pieces that used to be my heart feebly rumbled as if stirring—wanting to piece themselves back together. "Okay."

His strong hand continued to rub my back while the other held my hip. "How did he die?"

"Sickle cell. Dad had been sick for a long time before he died." I debated how much I should confess before adding, "He and my mom were both carriers." I waited for the implication to click into the place like it had the rare times I told anyone about it. I waited, but Rowdy seemed to take it all in stride. "It's okay if you want to ask me," I whispered when he reminded silent.

Rowdy frowned. "Ask you what?"

I pursed my lips, wondering if it truly hadn't occurred to him or if he simply didn't care. "If I'm sick, too." I inhaled deeply. "Sickle cell is genetic, Owen."

He blinked in surprise and then seemed to recover quickly. "Shit. I'm sorry, baby. I guess I was just processing."

It felt like a lie, but I let it slide. "It's okay."

Rowdy chewed on his lip before saying, "You know you don't have to tell me if you don't want to."

"I know." I waited a beat and then, "I'm not sick." I no longer had to wonder if he cared when I felt his chest cave with relief. "I guess Tyler and Kareena decided a one in four chance of their kids inheriting the gene was too risky for them to procreate." Rowdy's brows dipped in confusion again as he tried to decipher my meaning, so I decided to put him out of misery. "I'm adopted, Owen."

Rowdy jolted in surprise underneath me. "Word? Fuck," he breathed out. "I didn't know that."

I chuckled awkwardly. "It's okay. Why would you?"

I guess it was all too heavy for Rowdy because he reached around me and grabbed his drink. "Did you know?" he asked me after draining the glass.

"No." I wrung my hands in my lap. "Not until after Dad was on his deathbed, and I tried to donate my marrow to save his life. My mother refused and would never say why, no matter how much I begged. She just let him *die*."

"Your mom probably didn't want you to feel guilty if it didn't work or put you through that kind of procedure. I heard that shit was painful."

I already knew all of that but didn't care. It would have been worth it. I would have taken every ounce of pain even if it had only bought me one more day with him. Rowdy and I fell silent, lost in our thoughts. My voice was barely a whisper when I finally spoke again. "Do you know the odds of having a child with a negative blood type if the parents are both positive?"

He grimaced as he rubbed his forehead. "Probably low, but that doesn't mean anything, Atlas. Now, to be honest, science was a blur, but I do remember that much. It's a *recessive* gene, Dream. Invisible but still present and able to be passed on. You'd have to go back generations on both sides to be sure, and even then..."

"I'm sure."

I felt his hands tighten around me in silent comfort. "How?"

"My dad." I blinked away the fresh wave of tears at the memory of him using the last of his strength to bring me closure and beg my forgiveness. "My mom still refused to tell me the truth, but Dad finally admitted it before he died. He said he didn't want me living with the guilt of thinking there was anything I could have done."

"They wanted to protect you."

I shrugged as I stared at my hands in my lap. "Maybe."

Rowdy's hands began moving again, and I closed my eyes, enjoying the deep strokes all over my body as he used physical stimulation to distract me from the emotional pain. I didn't want to admit how much it worked. I just prayed he never stopped touching me like this.

It was more soothing than sexual. A reminder that he was here and wasn't going anywhere.

"What about your mom?" he asked me after a few minutes passed. "How does she feel about you dropping out of school?"

I knew it was impossible, but it almost seemed like he already knew the answer. I guess that, in a way, he did since I wasn't aware of too many parents who would be excited to learn their kid had dropped out of school and moved across the state without telling them.

"I doubt she's noticed," I admitted bitterly. After my dad passed, the grief took hold of her completely until nothing of the woman who'd raised me remained. I tore myself apart, trying to piece her back together until there was almost nothing left of me.

I remembered the day anger finally won, and I screamed at her, lying lifelessly in the bed she'd barely left in months. I told her that she didn't get to just disappear as if her life were over. I reminded her that I was still here.

The words she'd whispered back to me had delivered the final blow that shattered the illusion that she'd ever loved me.

Mama, please talk to me. So much is happening, and I need you. You can't just disappear. I need you. I'm still here. Please.

I know you are, Atlas, and that's the problem. I thought it would be enough.

I told Rowdy about that too.

He shook his head and rested his forehead against mine. "She didn't mean it," he tried to assure me. "It was the grief talking."

"Maybe. But when you have nothing left to lose, there's no reason for dishonesty." I shook my head to clear away the ugly memory. "I think my dad revealing the truth to me shattered the illusion for her. I could only be her daughter as long as I lived the lie."

Kareena had probably always dreamed of having a child, one she'd carried in her womb who looked like her or maybe my father—until one test shattered that dream. Physically, there had been no obstacles, but fear of the unknown and subjecting their child to my father's fate had kept them captive.

"Whatever the truth is, Atlas, know that she was wrong. You are enough. Don't ever let anyone tell you differently."

"I'll try."

"Nah, I don't need you to try. I need you to know it, and then tell me if anyone else says that bullshit to you so I can shoot them. I'll give your mom a pass because I know she loves you, but everyone else can get this work." He wore the most adorable frown as he stared off. His reaction was even cuter to me since I knew he was completely serious.

"I'm not going to tell you because I believe you really will shoot them and go to prison for it."

"Worth it."

I wasn't proud of my reaction, so I covered my flaming

cheeks to hide the evidence. Hearing a man say he'll shoot anyone over you was *not* something to blush over.

And yet here I was grinning like a fool.

I looked away and caught sight of the cocktail he still hadn't touched. "Can I try some of this?" I asked, gesturing toward the Passion Sunrise. "I heard their drinks were really good, and I can't order one for myself."

"Your ass had better drink this shit," he playfully spat. "I ordered it for you."

"Really?" I happily squealed before snatching up the drink and guzzling it down gleefully. "Oh, my God, baby, it's so good." Before my brain caught on to what I was doing and saying, I'd already tipped my drink toward him invitingly. "Taste." He held my gaze as he leaned forward and silently wrapped his lips around my straw, taking a drink and then leaning back. "Good, right?"

"It's straight."

I rolled my eyes and happily hummed as I took another sip before placing the straw at his lips again.

"Your ass better not tell anyone I be out here drinking cocktails and shit," he said after taking a second sip.

"I won't," I promised with a giggle.

We took turns sipping my drink until it was gone, and then I asked him if he could order another cocktail. This time I wanted to try the Blueberry Surprise.

Felicia returned with our food moments later, and her nose turned up at the sight of me in Rowdy's lap. We both ignored her as Rowdy ordered another Hennessy for himself and a cocktail for me. I tried to return to my seat so that I could eat, but Rowdy refused to let me go and instead fed me himself from his plate and mine.

After we cleaned our plates, he asked me if I wanted dessert. I declined since I was pretty full while he ordered strawberry cheesecake for himself.

As soon it came, he dumped my ass back in my chair none too gently and shoved up his sleeves so he could enjoy it fully. I watched him devour the delicious-looking cheesecake until my mouth started to water, and I wished I hadn't turned down dessert.

"That looks good," I said as I hungrily watched the generous slice become smaller and smaller.

"Mhmm."

"Are you going to eat it all by yourself? Aren't you full?"

Rowdy side-eyed me before spearing another piece on his fork and lifting it toward me. "Here, man."

I giddily accepted his reluctant offering, but when I begged for another, he shut my ass *down*. When Felicia returned, I ordered one to go, and Rowdy asked for the check. She returned minutes later with my cheesecake and the bill.

"Is there anything else I can do for you?" she asked Rowdy with a wink.

"No," I answered before he could. I watched her irritated gaze shift to me. "I can take care of his needs from here. Thank you. Bye." I waved and caught the smirk on Rowdy's lips as he pretended to study the bill.

"Okay, but I wasn't asking you," Felicia snapped back.

So the hoodrat wanted to go there. Okay.

"Aye, you can do something for me," Rowdy interrupted before I could curse her out. Usually, I'd refuse to argue over a man who wasn't mine, especially not one who gave me whiplash like Rowdy, but sometimes, you just had to check a bitch. "First, you can keep this shit." His ignorant ass crumpled up the bill and threw it at her forehead, where it bounced off and landed at her feet. "Even if I wanted to disrespect my girl *and* my dick by sticking it in you, I wouldn't need your number to do it. Now, go get the manager with your unprofessional ass."

What little sympathy I had left for her flew out the window when his words registered, and I realized she must have written her number on the receipt.

Felicia resembled the shocked man in that famous painting, *The Scream*, as she continued to stand there, jaw agape and dumbfounded that Rowdy hadn't fallen all over her.

"Oh. Okay, um, sure." She scurried away like her botched BBL was losing air, and we both cracked up as we watched her go.

"You ready, Dream?" Rowdy asked me after draining the last of his Hennessy.

I blinked at him. "We can't leave yet. The bill hasn't been paid."

"Nah, it's on the house," he said, taking my hand and yanking me out of my seat before I could protest. I just barely had time to grab my cheesecake before we hauled ass for the door. I caught sight of our waitress standing by the bar with the manager as they both watched us flee the restaurant with matching dumfounded expressions.

"Bye, Felicia!" Rowdy just had to yell before he pulled me through the door.

Out in the cold night air, we didn't stop running until we reached the Hellcat and dove inside. For a few moments, the only sound was of us both fighting to catch our breath, but then, once our gazes met, the momentary silence broke, and we both started cracking up.

I was the first to recover, and once the laughter subsided, the guilt started to hit me hard. "I cannot believe we just did that!" I squealed. I'd never dined and dashed before.

On the other hand, Rowdy felt no shame whatsoever as he laughed even harder at the look on my face.

"Yo, you look like Macaulay Culkin from *Home Alone.*" He snickered. I had my hands pressed to my cheeks as the horror of what I'd done sunk in. "Your ass is going to go to jail!" he teased, pointing his finger at me.

Believing him, I gasped. "Really?"

Slowly, his laughter eased as he stared at me from his side of the car and took his time answering. "No, not really."

"Oh." I released the breath I was holding and sat back in my seat. "Okay, good."

"You so damn square with yo' scary ass."

"So."

"That's all right," he said, leaning over and slipping me his tongue. I loved and hated how nasty he was. He didn't pull away until my panties were thoroughly soaked, and even then, it was only enough so that I could see the green of his eyes and nothing else. "I'm bad enough for both of us."

I couldn't even muster a reply until he pulled away fully. "A bad influence, you mean."

He shrugged as he pressed start on his car. The seat underneath me vibrated as it rumbled to life. "I'll be that if it means you have what you need."

My heart fluttered in my chest, but my guilt wouldn't allow me to let it go. "Still." I threw a remorseful glance at the restaurant. "That was wrong. What if it comes out of her paycheck? Waitresses don't get paid enough as it is."

Rowdy shook his head as if *I* were the disappointment and grabbed the blunt he had hidden in the middle console. "You got to stop setting your feelings aside to make room for people who wouldn't think twice about yours. *Clearly*. Earning chump change doesn't give her the right to hand you a shitty experience and still expect to be rewarded for it. What that bitch did went beyond bad service. I *still* would have paid and tipped her because I'm aware of everything you said, but she took it too far. The shit was foul, so I treated her as such. And if the owner wants to get paid, they can either come see me or hire more professional employees." Rowdy slipped the blunt between his lips and lit it before adding, "My money is staying in my pocket where it belongs either way."

"Okay, you're right," I agreed for expediency's sake and because, secretly, I knew he was right. I *had* been looking forward to eating there for weeks, and our waitress almost ruined the experience by hitting on my date right in front of me, so fuck her.

I'd never considered myself a pushover, but I guess the four people I'd loved most and lost tragically within the span of a few months had taken my fight with them.

"Can we go now before they realize we're still here and call the cops?" I urged.

Rowdy gave a light chuckle but didn't argue as he sped away from the restaurant. Of course, he didn't immediately take me back to Hooker's Cove. I made him stop at a pharmacy and buy me a new toothbrush to replace the one he destroyed. Afterward, we drove around getting to know each other without the heavy topic of my father's death ruining the mood.

"Yo, you're tripping," he told me after I listed my favorite movies. "*Die Hard* is not a Christmas movie."

"Yes, it is!"

"How, Atlas? Tell me one thing that made it a Christmas movie?"

"It happened during Christmas. Duuuuh!"

"Okay, two things," he said. "Name *one* more reason, and I'll believe you."

"How about three? It snowed the entire time, like every Christmas movie. It brought a family together, like every Christmas movie, and the soundtrack has Christmas songs, *like every Christmas movie.*"

"All right." He nodded. "I'll give you that."

"Thank you." I smiled gently at my small victory. "Just because it dared to be different doesn't mean it doesn't deserve to be included."

He cut his gaze my way as he turned onto a new street. It didn't seem like he had a destination in mind, and he seemed in no hurry to end our "date." "You think you're deep, huh?"

I shrugged. "I'm sure any new perspective will seem deep when you've been swimming in shallow waters."

"Yeah?"

"Yup."

"So, if I'm shallow, why did you agree to have dinner with me?"

I shook my head. "I don't think you're shallow, Owen. I think the company you keep—the woman you choose to *fuck*—are shallow, and it's made you a selfish, entitled, emotionally-stunted jerk."

I almost regretted my words when Owen Wray, the lion of Idlewild, honest-to-God flinched. "Tell me how you really feel."

"I just did."

I watched the muscle in his jaw jump as he strangled the steering—most likely imagining it was me. "Okay, Atlas."

We didn't speak again as we let Lil Baby's album drown out the tension. After my little admission, Rowdy drove me straight back to the motel, and while I couldn't say I was shocked that he wanted to get away from me, I was surprised by my disappointment.

Oh, well.

No matter which path we chose, we always ended up here—on opposite sides of understanding.

Maybe it was God telling us we weren't meant to be, and all we had to do to be happy was listen.

"Thank you for dinner," I said as I unbuckled my seat belt. He nodded but didn't say a word, nor did he get out to open my door like he had each time before. *Well, fuck you, too.* "Good night."

With his head down, he ignored me as he responded to a text on his phone.

I'd planned on leaving his presence with grace, but that option flew out the window now that he'd gone back to treating me like one of his hoes. I got out and slammed the door hard enough to make the glass rattle, but if I thought that would be enough to get a reaction out of him, I was sorely mistaken.

I could feel his eyes on me as I stormed to my door.

Key in hand, I stopped just short of inserting it into the lock.

The door was already ajar.

TWENTY-THREE

Atlas

I'D BARELY HAD TIME TO INTERPRET THE DANGER BEFORE ROWDY WAS at my side, gun drawn and wearing a scowl on his handsome face as he pulled me behind him.

"Go wait in the car," he told me with a look that warned me not to argue.

I gave a frantic nod before hurrying back to the safety of the Hellcat. My heart stopped as I watched Rowdy disappear inside the dark motel room, and I felt my skin crawl at the thought of him walking into an ambush. I chewed on my nails for a few minutes before I forced myself to stop fretting.

Fuck this.

Keeping my ears open, I searched the interior of his car until I found a spare gun in his glove compartment. I had no idea how to use it, but I didn't give myself time to worry over it as I grabbed his piece, hopped out of the car, and rushed across the parking lot.

I paused at the door, but when I didn't hear signs of a struggle, I pushed inside in time to see Rowdy walking out of the bathroom. It was scary how quickly he had his gun pointed at my head until I gave an embarrassing squeal that had him shaking his head and dropping his hand.

"Is anyone here?"

His expression was cold and blank as he stared at me. "I told you to wait in the car."

"I found this," I confessed, showing him the gun. "I thought you might need backup."

His brows shot up. The first real emotion he'd shown since I—well, I guess I'd hurt his feelings? It was trippy to think about. "Yeah?" He inched closer as he tucked his gun back into his waistband. "And what was you planning to do with that, Atlas? Shoot them in their kneecaps?"

I lifted my chin. "If I had to."

I could see the beginnings of a smile on his lips. "Oh, so you're hard now, huh?" he teased. "You think you gangsta?"

"No." I shook my head. "I just don't want to lose any more people."

He stood in front of me now, so he took the gun from my hands and secured it in the holster strapped to his ankle before rising to his full height again and taking my hips in his hands. "You won't lose me. I'm hard to kill."

I sighed and laid my head against his chest, taking comfort in his steady heartbeat. "Because you're crazy?"

"Something like that."

I closed my eyes as he rocked us back and forth. We stayed like that for a minute or two before I finally found the courage to ask, "Did they take anything?"

"I don't think so." He kissed my forehead before pulling away. "Come on. Grab your stuff so we can go."

Understanding it would be safer to stay in another room, I quickly did as he said, and luckily, I hadn't brought much with me from my old life, so I was done packing in under ten minutes. Rowdy grabbed all my bags, shaking his head when I offered to help, so I quietly followed him out the door.

My heart skipped a beat when he started toward his car with all my shit in tow instead of the front office.

"The office is this way." I pointed over my shoulder as I called out to him.

"Bring your ass on, Atlas," he commanded without looking back at me. Rowdy popped the trunk and threw all my shit inside like an asshole before locking it with his key.

"I can't leave, Owen. I already paid them for the week," I lied.

He sent me an impatient look. "Nice try. They only take payment by the hour since you're the only guest here *not* selling ass. Now get in."

"But what about my car?" A flimsy excuse, but the only play I had left to make.

"I'll have someone pick it up and bring it to you. Let's go, Atlas."

"Fine!" I stormed to the Hellcat, got in, and slammed the door. I realized my behavior was a little childish, but I was not sure many people could relate to being ordered around by a sexy psychopath to judge me.

Rowdy chose not to remark on it as he dropped into the driver's seat, started the car, and drove away. I watched the motel through the side-view mirror, and my belly flipped when it disappeared—like it knew I wouldn't be back.

"Where are we going?" I started to panic after he turned a couple of corners before hopping on the interstate. "There's another motel a couple of blocks from here."

"And?"

"I can't afford anything else, Owen."

He didn't respond, and neither of us spoke again until we pulled into a developing cul-de-sac, nestled between Maryle and King's Cross, twenty minutes later. Both sides of the street were lined with beautiful homes—most of them still being built—and I swear I even spotted one with a white-picket fence and a dog house with the name Spike painted on the front.

I was even more in awe when he pulled into the driveway of the largest one at the end. It wasn't a mansion or anything, but it looked like one of those Mediterranean-style homes you'd find in Spain with its tiled roofs, white stucco, and beautiful stonework. It even had a garage and driveway large enough to fit two cars.

The L shape of the house even offered some privacy, hiding the front door and lawn from the street.

"Where are we?"

"My crib."

I sucked in a breath. "Well, then, why am I here?"

"Because it's late, and I'm tired as fuck. I haven't slept in two days," he said, making me wonder why, "and I'm not going to get much of it tonight if I spend it worrying about someone kicking in your door."

I twiddled my thumbs as I responded quietly, "I would have been fine at another motel."

"And you'll be even safer with me, so come on." He climbed out of the car, leaving me no chance to argue. He had my bags unloaded and his front door unlocked by the time I talked myself into getting out and following him inside.

"Okay," I said as I walked inside his home. "But only for tonight."

Rowdy smirked at me before slamming the door closed behind me. Immediately, his scent, which was all over his home, enveloped me, and my muscles began to relax. That lasted until I heard the sound of the lock turning, and my belly sank. "If you say so," he teased before disappearing into the first room on the left.

Silly me. I followed.

TWENTY-FOUR

Rowdy

I HAD ANOTHER BLUNT LIT AND A GLASS OF HENNESSY POURED BY THE time Atlas tiptoed into the den after me.

You'd think I'd kidnapped her the way she was acting all skittish.

I guess I kind of had since that break-in had been one-hundred-percent staged. While Atlas was spilling her guts to me over dinner, I'd sent Britain and his crew to ransack her room so that I could bring her sexy ass home with me without all the kicking and screaming of *actually* kidnapping her.

I still couldn't believe how flawlessly I'd pulled it off.

From the moment she'd tried to kill me in a jealous rage three nights ago, I decided I was ready for a girlfriend, and I wanted that girl to be Dream.

Fucked up, I know, but the heart wants what the heart wants.

First, I needed to keep a closer eye on her to make sure I wasn't wasting my time, and since I wasn't a conventional man, I'd decided to skip all the courting the way she probably preferred and do things my way.

When I wanted something, I was all in, and I never took no for an answer.

"I thought you said you were tired," she whispered as she sat on the opposite end of the couch. She eyed me like I'd pounce the moment she let her guard down, and the shit was comical to watch.

"I am." Unfortunately, I had a routine, and I didn't like breaking it, no matter how close I was to falling the fuck over.

"You should go to sleep," she suggested quickly.

I sat back, spread my legs, tossed my arm over the back of the couch, and got comfortable as I eyed her pretty ass. "I will if you come with me."

Dream gently shook her head and tried to look stern, but she just looked like she had to take a shit. "That's not happening. I'll take the couch." She gave the soft cushions a loving pat.

"Suit yourself." I had a really nice spare bedroom that my mom spent a lot of time getting ready for guests after I bought the place, but I kept that little detail to myself. Atlas wouldn't be sleeping anywhere but in my bed.

We sat there in comfortable silence as I smoked, and she played around on her phone until she got bored enough to set it on the coffee table and scoot closer to me. "Why do you smoke so much?" she asked me.

I glanced at her and found no judgment in her eyes, only curiosity.

"I don't smoke that much," I answered honestly. "Only when I need to. You just always happen to be around when I do."

She tucked a dread behind her ear. "So you're saying it's my fault?"

"Most definitely."

Atlas kept her feet tucked beneath her as she scooted a little closer along the couch. "Can I try some?"

I eyed her skeptically. "You really never smoked weed before?"

She shook her pretty little head. "Uh-uh."

I took another toke and held it in before blowing it out slowly. "Come here." I patted my lap, making it clear where I wanted her.

She slowly stood from the couch and walked over to me in her heels. I could tell she was nervous but trying to hide it as I sat back and admired her frame in that dress. Her body was fucking perfect. Atlas was what black folks referred to as "slim thick." She had curves I couldn't wait to turn with no brakes and long thick legs I wanted to feel on my shoulders before the night was over.

True to her prissy personality, she primly perched her plump ass on my thigh and kept her legs closed and her hands folded in her lap. "Now, can I have some?"

I said nothing as I toked on the blunt and then gestured her closer. She obediently leaned in, an excited gleam in her gaze, and her lips slightly parted as she panted. I pressed our lips together, keeping my eyes open and watching hers widen when I slowly exhaled into her sweet mouth.

Once I gave her everything, I slowly sat back.

"Okay, what now?" she croaked before choking. A puff of smoke bloomed in the space between us as she coughed while holding her chest. "Oh, my God. It buuuuurns!"

"It'll be all right," I told her before placing the blunt between my lips and inhaling. "Want another one?"

Atlas eagerly nodded despite the fact that she was still coughing, so I gave her another shot gun. She coughed again, but it wasn't as bad as before. We went back and forth for a few minutes until only a roach remained. "When does the high start?" she asked me, glassy-eyed.

This girl, man. She was so damn innocent it made my dick hard as a brick.

"It depends. It takes longer for people with a higher tolerance, but it won't take nearly as long for a first-timer like you. A few more minutes tops."

"Okay." She giggled while grinning like a Cheshire Cat. I watched her reach up and palm her cheeks with both hands. "I can't stop smiling."

"Here you go." I groaned. I should have known her ass couldn't handle a little weed. "Don't be doing no crazy shit."

"Like what?" she asked curiously.

I rested my head back against the couch and just watched her.

She was so fucking pretty that I low-key found myself staring in awe at her at random-ass times of the day. "Like getting on your knees and sucking my dick."

She was quiet, chewing on her bottom lip while she twiddled her thumbs. When she spoke, her voice was soft and submissive, and I felt my crotch tighten with need. "You want me to?"

I kept my gaze on her as I lifted my hand resting along the back of the couch and took a sip of my drink. "Of course."

"I must be high," she mumbled as she slowly slid off my lap and knelt between my legs.

"Don't blame the weed," I said after polishing off my drink and setting it on the table behind her. "If I touched your pussy right now, would I not find it dripping for me?"

She nibbled on her lip before saying, "Maybe."

"Then what's the problem, Dream? Are we not both consenting adults? You don't need to make excuses for wanting this dick. Fuck what anyone else thinks. I want you just as bad—*if not more*—and unlike you, I've made that more than clear from jump."

"Okay, Owen," she whined and squirmed at my low-key scolding of her.

"Look at me." I reached down and gripped her chin when she disobeyed. "Do you want to suck me off?"

Atlas licked her lips and squirmed some more. I realized then it wasn't nerves at all. Her ass was horny. "Yes."

"And didn't I promise to give you everything you needed?"

Her head moved up and down in my hand when she nodded. There was a familiar spark in her eyes that said she was looking to get fucked. "So what's good, Atlas?" My thumb stroked her teeth. "What are you going to do?"

"I'm going to suck your dick." I gave her a close-lipped smile, and she lurched forward, her hands reaching for my belt, so I sat back and spread my feet apart to make more room for her.

I grabbed the small remote on the cushion next to me and hit play. "More & More" by Joe started playing as Atlas pulled my pants and boxers down. I lifted my hips to help her out, and my dick slapped my abs as soon as it was free.

Atlas scooted closer, and this time, there was no hesitation or fear before she wrapped her hand around me. "I still can't believe how big you are," she whispered.

My dick twitched in her palm, and she began to stroke the hard length.

Up and down. Up and down.

It seemed like it went on for hours.

Just as I was ready to tell her to stop playing with my shit, her tongue darted out, and she licked the tip.

"Mmh," I couldn't help but moan. It only seemed to spur her. A moment later, I was surrounded by her hot, wet mouth, and my head fell back as I fought the urge to take over and fuck the shit out of her mouth.

I could tell she was a little skittish about my size. Her hand wrapped around my base to keep me from going too deep as she gave teasing exploratory flicks of her tongue.

I forced my eyes open when I felt her trying to take me deeper, and after watching the mesmerizing vision of her head bobbing up and down in my lap, I nudged my hips upward a little to help her along.

Eventually, the tip of my dick reached the back of her throat, and my hands flew to her head as I felt my nut rising and forced it back down. I wanted nothing more than to come in her mouth, but not yet. *Not yet.* The feeling of her lips around me was too fucking good to give up so soon.

Atlas's hand gripped my thighs for balance, but she didn't complain as my movements gradually became rougher and wilder until I was outright fucking her mouth.

"Damn, bit—baby," I grunted, keeping her head in my lap as I thrust my hips upwards, making her choke and gag on my dick. I'd just barely remembered that she was my future girlfriend and not some random ho. I knew letting me fuck her mouth was a gift, and I didn't want to take it for granted. "Suck that shit."

I was vaguely aware of her hand leaving my thigh and reaching between her legs. A moment later, her hips writhed in time with my thrusts, fucking herself with her fingers like she was riding my dick while I brutalized her face.

Goddamn, I could hear how fucking wet she was as she played with her pussy. I wanted to tell her to stop—that her pleasure was mine alone—and at the same time, order her to keep going.

My gaze couldn't decide where to settle, and before long, it didn't matter. "Fuck!" I cursed when it got too fucking good, and I busted in her mouth prematurely.

Atlas's eyes were wet, and her lips were swollen when I pulled my dick out of her mouth. A long string of spit and cum stretched from the tip of my dick to her lips, prolonging our connection before breaking and landing on her chin.

She panted, trying to catch her breath, and I stole what little she'd captured when I leaned down and kissed her. "That was so fucking good," I hoarsely praised against her lips. "Thank you, baby."

"You're welcome."

"You good?" I checked in with her.

"Yes. I liked how rough you were. It was uncomfortable because you're so big, but it felt good too."

"Did you come?" She gave a frustrated whimper and then shook her head. I chewed my lip before saying, "Dance for me." I'd already guessed that pleasing me was a huge turn-on for her, so I was going to continue what I had started.

"I can't dance to this," she objected shyly.

I dug my phone out of my pocket and opened one of the playlists before selecting a random one.

"Wetter" by Twista & Erika Shevon came through the house speakers connected to my phone, and Atlas sent me a rueful look as she listened to the lyrics. "You had this all setup, huh?"

"Stop stalling."

I got comfortable again as Atlas rose unsteadily to her feet.

She was stiff and shy at first as she slowly moved her hips until her gaze dropped to my lap, and she noticed my dick, which she'd already sucked dry, slowly growing in my lap. I gripped my piece and started stroking, and seeing me turned on from watching her seemed to loosen her the fuck up.

Her dress came off soon after, exposing her apple-sized breasts and brown nipples that had been taunting me through the thin material since dinner. The entire outer curve of her right breast was a white patch where the pigment had been lost, and her left areola was a blend of white and brown patches that made my finger flex with want. Most of her stomach, starting around her belly button and reaching toward her ribs, had also lost its pigment. Her feet and thighs were much of the same, while the rest of her legs and arms had been mostly left untouched.

It was her face, though, and those start-shaped patches dotted in a particular pattern from the right side of her jaw to her left temple that always made my heart skip a beat.

Atlas's body was a work of fucking art. No one had ever gotten me this hard.

Naked, she climbed into my lap, still wearing the pearls, her heels, and glittery blue thong. I helped myself to handfuls of her plump ass as she twerked on my dick, getting it even harder.

"Are you going to be my new daddy?" she teased, referring to the lyrics as she pressed her wet pussy into my lap. The head of my dick pushed aside the material of her thong, brushing first her clit and then slipping and sliding through her wet pussy lips.

She was completely fucking soaked, getting my dick nice and lubed up to break her open later. I bit my bottom lip to keep from moaning like a bitch as I smacked her ass hard enough to leave a hand print. "Hell yeah. You're so fucking sexy, baby."

I pulled one of her tiny nipples between my lips and suckled hard, making sure it hurt as much as it felt good. Atlas might be sad and broken, but she thrived on the pain.

"You going to fuck me, Daddy?"

With my mouth full, I nodded as she wound her hips to the beat and threw her head back as she lost herself in pleasing me.

When she finally opened her eyes, I could tell she was ready for more but didn't know how to ask for it. Seeing that drop of innocence that somehow still remained after everything she'd been through shredded the last of my composure. I wrapped my arms tight around her waist before shooting to my feet. My slacks and boxers fell to my ankles, but I paid them no mind as I turned us both until her back faced the couch.

"Owen?"

I flipped her upside down without a response, and she yelped in surprise when her head hit the couch cushions. I pressed my palms to the back of her thighs, folding her in half so she couldn't move while I handled business.

I shoved her thong aside, and for a moment, I just gazed in awe at how fat and pretty her pussy was before diving in with a vengeance.

"Oh, my God...Owen!" she half screamed, half moaned, from the shock of me eating her pussy.

I attacked her clit as if it owed me money. I didn't want her to come yet, so I used my fingers to spread her ass and pussy before tunneling my tongue inside her and feeling her walls try to pull me in deeper. I might have spent ten minutes French kissing her pussy, stopping every now and then to watch how it throbbed and leaked her arousal before her body started convulsing.

"Oh, God. Oh, yeees. Owen, please!"

I finished her off quickly before the blood rushing to her head could knock her out and released her legs. Atlas collapsed on the couch and didn't move while I bent and yanked my pants up before scooping her sexy ass off the couch and carrying her out of the room and upstairs.

She didn't lift her head from my chest until we entered my bedroom, where I dropped her on my bed before removing my gun from my ankle holster and shoving it inside my nightstand.

"Is this your room?" she asked, sitting up and taking a sleepy look around.

"Of course." I stripped off my sweater and button-up, then kicked off my shoes before my pants and boxers followed to the pile forming on the floor.

Atlas's gaze immediately dropped to my dick, and I swear she gulped as if I'd just pulled my gun on her. I walked over to the bed and took her face in my hands before kissing her deeply until the worry lines disappeared, and then I pulled away.

"Lie down, Atlas."

And then I gave her a look that said I wasn't fucking around.

Atlas might have been young, but she was far from dumb. She knew where this night had been leading.

Dream chewed on her lip before obeying, scooting back on the bed and lying on her back.

I plucked a condom from my pants before strapping up and following her onto the bed. I hooked my fingers in her thong before pulling it down her legs and tossing it away. I then pushed her knees apart and stared at her pretty, swollen pussy that was still throbbing like it had a heartbeat of its own.

I almost did it.

For a split second, I almost said fuck the condom. I wanted to make that pussy mine in *every* way. I wanted to come inside her, write my name on her walls, and get her pregnant with my baby. I wanted to trap her ass so that she'd have no choice but to be with me.

But with one look into her trusting eyes, I knew she deserved better than me making her a baby mama. I was still trying to decide if I could be her boyfriend without eventually hurting her. It seemed inevitable. Bringing a kid into our complicated situation was a certified fuck boy move, and I wanted to prove her wrong about me.

Atlas was staring up at me, the worry back in her eyes as if she knew where my mind had wandered to.

"Don't hurt me, Owen."

"It's going to hurt a little," I told her honestly. Physically and emotionally, something told me it was inevitable that I would destroy her. And then I sealed the truth with a kiss. "But I'll try."

My dick was not only big, but Atlas was also tight as fuck, and no matter how ready I'd gotten her, I knew she hadn't been fucked in a while. She was one-hundred-percent the kind of female that required an emotional connection to have sex—pretty much the polar opposite of what I was used to.

"That's not what I mean," she whispered, only to gasp when my dick found her entrance and began to push inside. "After my dad and my mom and...everything else, there's not much of me left to give." She paused at the same time I did. "Please don't break what's left," she added when I didn't move or speak. "Please."

A tear slipped from the corner of her eye and spilled onto the pillow.

Fuck.

I hated making promises I couldn't keep, but something in my chest was pulling me to do just that.

"I'm not going anywhere," I heard myself say. "And neither are you."

She nodded and smiled sadly, a testament to what we both knew. That we could fight tooth and nail to be together and still most likely fail. This might all end badly no matter what we do.

I pushed forward and slowly sank to the hilt, erasing the sadness until there was only mind-numbing lust. And then I did it again.

Her eyes fluttered closed, so I nipped her jaw, and they immediately flew open. She gave me her gaze like I wanted, and I rewarded her by going deeper than I had before.

"Mmmmh," she moaned like I was killing her ass.

Her legs circled my waist while the heels of her feet dug into my ass every time I pulled back, only to push in again. I swallowed the choked cries that escaped her and bit back my own curses.

Her pussy was fucking heaven.

It took all of my control to fuck her slow and easy, delivering deep and long strokes while staring into her eyes. I fucked her exactly how I'd envisioned the first day I met her.

My muscles were straining from the control it took to hold back. I didn't want her to miss a moment or forget how good it felt to have me inside her. I wanted her to crave it—to be addicted to the idea of us.

I made love to Atlas Beck until her legs trembled around my waist, and she came on my dick, now crying for a different reason.

I wiped the sweat from my brow with my forearm before slipping out of her and rising to my knees.

"The first round was for you," I told her as soon as her eyes cracked open the tiniest bit. "This next one is for me."

TWENTY-FIVE

Atlas

I BARELY HAD TIME TO REGISTER HIS WORDS OR COME DOWN FROM THE euphoria before I was flipped onto my stomach and yanked to my knees. My ass was in the air now, and I was left dazed and confused.

I tried to look over my shoulder, but his hand locked around my nape and pressed my face firmly into the pillow. It smelled like him, but my heart was beating too rapidly to find comfort in that small mercy. I felt his dick prodding at my entrance, and it sent a little thrill down my spine because I knew what was coming next.

With none of the gentleness or care from before, Rowdy shoved himself inside me with a grunt. If it weren't for his hand on my nape, the force would have sent my head through the headboard. He didn't wait for me to adjust or get used to his invasion this time.

Rowdy began driving himself inside of me with selfish thrusts.

There was nowhere for me to go. Nothing for me to do but take the brutal strokes. The sound of our skin clapping echoed around the room as Rowdy pounded my pussy and had me questioning my sanity in letting his crazy ass fuck me.

It scared me how good it felt.

After only a few strokes, I found myself reaching back and placing a hand on his contracting abs in a futile effort to slow him down, but he only slapped it away with a growl before fucking me harder.

"Owen, wait. Wait! I—I can't," I cried. It was too intense. Too good. I felt like I was losing my mind.

"Yes, you can," he told me while biting back a moan. "Arch that fucking back."

I did as he said, and he rewarded me by slowing down a little and deepening his strokes. "Now, tell Daddy it feels good."

"It feels g-g-good, Daddy." The words had fallen from my lips too easily.

"Yeah?" He kicked up his pace again, and my eyes rolled to the back of my head as I let go and let him do whatever he wanted to me. I was surprised by how freeing it was.

And then there was nothing at all but him.

The sound of our skin smacking, my helpless cries, and him tunneling in and out of me echoed around the room. I was just glad there was no one living on the other side of the wall to hear every moment of Rowdy fucking me.

I felt another orgasm rising, and I chased the euphoria by throwing my ass back, meeting him halfway until I was fucking him almost as hard as he was fucking me.

"That's what the fuck I'm talking about. Fuck that dick." Rowdy smacked my ass in approval, and I moaned before digging my knees into the mattress and twerking on his pole with my eyes closed and my head resting on my arms.

It was mindless. Primal. So fucking *good*.

I didn't care if fucking my boss—a man nearly twice my age—was right or wrong. I didn't care about the unknown ties that connected us. I didn't care about betrayal or grief. I felt only him.

My body seized, and with a startled cry, I came so hard Rowdy hissed when my walls tightened around his dick to keep him inside.

"Ah, fuck, Dream," he moaned. "You tryin' to make me come, huh?"

"Yes." I looked over my shoulder and purposely squeezed my walls around him when our eyes met. "I want you to come for me, Daddy."

His fingers dug into my hips, my only warning before he took over. This time, I didn't fuck him back.

I was too spent, and he didn't seem to care as he folded himself over me and drove me into the mattress with short, hard punches. I could smell my pussy and the Hennessy on his breath—feel the harsh puffs of air on my cheek—as he used my body to chase his nut without any regard for me. Somehow, it turned me on even more, and I came again with a soundless scream that mingled with Rowdy's choked groan as he thrust inside me one last time and flooded the condom.

I had this crazy thought as I lay there—this momentary lapse in judgment when I wished there was no barrier between us, and it had been me he came inside.

I wasn't even on birth control.

Sutton and I had stopped fucking months before I found him in bed with Sienna, and I'd been too distracted by my dying father to keep up with doctor's appointments.

"Goddamn."

The sound of Rowdy's voice was like the ring of a bell. It signaled my brain back from the mental smoke break it had taken while Rowdy was fucking me senseless.

What the fuck had I done?

It wasn't regret that curled in the pit of my stomach. My pussy was too content, still throbbing from the aftershocks of three orgasms, to feel remorse. But it was something else. A dire acknowledgment that I had done something irreversible.

"Atlas." He kissed my shoulder, distracting me from my rising panic.

"Yeah?"

"What we did," he said, slipping his hand between my thighs

and cupping my pussy as if his monster dick still lodged inside me wasn't possession enough, "I don't want you to do this with anyone else."

I turned my head enough to meet his gaze, and the promise of violence if I disobeyed sent a fucking chill down my spine. Meanwhile, my heart jumped up and down in my chest, waving pom-poms around like we'd scored some kind of victory.

"Are you saying you want me to be your girlfriend?"

"I'm not sure we're there yet," he answered carefully, "but if you fuck someone else, Atlas, we'll never be."

All of a sudden, I couldn't breathe, and it wasn't entirely because of his crushing weight on top of me. It hadn't escaped my notice that he'd chosen to have this conversation while he was still on top of me. I was trapped with nowhere to go until I met his demands. I guess he'd forgotten backing me into a corner only made me bite.

"And while I'm carving your name on my pussy, how many women will I be sharing your dick with?"

Suddenly, Rowdy couldn't get away from me fast enough. He pulled out of me, stood, and then lifted me from the bed. I didn't fight him when he carried me to the bathroom. I was too weak to do more than lay in his arms like a limp doll.

Seeing my temporary supplication, Rowdy chuckled. "We got to get that pussy used to me."

"You won't have to worry about that if you're still going to be fucking other women."

Again, Rowdy said nothing, and I pursed my lips. He set me on my feet inside the glass shower stall, then turned on the water before moving away.

I didn't move, standing just out of reach of the cold spray while I watched him snatch off the condom and trash it.

Afterward, he left the bathroom, and I strained my ears to hear him leaving the bedroom too. Before I had a chance to feel uncomfortable at being left alone in his private space, he returned a couple of minutes later with my toiletry bag in tow. I watched as he set it on the counter before rifling through it until he found my body wash and sponge.

"Anything else you need?" He peered over his shoulder and waited for my answer.

I shook my head, and he rejoined me in the shower, silent as he crowded me underneath the spray, his green gaze intense and looking like he could go another round or two. Attitude still on ten, I turned my back on him.

"We're not in a relationship *yet*," he mumbled, picking up where I'd left the conversation and finally putting me out of my misery. I looked over my shoulder in time to see him squirt some of my body wash on my sponge. I swear to God it should have been in a porn commercial for soap. "But we're moving in that direction. I think this is what corny fucks like you call dating." Rowdy kissed the top of my head and gently began soaping my back. "Or am I wrong?"

Against my will, I slowly smiled. "You're not wrong." When he was done, I turned in his arms and tilted my head back to meet his gaze. "But if I can't fuck anyone else, you can't either."

Rowdy smirked as he stared down at me and slapped my ass so hard I inhaled sharply from the sting of his wet hand. "What's understood doesn't need to be explained. After the way you just put that pussy on me, I don't *want* to fuck anyone else. Believe that shit."

I liked the sound of that, so I held his gaze as I slid to my knees and showed him just how much.

TWENTY-SIX

Atlas

When I awoke, my first thought was that I hadn't slept that well since before my father's first stint in the hospital. My second thought was that I didn't know where I was.

I was naked.

My pillow was warm and hard and smelled like Irish Spring.

I couldn't see much since the sun hadn't risen yet, but it felt like I'd slept for years. I knew it must have been early morning, at least.

From what I could see, the bedroom was simple yet far too nice to belong to the motel.

And that was when I remembered.

The date with Rowdy, the break-in, and Rowdy driving me to his house. Then the amazing, wild, rough, and wholly unforgettable sex.

I lifted my head and saw that he was still out of it and, somehow, even more handsome while asleep. His long lashes swept his cheeks, and his lips were parted as he lightly snored.

I smiled to myself as I grabbed my phone off the nightstand and laid my head back on his chest. I'd made him get it and my cheesecake from downstairs after he fucked me stupid for a third time—

By the time I was done checking my notifications, I was bored and stuck in a house I didn't know.

I needed attention.

Rowdy must have been more tired than I thought because he was still sleeping heavily. I pressed my lips to his chest, keeping my focus on his face while I kissed my way down his abs.

"Don't start no shit that I'll have to finish, Atlas." I nearly jumped out of my skin at the sudden sound of his groggy warning. He must not have been sleeping as deeply as I had thought. "If I wake up, you're sucking my dick."

I giggled while shaking my head. He could be so damn ignorant. "You're already awake, silly."

He popped one eye open and looked at me. "Then why are my balls still full?"

I sat up and wrapped my arms around my stomach. "Because I need romance, and you're not treating me like you want me to be your girlfriend. You're talking to me like I'm a ho."

Rowdy stared at me for a second before sighing and stretching. I cringed when I heard his bones pop, and then he sat up too and pulled me into his lap. "I apologize," he shocked me by saying. He kissed my forehead and then my lips as his thumb rubbed my naked hip. "Good morning, beautiful."

I blushed even though I didn't want to forgive him that easily. "Good morning."

"If I thought you were a ho, you wouldn't be here right now. Believe that shit."

I stared at him. "Because you don't let girls sleepover?"

"Because I don't bring them here, period."

"Oh." I stared at the comforter as he kissed my neck. He seemed to like doing that, and I had the feeling covering up hickeys would become a part of my morning routine. "Can I ask you something?"

His lips paused on my neck before he sighed and lifted his head. "Don't think I don't know your slick ass is stalling on getting this dick, but fine, go ahead."

"Why did you bring me here?"

I could tell it wasn't the question he expected when he frowned. "Because you needed somewhere safe to stay, and I had protection to give."

My nipples tightened, and my belly warmed. I ignored them both. "Are you saying you'd kill for me?"

Rowdy stared at me for a really long time, and I could tell by the way his hold on me tightened that he was questioning if the truth would scare me. "Just give me a name."

"Just like that?" I eyed him skeptically.

But we both knew he didn't need to convince me. I already believed him.

Rowdy answered by lifting me and forcing me down on his dick. I gasped and closed my eyes, my fingers digging into his shoulders as a whimper escaped me. I tried controlling the pace and depth, but his hands were unrelenting as they cupped my hips, pressing me down, down, down.

"Wait. Owen, wait," I pleaded when I was sure I couldn't take anymore. I could feel him in my stomach, and my sore pussy burned from the tight stretch.

"All the way down," he ordered, only to force the last inch or so with a mean upward thrust. "You want this dick to be yours, you got to ride it like it's yours."

"I am," I whined.

"No, the fuck you not," he barked and then slapped my ass hard to get me going.

I rolled my hips despite the pain, and because it was him and I wanted to please him, it didn't take long before it started to feel good. I was riding him in earnest now, so Rowdy leaned against the pillows with his hands behind his head. At this point, it was me fucking him while he watched me lose my mind on his dick with a cocky grin.

"I thought you didn't want it," he teased and then slapped my ass.

"I want it! I want it," I chanted as I bounced up and down.

Feeling freaky, I leaned back, bracing my hands on the mattress and resting my weight on my palms before throwing my pussy up and down on his pole. I'd never been this bold before, but I'd had plenty of lonely nights in my motel room to think about how I wanted to ride his dick if I ever let myself.

I knew Rowdy would hijack my whole world and not just my body if I did, so I never thought this day would come.

"Ah shit," he let slip. His moans, which he usually held back, became more and more frequent as I rode him. I watched through half-lidded eyes as the arrogance slowly fell away, and his brows dipped in concentration as he zeroed in on where his dick was disappearing in and out of me.

A moment later, he bit his bottom lip *hard* as he held back his nut. He sat up, and his thumb found my clit, circling and teasing until my knees flew together when I felt the beginnings of an orgasm stirring low in my gut.

"Oh, my God."

"You gonna come for me, Dream?"

"Yes, Daddy," I promised in my sweetest voice. Rowdy had stamped his ownership all over my body last night. This time, I wanted to do the same, so I sat up and placed my lips to his ear. "I'm going to come so hard for you. Can I have my morning protein first?"

His curse was my only warning before I found myself flat on my back and his dick slipping out of me as he straddled my chest and began jerking himself furiously.

"Open your fucking mouth."

I happily obeyed, and a moment later, his warm cum landed on my tongue. Overwhelmed by the sight, Rowdy tossed his head back, and I felt a couple of drops carelessly land on my cheek, chin, and chest. Not wanting to waste a drop, I scooped them up, and when he opened his eyes, I held his gaze as I slipped my fingers in my mouth.

Rowdy groaned like I was killing him. "You so fucking nasty, little girl."

I didn't have a chance to respond before he grabbed my legs and folded me in half. My knees were touching my ears while he held the back of my thighs, keeping me open for him. The sounds he made as he licked and sucked my pussy told me he had a ferocious appetite that wouldn't be stated.

And just when I thought there was nothing else he could do to turn my world inside out, I felt his tongue dip dangerously low. And then…

"Oh my…Owen…fuuuuck!"

His tongue rimmed my asshole, and I screamed.

I screamed as my orgasm ripped through me so fiercely all I could do was take it.

I screamed as Rowdy pushed his fingers deep inside me until he found my G-spot and worked it relentlessly until I came again on the heels of my first orgasm.

This one was different but newly familiar. More intense. Messier. It was the same pressure I'd felt in the stockroom. It built low in my pelvis just before I lost against the urge to push, and I squirted his fingers, abs, and thighs with ejaculate, making a mess of the sheets and…him.

God, I was all over him.

His skin was glistening with my arousal, but then, so was mine. We'd taken turns defiling one another.

I was still shaking long after Rowdy pulled away. It was another few minutes before I returned to Earth and heard him snickering.

I grabbed one of the pillows that had been kicked to the foot of the bed and threw it at him.

"Shut up! It's not funny!" I whined. My body was still trembling, and I was embarrassed as hell. I still wasn't entirely convinced I hadn't peed on myself despite Rowdy's insistence that I hadn't. "I think I'm having a seizure." Wide-eyed, I turned my head toward him since it was the only other part of me I could move.

Rowdy sucked his teeth before saying, "Your ass is not having a seizure. You just busted a good-ass nut. That's all." He stood from the bed and scooped me up before I could protest. "Come on. Let's take a shower."

After our shower, I helped Rowdy take out his braids as he sat on the edge of the bed and watched the news. I think a few drops of drool landed on his back, which I blamed on the water from the shower when he flinched and turned to look at me questioningly.

He truly looked like the lion he portrayed, with his hair wild and sexy around his powerful shoulders. I wanted to go another round, but the throbbing soreness between my thighs told me it wasn't happening.

A moment later, sex was the last thing on my mind when a thought shifted the desire in my belly to despair. "I have a question," I said after I finished detangling his hair.

"What else is new?" he returned dryly.

I ignored his sarcasm and cut to the chase. "Who braids your hair?"

Rowdy kept his gaze fixed on the TV, but I was watching him so closely I'd clocked his small pause. The news wasn't that damn interesting. "Why, Atlas?"

I moved to stand in front of him and folded my arms. "Because I want to know."

His green eyes slowly slid up to meet mine since I blocked the TV. "Just some bitch I know."

"A girl you're fucking?"

"I'm only fucking you," he hedged. "Remember?"

Lord, why did you only give men half a brain? "You know what I mean, Owen. *Have* you fucked her?"

Rowdy didn't respond as he stood and gently pushed me out of the way before disappearing inside his closet. He emerged a few minutes later dressed in his work clothes.

I guess I had my answer.

Since I had no words left for him, I walked over to my stuff, already neatly piled in the corner courtesy of Rowdy, and began searching through them for something to wear. I'd chosen speed over convenience when packing last night, so it took me longer than I liked to find a clean uniform.

"What the—Well, that's weird," I mumbled when my hands landed on a familiar white envelope with my bank's logo on the front.

"What is?"

Not wanting to speak to him, I wordlessly pulled out the envelope full of cash. Because of their clientele, Montrose Inn only accepted cash, and I had just taken out three hundred dollars that day. It was even riskier walking around Idlewild with that much cash, so I'd left it in my purse that I'd switch out for my cute evening clutch.

There was no way whoever had broken into my room at Hooker's Cove would have missed it. It wasn't like I had a lot of stuff or even places to hide it. The cheap room didn't even have a safe.

I could feel Rowdy's gaze on me even though he said nothing, and I realized he was waiting for me to explain. I sighed, deciding to be a grown-up and end the silent treatment.

I told him about the cash that I'd just withdrawn that day.

"It was still in my purse when my room was broken into, but the robbers…" I shook my head in bewilderment. "They didn't take it." I forced myself to turn and face Rowdy, only to see no expression on his face whatsoever.

"That is strange." It was all he said before he turned away and retrieved his gun from the nightstand. I watched him tuck it inside his waistband. "Get dressed so we can go." Without another word or glance my way, he quickly left the room.

I wrinkled my nose at his retreating back and tried to make sense of this riddle. Why would someone break into my room but not take anything?

Could it have been Unrequited? Had they done it to scare me? They hadn't shown any hostility toward me before, so it didn't add up.

Deciding to put it off until later, I shoved it to the back of my mind and dressed for work.

Rowdy was standing by the door, guzzling down a bottle of water when I hauled all of my stuff downstairs. I felt him eyeing me out of the corner of his eye as I approached, and when his gaze dropped and he noticed me holding my bags, he pulled the bottle away from his lips with a frown. "Fuck you doing?"

I blinked at him. "I don't know what you mean."

"Why do you have your stuff, Atlas?" His tone was impatient and pissed off, but since he hadn't given a damn about my feelings, I decided to match his energy.

"Because it's easier than driving all the way back here after work to get it."

Rowdy lived clear on the other side of town. In other words, he had me fucked up.

"Take your stuff back upstairs, Atlas."

It was my turn to frown. "Why?"

"Because I said so."

"I suggest you think of a different reason."

Rowdy closed the gap between us until I was forced to lean my head all the back just to hold his gaze. "You really want to put yourself in danger just to prove a point?"

"I highly doubt last night was personal since I don't know anyone in the city," I half lied. Did Unrequited live in Idlewild? Why hadn't I considered that before? They had to have been watching me at least if they'd known I'd gotten a job at the shop. "I think I'll be fine at a new motel. Excuse me."

"You're not leaving until you do what the fuck I said, and if you think I won't write you up for being late, think again."

My lips parted. "That's not fair."

He took another menacing step closer. "Does it look like I give a fuck?"

"You can't just bully me into doing what you want! You can't even call me your girlfriend without stuttering and making excuses, but you want me to move in? What sense does that make, Owen?"

"I don't give a fuck about any of that," he said with a curl of his lips as he pressed his forehead against mine. Rowdy was standing so close now that all I could see was the white of his eyes. "Take your motherfucking ass upstairs before I lose my motherfucking composure."

I inhaled, and right before I let the air go, I knew what my answer would be. "No."

TWENTY-SEVEN

Rowdy

I WAS RUNNING HELLA LATE WHEN I FINALLY PULLED INTO WORK ALMOST an hour later.

Atlas thought I was crazy before, but she hadn't really seen anything—not until she tried me this morning.

We ended up tussling over her stuff from one room to the next until it ended with me throwing her shit all over the backyard and in my pool while she screamed at me to stop and called me every name but a child of God.

I'm sure the neighbors had gotten more than an earful.

For the first time since I left home, I glanced to my right and saw Atlas still pouting and fuming silently in the passenger seat.

Fuck, she was pretty.

I had no idea what the fuck she was so upset about, though. I was the one with a black eye and busted lip. She didn't even have a fucking scratch on her.

Secretly, I wore that shit like a badge of honor. I didn't want my girl to be afraid of me, and it made my dick and heart proud that she wasn't. There were grown men twice her size who couldn't say the same.

I touched my lip and winced as much from the memory of

the mean slug she'd hit me with as from the pain of the wound itself.

"I'll be back before lunch," I announced as I watched her. "Maybe we can grab some food on your break."

Atlas resembled a damn psychopath when her head slowly turned my way like she was Annabelle or some shit. She was looking at me like she wanted to disembowel me. "Aww, that's sweet. Eat a dick. I'd rather chew my arm off than talk to you."

"That's okay, Dream. I'll still fuck with you with one arm."

My baby spat a string of curses and insults that would make the devil blush before shoving her door open and leaving my car. I thought about running her ass over when she slammed my damn door closed, but I refrained since I knew she'd probably never fuck me again if I did.

I waited until she disappeared inside the shop before speeding off the property and back into heavy traffic. I reached my destination on the south end of King's Cross just before you crossed into the Battery. King's Cross was the second roughest part of town—Unity Garden being the first—and the place I'd first called home before my parents decided they wanted better for me and moved us to the suburbs.

Sunnyside was known around Idlewild as the Black suburbia since that was where all the well-to-do Black folks moved as soon as they came across a little money.

Maryle was the same, except it was mostly White people upgrading from the high rises in the inner city or escaping the Nine Hills bikers who ran Hilltop.

The two suburbs were separated by Midtown, Unity Garden, and King's Cross. KC used to be called Third Ward until Joren, Roc, Golden, and I took over. The interstate ran directly through it from all four directions, so if any player wanted to move their product in and out of town, they had to go through us, hence the name King's Cross.

"I thought you weren't coming," Giselle greeted me as soon as I got out of my car. Despite how cold it was, she was standing on her stoop in blue cotton shorts that looked more like panties, with her arms crossed over her braless chest covered by a thin tank top and a pink bonnet on her head.

Knowing what type of time she was on, I sighed and rubbed my brow. I know I promised Atlas I'd be good, but I didn't expect to be put to the test this soon. I didn't have a type, but if I did, it would be girls like Giselle.

Hoodrats were my fucking weakness.

They gave the best head, and I could get my dick sucked without them thinking they were my girl just because they made me come. They were just trying to survive from one day to the next and understood the game. Every encounter was transactional rather than emotional. They took what they needed from men and kept it pushing. But most importantly, they played their fucking position.

Clout chasers—suburban private-school princesses like Savannah, who'd had the world handed to them on a platter—expected me to fall at their feet just because they looked good and had okay pussy. They were shallow, couldn't hold a real conversation for shit, and were the easiest to use. They were doormats, willing to do whatever I wanted because they were either looking for a thrill, wanting to piss off their rich fathers, or thinking it would make me wife them.

And then there were girls like Atlas.

Head in the clouds. Sheltered. Naive. Young. They demanded the fucking world based on absolutely nothing and couldn't fuck without getting their feelings involved. I'd always stayed far away from her kind.

That was until my girl showed up on my doorstep and stole all my fucking focus with her fucked-up attitude and smart-ass mouth. Atlas didn't fit firmly in one box, which might be why I couldn't stay away, and why it felt like I couldn't breathe when I wasn't in the same room as her.

"What's up, Giselle?"

"Nothing. Come on inside. I'm ready for you."

Out of habit, I admired the way her ass cheeks hung out of the bottom of her shorts as I followed her inside the ramshackle house. Giselle had a makeshift salon set up in one of the back-rooms. Yeah, I could have gotten my hair done at an actual salon, but I'd grown up with Giselle, and she'd been braiding my hair ever since I decided to grow it out in high school. She was talented as fuck, so I never had any reason to switch up on her.

And, yes, okay, I fucked her *occasionally*.

I knew it wouldn't matter to Atlas that it was before her time, so I'd avoided the subject altogether so that I wouldn't be tempted to choke her ass when she got mad over nothing and pissed me off.

I sat at the bowl and let Giselle wash my hair as she filled me in on everything going on around the hood—mostly who was fighting, fucking, or getting money now. Giselle was my little spy, and I paid her well to keep her eyes and ears open.

When she was done shampooing and conditioning my hair, she blew it dry before oiling my scalp.

"So, what about you?" she asked me as she began sectioning my hair to braid.

"What about me?"

"Is it true?"

"Be specific." I could feel myself getting irritated, especially after the morning I had. Fortunately, I was trying to change and become someone Atlas would be proud to call her man, so I took a deep breath and forced myself to chill.

"Is it true you're fucking some young bitch now?"

I didn't even try to pretend I didn't know who she was talking about. "Aye, watch who you call a bitch. Matter of fact, who told you that shit?"

"It's all over the city, Rowdy."

"Aight." I didn't bother to confirm or deny it since it was no one's business but mine and my girl's.

My girl.

Fuck.

Even though I told Atlas I wasn't there yet, I couldn't help thinking of her as mine already. I didn't know why I was stalling on making it official. My dick and mind were already there. I just couldn't get my heart to cooperate. It had been a steel vault before her.

"Some people even said you were fighting over her last weekend," Giselle prodded.

"Okay."

Giselle sighed when she realized she wasn't going to get anything out of me. I didn't owe her or anyone else an explanation about where I stuck my dick. "I just hope this doesn't interfere with what you and I have going on," she added.

I didn't respond at all this time, and thankfully, Giselle caught the hint and shut the fuck up.

An hour later, she finished braiding my hair to my scalp in six neat rows, secured the ends in a knot, and freshened up my fade. I handed her the cash I owed her plus a little extra since I knew she was saving up for her own salon one day. She thanked me before tucking the money inside her handheld safe and reaching for my belt.

"Stop." I knocked her hand away.

"Stop?" she echoed with a bewildered look on her face. "Since when do you turn down head?"

Never.

Not once had I ever turned down a blow job—especially not one from Giselle, who sucked dick like it was her main job.

"Since now," I said as I made a beeline for the door. "I'm good. Thanks anyway."

"It's because of her, isn't it? I know you're not really going to walk away from our thing because of that pigment-challenged bitch!"

I'd been one foot out of the room with Giselle on my heels when she said that hot shit. I turned and snatched her up by her shirt before lifting her until we were at eye level—so much for turning a new leaf. But, for Atlas, I'd be a monster if I had to.

"Let this be the last time you disrespect my girl, or I'll snap your long neck and leave those badass brats of yours without a mother. Are we clear?" She started crying, but it didn't faze me one bit. The only tears I cared about were Atlas's. "Are we clear?" I roared when she didn't answer me fast enough.

"Yes!"

I dropped her ass and left her crying on the floor as I left her house.

I broke every traffic law on my way to the shop. I needed to see my baby ASAP and make up with her but also break it to her as gently as I could that her home was with me now and she was never leaving. I was almost there when I got a call from an unstored number. Already knowing who it was and that I couldn't ignore it, I pressed accept.

"I hope I didn't catch you at a bad time," mayor Norwood greeted from the other end of the line. "We need to talk."

Knowing whatever it was couldn't wait, I disconnected the call without responding and hopped on the interstate to head west.

TWENTY-EIGHT

Atlas

LUNCH HAD COME AND GONE WITH NO SIGN OF ROWDY, AND BY THE end of my shift, when he still hadn't shown his face, I was forced to accept reality.

I was stranded at work with no ride home.

No.

Not home, just a place with four walls, a roof, and a crazy man who wouldn't let me leave.

I was mustering the courage to ask one of the Kings for a ride since Tuesday's shift didn't end for hours when I got a text from Ruen.

Ruen: Got a gig 2nite. VIP + booze for moochers n tagalongs. U n?

I hesitated in the space of time it took me to remember this morning before I texted back.

Sure.

Ruen: Cool. C u 2nite.

Or sooner? I texted back. *I'm sort of stranded at work and need a ride.*

Ruen: ?

Long story.

Ruen: Lucky 4 you, I'm good with damsels :)

I grinned and shook my head as I texted back. Ruen was a relentless flirt but also a bit of a player.

Even better, you're not crazy

Ruen: Get to know me

I was still figuring out how to respond to that when she sent a second text.

Ruen: ur pumpkin is on the way, Cinderella

Okay. Thx.

Ruen: U owe me

I must have read the cryptic text a hundred times, trying to figure out how to respond. I came up empty every time.

"Fuck, there you are," I heard after ten minutes had gone by. I looked up from my phone to see a disgruntled Joren emerging from the side entrance. "I've been looking all over for you," he grumbled. I was currently standing outside by the valet booth where I'd been shooting the shit with Tommy and Dre. "Come on," Joren ordered as he started for the parking lot. "Let's go."

"Go?" I echoed to his retreating back. "No, sir. I'm not going anywhere with you. I'd rather joyride with Ted Bundy."

Joren stiffened, pausing mid-step at my words. He looked more than a little irritated when he turned back to face me. He looked like someone had forced him to swallow shit.

I guess that would make me the turd.

"Look, little girl. I'm not fixing to go back and forth with you. O had some shit to take care of, so he asked me to give you a lift. You can continue to stand out here in the cold, or you can get your narrow ass in the car. Your choice."

"Well, I think my *narrow* ass will take option C, but thanks anyway."

"There is no option C," he snapped back.

"That's what you think." As if God was on my side, a car I didn't recognize turned off Temperance and pulled alongside me. I did, however, recognize the face behind the wheel of the Pontiac. I'd only seen it once before, pale and pinched as Rowdy slowly strangled the life from him.

That messy bitch had sent her friends to my rescue in her stead.

"Get in," Ky said before rolling up the tinted window. It was so dark I couldn't see the other occupants inside, but I had caught a glimpse of a muscular arm in the seat next to him.

"Little girl, don't you get in that fucking car," Joren warned.

Ignoring him, I tried the back door closest to me and found it locked. I rounded the back of the car, my eyebrows rising at the sight of the bullet-riddled paint and the missing back windshield boarded up with cardboard and plastic. It was either desperation or stubbornness that drove me to climb in anyway.

I didn't get a chance to second guess my decision before Ky peeled away from the shop at a hair-raising speed. The reversing car swerved onto the busy street, sharply turning at the last minute and throwing me across the back seat despite my seat belt before shooting forward and racing down Temperance.

"Stop being an asshole, Ky," the blond with the ripped arms and sad disposition scolded from the front seat.

Ky laughed mockingly before turning his head and letting his assessing gaze sweep me slowly. "You're not afraid, are you, beautiful?"

"I'd be an idiot not to be. I don't know you and don't have anything to prove to you," I said, earning a snort from Roc's nephew, Malik.

He'd been quietly surfing on his phone next to me and hadn't looked up once. Suffice it to say, I was surprised he was even aware of my presence.

I wondered where Britain was lurking. He was the only one of Ruen's crew not present. And it was clear he was their leader. Well, except for Ruen. I didn't think anyone could put a leash on her.

"Touché." Ky faced forward before speeding through the light that was clearly red and narrowly missing getting us T-boned by a garbage truck. "Although, considering the stick you chose to ride," he quietly mused, "I assumed you liked a little peril in your life."

"I'm not discussing my sex life with you."

Ky seemed to think that was especially funny, swerving and nearly losing control of the car as he laughed like a hyena at my expense.

Christian turned in his seat to peer at me through sad yet sympathetic eyes. "Atlas, isn't it?" I forced myself to nod. "It's all over the city," he confessed warily. At my confused look, he added, "Rowdy put the word out on you. Your property of the Kings."

"His, to be specific," Ky added gleefully.

"We probably signed our own death warrant just for giving you a ride," Christian mumbled. He turned around and mercifully left me to process this news.

Rowdy, who couldn't even define who we were to each other, had apparently told everyone I was his while leaving me in the dark as to where I stood with him.

Fuck…that.

If there was one thing I'd learned after my father died, it was that I was alone in the world. And now Rowdy knew it too. I'd bared my soul to him, and he'd decided to use the knowledge to take advantage. He wanted to keep me all to myself while letting me dangle hopelessly with nothing to catch me when I eventually fell.

I couldn't decide which truth hurt more.

"I see you made it one piece." Ruen was waiting for me when I walked through her front door.

Britain had taken one look at me and then Ruen before swearing and storming out the door, wearing a fierce scowl. A little mesmerized, I watched him eat up the distance to Ky's car before climbing inside. They wasted no time taking off. I guess they wanted to get out of dodge before Rowdy figured out where I was, and shit hit the fan.

Their truce with the Kings was tentative, and Ruen and I were threatening it with our friendship.

"Yeah, no thanks to you." I sat my purse on the kitchen counter full of baked goods and smiled softly at Remedy, who had just pulled a fresh batch of scones from the oven. "Hey, Rem," I fumbled to sign.

Ruen had given me a crash course on sign language, and so far, I knew how to say "hi," "bye," and "this tastes amazing." Remedy was an amazing cook and loved baking even more, so the last one had been crucial to winning brownie points with the cloistered beauty.

Remedy set the tray of cookies down and began a long string of hand gestures that I couldn't follow after hello.

"She asked if you like snickerdoodle," Ruen supplied after I threw a helpless look her way.

"Does Nick Cannon own a condom?" I wrinkled my nose at the perfectly round and yummy-looking cookies. It was too bad I hated the taste of cinnamon.

Ruen shrugged and reached for one. "More for me." Remedy slapped her sister's hand away before signing something that had Ruen huffing. "Who cares if they haven't cooled yet? They're going to break apart in my mouth anyway, Rem."

Remedy answered with a withering look before transferring the cookies to the cooling rack. She then moved over to the cupcakes that had already cooled and picked up the piping bag filled with green frosting.

"What is all of this for anyway?" I asked, surveying all the delicious treats covering almost every inch of the counter's surface.

"Oh, this?" Ruen waved a dismissive hand. "This is nothing. You should see our kitchen after Rem gets inspired and tries out a new recipe. She'll spend all day and hundreds of dollars perfecting it, or she'll get it right after a couple of batches and then bake whatever comes to mind until she scratches that itch."

"Oh."

Ruen took advantage of her sister's distraction and snatched a snickerdoodle from the cooling rack. "Fuck, that's hot," she complained, bouncing the cookie from one hand to the other until her skin adjusted to the high temperature. She wasted no time stuffing her face before chewing happily.

I caught Rem rolling her eyes at her twin, all the while keeping her focus on the complicated-looking flower she was placing on her fifth cupcake.

"Want to go up to my room?" Ruen eventually asked around a mouth full.

"Sure."

I started to rise which caught Remedy's attention. She promptly abandoned the frosting to sign something to her sister.

"Relax. We're not those kinds of friends," Ruen responded. Oh, boy. I guess I was the cause of the worry lines now marring Remedy's youthful appearance. Ruen's gaze shifted to me, and I didn't like the challenge I saw there. "Right, At-las?" She'd said my name slow and teasingly. "You're not into girls, are you?"

"Right," I confirmed. It felt not entirely like a lie.

Ruen Quintana had somehow made it seem less simple than preferring one sex to another. *She* was just too magnetic to stay away from.

"See?" Ruen shifted her focus back to her sister. "Nothing to worry about. She's safe all alone with me." Ruen left the kitchen and headed upstairs. I took one step to follow and stopped to look back at her sister, who was shaking her head.

Now this was awkward.

I knew Remedy meant well, but Ruen was my friend and had helped me out of a bind. The least I could do was trust her when she said I was safe with her, right?

It was probably fine.

Said no smart hero or heroine ever. And wasn't that what we all were? The main characters of our own story?

I smiled at Remedy placatingly before following after her sister.

I'd no sooner stepped over the threshold of Ruen's room

when my phone rang, and Rowdy's name and frowning mug appeared.

The photo was a candid close-up from this morning after our shower—before things had gone horribly wrong. I had just told Rowdy that I lied about my age and had been telling the truth when I said I was fourteen the day we met. I even told him the driver's license I'd shown him was a fake that had cost me a lot of cash to look real.

I had only just managed to capture his reaction before he slapped my phone out of my hand and threatened to dunk my head in the toilet bowl if I wasn't bullshitting.

I had never laughed so hard in my life.

There had been tears in my eyes by the time I managed to convince Rowdy that I was joking. And to *not* give me a swirly like we were in freaking middle school.

After I had retrieved my phone from the floor where it had fallen, I'd taken one look at the adorable glower I'd managed to capture and made it his contact photo.

I stared at it now for a moment before hitting *ignore* and pocketing my phone where it rang five or six more times—I'd honestly lost count—before blessedly falling silent.

When I gave Ruen my full attention, she was holding up a silver sequined top cut like a bandana with strings to tie around the neck.

"What was that about?" I asked her, referring to Remedy's mini-freak-out downstairs. "Does your sister not trust me with you?"

"More like she doesn't trust *me* with *you*." She finished examining the top before throwing it on the bed next to me and disappearing through one of the open doors. "I can be pretty persuasive," she called out from what I assumed was her closet.

"I actually thought your tattoo was more accurate," I teased her. Ruen was indeed *bad news*.

And her room was still a fucking mess.

The clothes, records, expensive-looking equipment, and even

pricier bottles of alcohol lying around were now a permanent part of her floor. I thought I even spotted a purple dildo with a wicked curve peeking out from underneath a pair of discarded boxers. Lying next to it was an empty condom wrapper.

My brows shot toward my hairline as I gawked at the unmistakable evidence of a male lover. It was weird to see, considering Ruen was unapologetically a pussy hound.

Or perhaps it was just mine that she couldn't stop sniffing around.

I knew part of her interest was just to piss off Rowdy, but I think she genuinely liked me too. As a friend? As a potential lover? I didn't know. Ruen didn't strike me as the type to take in strays for the kindness of it. Her sister, maybe, but Ruen? She had a cruel side to her.

I debated whether it was rude or even my business to ask for all of two seconds before blurting, "You're not a lesbian, are you?"

I heard a snort just before she said, "I never said I was, Twinks."

"Bisexual?" I threw out, ignoring the nickname she'd given me—Twinkle, inspired by the star-shaped vitiligo on my face.

Ruen sighed as if the topic of her sexual preference was too tedious to bear. And then I remembered her calling me a boring heterosexual when we first met. "I like sex, and I like having it with people," she said matter-of-factly. "Their gender is irrelevant."

"Sure." I nodded as if she could see me while wondering what label I could use to explain my confusing attraction to Ruen. I definitely had a preference, and it wasn't for my own team. I'd never been attracted to another girl before, and it wasn't as if my heart was torn between Ruen and Rowdy.

Nope.

My pussy might be a free-for-all buffet, but my heart only had room for one forbidden relationship at a time. My much older boss had already commandeered my every waking thought. Fuck, he followed me into my dreams too.

Still…I was curious about Ruen too. Usually, it ebbed and

flowed based on my proximity to her. I didn't want to admit that Rowdy had every reason to want to keep us apart. I was flirting with fire being here.

"So, where is this party?" I called out. I desperately needed a change of subject.

Ruen walked from the closet with a red faux leather mini skirt and matching choker. "After Dark. It's only been open for a few weeks and has been generating a lot of buzz. They have an in-house deejay, but he caught that virus going around, so he put in a good word for me with the owner. It means I'll have a steady gig for the next few weeks while he's home recovering."

"Wow. Congratulations, I guess?" I thought about it and asked, "Aren't you worried, though, since the crowded club is where he probably caught it?"

"No." She shrugged. "The chances I take every day are riskier than some virus. You know?"

No, I didn't know, but I could understand her point of view.

The night of my welcome party had opened my eyes to just how different the worlds we lived in were. Ruen was very much the queen of her realm while I was still searching for a place in mine.

"VIP or not, I don't know how I'll feel partying all alone while you work," I confessed.

"You won't be alone," she reassured. "I invited some people."

That didn't make me feel any better. Meeting new people? Gross.

"I don't have anything to wear." I gestured to my work clothes, which wouldn't pass for club attire in any kind of light.

"Way ahead of you." Ruen pointed to the outfit I'd watched her put together. "We're about the same size, so it should fit. What size shoe do you wear?"

"Eight."

"I'm a little bigger than you," she said before disappearing inside her closet and returning with spiked silver boots. "Throw on an extra pair of socks, and these should fit."

"Okay."

My phone rang again, so I silenced it without looking at the screen. I already knew who was calling.

"Seriously, is everything okay, Twinks?"

I shook my head while staring at the floor. "Not really. My room got broken into last night, so Owen took me home with him after our date. It was only supposed to be for one night, but now he seems to think we're ready to move in together, and nothing I say will persuade him otherwise. I can't afford a room outside the Cove, and even if I could...he'd find me anyway."

"So stay here," Ruen offered easily. My head shot up, but before I could form words, she shrugged. "We've got a guest room Rem would love to put to use, and I've got no problem helping you kick your boyfriend's ass if he tries to drag you back to his cave."

I didn't bother to correct Ruen's assumption that Rowdy was my man. Instead, I said, "Ruen, I...I can't ask you to do that."

My loyal but crazy friend sighed. "You didn't. I offered." Without warning, Ruen stripped down to nothing but her thong, giving me a naked view of her perky tits and tight belly before sitting at her cluttered desk and powering on her laptop. "Feel free to use the shower if you need it," she offered with her back to me.

I sighed before standing and wordlessly disappearing inside her ensuite. I shut the door, and after being real with myself for once, I locked it just in case. A moment later, Kehlani began to sing her woes about her lover choosing to be with a man over her.

TWENTY-NINE

Atlas

I'D LEARNED SHORTLY AFTER TURNING LEGAL THAT CLUBS WEREN'T FOR me.

Dressing up to be herded into a shoebox-size room with no air-conditioning to stand around for hours in heels designed by someone who hated women just to be groped by men blowing their rent money for a chance to fuck and having random crotches shoved against your ass?

Yeah, no thanks.

After Dark made those hole-in-the-wall hot spots around my old campus seem like after-school programs in comparison.

The lounge had an entry age of twenty-one and up, so the crowd was more mature and less rowdy. Thanks to Ruen's connections, I hadn't been carded at the door or when the two waitresses brought over the free bottles to our VIP section as promised and agreed to mix any cocktail we wanted.

I was even able to dance the night away without being pressed by some broke loser looking to cop a few feels.

A girl could get used to this.

Ruen's friends…not so much.

"Oooooh, guuuurl," her most annoying friend drunkenly slurred. "Where did you get them boots?"

Breana, I think her name was, had taken advantage of the bottomless mixers and had gotten sloppy drunk. Her dress had long ago risen above her waist from stumbling all over the section. None of the friends she came with seemed to notice or care that their friend's bare bottom was on display for the entire club to see. Their carefully painted faces were glued to their phones as they filmed and took pictures of themselves sitting in the high-dollar section for Instagram.

"I don't know," I replied as I swayed to the music. "I borrowed them. You'd have to ask Ruen."

Realizing the guys in the section next to us were ogling and filming her bare ass, I reached over—no longer caring if it was my place—and yanked her dress back over her ass.

Some of those creeps sucked their teeth and called me a bitch under their breath, but I flipped them off and continued vibin' to the music.

"Oh, shit," Breana said, slurring. "Thanks, girl." She hiccupped before stumbling to get another drink.

I was about to intervene before she mistakenly poisoned herself when I spotted a familiar face walking by.

I wasn't sure what compelled me to go after her, but I left the guarded section without a word, dodged the waitresses speeding by, and pushed through some of the people whose sections had spilled over into others until I caught up to the small group of women the plus-sized beauty was leading to a section of her own.

"Demi?"

She stopped, hearing her name, and turned. A warm smile instantly appeared when she saw me. "Atlas? What are you doing here, girl?"

I accepted the hug she offered before shrugging. "Having a good time like everyone else."

"Yeah, except you know that your ass is too young for this club. Be real with me." She gave me a stern look. "Did you sneak in?"

I flashed a secret smirk before shaking my head. "No. I just know the right people."

"Okay, girl. I see you." Demi looked me up and down and nodded, silently giving me my props. I didn't tell her it was Ruen that put tonight's fit together since it was the woman that made the clothes and not the other way around. "Did you come alone?"

"Not exactly," I grumbled before pointing to my section where Ruen's friends now had a gang of hardheads commandeering the space. Breana was now twerking her ass on the same guy that had been recording her while her friends were busy snorting the white powder piled on the table and arguing with the girls from the neighboring section that the guys had wandered over from.

Clearly, the men were freeloaders willing to pit women against each other for their own entertainment, but there was no seeing the light once the first punch was thrown. An all-out brawl started between the group of girls while the men, drinking up their liquor and occupying their space, laughed and filmed the whole thing.

They'd be viral by morning. I was sure of it.

Demi winced when she peeped the scene, confirming what I already knew. Ruen's friends were ratchet as hell.

I silently weighed my options. I could leave or go up to the deejay booth to watch Ruen work. I was still thinking it over when Demi tapped my shoulder. "I can see the wheels turning, and no. You don't need to be around all of that. Come chill with me and my girls. We have a section."

I hesitated. "I don't want to impose."

"How can that be when I offered?" Demi turned away to rejoin her friends, and I reluctantly followed, feeling curious gazes on me as I entered the section. "Ladies, this is my little mama. Atlas, these are my girls—Chrissy, Mylah, Zoey, and Kingsley."

They all waved, and I returned the gesture as I sat next to Demi.

"Atlas," Kingsley mused with a continuous snap of her fingers. "Where have I heard that name before?"

"Probably from geography class, you dumb bitch. What do you mean?" Chrissy immediately roasted her friend.

"Don't do me," Kingsley said with a roll of her eyes. "I've been hearing that name in more than a few circles. Word on the street is that Rowdy's whorish ass has a girl now." Her gaze finally traveled to me, and I saw the budding hostility she tried to hide under the guise of harmless curiosity. "Same name as you."

"Be so for real," Zoey interjected. "This girl looks like she's twelve. No offense," she offhandedly threw my way. I was very much offended, but it wasn't worth arguing over, and with a stranger, no less. "She doesn't even look like she's old enough to be in this club, much less date that green-eyed monster."

"That's the thing. Everybody's saying his girl is young. Like *real, real* young. And I don't know about you, but I don't know too many bitches walking around with her name."

I said nothing as I listened to their back and forth.

What was there to say? I'd risked complicating my friendship with Ruen in order to avoid an even more complex situation with Rowdy, and somehow, someway, that overbearing negro had found a way to disturb my peace without even being here.

Call me crazy, but at least two of Demi's friends sounded like they'd known him intimately. Kingsley was the most obvious of all. She looked seconds away from crying in a corner while Zoey seemed resigned to the fact that Rowdy belonged to neither of them.

The jealousy and frustration amalgamating in my gut nearly came to a head when Mylah, the fourth and most quiet of Demi's friends, spoke first. "Um, ladies? She's sitting right there. You can just ask her who she is."

All four sets of eyes turned to me while Demi pointedly focused on mixing herself a drink. I was sure she already knew the answer but was allowing me the space to decide if I wanted to expose myself or not.

"So?" Chrissy prodded when too much time passed without a peep from me. "Are you her?"

I swallowed. "Yes…and no."

"Well, what does that mean?" Zoey asked with a frown. "You're either *the* Atlas or you're not."

"As I've already told you, I am she, but it sounds like a few details were embellished, so I cannot and will not confirm anything other than my truth." I rolled my eyes.

"Such as?" Kingsley interrogated.

The other three had backed off, understanding that I wasn't open to discussing my relationship with Rowdy. Kingsley, on the other hand, couldn't seem to catch the hint.

"We're not dating." I made sure to meet each and every one of their gazes so they could see my sincerity and drop it. "I only work for him."

Chrissy and Zoey exchanged confused looks while Kingsley held my gaze. "What kind of work do you do for him?" she inquired. "I heard you stayed over by the Cove."

"What does where she stays have to do with her job, Kingsley?"

She waved Mylah off before saying, "I just want to know if she works for him as she says or if she's just another ho that takes credit cards."

I'd already guessed the root of Kingsley's problem, but I knew for certain she had me fucked up.

"Chill, Kiki," Demi snapped, finally speaking up and checking her friend before I could. "You asked a question, and she answered. Now let it go! All this shade you throwing is unnecessary. You're doing way too much for a man you only fucked once," she added, letting me know on the sly what Kingsley's problem was.

"There's no shade," Kingsley said with a false smile. "You guys know I like to joke around." She waved Demi off before grabbing her drink and watching the crowd on the dance floor below as she rocked her hips to the beat.

"Anyway." Demi rolled her eyes at her friend before turning to me. "I'm so sorry," she mouthed to me. "You okay?"

I nodded as I searched for the words to assure Demi that I appreciated her help but could handle my own. I knew girls like Kingsley would only keep coming, hitting harder and cutting deeper unless you nipped it in the bud from the start.

Ruen appeared a moment later, and I exhaled my relief.

"Oh, shit. There you are. I've been looking all over for you. I thought you ditched me again."

I shot to my feet and met her at the bottom of the stairs that led up to Demi's section. "I'm here," I reassured her. "What are *you* doing here? Shouldn't you be working?"

Ruen waved me off. "Someone told me about the fight, so I came to see if you were okay."

"I'm fine. I ran into a friend," I said, pointing to Demi, who noticed and waved hello at Ruen before focusing on Zoey, who had asked her a question.

"Oh, cool. I was going to invite you up with me, but I'm sure you'll have much more fun here with your friends."

It seemed petty to correct her and tell her that they were Demi's friends and not mine, so I let it go. "Speaking of friends, yours were… interesting."

"Who? The girls from the section?" Ruen wrinkled her cute freckled nose. "I don't know those bitches. Breana did me a solid, so I owed her one. That's all."

"Oh." That made a lot more sense than Ruen associating herself with those gutter rats.

"Anyway, I have to get back. This set is almost done."

"Okay."

Ruen kissed my cheek, and I blushed a little. Thankfully she didn't notice as she quickly disappeared into the crowd, heading toward the deejay booth.

I realized I had to pee, so I told Demi where I was going before fighting my way through the crowd to the long line waiting outside the bathroom.

It took ten minutes before my turn came.

The bathroom only had three stalls, so I took the only free one in the middle. I must have drunk more than I thought because it seemed like I was peeing forever.

I was alone in the bathroom by the time I was done, so I pulled out my phone and sat on the toilet lid to enjoy the peace and quiet for a few moments.

There were a few texts from Rowdy, but I chose to ignore those. Instead, I checked my email and saw that I had one from Professor Saunders asking how things were going.

She was so sweet.

I smiled as I typed back a reply. I was still typing when the music outside became louder and then muffled again as the bathroom door swung open and then closed. I paid no mind to the footsteps traveling across the tile until the shadow they belonged to darkened my stall.

A moment later, the door rattled when the person pulled on the handle.

"Someone's in here," I called out.

Instead of trying the next one, the person yanked on the handle even harder as if they were trying to tear the entire door off.

"Uhh, helloooo? What part of occupied do you not understand?"

The nut job didn't respond and yanked on the handle again. This time, a screw fell loose.

Oh, shit.

Another hard tug, and they'd be in.

Done with this day, I shot to my feet and unlocked the door. "Is it really that serious? There are two other stalls that are empty, weirdo. Just—" I ripped the door open without thought, and the rest of my rant died at finding Rowdy's scowling mug on the other side.

He was no longer in his work uniform from this morning. He was dressed in all black with the hood of his sweatshirt thrown over his head and concealing part of his handsome face.

My brain shouted, *Run*, and I jolted into action.

Before I could shut the door in his face, however, Rowdy slowly stepped into the stall with me, pushing me back until we were both closed inside.

"Wha—um—what...what are you doing here?"

Without saying a word, he slipped my phone out of my hand. "I guess you don't need a phone since you don't like to answer this motherfucker, huh?"

My eyes widened, and I silently shook my head, but he held it up in my face anyway, gripped each end with both hands, and snapped it in half.

He *snapped it*...in *half.*

I didn't even want to know what he could do to *me* if he could do *that*.

A choked gasp escaped me, and then I quickly found my voice. "Why did you do that?" I screamed.

"Who the fuck you raising your voice at?" he barked back while getting all in my face. I swallowed my retort since I didn't relish a repeat of this morning. "Next time, you answer when I call, Atlas. If I have to track you down again, I'm putting my foot in your ass."

I didn't really believe he'd hurt me, but I did believe he'd make me sorry. Either way, I was beyond caring. "Fuck you. You're not my father."

It was the straw that broke the camel's back.

One angry kiss in the heat of the moment led to him shoving up my red leather skirt and throwing me against the stall door. Rowdy turned me until my front was pressed against the door and he was looming behind me.

Rowdy quickly ripped open his belt, and then his jeans and boxers were shoved down around his ankles. I felt his chest at my back a moment later, his dick poking around my wet hole, and when he entered me, it was rough and ruthless. He made me take it all, filling me up, and then he pummeled my pussy from behind and talked shit.

"You..." *Thrust.* "Gon'..." *Thrust.* "Learn..." *Thrust.* "Not..." *Thrust.* "To..." *Thrust.* "Play..." *Thrust.* "With..." *Thrust.* "Me."

I was mid-scream when I heard the bathroom door swing open and heels clicking on the tile as someone entered. I knew Rowdy heard, but he didn't care as he continued to fuck me without discretion.

"Atlas?" the intruder called out.

I squeezed my eyes closed when I recognized the concerned voice and realized it was the worst possible person standing on the other side listening to Rowdy screw me.

"You gave her my pussy?" he asked me for the third time. His voice mixed with the sound of our skin clapping together, the stall door rattling under our weight, and the music outside as he fucked me.

"Nooooo."

"Why you lying?"

I squealed when he paused, bent his knees slightly, and slammed inside me from a different angle. "Oh, fuck! I'm not! I'm not!" He was simply hitting it too deep for me to sound convincing.

"But you want to, don't you?"

"N-no."

"Yes, you do," he said calmly and matter-of-factly as he kissed the side of my face. "I know you do."

"Mm-mm," I continued to deny. Rowdy was much too jealous for me ever to admit the truth. I was curious about Ruen, but it wasn't worth the bloodshed.

This, fucking me in a public bathroom while she listened on the other side, was bad and embarrassing enough, thank you. Neither of us was even attempting to be discreet as the force of Rowdy's thrusts threw our bodies against the door, making it rattle violently.

"Atlas!" Ruen tugged on the broken door handle, but Rowdy was stronger. His hand was gripping the top, holding it closed while he continued to brutalize my body. An alpha in her own right, I knew Ruen wasn't letting it go until she knew that whatever was happening on the other side was consensual.

I'm sure it sounded bad, but it felt so fucking good.

"Answer her," Rowdy goaded, hitting me with a particularly mean stroke and stealing the words before I could. My eyes had rolled to the back of my head. "Tell her how much you love this dick."

"I-I'm fi-i-ine!"

He chuckled, but it was dry and without humor when I pointedly left out the rest. It didn't matter in the end. He made sure it was obvious how much I loved being used by him.

I came so hard that it was impossible to hold back when I screamed his name.

Satisfied, his rhythm slowed—changed. His hips began jerking against my own, and I knew what it meant.

"Wait!" I struggled to free myself from his arms, but they tightened around me, making my heart drop when he held me still. "Please don't," I begged. "Please, Owen. I'm not—you can't—"

Rowdy shoved inside me one last time and came inside my unprotected body with a long groan that was both barbaric and obscene.

I knew it was all for Ruen's benefit.

And to teach me a lesson.

The bathroom had fallen quiet, but I knew. She was still on the other side, waiting, listening.

"Oh, God." I palmed my face as I struggled to catch my breath. Why couldn't she have left? There was no way I could face her now.

Unfazed, Rowdy didn't say a word as he slowly pulled out of me. He then dug inside my clutch hanging on the hook and pulled out a couple of the wipes he knew I kept inside before cleaning himself and then me with a fresh one. Tossing them both inside the toilet and then flushing, he pulled my skirt back over my ass before reaching around me to unlock the door, but I refused to move so he could open it.

"Don't be shy now." He pressed a gentle kiss to my cheek. "Come on."

I finally shifted to the side and let him open the door.

My gaze was stuck on the floor as Rowdy forced me from the stall with a firm hand on my waist.

"The next time you two want to fuck on my behalf," Ruen said, coming into view when she abandoned her perch on the sink and rescued my tattered thong that had fallen from my leg. "Either invite me to join or leave me out of it."

"Thanks," Rowdy said as he snatched my torn panties from her and trashed them. I swear it was like déjà vu with these two quietly pissing over me. "I'll remember that."

Oh, God.

Wait...

What?

I looked up at Rowdy, who was already staring down at me, watching carefully for my reaction, but I didn't give him one. Instead, I moved away from him over to the sink while being careful not to stand too close to Ruen.

Why wasn't she leaving?

I risked a glance her way and found her watching Rowdy, a mocking sneer on her lips. As if she felt me watching, I saw the minute shift of her gaze my way—long enough to see me mouth, "Please don't."

Her lips twisted wryly before she finally straightened and started to leave. At the door, she paused with one foot over the threshold as she looked over her shoulder at me. "I guess this means you won't be sleeping over?"

Before I could tell her no, we both heard the unmistakable sound of a gun being cocked.

Ruen laughed like we didn't both know Rowdy wouldn't hesitate to kill her before calmly leaving with a dainty wave of her fingers.

My gaze flew to the mirror in time to see Rowdy tucking his gun back inside his waist.

"Is it really that serious?"

"Hell yeah. I didn't write my name all over that pussy for nothing." He jerked his chin toward the sink to get me going. "Wash your hands so we can go."

"Okay." He pressed a kiss to the top of my head, and I tried not to simper like a love-sick fool.

I wasn't in love. Not yet. But I was a fool.

I dried my hands and then moisturized them because there was nothing cute about ashy knuckles, and then we left the bathroom together, hand in hand.

Rowdy might not have cared about the dirty looks thrown our way, but I did. I knew he must have threatened to shoot the women waiting if they came inside, which was why the line had become twice as long as it was before. It felt like I was doing the walk of shame as the women turned up their noses at me. One high-fived me though.

They probably all heard me taking that dick.

"Wait." I stopped in my tracks when Rowdy attempted to pull me toward the exit. "I need to let Demi know that I'm leaving so she doesn't worry."

Rowdy scowled, but he didn't argue as he followed me back to the VIP area, where Mylah, Chrissy, and Zoey stood on the couches, shaking their asses like they were being paid for it. I couldn't help smiling at their antics and would have joined them if Rowdy hadn't chosen that moment to rest his arm around my shoulder, keeping me by his side.

"Don't even think about it," he whispered in my ear. "Now, say what you got to say, and let's go."

"Whatever."

I searched the section for Demi but didn't see her or Kingsley. My gaze roamed the surrounding area until I found them standing a few feet away near the glass half-wall overlooking the dance floor. I escaped from underneath Rowdy's arm and approached them with caution since it looked like they were having a private conversation.

"Demi, I'm just saying," I overhead Kingsley say. "You my girl and all, but you know he's the reason I had to start getting my hair done across town." She fluttered her lashes while patting her weave. "That dick was too damn good to say no to."

I didn't have to question if Kingsley had meant Rowdy.

"Keep it real, Kiki, and I will do the same," Demi retorted with her back to me. "That man wanted you even less after he had you than he did before you forced yourself on him. You basically begged for the dick, and now you're stuck in la-la land, hoping that man even remembers you."

"At least I had the guts to go for what I wanted, unlike you, who let a *White* girl steal her man."

"What does Harper being White have to do with anything, Kingsley?"

"It's just so cliché."

"That would be true if Roc had been mine, but he wasn't, no more than he was Harper's. He's for the streets, and that's where I left him. My worth transcended anything he could offer me, and I knew it. Can you say the same, Kingsley?"

Rather than answer her, Kingsley chose that moment to notice me. "Uh…can I help you?"

"You can't even help yourself, so no."

Her hackles visibly rose as she attempted to step around Demi, who promptly placed herself between us. "Excuse me, bitch?"

Ignoring her, I shifted my attention to Demi. "Look, I didn't mean to eavesdrop. I just came to let you know I was leaving."

"Leaving?" she protested. Before Demi could ask why, her gaze suddenly shifted above my head.

I smelled his cologne a heartbeat before I felt his warmth at my back. My body liked having him so close to me and shivered in pleasure.

Unfortunately, it was all witnessed by Demi, whose gaze was flitting back and forth between us before narrowing on Rowdy.

"Atlas, do you want to go? You don't have to if you don't want to," she assured me while inching closer like she would protect me from Rowdy if need be.

It made my heart clench for two different reasons—overwhelming gratitude and fear for her safety. I knew Rowdy had no limits when pushed, and I was beginning to understand that I was one of those triggers.

It was a reality I was unused to since I hadn't come first for anyone in a long time.

"Chill, Dem," Rowdy told her, calmer than I expected. "No one is forcing her hand."

That wasn't entirely true, but I chose to let it slide. I *wanted* to leave with him, but I also knew I had no choice even if I didn't.

"What's the matter, Rowdy?" Kingsley taunted while stepping forward and making herself the center of attention. "You couldn't find a *woman* your own age?"

Instead of rising to her obvious bait, I looked up at Rowdy, watching for his reaction.

He was staring at her like he smelled shit in the air.

"It's wild that you're pressing me like I owe you an explanation when I don't even know you," he flatly stated.

Kingsley's jaw dropped as red flooded her high-yellow skin. "Oh, no, negro. Don't pretend you got amnesia just because your little girlfriend is standing here. She don't even look legal. I should call the police and tell them you're dating preschoolers."

Rowdy placed his hands on my hips as if he were about to push me out of the way, so I spun in his arms and wrapped mine around his neck. I knew what he would do to Kingsley if I let go, so I threw caution to the wind and rose onto my tiptoes, pressing my lips against his.

He didn't kiss me back right away.

Instead, he stared at Kingsley as if he would actually murder her in a club filled with hundreds of witnesses.

I licked the seam of his lips, and my stomach tightened when his lips parted ever so slightly, granting me access a heartbeat before he took over.

With one kiss, I'd confirmed the rumors.

Panicking a little, I pulled away, and his nasty ass chased me to continue. I pressed my finger against his lips and said, "Take me home so we can finish this in your bed."

He stared at me like he was debating taking me right here before seeing the light and pecking my lips twice. "*Our* bed. And that's a fucking bet."

THIRTY

Atlas

We were standing in front of a hot-air balloon.

After playing hooky from work for the last two days and spending an entire day fucking, Rowdy dragged me out of bed, sore and half-alive, to this empty golf course just before sunset. He whispered to the pilot while I silently mustered the courage to tell him I wasn't climbing in that damn thing.

But I didn't want to fight after the peaceful day we'd had.

We didn't just fuck.

Rowdy and I had talked about everything under the sun and had gotten to know each other in a way we hadn't been able to before, and well, I *really* didn't want to fight.

As if my pushy, not-quite boyfriend could sense my unease, he glanced back at me and frowned when he noticed me still standing there. I chewed on my lip as I watched him shake hands with the pilot before swaggering over to me, the furrow in his brow increasing with each step until he stood in front of me.

"What's the matter, Dream?" He grabbed my hips and pulled me close while kissing my forehead and cheek. I sighed and leaned into the protection of his body. His chest felt so warm and strong under my hands.

"Oh, nothing. Just…I think I'm afraid of heights. Please don't be mad."

His cut brows rose toward his freshly lined-up hairline. I tried not to focus on it, knowing that some bitch had her hands in his hair, and there was nothing I could do about it. For *now*. "You think?"

I gulped and shifted on my feet. "Well, I've never been in a position to test the theory before, but…yes."

Rowdy was quiet as he searched my gaze, and for once, I couldn't tell what he was thinking. "Do you want to go?"

My surprised gaze shot from his chest to his face and then to the blue and white striped balloon and the pensive middle-aged White man with a thick graying mustache readying it for flight.

I gulped again before nodding slowly.

It took me longer to meet Rowdy's gaze this time since I'd already guessed how much trouble and money he'd probably spent on this date. "Are you mad?"

"Give me your mouth."

My heart stuttered in my chest as I lifted onto the tips of my toes and did as he ordered. He kissed me long and deeply until all I wanted him to do was drag me inside those trees and fuck me against a tree.

When he ended the kiss, I chased him, but he stopped me with a hand on my nape. "I know you've been through some shit, so it might take you a while to believe me, but your back is my back, Atlas, and I'll always have it."

It took a moment longer for the lust fogging my head to lift, and when it did, my belly filled with butterflies. Suddenly, a hot-air balloon seemed unnecessary.

My feet were already floating off the ground.

"But—"

"Nah, no buts," he cut me off sternly. "You don't want to do it, so we won't. Let's go."

I pushed away from him to eye him skeptically. "Just like that?"

Rowdy tucked his bottom lip between his teeth and nodded. "Just like that."

"It looks expensive, Owen." And nonrefundable.

He slapped my ass for arguing before pulling me close again. "So suck my dick while I find us something to eat, and we'll call it even."

I didn't need to ask if his nasty ass was serious. I already knew he was, and it took all my effort not to fall to my knees and suck his big, black dick right here.

Rowdy kissed me again and then looked over his shoulder at the pilot. "Aye, bruh, we out. My girl said I got her fucked up," his ignorant ass called out.

The pilot chuckled and waved us off while I hid my face out of second-hand embarrassment. Rowdy could be so damn ghetto.

"Come on." He grabbed my hand, and we started the long trek back to the car.

We might have made it five steps before my head turned, and I stared at the large balloon blocking out the setting sun.

Why did he bring me here?

That question kept echoing in my head, and it wouldn't stop. It grew louder with each step until I stopped in my tracks. "Wait."

Rowdy obliged me and looked down at me quizzically. I inhaled and exhaled slowly, knowing that once I let the words free, I wouldn't let myself take them back. "I want to do it."

Rowdy's expression turned skeptical, so rather than trying to convince him, I let his hand go and marched back toward the balloon.

"Changed your mind?" the pilot asked in a thick Southern accent when he noticed my approach.

I squared my shoulders and nodded. *God, I want to fucking puke.* I ignored my queasiness and grabbed the edge of the basket.

"Fuck is you doing?" Rowdy snatched me back without an answer before I could begin my graceless climb inside. His long body was like a furnace as he kept my back pinned to his chest.

I looked over my shoulder at him. "I told you. I can do this."

"I know you can. I never doubted it for a second, so what are you trying to prove?"

"Nothing," I answered honestly. "According to you, as long as I'm with you, I have nothing to fear, right? So let's go, hero."

"I'm not Superman," he returned flatly. "I can't fly us away if this shit crashes."

I grinned and wiggled against his dick lodged against my spine. God, he wasn't even fully hard. That damn dick of his should be classified as a lethal weapon. I truly hoped this ride wouldn't last long because I couldn't wait to get him alone so I could bounce all over it. "I bet that killed your soul just a little to admit, didn't it?"

The lion of Idlewild was far from humble.

Rowdy's stern expression broke, and he smirked. His grip on me gentled before he pecked my lips. "You sure?" he whispered. "Don't do this for me, Dream. I'm too far gone. Nothing you do will make me less obsessed with you."

I reached up and pressed my hand to his cheek. "I'm doing it for us," I whispered back. Besides, my heart wouldn't let me leave. There was a reason he'd brought me here.

"Bet." It was all he said before that asshole lifted me without warning. I yelped when he dumped me inside the basket before basically stepping in after me, thanks to his freakishly long legs. "We're ready," he announced to the pilot.

The pilot spat out his chewing tobacco, then quickly ran through a safety demonstration.

Minutes later, we were lifting off the ground.

My eyes immediately snapped closed, and my fresh acrylic nails that I made Rowdy un-ass eighty dollars for after embarrassing me at the club dug into his arms as I clung to him. He didn't complain, just rubbed my back as he tried to coax me into enjoying the view.

"Oh, shit. Look, baby, birds."

"Mm-hmm. They're so pretty," I lied as I burrowed my face

deeper against his chest. Rowdy snickered, knowing full well that I was not about to open my eyes for some damn birds.

He tried a little longer to coax me into looking before abandoning his patient approach…and me.

My heart tightly clenched when Rowdy pried himself away from me. I whimpered and made a desperate grab for him, but he stepped out of reach, forcing me to blindly chase after him.

"Owen!" I pleaded when my search came up empty.

I collided with the low wall of the basket, my hands grasping the wicker edge for purchase at the same time that I felt a punishing grip around my nape, keeping me from spilling over.

My eyes flew open, and words lodged in my lungs, my fear overshadowed by wonder as I gaped at the breathtaking view.

"Oh. Wow." I was only vaguely aware of Rowdy pressing himself against me from behind, his arms caging me in protectively as I admired Idlewild and the mountains that surrounded it from twenty-five hundred feet in the air. "It's so beautiful, Owen."

Up here, out of reach and away from it all, it felt like anything was possible.

It felt like *we* were possible.

Rowdy hummed his agreement, nuzzling my hair before kissing the top of my head. "I knew your scary ass would like it."

"Yes, you did." Nodding, I took a page from his book and reached back, taking a firm grip on his nuts without warning and squeezing until I felt the strained puff of air on my cheek that told me I had his undivided attention. "But do me a favor, and don't play with me like that again."

"Let me go, Atlas." Feeling his hand around my wrist, I squeezed harder, digging my sharp nails in for good measure. A moment longer, and I'd probably even break the skin. "Fuck, baby. Aight." His pitch raised a little when I still didn't let go. "Aight, aight, damn!"

Satisfied that we understood each other, I released him and smiled to myself, tuning Rowdy out as he grumbled and talked shit. I was too busy admiring the view he'd tricked me into enjoying.

It really was gorgeous.

Not even Rowdy could resist its call. He stopped fussing eventually to join me in the moment.

"Will all of our dates be this adventurous?"

I felt him shrug and kiss the skin behind my ear, a delighted shiver working down my spine. "If you want it to."

My lips parted, but no answer came. This was not something I would ever have done—alone or even with a friend.

But with Rowdy?

Somehow, I knew I'd dive off a cliff if only he said he was coming too. With him, I felt so vulnerable yet so fearless at the same time. I knew nothing could touch me as long as he stalked my shadow.

Rowdy cleared his throat before I could fall too deep down the rabbit hole.

"I have something I wanted to ask you." He sounded uncharacteristically nervous, making me suck in a break a moment before his arms slipped around my waist, anchoring me to him.

Whatever Rowdy wanted to ask me, he wasn't certain my answer wouldn't be no. He wanted to assure himself I couldn't run away—as if being stuck in a hot-air balloon with him wasn't enough.

"So, ask," I said with more confidence than I felt.

Rowdy pinched my butt and tightened his hold when I tried to turn around. "I like you, Dream, more than I've ever liked anyone. I think about you all day, and even when I try to stop, I just wonder if you're thinking about me too. I love making you smile, and I'm obsessed with making you come. I have no intentions of stopping anytime soon, so running away from me is a big fucking problem. I'd rather spend that time giving you what you came to Idlewild looking for."

I stiffened in his arms as my heart began to race. Did he know about the letter?

No.

He couldn't know.

"I want to give you shelter and be your peace. I want to take care of you, Dream. I want to be yours. I won't ask if you like me too because I don't waste time with stupid questions. Instead, I'll only ask one." I held my breath and waited even though I already knew what his question—and what my answer—would be. "Can I be your boyfriend, Atlas Ilana Beck?"

My heart stuttered in my chest at the same time that a startled laugh broke free. "Um, don't you mean will I be your girlfriend?"

"No."

When he didn't elaborate, I sighed. "Explain."

"Aight, it's simple. You were mine from the very first day. From the moment I tried to fire you, and you begged me not to. Deny it or reject it—it makes no fucking difference. I'm the unshakable truth that will haunt you forever."

I stared out at the gorgeous mountain peak that seemed so close yet so far away.

That was the reality of Rowdy and me.

We were so close to something real yet still so far away. Our foundation was still building and could crumble at the slightest wind.

"Even if I turn you down?"

He was quiet for so long I was afraid he wouldn't answer—or say something crazy and ruin the moment.

And then he spoke.

"I thought fucking you would be enough, but I was lying to myself. I started to enjoy the chase a little too much, Dream. Suddenly, I had this endless patience like I'd follow you forever until you said yes, and I knew I wasn't running you down just to fuck you. I was looking to make you mine. I kept forcing myself inside your head, not knowing I was pulling you into mine. His lips brushed my ear, and then he whispered, "You own me." My lips parted, and I couldn't quite catch my breath after his quiet confession. "You temper this animal inside of me, Dream, but you match it, too. My obsession with you…it's violent and ugly, but it's *real*. You're the most honest thing I've felt in a long time, and

I'm begging you for one more chance. We can't go back in time, but we can change our future. Ask me not to let you go again, and I promise I won't."

My stomach dipped and my breath left me in a rush as relief flooded my veins and silent tears ran down my cheeks. Everything he'd confessed to…I'd felt it too.

I'd been obsessed with him ever since I found his picture waiting for me. I knew I was coming to find him even before I read the letter.

I came to Idlewild for *him*.

Rowdy's arms loosened enough to pass a soothing hand over my stomach as if he could sense my inner turmoil, and the truth I'd hidden even from myself.

"Fucking you, taking care of you, coming home to you every day…I haven't felt this passionate about something since I fixed my first car. I can't stop, Atlas. I will *never* stop. I need you to claim me too."

I sucked in a breath when that same hand traveled beneath my dress, finding my panties with ease and slipping inside…

Remembering we weren't alone, I grabbed his wrist. His next words loosened my grip, however, before I could stop his fingers from finding my clit and stealing away every rational thought until there was only him.

"You think this will end with you in love and alone, but what if you're wrong?" His fingers sailed through my wetness, dipping lower until he found my entrance. He circled my wet hole, taunting me until I whined, and then he pressed inside. Rowdy filled me up until my hips answered, winding to get him deeper.

"You always said you hated how I treated the women I've fucked, but you never asked me why," he continued. I gasped when he added a third finger. "It's because of you. I didn't just wait my entire life for you, Atlas. I saved all my kisses and compliments. I swallowed every promise. I guarded my loyalty…for you. I kept my heart hard as stone so that when the day came I found the woman I couldn't hold any of that back for, I'd know without a doubt that I'd found the one."

"Oh, Owen."

He growled and stabbed his fingers in and out of my abused pussy. It hurt so fucking good. I was so obscenely wet for him that nothing else mattered. "Fucking say it, Dream. Say yes. Make me yours."

The heel of his palm slammed against my clit, and my mouth fell open when he held it there. "Oh, my God," I whined. The answer he sought mingled with my gasp that slipped free as I came. "Yes!"

The burner keeping the balloon in the air roared to life at that moment, drowning out my ecstasy.

"Fuck." I heard Rowdy's mumbled curse a second before I felt his fingers slip free. Spent, I leaned back against his chest and stared through lowered lids at the view before me. My bliss was momentary, interrupted only by the unmistakable sound of his belt loosening and then his zipper lowering.

I stiffened in his arms.

I know he didn't think he was about to fuck me *now*.

"Owen?"

"Hush, baby." He hiked my dress over my ass and pressed closer.

"No, really, wait." My heart was racing even as I tried not to panic. "The pilot," I reminded him.

Ignoring me, Rowdy wrapped his hand around my throat, keeping me in place with one hand and shoving my panties aside with the other. I tried again to reason with him when I felt the flared tip of his dick pressing against my swollen lips.

"He'll see us!" I squawked.

Rowdy groaned as he pressed forward and entered me with one long stroke. The rest of my protests died on my lips as my lashes fluttered, and I fell under the spell of his magical penis.

Fuck, the view was beautiful.

Still not quite used to his size, I whimpered when he shifted, and then I closed my eyes, knowing what came next.

However, instead of the ruthless pounding, Rowdy wrapped his arms around me before resting his chin on my shoulder.

"Still enjoying the view, dear?" the asshole mocked in a "proper" voice loud enough for the pilot to overhear.

"I hate you," I whispered as I stared at the setting sun.

Rowdy chuckled and pressed his lips to my ear. "No, you don't." His hips flexed with a small, imperceptible pump. "You love this dick, don't you?" I kept my mouth stubbornly closed. "Say it before I make you scream it." The next punch of his hips was more forceful, stealing my breath while keeping our activities hidden.

"I love your dick," I admitted breathlessly.

"What was that? I can't hear you."

"I said I love your dick, asshole."

Rowdy pressed his mouth against my temple, his perfect teeth bared and cutting against my skin, his voice rough from holding back. "You want me to stop fucking you?"

"No, Daddy." I fought the urge not to say fuck it, bend over, and let Rowdy go to town on me. I wanted my pussy pounded, not this gentle covert bullshit.

"Throw that ass back then."

"I can't. He'll see," I whined.

Rowdy's grip tightened around my throat as he angled my head back enough to look into my eyes. "Where am I right now, Atlas?"

"Behind me."

"Which means?"

I swallowed, knowing what he wanted to hear. "You have my back."

Rowdy kissed my temple. "Then do as I said. Give me that puss."

I sucked in a breath, my walls pulsing wildly around him at the authority in his tone. It kick-started my hips as they began to move freely. I knew Rowdy would preserve my modesty as much as possible.

As good as this felt, that old man could watch for all I cared.

It wasn't long before I truly threw caution to the wind, and I found myself bent, arms resting on the wicker rail as I stared out at the city approaching slowly from our descent.

"Oh, God, yes!" I cried under the cover of the burner and the wind. I'd abandoned all reason and wildly threw my ass and hips back, fucking myself on his monster dick the way Rowdy had known I needed to be taken.

The only thing that could have possibly made it better would have been losing our clothes, too, so I could feel his skin against mine. I already knew it wasn't happening, though. Rowdy was not about to let another man see my naked body.

"Fuck me, Daddy! Fuck me, Daddy! Yes, yes, yes!"

Rowdy and I grunted in harmony as he held onto me. I could feel him watching me and the struggle it took to hold himself still as I lost myself in the pleasure of using him so shamelessly.

It only made me that much more eager to please him.

My second orgasm came swiftly, and I didn't fight it or try to prolong it this time. I straightened on weakened legs, letting his hard dick slip free of my pussy, and turned to face him.

"Daddy?"

"Fuck," he groaned. "Why'd you stop?"

"Because…" I stared into his green eyes as I slid my hands up his hard chest. "I've been a good girl, right?"

He wordlessly nodded.

"And good girls drink their protein?" The confused frown slowly disappeared from his face as I lowered to my knees.

"Ah, shit," he moaned when I swallowed him whole.

There was no need to let my saliva build—not when my arousal still coated him, making the head nice and sloppy the way he liked it. I pulled back, my tongue lashing his frenulum, where my taste still lingered before taking him deep once again.

I couldn't quite describe the look in his eyes as he watched me suck him off. Vulnerable? Awe? Obsessed? Whatever it was, it made me feel powerful even while on my knees.

I used my free hand—the one not wrapped around his shaft to keep him from going too deep—and cupped his balls while I moved my mouth up and down. My lingering arousal and saliva mixed with his pre-cum gargled noisily at the back of my throat, and the gleam in Rowdy's eyes told me he liked it.

He was holding back still, refusing to fuck my face, and I wondered if it was to keep what we were up to a secret or if he was being a gentleman and letting me keep control.

He busted down my throat before I could discover the answer.

"Mmmh." I loudly smacked my lips after I swallowed his cum. "Yummy."

"You so fucking nasty," Rowdy praised. He rubbed the fat head of his dick, still dripping cum, on my bottom lip, and I dutifully licked it away before he helped me to my feet and immediately shoved his tongue in my mouth, groaning when he tasted himself on my tongue. "Come on," he told me when he broke the kiss. "Let me get you home so I can eat and fuck that pussy right."

"Okay."

I looked around and realized we'd landed and were now alone in the basket. Rowdy hopped over before helping me out, and I spotted the pilot returning from speaking to another couple already waiting for their turn a few feet away.

"Appreciate it." Rowdy slipped him a fat wad of cash when he shook the pilot's hand.

"Happy to help," the blushing pilot drawled. "Good luck."

"Oh, my God," I whispered as soon as he walked away. "I think he saw us, Owen."

Rowdy gave me an incredulous look as we started the long walk back to the car, hand in hand. "Of course, he saw, Atlas. That basket ain't but fifty feet long, and we were the only people in it. What did you think the tip was for?"

My mouth fell open, and I covered my face with my hands. "Kill me. Just…kill me."

"Chill. He's not trippin' about it, so why are you?"

"Because it's embarrassing! He probably thinks we're weirdos."

"Then you haven't seen yourself when you're being fucked, Atlas. If you saw what I saw, you would know there's nothing to be embarrassed about."

"Whatever." I rolled my eyes. I was pissed at him but not more than myself at him for letting him break me down so completely.

Rowdy sighed. "The pilot knew all along, Atlas. The only one who wasn't in on it from the beginning was you."

"What?" My mind raced as I replayed every interaction from the beginning. "Is that why he wished us good luck? What did he mean?"

Rowdy grinned. "I told him you and I were recently married and having issues rekindling our flame after having our first kid. His only condition was that we keep our clothes on, and we keep him out of it." Rowdy bucked his eyes at me, and I couldn't help laughing at the outrageous yet kind-of-genius lie.

Our obvious age difference made it much more plausible that I was Rowdy's daughter, not his wife, though.

My smile slowly fell, and then I was hit with a sudden tsunami-sized wave of nausea that ended with me hurling my guts all over the golf course.

"I'm fine," I said, waving off Rowdy when he immediately crowded me.

Oh, God. I wasn't fine. What the hell was that?

Maybe it was the change in elevation or motion sickness. Or...something. I stood and forced a smile that made Rowdy narrow his gaze for a split second before he carefully lifted me in his arms and carried me the rest of the way to the car.

"I can walk, you know."

"I don't know shit," he told me and then tightened his hold.

I sighed and rested my head on his shoulders, letting him do what I was beginning to understand he did better than anyone else, including me—take care of me.

"What changed your mind about us?" I sleepily asked after a few minutes of getting lost in my thoughts.

Rowdy took so long to answer that I thought he hadn't heard me. We reached the car, and he placed me in the passenger seat before squatting until he was eye level with me.

"Ever since I brought you home, you've had one foot out the door, and I didn't like that shit. I kept telling myself you weren't going anywhere, and it wasn't because I wouldn't let you but because you wouldn't want to. And then you did. Keeping it real, you proving me wrong wasn't even that big of a shock. Fear of who I am doesn't stop you from calling me on my shit. It's what drew me to you. That...and this," he said, lightly tracing the discoloration on my face that, until recently, had been a great source of insecurity for me.

I wasn't blind, and I wasn't going to be fake humble by pretending I didn't know I was a beautiful brown girl. Still, no one had ever made me feel as beautiful as Owen did every day since I'd met him—not even Sutton's bitch-ass.

"My birthmark?" I asked, even though it was so much more than that. I'd been born with a rare case of congenital vitiligo that was mostly present on my breasts, thighs, belly, and feet.

The markings on my face, however, were different.

They were smaller and lighter, but the star-shaped patches couldn't be missed. They traveled from my left cheek to my right temple in a pattern I could never quite put my finger on.

My mother said it reminded her of how sailors once used the stars to navigate and had named me Atlas because of it.

"Why?" I asked when Rowdy nodded.

"Because it's proof that I was meant to find you."

I gave him a crooked smile. "Technically, I found you."

"You did," he agreed with a nod. "And you were the map all along." I blinked at him in shocked silence, wondering if he'd read my thoughts. "Do you believe in fate?" he asked me when I just gaped at him.

"I'm not sure. Maybe?"

"What if I told you the markings on your face follow the same pattern as one of the constellations?"

My belly dipped, and my breath rushed out of me as I searched his gaze for the answer. "I'd ask what constellation you're referring to."

But I didn't. Because I already knew.

Leo.

The markings on my face made the Leo constellation. I'd known the moment he'd posed the question.

Seeing the answer on my face, Rowdy smiled, then stood and closed my door before rounding the hood and climbing into the driver's seat.

In nineteen years, Rowdy had been the only one to ever figure it out, the only one who'd ever truly seen me.

I expected him to gloat about stunning me into silence, but he didn't. He just turned on Summer Walker even though he complained whenever I played her music, saying she made his ears bleed.

We rode in silence, vibin' to her album *Over It,* before a thought struck me, and I turned down the music, stealing his focus for a moment before it was forced back to the road. "What was the biggest shock?" At his confused frown, I added, "You said before that my trying to leave wasn't the biggest shock. What was?"

I could tell he didn't want to answer but did anyway after stopping at the light. He knew I wouldn't let it go. "Realizing I'd do anything to make you stay. Nothing was off limits, Atlas. Nothing. I let someone I wasn't sure about into my kingdom because it meant I could have you instead."

I held his gaze as I turned over his confession in my mind, and he stared right back at me until I couldn't take the distance anymore, and I found my way into his lap. Safe in his arms, the place I'd abandoned everything I knew to be, I kissed him, forcing traffic to go around us with an angry blare of their horns.

THIRTY-ONE

Atlas

WINTER LEFT, SPRING HAD COME AND GONE, AND NOW SUMMER was nearing its end as well. I wish I could say the six months since Rowdy and I became official had been pure bliss, but…I hadn't considered the backlash.

And since I was the first to hold that title, there had been no one to warn me.

Rowdy had put the word out on me long before he'd made his intentions known, but it was a different story when people saw the truth with their own eyes and knew it wasn't a rumor started by some clout chaser.

Nope.

I, Atlas Ilana Beck, was Rowdy Wray's official girl.

The position came with endless adoration, affection, respect, care, security, that big, beautiful Black dick, and the long list of enemies I'd inherited overnight.

I couldn't go anywhere without some girl Rowdy had fucked in the past trying to befriend me or fight me. Usually, it was the latter. It had gotten so bad that Rowdy now forbade me from going anywhere alone. Since I didn't have anyone else, it meant without *him*.

I sighed as I studied my reflection in the floor-length mirror.

My faux locs were a thing of the past, and I now wore my natural hair in two long stitch braids with my baby hair softly curling around my hairline. I admired the nude halter bikini clinging to my body one last time before grabbing the matching cover-up and tying it around my waist.

The decorative mirror leaning in the corner of the master closet was just one of the many additions I'd made to Rowdy's barren bedroom.

His room, along with the rest of his house, had been the picture of bachelorhood, bereft of furnishings and a personal touch. When I'd asked him why, he'd said there was no need when he was never home.

Rowdy then handed over his credit card and told me to buy whatever I needed to feel at home. I'd swallowed my rejection, knowing it would only lead to an argument. The last time we'd argued about money, my returning to school had been the cause.

We had been cuddled up on the couch, watching a scary movie, and at some point, during the new *Conjuring* movie, my mind had drifted to money. I'd made the mistake of asking him about his household bills.

Still facing the TV, his wary gaze slid to me, curled up next to him. "Why, Atlas?"

"Because I feel weird living here without contributing anything. It feels like I'm mooching off you."

Grabbing the remote, Rowdy pressed paused before giving me his full attention. "Do I strike you as a person who can be taken advantage of, Atlas?"

I didn't even need to think about the answer. "No."

"Then why are you sitting here thinking of ways to piss me off? What's the matter?" His brows dipped in contemplation like he was really trying to uncover my true motive for asking. "You want me to pipe you or something?"

I rolled my eyes. Of course, his mannish ass thought everything I did was to get him to fuck me. I mean, occasionally—most of the time—yeah. Definitely. *But not now. Not this time. "No, Owen. I'm serious.*

My paychecks aren't much—as you know—*but I can help out with the smaller bills like the electricity or groceries."*

"Nah."

"But—"

"I said no. If you want to help me, work on getting that school transfer, as we talked about. Your ass is stalling like you thought I wouldn't notice, so let's get this shit understood while it's in the air. When it comes to you, I'm always three steps ahead. Live it, breathe it, and don't ever doubt it. I didn't say anything before because, while I have no problems whatsoever steering this boat, sometimes, *I want you to choose us without feeling like I forced your hand. That's for you, not for me. I kicked morals to the curb a long time ago. You're young as fuck—so young that some days I struggle to convince myself that wanting you isn't an affront to nature. Most days, I forget you're only nineteen with your whole life ahead of you, and I'm back to square one—chasing your bumper. There's no me without you, so fuck it. Bills are the last thing you should be concerned about. Work on getting that degree, stacking your money, and fulfilling your dreams. I got the rest."*

He stared me down until the blazing warmth that traveled from my cheeks, pooled in my gut, and set my pussy on fire *before tickling my toes, finally settled enough for me to whisper, "Okay."*

"Cool." Rowdy reached for the remote and hit play, his gaze on the screen when he spoke again. "Oh, and, Atlas?"

"Yes, Owen?"

"Don't ever insult my manhood again."

Whatever that meant.

When the subject of money came up again, I didn't bother to suggest I use my own to make this house a home. I just smiled, thanked him, and started making a list.

Still, I started off small by buying a trash can.

While I didn't mean to disparage anyone's lifestyle or journey, I could no longer live with a store bag hanging from a random door handle as the trash.

I mean, *come on.*

The man was almost forty.

I considered ordering a simple ten-dollar one from Target but decided to test the limits of Rowdy's generosity by buying a ridiculously over-priced stainless-steel gadget that opened with a wave of your hand.

It was hard keeping a straight face when I demonstrated the trash can's magical powers to Rowdy—especially when I told him how much of his money I'd used to pay for it.

I was both excited and disappointed when he barely reacted with a "That's what's up" before leaving the room.

As far as I was concerned, he'd given me the green light to do whatever I wanted, so once the necessities were taken care of, I really started to get creative.

The first argument didn't start until I bought candles.

Apparently, I could spend a ridiculous three-figure amount on a *trash can*, but he drew the line at scented candles, saying he didn't want his house smelling like the back room of a strip club.

Now, I'd never been to a strip club—much less the back room—but I somehow doubted it smelled like strawberry pound cake from Bath and Body Works.

The final straw came when I tried to spruce up our bed with these cute decorative throw pillows I'd found. Rowdy made me watch while he cut them up with a kitchen knife until the stuffing and feathers littered our bedroom floor like a second rug.

Luckily, I'd gotten my period that week, so I was super hormonal, which made it easier to turn on the waterworks. I reminded him through my "uncontrollable sobs" that Ruen's empty guest room came with an open invitation if he couldn't get past our creative differences.

We haven't had any more issues since.

I grabbed a pair of sunglasses and my brand-new beach bag before leaving the huge closet that had been mostly empty before I moved in.

Rowdy, for all his brutish ways, spoiled me rotten.

I now had triple the amount of clothes, shoes, and accessories than when I'd arrived in Idlewild.

Wearing his signature frown, my boyfriend—*still getting used to that*—stepped into the bedroom at the same time I did.

"Damn, Dream, you ain't ready yet?" he immediately griped.

"I told you I could drive myself since you're in a hurry, but no. You act like it's a crime for me to go anywhere without you. I mean, are you my man or my babysitter?"

Rowdy stepped further into the bedroom and kept coming until he'd herded my ass right back inside the closet, where he crowded me in a corner without ever laying a hand on me. "Who the fuck are you talking to, Atlas?"

My gaze dropped, and I mumbled submissively, "No one."

Rowdy hooked his finger under my chin and immediately lifted my gaze from the floor until it met his once again. "Nice try. My eyes are up here. What's wrong? Talk to me."

"I—nothing," I said, which was only partially true. Something *was* bothering me, but Rowdy wasn't to blame. It wasn't his fault or mine that everyone seemed determined to tear us apart. "I'm just cranky, I guess. It's been a long weekend."

Rowdy searched my gaze for signs that I was lying before his lips tilted. "You should have taken your ass to sleep like I told you to, but no. Your hardheaded ass wanted to ride my dick all night."

I giggled before cupping him through his Burberry trunks that matched my bikini. "My pussy can't help that you stretch her so good."

"Atlas," he groaned while grabbing my wrist and stopping me from pulling him out. "No, and I mean it this time. We're already late. We have to go, baby."

"Please, Daddy? I'll be quick. I promise." I felt his dick twitch in my hand and knew I had him.

Rowdy rubbed his brow before sighing and taking a step back. "Take this shit off." He gestured to my bathing suit. "And go bend over the bed."

I squealed before running out of the closet, losing my bikini bottoms along the way. Rowdy followed me into the bedroom a second later. He was naked with his dick in hand and his bottom lip trapped between his teeth when he spotted me in position—face down, ass up.

"Hurry," I whined, wiggling my ass when he stared at my wet pussy with that look in his eyes that said he wanted to eat it for lunch.

Ignoring me, he ran both hands over my ass in reverence before he pushed two fingers inside me, testing my readiness even though I was visibly dripping all over the damn sheets.

I knew he only did this when I was truly in for a pounding, so my heart and pussy both gave an excited clench. The amused glance Rowdy gave me told me he'd felt it.

"We got to put your thirsty ass on a schedule before you fuck my dick off, Dream, damn."

"Yeah, yeah. Shut up and fuck me, Owen." He brought his dick to my pussy, teasing the entrance with the flared tip before pushing inside and making my jaw go slack as he slowly filled me up. "Mmm, fuck," I moaned when he reached the hilt and sat inside me, making sure I felt every one of my muscles stretching to accommodate his length. "Oh, fuck. Oh, fuck, *yes*."

"You like that?"

"Yes, Daddy. It's so good."

"Yeah?"

"Please," I whined.

"What about this?" Rowdy teased as he slowly withdrew to the tip only to surge back inside me so deeply, his pelvis smashed against my ass, forcing me forward on the bed and a long, tortured moan from my lips. "You like that too?"

"Harder."

"Harder?" He quickened his pace until the only sound was the wet chorus of our skin slapping together and his dick pummeling my pussy. "Why," he damn near growled. "Are you always… so goddamn…wet?"

Unfortunately, I couldn't answer him while he was fucking me so good, which only seemed to spur him to fuck me harder.

Rowdy climbed onto the bed, pinning my front to the

mattress as he covered my body with his. He hooked his arms under mine, grabbed my shoulders for leverage, and proceeded to beat my pussy to a pulp while I could do nothing but lie there and take it. He was so deep now that I swore I could feel him in my goddamn *throat*.

I quickly came as I promised, but he wasn't done with me yet. Rowdy flipped us over until he was lying on his back with me on top and facing away from him.

"W-waaaait!" I cried as he pummeled me from below. I knew what he was after, but I was absolutely sure I wouldn't survive a second orgasm.

"Ain't no wait," he huffed underneath me. "You wanted this dick, right? Take it like a big girl."

My plea fell short when I glimpsed us in the mirror above the dresser.

Rowdy held my legs open, giving me an unobstructed view of his dick driving into me. I saw and felt each time he sank so deep his balls slapped my pussy. I saw my tits bouncing from each movement and the slack, helpless look on my face as I became lost in pleasure.

The visual of us together, wild and uninhibited, was such an aphrodisiac that I came again even faster and harder than the first. It was only intensified by the feeling of his warm cum coating my walls in violent spurts as he came with me.

I was just glad I'd gotten back on birth control. There were times I swore Rowdy had been trying to knock me up on purpose.

As soon as we both caught our breath, Rowdy scooped me up before carrying me to the shower, where he had to clean us both since I was basically comatose from the super intense dick down.

Once again, I'd bitten off more than I could chew, and I'd loved every second of it.

After we were clean, we were both all smiles as we put our bathing suits back on.

Rowdy started mean-mugging me as soon as he caught a glimpse of how little my bathing suit actually covered.

I'd purchased this bathing suit months ago when it first started to get warm, but I'd gained weight recently—mostly in my butt and thighs—which Rowdy loved and hated since I still tried to squeeze into my old clothes that were now a size too small.

The bikini bottoms were digging so far up my ass that it might as well have been a thong. The tiny triangle tops barely covered more than my nipples, but it still wasn't anywhere as racy as the suits I knew those bitches hoping to catch his eye would be wearing.

"Make sure you keep that shit on all day," he ordered when I tied my cover-up around my waist.

I rolled my eyes as I followed him out of our bedroom, downstairs, and into his car, but I didn't argue. It would only end with him destroying yet another piece of clothing of mine, and I really liked this suit.

Today was the last day of the Pride of Kings festival. It was an annual weekend-long birthday bash for the Kings that both raised money to buy school supplies and clothes for low-income minorities around the way and stroked the Kings already inflated egos.

The festival was how I'd found out that Rowdy, Joren, Roc, and Golden were all Leos, which explained the matching tattoos.

Since their birthdays were so close together, they'd decided that it was easier to have a collective celebration than a huge and expensive party every week for a month. The festival was always held during one of the Kings' birthday weekends, and this year was Roc's.

Rowdy's thirty-sixth birthday—which he'd spent alone with me like he wanted—had come and gone, leaving the gap between our ages even wider.

My twentieth birthday was less than three months away, but I knew that even then, it wouldn't silence the whispers and constant judgment.

Of all the available women, the lion of Idlewild had chosen a teenager. It didn't stop the men from worshipping the ground he walked on or the women from wanting to take my place, but it gave them stones to throw nonetheless.

I was beginning to understand why Rowdy had kept everyone except his parents, the other Kings—and now me—at arm's distance.

Sometimes, not even that was enough, and he was forced to extend that radius to however far his gun aim allowed.

It was a thirty-minute drive to the Idle Lakes. The last party of the weekend was in full swing by the time we arrived at the huge lake house. It was more of a staging area, really.

There were people lined up near the shore, waiting their turn to be taken out on one of the motorboats to the huge platform in the middle of the lake. From here, I could just make out a DJ booth, bar, and water slides at both ends that the drunken partygoers were riding down and into the lake.

Hilltop, the heavily guarded territory of the infamous yet rarely seen Nine Hills gang, was perfectly visible from the deck overlooking the water.

The mountains had looked so beautiful during our balloon ride in the sky. I had asked Rowdy days later if he could take me up there one day, and he told me under no circumstances should I ever cross the boundaries of the Battery unless I wanted the entire city at war. Apparently, outsiders who wandered where they didn't belong had a habit of never being seen again.

"I see you two finally made it." The deep voice those words belonged to were drunken and familiar.

I turned my head and spotted Joren stumbling up the wooden stairs toward us and wrinkled my nose before I could remember to play nice. Unfortunately, he'd been looking right at me, so he hadn't missed my disgust and glared right back.

It had been several months since I started working at Pride of Kings, and Joren and I still hadn't warmed up to each other. In fact, things had become even more tense since I started dating his boy. Rowdy tried to keep out of it and not take sides, but I could tell he was becoming annoyed with us both since neither Joren nor I had no cause to dislike each other.

Golden was now speaking full sentences to me on a regular basis, but Joren, who thought the sun rose and set on his bald head, couldn't be bothered.

I didn't know what it was, but I couldn't stand his ass, and the feeling was mutual, so we stayed out of each other's way.

"It ain't even noon yet," Rowdy snapped from beside me. "How the hell you drunk already, and the party just started two hours ago?"

Good question.

Joren waved him off, which made him lose his balance, sending him tipping forward. He would have fallen on me if not for Rowdy's quick reflexes. He lifted me out of the way, leaving Joren to collapse on the blue and white striped couch, where he ended up lying face down and snoring seconds later.

"Dumb ass," Rowdy spat at his friend's unconscious form.

Usually, I would concur, but I was starting to suspect that there was more to Joren's drinking. Whatever it was, judging by Rowdy's reaction, I'd also guessed that Joren hadn't shared his woes with his friends.

I still didn't like his ass, but I could empathize, which was more kindness than he'd ever shown me. Joren hadn't been cruel necessarily, just indifferent. I couldn't understand why it grated on me.

Nevertheless, I knew what it was like to walk through hell and feel like there was no one or nothing to turn to except your own self-destruction.

The very reason I'd been reckless enough to follow an anonymous note into this lion's den. I'd left everything behind to find the Kings, and I still didn't know why. I stopped caring months ago, and I wasn't the only one.

I haven't heard from Unrequited since their warning.

"I can keep an eye on him if you want," I volunteered.

The last two days had taught me that it wouldn't be long

before my boyfriend's attention would be split between keeping a controlling eye on me and the adoring sycophants who desperately wanted his attention.

It took him even less time to hunt me down after I grew tired of watching them dick-ride and did my own thing. Why not save him the trouble and stay where Rowdy knew he could find me later?

"Hell nah. Where the fuck is Jada?" he asked no one in particular.

My heart dropped, and my ears started ringing at the sound of that familiar name.

Jada.

Could this be the same girl from the photo? Could Jada be Unrequited? I'd already figured out that the sender had to be someone who knew the Kings personally—someone who knew all their secrets. Who better than the girl who'd been their centerpiece for so long?

"I'm here," a lilting voice purred a moment later.

I followed the sound, something in my chest tugging me toward it until my eyes landed on the statuesque beauty strutting toward us in gold heels.

The sexy red halter one-piece she wore was cut out on the sides to show off her flat belly and golden skin tone. The curly copper hair I remembered from the photo was now bone straight, not a strand out of place, making it clear the bathing suit was for show only.

After our hair had been freshly pressed, sweat, water, or moisture of any kind was an absolute no-no for Black women.

The humidity in the south was so bad that I didn't even bother during the summer months, preferring to wear my hair naturally or protected by braids. I'd tried wearing extensions once but hadn't lasted more than a week before cutting them out.

"What's the problem, Owen?" she asked as she stopped in front of us.

Jealousy as green as Rowdy's eyes reared its ugly head at

the casual way she stood so close to him and uttered the name his mother had given him. The fact that Rowdy hadn't corrected her as he was known to do only fed the monster awakening inside of me. Not even his friends called him Owen, preferring O or Rowdy instead.

I took a deep breath, reminding myself that Jada had known him longer than I had even existed. A *very* long time. Probably years before he'd earned his moniker.

"What else?" Rowdy returned sarcastically, gesturing to a passed-out Joren.

Jada's gaze barely flicked in his direction before she waved Rowdy off. "He'll be fine. Let him sleep it off, and he should be awake in a couple of hours." Her attention shifted to me, and she smiled. "You must be Atlas. I've heard a lot about you. I'm Jada. Joren's wife."

My smile wavered.

Wife.

I'd known Joren was married, but I hadn't known it was to the girl in the photo. He barely mentioned her—none of them did—and she never came by the shop. She hadn't even shown her face all weekend until now.

"Nice to meet you," I forced out with a strained smile. It wasn't a lie per se. There were just too many warring emotions rioting inside my head to focus on anything but quieting them.

Even now, I could see the curiosity in Jada's gaze as she tried to keep her own polite smile on her face.

For fuck's sake.

I hoped Rowdy hadn't fucked her too.

No.

That would be too trifling—even for him.

I started to excuse myself under the guise of getting a drink when an argument nearby delayed my quick exit.

"How many times do I have to tell you? Stop following me, stalker."

I spotted Demi strutting through the sliding door with Halo

riding her hip and Roc hot on her heels like a puppy eager for any ounce of affection from its owner. He was wearing one of those plastic crowns on his head and a T-shirt that read Birthday Boy on the front.

Roc sucked his teeth at Demi and threw his arms up in mock defeat. "How you gonna tell me I can't follow you when you got my damn daughter, Demetria? Anywhere she goes, I'm going."

"Try again, loser. If you didn't want to grow up, then you should have worn a condom. Your daughter had no business being here in the first place. There's not one other child around. Why? Because this is a grown folks' party. You didn't even invite half these people, yet you had the nerve to have her sleeping in that room alone with the door *unlocked*."

"I told you I thought I locked it!"

"And I told you to do better."

Well, damn.

It was hard to believe that Demi and Roc hadn't created Halo together. They weren't even dating, fucking, or anything in between, yet they insisted on upholding this weird dynamic where they argued incessantly to hide the sexual tension so thick it was almost stifling.

Unfortunately, Demi was loyal to the bone, and Roc had fucked up any chance they might have had when he knocked up her best friend. Now, I think the two of them punished one another for the other's perceived mutual transgressions by constantly finding a reason to stay in each other's orbit.

The way Demi told it, she hated the air Roc breathed yet never balked at stepping in whenever he fell short as a parent. Meanwhile, Roc, who was a *great* father and a single one at that, constantly placed himself in her path and even resorted to using his daughter as a pawn.

Halo, who was still rubbing the sleep from her eyes, must have grown tired of listening to their bickering because she started looking around until her sleepy gaze traveled in our direction, and she began squirming to get down.

Demi let her down when she started to whine, and before either of them could tell her to stay put, Halo darted away.

"Uncle O! Uncle O!" she screamed right before colliding into his legs.

Rowdy pretended to almost fall over before scooping her up and tickling her belly through her jumper, making her laugh uncontrollably.

"Aye," he said once she quieted down. He was frowning deeply now as he held her up by her armpits until she was at eye level. "You still owe me six lollipops for that race I won last week."

"Uh-uh! You cheated!" Halo shouted back.

"I what?" He darted to the railing before flipping Halo upside down and holding her over it. "Let's try that again, you little gremlin. I gave you a week and not a day more to pay up. Where's my candy, Killa?"

"Daddy!" Halo could barely call out for her father from laughing so hard. She looked so comical with her long curly ponytail damn near touching the ground.

"You better stop," Rowdy warned when she started to wiggle around. "I might drop you." The asshole pretended to let her slip, making her shriek and call for her father again.

"Okay! Okay!" she finally agreed when she realized her father was still too preoccupied with Demi to pay his daughter any mind.

Rowdy lifted her back over the railing before setting her on her feet. "I'm waiting," he told her when all she gave him was a playful pout.

"Um…I don't have any candy. Not really," she confessed with a shrug. Rowdy reached for her again, but Halo shrieked, darting out of the way and running to me, of all people, for protection before wrapping her little arms around my leg. "Atlas, help me!"

"I don't know. He seems pretty serious." I played along. "Maybe if you got a dollar from your dad, Uncle O could buy his own lollipops?"

Halo's eyes brightened a second before she dug into the pocket of her jumper.

I watched her pull out four crumpled bills and wondered just how strong a spell Rowdy had me under that I was willing to help him extort a four-year-old. I didn't even think it was possible to dig myself into a hole this deep.

"Here you go!" Halo said, handing over her fist full of cash. "You buy lots of candy!"

"Bet," Rowdy said after pretending to think it over. He took the cash from Halo and counted it out. "Yeah, this should be enough. Oh, wait. I owe you change." He went into his own pocket and pulled out a crisp one-hundred-dollar bill before handing it over. "Pleasure doing business with you, Killa."

Excited for her new prettier money, Halo jumped up and down as Roc finally wandered over, looking stressed. Demi was standing alone, staring blankly out at the lake. She looked like she had nothing left, and if his daughter wasn't standing here, I'd slap the shit out of Roc.

"Look, Daddy. I have a new dollar!" Halo boasted, showing off her hundred-dollar bill.

"I see," her father said while Rowdy was busy cracking up that Halo didn't understand she had way more than just a dollar.

Remembering the lone tear Demi had wiped away before anyone could see, I crouched and whispered, "Hey, Halo. Maybe your Daddy can give you a few more dollars just like those."

"Really?"

"Mm-hmm." I squeezed her little nose, making her giggle.

"Yay!" She turned to her father. "Daddy, can I have some more?"

Roc shot me the nastiest look he could muster while I kept my expression the picture of innocence. He shook his head before looking down at his daughter. "Yeah, baby. I got you later."

"No, now," Halo whined.

Roc frowned, going into stern father mode. "What did I say, Halo?"

"Waaaaaaaa!" Halo cried, falling on her butt like an award-winning drama queen in the making.

"Come on, Halo, stop that," Roc pleaded as he picked her up and wiped her tears. "I thought you were a big girl. Don't you want cake later?"

"No, I want more dollars."

Everyone in hearing distance roared. There was no fooling Halo High.

Roc carried his daughter back inside the house before she could throw another tantrum, and seeing the coast was clear, Demi finally made her way over.

"Well, if it isn't my little cousin," Jada called out, reminding me of her presence. At first, I didn't know who she was speaking to until I realized her gaze was on Demi, who had been staring at me, her mouth poised to speak. "I haven't seen you in months, but you just walk past me like I'm not here? What would Aunt Candace say?"

Demi spun on her heel, giving me her back to square off with her cousin. "She'd probably tell your bourgeois ass to get that false nose out of the air and stop acting like you're too good for your family. Maybe then you'll see me more. But, yeah—hey, girl!" Demi mocked in a fake tone.

"Girl, bye," Jada said, looking away and abandoning the confrontation she'd started but apparently wasn't ready to finish.

"Yeah, I thought so," Demi mumbled, flipping her cousin the bird before facing me. A sweet smile slowly graced her face as she gave me a once-over. "Hey, munchkin. You look cute."

I blushed at the compliment.

It was nothing new for Demi to give them freely. She had genuine energy, and I guess that was why we instantly clicked from the moment I walked into her shop all those months ago.

She'd even taught me how to cornrow after I made it clear to Rowdy that letting other bitches touch his hair was a no-no. I couldn't have him walking around looking busted either, so I did something about it. Demi and I had gotten to know one another better during those sessions, and I learned just how small the world truly was.

It turned out that Demi wasn't a native of Idlewild either. She'd moved here after graduating high school.

From Ossella.

Apparently, her family still lived there, but Demi had never looked back, preferring the big city to our small town.

I still couldn't believe we'd never run into each other before, but our ten-year age gap and Demi leaving so young made it plausible.

"Thank you, but I look like a toddler compared to you. You are killing that swimsuit."

"Ain't I, though?" she boasted. I loved that she wasn't fake humble. Demi's body was *sick*. But Demi's body in a bikini?

It should have been illegal.

At a voluptuous size eighteen, her curves were outrageous, but it was the blinding smile she wore that completely stole the show, making it impossible for anyone with twenty-twenty vision to keep their eyes off her—including Roc, who had one eye on his daughter and the other on Demi, tracking her movements from the panoramic window overlooking the deck.

"So, we were getting ready to take the four-wheelers out. You coming?" she asked me.

I hesitated since I'd never ridden one before and didn't know how. "Sure," I slowly agreed when she pouted and gave me puppy eyes.

How hard could it be?

The wind whipped through my hair as Rowdy, Roc, Demi, and I followed the shoreline to the other side of the lake. I wasn't sure how or when it turned into a race, but I could barely steer from laughing so hard that tears blurred my vision.

Rowdy and Roc had teamed up at some point and were trying their hardest to run Demi, who had held the lead, off the road. She screamed, calling them everything but a child of God when they sandwiched her in, not caring about the damage they were causing.

I just hoped the ATVs weren't rentals.

Rowdy had given me a quick tutorial back at the lake house before that asshole gunned it down the dirt path and left me in his dust.

Fuck it.

I hit the gas, increasing my speed until I finally began to gain on them. The path ended up ahead underneath a pair of broken bridges with their centers blown out. Apparently, it was the only public access to the passable side of the mountains.

I could see Golden standing underneath one—shirtless, blonde-tipped dreads hanging around his powerful shoulders and his light skin competing with the sun.

I pictured his signature brooding frown as he watched us race toward him and grinned as I gunned the ATV, earning a startled look from Rowdy when he glanced over his shoulder and noticed too late me closing in.

I didn't slow down even as I ate up the last of the gap.

His lips parted to warn Roc when he caught on to my intent, but it was too late as the front of my ATV collided with the back of Demi's, the hit nudging her ATV forward and freeing her from their clutches.

The impact had my butt lifting from the seat, and I just barely kept from flipping over the handlebars when Rowdy thrust his arm out and caught me before I could.

He shook his head in disapproval, so I blew him a kiss and gunned it past them both. I followed Demi across the invisible finish line and slowed to keep from hitting the partygoers as I circled the ATV around.

Roc and Rowdy raced across the finish line, hopped off, and immediately came to blows over who came in last.

"They so damn childish," Demi told me after cutting the engine and climbing off.

I nodded my agreement and did the same, waving hi to

Golden. In typical Golden fashion, he wordlessly tipped his head at me as he took his time heading over to break up the fight happening between Rowdy and Roc in the sand. I stuck my tongue out at him as I followed Demi over to the food.

Fred was manning one of the three smoking grills while people sat around the picnic tables enjoying the food or playing Spades. There was even a volleyball net set up with a game currently in play as the rest danced to the music, swam in the lake, or swung from ropes. One rope was tied underneath the bridge closest to the water line, and another was hidden higher up somewhere in the trees on a small cliff.

There were basically three different parties happening at once—one at the house, another in the middle of the lake, and here at the far end underneath the abandoned bridges.

Joren was still passed out drunk, so Jada, thankfully, had agreed to stay behind with her husband and look after Halo until Roc's mother came to get her. I didn't know why, but like Joren, I felt uneasy around her. I needed time to process the feeling.

God, however, must have had time to play today.

As soon as Demi and I were done stuffing our faces, Joren—awake and sobered—arrived with Jada on the back of his ATV. Apart, they were both stunning. Together, their beauty was blinding. Joren and Jada both looked like they belonged in a magazine.

I wondered if they had kids. Joren never mentioned them, but then again, he never really talked about his wife, either. It would be a shame if they didn't since no one could argue that the two of them would make some beautiful babies. I just hoped neither passed on their personalities.

Demi and I got the bright idea to challenge the guys to a game of volleyball—girls against guys. We lost horribly. I even had to endure endless ribbing after I tried to keep the guys from scoring the winning point and ended up with a face full of sand.

With my makeup ruined, I figured I might as well get wet, which somehow led me over to the rope. I remembered thinking what a bad idea it was as I waited for my turn and, again, once it came and I stepped up.

"You sure?" Rowdy asked, hand on the rope, keeping me from running to the edge of the cliff. I was feeling daring today. "Don't expect me to jump in there and save you if your scary ass drowns."

I spat out sand for the umpteenth time since the game ended and glared over my shoulder at him. "Shut up, Owen."

He chuckled, and my heart galloped in my chest when he finally let go of the rope. "I'm fucking with you, baby. You know Daddy got you." With a stinging slap on my ass, Rowdy stepped back, slipped his hands in the pockets of his trunks, and with a nod toward the water, he sent me on my way.

Here goes nothing.

I gripped the rope tighter and sprinted toward the water.

Time seemed to stop once my feet left the safety of the small cliff.

I forced myself to let go of the rope, throwing my body backward in that split second between suspension and dropping and executed a perfect flip.

After, I watched the glistening expanse of the water rapidly approach and thought, *Wow, this is a really bad idea.*

And then I plunged underneath the surface.

THIRTY-TWO

Atlas

IT WAS DARK.

As I came to, I realized I was lying on my back, the sand from the shore digging into my wet skin.

There was an unbearable pressure on my chest as someone pressed it repeatedly while screaming my name.

How did I get here?

The last thing I remembered was diving beneath the water and then…nothing.

I couldn't resist the urge to cough, feeling water pour from my mouth and run down my jaw before I greedily drew in enough air to fill my burning lungs.

"Dream? Open your eyes. Please, baby. Let me see your fucking eyes!"

The sound of Rowdy's frantic voice had me rushing to obey. At first, all I could make out were shapes—blurry, chaotic shapes closing in around me. I blinked, breathing in more air—as much as I needed to feel like I wasn't two seconds from death.

Slowly, my vision cleared until I could make out Rowdy leaning over me and dripping water everywhere. I was so tired. I wanted to close my eyes and sleep, but Rowdy looked like he'd lose his shit if I tried.

"Mmmm," I groaned. "What—"

The sound of someone sobbing drew my attention away. It took some effort to turn my head enough to follow the sound.

Demi was standing a few feet away, crying uncontrollably and being held back by Roc, who was also staring at me as if someone had died.

Joren and Golden were busy keeping the crowd back, making sure they didn't try to film me and post it later for views.

Surprisingly, it was Jada who had remained close. Her light skin was now deathly pale as she stared down at me like I was a ghost who had come to haunt her.

I couldn't look away from her any more than she could me. Her gaze traced the lines of my face over and over like she was seeing me for the first time.

I felt something warm and wet pooling near my hairline and pressed my fingers to my temple. Hissing from the pain, I drew my fingers back and examined the blood mixed in with my foundation that had mostly washed away from the water.

Oh, right…

Jada was probably staring at my birthmark.

I wasn't ashamed of it, but lately, I'd started wearing makeup to hide it. Being Rowdy's girl had thrust me into the spotlight, and the first thing strangers usually asked me about was the star-shaped discoloration on my face.

My condition had only made me easier to spot in a crowd, leaving no doubt in their heads regarding my identity.

I forced myself to look away from Jada and turned to Rowdy. "What happened?" I croaked.

Rowdy, who was soaking wet now, closed his eyes and drew in a shuddering breath before answering. "You drowned, Atlas."

My lips parted just as his eyes opened, taking the breath I'd only just acquired when I saw they were wet with unshed tears. It was the fear mingling there that made him look uncommonly human.

I knew right then I never wanted to see it again. I wanted the man, not the legend, just...not like this.

Still, there was no way I'd drowned. Rowdy must have been mistaken. I'd been swimming since I was five.

And then I remembered what happened after I'd plunged beneath the water.

How I'd sunk to the bottom, feeling the air in my lungs dissipating the longer I lingered. How I'd looked to the surface and salvation but saw only my father's and mother's ethereal faces and decided to stay with them a little longer.

Even when my lungs had begun to burn, and I knew I'd stayed too long, I still didn't swim for the surface. I'd let myself drift away until all the pain, grief, and uncertainty of where I belonged finally, blissfully, stopped.

It was yet another truth I would have to take to my grave.

But as I stared up at Rowdy and the growing suspicion in his gaze, I wondered if he knew my secret.

After learning that I'd hit my head on some underwater rocks—which might have explained my hallucination—Rowdy took me to the hospital, where I was admitted for observation. I not only suffered a concussion but had technically died before Rowdy rescued me from the water and performed CPR.

The next morning, when I woke feeling like crap, I still found it in me to smile at the adorable picture Rowdy made bundled up in his Idlewild's Finest hoodie and thin blanket. He'd been snoring with his mouth open and looked so uncomfortable in his cramped recline on the too-small couch. He had refused to go home, where he would have been more comfortable in his bed.

My smile only deepened when I noticed the flowers and card waiting for me on the nightstand. I'd already guessed they were from him, but I eagerly plucked the card up anyway, my smile dying as I read the words. The light feeling and knowledge that everything would be okay dying with it.

Heard about the nasty spill you took.

That's what happens to whores who take what doesn't belong to them.

I have to say, I'm disappointed in you, Atlas.

I thought we were friends.

See you soon.

Love,
Unrequited

THIRTY-THREE

Rowdy

I stopped the Hellcat at a light and discreetly checked my phone when I caught the name on the screen.

Sissy: Hey, stranger.

Sissy: Are you going to ignore me forever? I thought we were cool.

I cut my gaze to the right and made sure the coast was clear before texting back. She'd been texting and calling for months, but this was the first time I'd responded. It was as if the moment I made Atlas my girl, all sorts of bitches from my past had come out of the woodwork to test me.

Fuck u want? Where's yo' husband?

Her response came immediately.

Sissy: He's not my husband anymore. Why? Were you jealous?

I deleted the thread without responding and slipped my phone back into my pocket just as the light turned green.

I had better things to think about, such as the grand reopening of Harry's car wash.

I hid it well, but I was as nervous as fuck.

I'd turned the reopening into a whole event, inviting the entire city out with the promise of a one-time free service.

I'd taken Harry up on his offer and threw in my own

stipulation, which allowed him to keep a generous share of the profits for as long as he lived.

After that, those shares would help fund a scholarship of his choice to help keep young Black boys off the street and give them options I never had.

I not only had the wash renovated and expanded, upgrading all of the equipment, but I added both an on-site and mobile detailing service and hired only the best who could handle any job—small or big.

I also changed the name to Harry's so that his legacy could live on.

Atlas and I were on our way there now, but first, a detour.

I bypassed our turnoff for Harry's, which hadn't escaped Atlas's notice with her nosy ass.

"Where are we going?"

It was her first time speaking since we'd left the house.

Atlas had an attitude because I made her change after she tried to walk out of my house wearing a mini dress so thin it was see-through.

She didn't put up that big of a fight when I made her change, and I learned why when she returned, wearing a crop top that only covered her tits, tiny shorts that left her ass hanging out, and a smirk.

Realizing she was testing my gangsta, I said nothing and only smirked back as I held the front door open and let her ass walk out like that.

"You'll see," I told her when she waited for my answer.

A few minutes later, I pulled into a quiet neighborhood nestled deep in Sunnyside, turning a few corners until I reached the house I'd partially grown up in. I could feel Atlas's gaze on me and her nervous energy as I pulled into the driveway.

"Where are we, Owen? Whose house is this?"

I killed the engine and made sure to pocket the keys before I answered her. "It's my parents' home."

Atlas's reaction was about what I'd expected.

She visibly balked. "Your…*what*?"

This girl is trying me today, I swear.

"I'm not going to tell you again!" I yelled from the front door of my parents' home. "Bring your ass in here, Atlas!"

"I don't know what the hell all of this yelling is about," my mother scolded from the kitchen, "but I know you're going to stop cussing in my goddamn house."

I didn't point out that she was cursing herself since I knew that would only get me cussed out worse. "Sorry, ma."

Shaking my head, I laughed as I continued to watch Atlas. Her stubborn ass was still sitting in that hot car with her arms crossed since she refused to get out after I made it clear I wasn't just stopping by.

I'd brought her here to meet my parents.

"Are you crazy?" Atlas shrieked. "I can't meet your parents dressed like this. Take me home so I can change."

"Nah, I gave your ass a chance. You didn't want to listen."

"Because I thought you were being a controlling jerk—like always!"

"Well…" I snickered. "Now you know."

"Hey, hey. What's going on?" my father demanded. His deep and authoritative voice had drifted from one of the back rooms where he'd been chilling.

I looked over my shoulder to see him leaving the den and swaggering down the dark hallway toward me. His head damn near touched the ceiling since he was the only man I knew whose height matched mine.

I sucked my teeth and grumbled, "I brought my girlfriend to meet ya'll, but she won't get out of the car."

My father's green eyes, which I'd inherited from him, assessed me. "Why? What did you do to that girl?"

"Me? Pops, she's the one you need to talk to. I swear this girl wakes up every day thinking of ways to piss me off."

"I see." He chuckled. "Well, your mother mentioned that she was young."

Inwardly, I cringed since I hadn't told them just how young Atlas was. I was already preparing myself for a lecture from my pops once he got me alone, mostly because my mom would make him.

"I can tell you from experience that it's because your girl wants to know she can. You're my son, so I know you," he said—a fatherly way of admitting he knew I wasn't shit. "If you didn't care this deeply about her, you wouldn't get so upset, and she knows it. I'm guessing you haven't told her you loved her yet?"

Uncomfortable with the subject, I shifted my feet. "Nah."

My father nodded. "Then, for now, this is her only way of assuring herself that you do."

"If you say so."

My dad sighed and shook his head at me the same way I often found myself shaking mine at Atlas whenever her skull got too thick to penetrate. "Move, boy."

I shifted to the side, letting him step out onto the porch. My scowl only deepened when my father slowly approached the car, like he was afraid Atlas would get spooked and run away.

She absolutely would, which was why I made sure to take the keys.

Pops knocked on the window, and I bit my lip to keep from telling him he was wasting his time. I saw Atlas's hesitation just before her scary ass cracked the window barely an inch. The opening was just enough for my father's voice to reach her clearly but not enough for him to see inside.

"Hey, there," his smooth-talking ass greeted.

For as long as I'd been alive, I'd never known a woman who could resist my father's charm.

It used to drive my mother crazy until her accident. After, it became clear that in sickness or health, my father had eyes only for her—nothing and no one could change that.

It was wild how I looked exactly like his ass, but our personalities were polar opposites.

Michael Wray was what some would call a gentle giant—quiet, unassuming, respectful, and patient. The only thing we had in common besides our reflections was that he was a beast with his hands.

"Hi," Atlas shyly replied. I couldn't quite hear her, but I'd read her lips just fine.

"I don't know what's going on between you and my son, but I'm sure it's nothing that can't be resolved inside and away from this hot sun." Still, Atlas hesitated, and my father noticed. "You like pancakes? My wife made some that will make your mouth water and forget all about whatever my son did since I'm sure this misunderstanding is his doing. If you like, I can make him leave while the three of us get to know each other better."

"I like pancakes," Atlas admitted, but she still didn't agree to come inside.

"Good. My son has never brought a girl home to his mother before, so she's dying to meet you. Been cooking all morning. Nice girl like you, I'm sure you wouldn't want to disappoint her, would you?"

I swear I could see Atlas blushing from here. "No."

My father smiled gently. "Excellent. May I?" He stood and gestured toward the car door, which he only opened after earning Atlas's slow nod.

It wasn't until she climbed out of the car that I realized she'd found my Idlewild's Finest hoodie in the back seat and had thrown it on. The sweatshirt was so big on her that the hem damn near fell to her knees, completely swallowing her curves and the bare skin she'd put on display to piss me off.

I watched her look around as she followed my father to the front door, taking in the immaculate front lawn and the house I'd grown up in. Her head tilted in contemplation when she noticed the paved ramp perpendicular to the stairs leading up to the small porch.

It had been the selling point for my parents when they bought this house after moving out of the hood.

His back to Atlas, my father gave me a warning look to behave before leaving us alone so he could help my mother in the kitchen.

"Aye, you better stop looking at my pops like that before my mom fucks you up," I whispered, yanking my girl to me when I caught her drooling over my father.

Atlas's mouth, which had been hanging open, snapped closed with a guilty squeal and audible click of her teeth. "Baby…he looks just like you."

"Yeah, yeah," I dismissed.

I'd heard that shit all of my life. My father could pass for my twin, especially since he looked nowhere near his fifty-nine years and more like an older brother. I let my hands wander under my hoodie and helped myself to two handfuls of her ass, which was still hanging out of her shorts.

"Who told you that you that could wear my shit?" I teased as I kissed and sucked on her neck.

I'd probably never get my hoodie back now, but that was okay. I liked seeing her in my shit more than I'd ever admit aloud. Atlas and I had been together for six months, but I was still learning how to express emotions other than anger and lust. I wasn't about to turn into some purse-holding sucker-for-love, but I had no problem whatsoever letting my girl know how precious she was to me.

"Stop, Owen," Atlas whined as soon as I got a little frisky. My hands were shoved so far up her shorts now that my fingertips had burrowed under her thong, teasing her wet folds and spreading her arousal around. "You're going to get us in trouble."

It was times like this that I was reminded of her age—*more like punched in the dick with it.*

"I'm a grown-ass man, Atlas."

"Owen Rashaad, leave that girl alone, and ya'll come get this food," my mother called from the kitchen.

Atlas lifted a brow, looking smug now as she waited to see what I'd do.

"You got it," I told Atlas as I let her go. "*This* time."

I took her hand and led her into the dining room. The table my parents cappin' asses never used—preferring to eat in front of the TV—was already set with platters of pancakes, eggs, bacon, sausage, and biscuits waiting in the middle. Steam still rose from each of the dishes.

My father hadn't been bullshitting when he said my mom was excited to meet Atlas. Since becoming a man, I'd had to listen to her guilt trips over never becoming a grandmother when it became clear her only child hadn't been interested in marriage and babies.

"Sit down, baby." I pulled out her chair before copping a squat beside her.

My beaming mother entered a moment later, carrying a pitcher of orange juice in her lap. My father was behind her with his hands around the handles of her wheelchair as he pushed her toward the table.

I took a sip from the glass of water already waiting for me as I watched for Atlas's reaction out of the corner of my eye.

To someone who didn't know what to look for, her soft smile would have been the only thing she gave away, but I could see the wheels turning in her head as she slowly pieced together everything I'd shared with her about my parents and upbringing.

Back when my Pops and I were beefing heavily over how I was getting money, my mom had gotten hurt in a hit-and-run that left her paralyzed from the waist down. Everyone assumed the accident was the reason my father and I had set our differences aside, but it was only part of the truth.

The other half was scattered six feet deep around the mountains of Hilltop. It was where my father and I had left the motherfucker who had ran my mother off the road.

"Oh, my word, Michael," my mom gushed as she stared at Atlas. "You didn't tell me how pretty she was!"

"I might have taken a few hits to the head during my fighting days, but that didn't make me a fool, woman." My mother playfully hit my Pops on the arm before giving her full attention back to my baby.

Like Atlas, if my mom was shocked by her age, she didn't show it, meaning my father had already warned her before they came in.

"Hello, Mrs. Wray. It's nice to meet you."

"Oh, please, child. Call me Heidi."

"Okay, Ms. Heidi."

The four of us cracked up over Atlas's insistence on being respectful, no doubt an influence of being raised by Black parents. We never called our elders by their first name; it was always Ms., Mr., Aunt, or Uncle, according to whatever role they parroted in our lives.

"You are beautiful," my mother said again.

True.

"Owen has told me so much about you that I couldn't wait anymore. I told him if he didn't bring you over soon, I was going to pay a visit myself."

Also true.

I had been planning to anyway, but fear of spooking Atlas had made me hesitant. Since I'd never been in a relationship before, I'd found myself second-guessing if it was too soon.

My mom had essentially taken the choice out of my hands when she tried to come to the hospital after I told them about Atlas's accident.

It had only been my reminder that the stress of meeting her boyfriend's parents for the first time was the last thing someone with a fresh head injury needed that had kept my mother away. My father had been no damn help since his soft ass couldn't seem to ever say no to my mom. I knew he was firmly on her side for whatever she chose to do.

I could still hear my mother's threat ringing in my head.

"As soon as she's healed, I want you to bring her by the house. Don't make me have to get your father involved, Owen Rashaad."

Like me, my mom never issued a promise she didn't mean, so I'd given her a date and time as soon as the doctor cleared Atlas. I made sure to schedule it before the reopening so that if things went south, we'd have an excuse to leave as soon as possible.

Kareena's panic had been easier to manage since she was too weak to travel. I'd been sneaking down to Ossella these past few months to check on Atlas's mom and make sure she was seeing a doctor as agreed. I also tried to talk some sense into her about telling Atlas the truth to no avail.

I had almost broken my promise after Atlas's accident.

I hadn't believed that Atlas was telling the full truth about hitting her head and losing consciousness. The doctor and the cut on her head had already confirmed she'd hit her head, but I wondered if it had occurred *after* she'd passed out.

The underwater current had been strong enough when I dove in to save her that anything was possible.

"Thank you. And I'm sorry about earlier," Atlas apologized. "Owen didn't tell me we were coming, so I was caught off guard and reacted badly. I hope I didn't disrespect your home or make you think less of me."

My mother waved her off. "Don't worry about it. While I love my son more than any mother could, I'm under no impression that he's an angel. I'm sure you were right to feel cornered."

"Sometimes I think he's the teenager, and I'm the dirty old man," Atlas teased, making water squirt out of my nose while my father pounded the table as he roared his amusement at my expense.

My mother, who had a great sense of humor, let out a trilling sound that I hadn't heard in a long while—so long my father's green eyes were practically glowing with awe as he watched his wife laugh.

His head slowly turned, and then he stared at Atlas like she was the second coming.

Ever since my mom's accident, her days alternated between extreme highs and lows. Still, nothing had made her as happy as her only son bringing a girl home finally.

Or anyone really.

I'll never forget that time my mom had gotten it into her head that I was gay, and that's why I hadn't brought anyone home to meet her. She made it clear that she and my father loved me no matter what, and after I caught on, I made it clear they had no choice and that my sexual preferences steered firmly toward women.

"Oh, Michael," my mother said after we started to dig in. "I forgot the syrup."

My father immediately set his fork down to do her bidding.

"Oh, no, Ms. Heidi," Atlas said when my father started to stand. "You and your husband worked so hard already. Owen isn't doing anything. He can get it."

My chewing slowed as my gaze slid to Atlas, who tilted her head and silently dared me to object.

Sliding my tongue over my front teeth, I nodded and stood to do *her* bidding.

"Oh, I like you," my mother said with a wink. "I think you're exactly what my brutish son needs."

THIRTY-FOUR

Atlas

NOW THAT I'D MET ROWDY'S PARENTS AND IT HAD GONE BETTER than expected, I was just grateful to have it over with. Meeting Sutton's parents hadn't gone nearly as well since I'd met ice cubes warmer than his mother, and his father had wandering eyes.

It was just after noon during my shift when I heard the shop's front door open.

It was my first day back in two weeks, so I was behind the reception desk, catching up on emails and paperwork that Tuesday had understandably been too overwhelmed to keep up with.

I was currently dealing with a particularly nasty email from a customer inquiring about the status of his repairs. I was trying—and failing—to find a non-snarky way to remind the pushy customer that the agreed-upon timeline for his repairs was two weeks, and it had only been three days.

I read over my response one last time and hit send.

The man's questions were just too stupid for me to answer honestly without sounding sarcastic. I'd probably get in trouble, but I wasn't worried. Rowdy would lecture me even though he was *worse*, I'd pout, and then he'd kiss me and tell me to behave before sending me on my way. Now that we were dating, the other Kings always let Rowdy handle me, so they wouldn't say anything either.

"Hello, welcome to Pride of Kings. Do you have an appoint—" The question died on my lips when I looked up and saw who was standing there. "Oh. Hi."

Jada flashed a dazzling smile that I didn't buy for one moment. The gesture was too strained, her eyes too assessing. "Hello." Her shaped brows bunched contemplatively. "Atlas, right?"

Bitch, you know my name.

"Yup."

"It's nice to see you again. I, um, I hope you're feeling better."

Detecting the first morsel of sincerity from her, I forced myself to relax.

Jada hadn't done anything to me, so there was no reason not to like her. I just didn't trust her, and I had no reason for that either.

Jada, Joren, and the rest of the Kings had come to see me during my short stay in the hospital, and she'd acted just as phony and withdrawn then as she had on the lake. Jada and Joren had barely stayed a full hour, but I often caught her studying me like I was a ticking time bomb that could explode at any minute.

"Thanks. I am. Did you want me to grab Joren for you?" The sooner I could get her out of my face, the better for both of us.

Even now, her flawless face was pinched as if she could barely stomach the sight of me.

There were few reasons a woman would act this way toward another woman they barely knew. Usually, when they thought you were fucking their man.

The thought of Joren and I having sex was almost laughable, and it wasn't because he wasn't attractive. Each time I tried to put myself in Jada's head by picturing Joren and I naked and writhing together, my mind instantly revolted, shutting it down while I fought the urge to hurl. I hated him, so it made perfect sense.

Then again, I'd initially hated Rowdy too, and I'd had no problems fingering my pussy to thoughts of him so…

Whatever.

Jada's life as a trophy wife must have truly been dull to go looking for drama where there was none.

I couldn't get much out of Rowdy since he wasn't the type to gossip and had firmly shut down all my attempts to discuss her. Demi, on the other hand, had been all too willing to spill.

I knew Jada didn't work, and for some reason, in the seventeen years Joren and Jada had been married, eloping straight out of high school, they hadn't made any kids together either.

It was truly a shame since I knew this freakishly gorgeous and seemingly healthy couple had the potential to make some beautiful babies.

Truly. A. Shame.

"Actually," Jada responded to my question, "I'm here to see you."

Errr, what? I tried to think of a polite response and failed, my brows shooting to my hairline and my fake smile becoming even more strained. "Me? Really? Why?"

Subtle, Atlas.

Uncharacteristically nervous, Jada fingered her reddish-brown hair behind a delicate ear. It was then I noticed the tattoo of a lone star—a shooting star—on her right forefinger. "I thought we could have lunch. Get to know one another." At my blank look, she added, "My husband told me you're new in town, and since you're dating Owen now—"

"Rowdy," I corrected, not caring if I was being petty. She might have known him longer, but he was mine.

"Oh…yeah, sure. Rowdy." I still didn't relax, so she reached out and touched my hand. "You okay, sweetie?"

I sucked in a breath and pulled away when it felt like the blood in my veins began to sing. I'd just barely managed to keep from snatching my hand back when I pulled away.

"Fine. Lunch sounds…" *Unbearable. Horrible. Awful.* "Nice."

Joren's wife forced a smile. "Great. Are you free now? I took the liberty of booking us a table for two."

Before I could tell her that now wasn't a good time, a masculine voice called out. "Jada?"

Speak of the devil.

Joren, dressed in overalls and hands stained with oil like he'd been hard at work for once, was standing at the Employees Only entrance to the workshop looking shell-shocked.

In the seven months that I'd been working here, Jada hadn't visited the shop even once, so I knew it must have been even longer since Joren had been graced with a visit from his wife.

His ebon gaze bounced between us before settling on his wife. "What are you doing here?"

Jada's manicured nails flicked toward me. "I came to take Atlas to lunch."

As if these unexpected and disastrous events were my fault, Joren's gaze flitted to me before narrowing suspiciously.

Of course, he thought this was my doing.

Or maybe he was afraid I'd spill the beans about the stripper he'd snuck out of his office early this morning. I guess Diamond hadn't even been worth the thirty bucks it would have cost for a few hours at one of the motels in Hooker's Cove.

"You know what?" he said with a smile that didn't reach his eyes. "I'm feeling a little hungry myself. Mind if I tag along?"

Oh, hell no. While the two of them were occupied, I quietly grabbed my phone off the desk, ducking my head as I quickly typed out a one-word text.

Help.

I nervously tapped my foot, tuning out Joren and Jada's bickering as I watched bubbles appear on the screen before a reply came seconds later.

Mine: Omw

I released the breath I'd been holding and pocketed my phone just as Jada said, "But, baby, I wanted it to be just us girls."

"Fuck is going on here?" Rowdy's booming voice barked, startling a few of the patrons lounging in the waiting room *and* me with his sudden appearance. I had no idea how he got over here so fast when he'd been next door overseeing operations at Harry's.

Maybe calling him in for reinforcements hadn't been such a great idea since I knew my baby lived on *Go*—his moniker wasn't for nothing.

"Rowdy, there you are." Jada lost what few points she had in her favor when she fluttered her lashes and smiled. "I was just inviting Atlas to lunch. Can you please tell my husband that he can't come along? It's a girl date. You understand."

Ignoring Jada, Rowdy's gaze immediately slid to me.

Whatever he saw on my face had him shaking his head a moment later. "Nah. I don't understand shit. Tuesday is off today, and the shop is too busy to leave the desk uncovered."

At least it wasn't a lie.

Even now, the waiting room was full, and the phone was ringing off the hook. The Monday morning rush had yet to abate, so I'd already made plans to work through lunch.

"I need Atlas here. Maybe some other time."

The feigned pleasantness instantly melted off Jada's face. "Really? Are these the games you two want to play?" Her head tilted to the side, and the look in her eyes as she silently communicated something to Rowdy said she was in on a secret that only the two of them knew. "Why can't your girlfriend have lunch with me, O—Rowdy? I'm harmless."

Somehow, I doubted that.

"Jada, kill that noise," Joren ordered. He stepped forward and grabbed his wife's thin arm. "That man just told you why. Come on." He guided her toward the door, safely out of Rowdy's reach. "I'll take you to lunch. My treat."

"Of course it is, husband," Jada snapped. "It sure as hell won't be mine."

Inwardly, I cringed as I watched them go, their heated argument reaching my ears from across the shop.

There wasn't much I knew about marriage.

In fact, I knew nothing at all, including how the hell those two had stayed in it together for so long. Clearly, they were both unhappy, finding contentment only in making each other miserable.

"Wow," I drawled as soon as the side door closed behind them. Still arguing, they headed for the employee parking lot. My gaze slid to Rowdy, who was looking everywhere but at me. "Are they always like that?"

"Pretty much," he mumbled. He then checked the time on his watch before finally meeting my gaze. "So come on. Let's go."

I frowned. "Where are we going?"

Rowdy gave me an impatient look as if I should have already known the answer. "I'm taking you to lunch."

A conspiratorial grin spread my lips despite my hesitating long enough to say, "But you said I had to stay since we're busy." The phone was still ringing off the hook.

"I know what I said, Dream. Fuck that phone. My only concern is you, and right now, I want to feed you."

All the air left me, leaving me breathless. "Okay."

Blushing, I quickly routed the phones to voicemail before grabbing my purse and leaving the desk. The current repairs wouldn't be completed for a couple of hours anyway, so I had plenty of time to let my boyfriend take care of me.

As if reading my thoughts, Rowdy grabbed my hand, stopping me when I started to walk past him in my skintight jeans. "Hold that thought," he murmured, kissing me when I looked at him. "I need to take care of something really quick. Go upstairs and wait for me in my office. I want to pound that pussy for a few before we go."

The visible shiver that turned my bones to jelly had him smirking cockily.

"Okay."

The moment I closed Rowdy's office door behind me, my smile took on a different form.

Sneaky.

Conspiratorial.

I'd never been alone in here before.

Sure, I'd snooped all through his home but hadn't found any skeletons hiding in the closet, which had been suspicious enough since everyone had them.

It made sense that whatever buried secrets he was hiding would be kept here since Rowdy was a workaholic, and until me, he'd spent all his time at the shop—his real home.

Knowing I only had minutes until the window closed, I darted straight for his desk. The top drawer revealed nothing—some spare change, a rolled blunt, loose bullets for his AK, and rubber bands that he often wore around his wrist for quick access.

I checked the next drawer, but it was completely empty.

The last drawer held various forms for the shop, including blank copies of the Misconduct Form he made me fill out almost every day before we started fucking.

I started to shut the drawer when something at the bottom caught my eye.

It was a large black folder tucked and hidden underneath the mountains of boring forms. I removed the stack from the drawer and set them on the desk out of the way.

Stamped on the glossy front in gold Blackletter font were the words *Idlewild Technical College.*

I only hesitated a moment before carefully lifting the folder from the drawer and flipping it open. Small triangular blue ribbons decorated each of the four corners, while more of the Blackletter font was inscribed on the cream-colored parchment.

On the recommendation of the faculty and by virtue of the authority vested in them, the Trustees of the College have conferred upon
Owen Rashaad Wray
the degree of
Associate of Business
in Business Administration

The rest of the words printed in black blurred together as my mind drifted. We would often spend hours talking about our past and our hopes for the future.

Why would Rowdy not tell me about this? And why would he stuff his degree inside a drawer like he was ashamed of it?

Knowing him, he probably thought he was too gangsta to let anyone know he was really a closet nerd. I stuffed the folder and the forms back where I found them, making a mental note to come back for the folder.

Shutting the drawer, I turned and scanned the bookcase until my eyes fell on a small metal tackle box. The teal paint was peeling in some places and rusted in others, making it clear he'd had it for some time.

Eyeing the keyhole suspiciously, I tried my luck anyway, my stomach twisting violently when the lid wouldn't budge.

Got you.

One of my most hated and admired qualities about Rowdy was how open and upfront he was. He never even bothered to lock his car door because every car thief and jack boy in this city not only knew Rowdy but feared and respected him. If Rowdy had gone through the trouble of locking this tackle box, he must not have wanted anyone to see what was inside.

I lifted the box to my ear and shook it, frowning at the quiet shuffle that emerged from within.

I was still ruminating over the possibilities of what it could be when the office door banged open behind me, and I jumped with a guilty squeal.

"The fuck you in here doing?" Rowdy demanded.

Stupidly, I spun around with the tackle box still in hand and found Rowdy standing in the open doorway of his office.

"I—What is this?" There was no point in lying or trying to hide that I'd been snooping. He'd caught me red-handed.

Rowdy gave me a blank look in return. "It's a toolbox, Atlas. What does it look like?"

"Why is it locked?"

He gave a petulant shrug of his powerful shoulders and then closed the door behind him as he stepped inside. My gaze narrowed on him when he wordlessly walked over to the sideboard on the other side of the room, giving me his back as he grabbed a bottle of water from the fancy built-in cooler. I could see the rigid tension in the muscles of his back and knew that his ass was lying.

"Well, where is the key?" I asked as soon as he faced me.

He took the time to drain his water before tossing it in the recycling bin and closing the gap between us. "I don't know, Atlas. I haven't used that shit since before I opened the shop. It's the first toolbox I ever had. My grandfather passed it down to me before he died, so I kept it for sentimental reasons. Now put it back and come here."

"No." I held the box tighter as I backed away. "You're lying to me. What's in here that you don't want me to see?"

Rowdy growled, looking and sounding so much like the lion of Idlewild as he stalked me around the room. "Your front teeth if you don't stop playing with me."

"Try again." I didn't trust a word he was saying, including his threat to hurt me. *Then why are you running, dummy?*

Because…

I knew the moment he got his hands on me, I'd fall prey, not to the wrath brimming in his green eyes but the promise of sex simmering underneath.

I *absolutely* wanted him to fuck me senseless, but first, I wanted answers, which meant I had to keep a clear head.

"All right," he said, suddenly stopping in his tracks. "I got work to do, and so do you, so get back to work since you want to play games."

My jaw dropped when he started for the door. Rowdy had his hand on the doorknob, poised to open it and leave, when I yelled, "You selfish asshole!"

I dropped the tackle box and charged across the room.

Rowdy had one foot out the door by the time I reached him. My teeth were clenched when I stopped him—but not *really*—with one hand clutching the back of his work shirt. He could have easily overpowered me if he wanted to leave, but no.

I'd played right into his hands, and I knew it the moment he turned and looked at me like he wanted to eat me alive.

I didn't care. My body was thrumming, and I knew there was only one fix.

"You're not going anywhere without fucking me first," I told him with a growl that rivaled his own.

Rowdy said nothing as he stepped back inside and closed the door behind him.

I ripped his belt and pants loose as he backed me toward the desk. As soon as my legs collided with the edge, Rowdy yanked me around, and I had only seconds to get my jeans out of the way before he planted an unforgiving hand on my back and shoved me face down. My cheek smacked against the wooden surface of the desk as he yanked my panties down to join my jeans around my thighs.

A moment later, he was filling me up, stealing my breath as he stretched my walls and made me take every inch.

He felt so fucking good.

"Oh, fuck. Fuck yes. Fuck me!" I screamed as he pounded me relentlessly. The heavy desk rocked underneath our rough movements while Rowdy's belt buckle jingled noisily in time with his skin slapping against mine. Anyone walking by would know *exactly* what we were up to.

"You better take that dick," Rowdy talked shit. "What did I tell you about misbehaving, huh?"

"I'm sorry!"

He gave my ass a punishing slap hard enough to make me gasp. "No, you're not."

My gaze traveled to the teal box just inches away from my face. No…I wasn't.

An hour later, after I'd torn off both our clothes and he was done fucking me like on every surface in his office, I stood alone while he finished cleaning up in the bathroom.

I was smiling, and it wasn't just from the orgasm.

Crumpled on the floor at my feet were his work pants. I peeked over my shoulder to make sure he was still occupied before bending and scooping them up. I quickly checked both pockets until I located his keys and pulled them free.

I eyed them all, eliminating them one by one.

House.

Hellcat.

Charger.

Shop.

Office.

Bingo.

I freed the last key—small, thin, and cylinder shaped—from the ring before slipping it into my own pocket and returning his keys to his pants.

There were two things I knew for certain…

One, Rowdy was hiding something.

And two, he had me completely fucked up if he thought he could keep it from me.

THIRTY-FIVE

Rowdy

"OWEN, I'M LEAVING NOW," ATLAS ANNOUNCED AS SHE WALKED into the living room, her new heels I'd spent nine-hundred damn dollars on clicking against the wooden floor and interrupting my game.

Between my girl, the shop, ruling Idlewild's underworld, my side business customizing cars, and now the car wash, I didn't have a lot of free time just to sit back and kick it. I was excited as fuck when Atlas asked me if she could go to a party with her little friends she'd met on campus.

I made sure to get the hoe and the hood fax on every one of those thots before I gave Atlas the green light to hang with them, though. Even after she'd been burned in the worst way, my girl was still too damn trusting.

That was where I came in.

Atlas called me controlling, but I tuned her ass out and did what I did best. I looked out for her.

"Okay. Bye, baby," I said without taking my eyes off the TV. This was my third time trying to beat this damn level.

"I should be home by one."

"Cool."

"You going to miss me?"

"Yup."

"Are you giving me short answers so that I'll leave faster?"

"You so pretty, baby."

Atlas giggled and mushed my head as she left the room. Me being me, game be damned, I glanced over my shoulder to get a good look at that fat ass as she walked away.

What the—

I paused the game when I saw what the hell she was wearing.

"You got me fucked up!"

Realizing she'd been caught, Atlas darted for the door.

I threw the Xbox controller down and hopped over the couch to give chase. By the time I reached the door, she was already in the car and gunning it down the driveway.

Atlas was supposed to have left an hour ago, and now I knew why. Her ass had been stalling until I was into my game so she could sneak by me.

Whipping out my nine, I aimed for her front tire, making Atlas scream when I pulled the trigger twice. I was so mad I missed both times, which only pissed me off even more—that and the two bullet holes in my pavement.

"Fuck!" I roared. All I could see was Atlas's taillights as she raced down the street. "The fuck you looking at?"

I'd caught my neighbor staring at me, and once he noticed the gun in my hand, he hurried his old ass back inside.

It was times like this I wished I'd splurged a little more when I bought my home. Preferably one that didn't come with neighbors. I just hadn't seen a need for a big ass house way out in the suburbs when it was just me.

I stormed back inside the house and called Atlas's phone. Surprisingly, she answered.

"What do you want, you psycho?" she screamed at the top of her lungs.

I rubbed at my brow and sighed. "You know what I want, Atlas. Bring your ass back here."

"No." She whimpered. "You tried to kill me."

"I *did not* try to kill you, you fucking crybaby. I tried to kill your car. Why would I hurt you when I love you? Just come home to me so we can talk about this." I didn't realize what I'd let slip until I heard her tiny gasp. "Fuck," I mouthed.

This was not how I'd pictured telling her.

It was the first time I'd ever uttered those words to anyone other than my parents. Atlas deserved better than a clumsy slip of the tongue. I wanted to do something big like take her to Paris or buy her a diamond ring. Not…this.

"What did you say?" she whispered.

I paced the floor, feeling my lip curl. "I said come home."

"Owen…"

"IsaidIloveyou," I rushed out.

Atlas giggled and then said, "I love you too, Owen."

Even though I wanted to do cartwheels, I decided to play it cool. "That's what's up."

"I'm still not coming home, though." The line clicked when she hung up.

I tried calling her back, but she sent me to voicemail all seventeen times before turning off her phone completely.

Two new texts arrived a moment later.

Sissy: I'm in town for a few days…

Sissy: I thought we could hang out again…like the old days.

I sucked my teeth, and after thinking about it for a moment, I decided to block her thirsty ass. Sissy and I had mutual acquaintances, but we'd never been cool like that. Yeah, she was cute—a little nerdy—but cool.

Back in the day, I'd always catch her weird ass staring at me on some fatal attraction shit, so I tried to give her the dick. When she told me she was saving her virginity for love, I backed all the way off and never thought about her again.

After high school, Sissy had left town to go to college up north, and then I heard she'd gotten a teaching job a few hours away, but we didn't keep in contact.

At least until a few years ago, when I enrolled in night classes at the community college, and Sissy found out—probably from Joren's gossiping ass. She had reached out with an offer to tutor me, which I took her up on. After I graduated, we'd kept in touch here and there until she went radio silent out of the blue a few months later.

I didn't really ask questions, but I'd heard from Joren that she'd gotten married.

After blocking Sissy, I pulled up the app for the tracker I'd installed in Atlas's car before throwing on a shirt and grabbing my keys.

I snatched open the front door and swore when I saw the woman standing there, fist poised ready to knock. I'd been so wrapped up in trying to get hold of Atlas that I hadn't even heard a car pull up.

I frowned at my late-night visitor, knowing it would not be a good look if Atlas pulled up right now. "The fuck are you doing here?" I asked the woman standing on my porch, looking like her dog died. "Joren isn't here."

"Good, because we need to talk," Jada replied.

She tried to invite herself inside, but I stepped out and pulled the door firmly shut behind me. "I doubt it."

"You can't ignore me forever. We need to talk about *us*. We need to talk about *her*. There's something you don't know, Owen." Jada paused and inhaled deeply when she realized she had my attention. "Atlas isn't who you think she is."

I cackled and stepped around her before she could say more. These bitches would find any reason to stay on my dick.

I kept walking to my car while Jada's thirsty ass followed me. "One, there's nothing you can tell me about my girl that I don't already know." Not only did I eat, sleep, and fuck everything Atlas Beck, my baby had made it clear early on in our relationship that pillow talk was mandatory. Most nights, I couldn't even get the pussy without sweet-talking her ass first, but I didn't mind now as much as I did in the beginning. "Two, there is no *us*," I told Jada. "Get off my dick, and go find your husband."

"Contrary to what you believe, not everything is about *you*. I did something, Owen. A long time ago when we were kids."

I kicked myself for parking on the street and not in the garage. I could have avoided this whole interaction. I sighed and pinched the bridge of my nose when I stopped abruptly and turned to face her. "What does this have to do with me, Jada?"

Instead of answering, she shook her head and looked off with her arms crossed protectively. "I can't tell you that. You'll just have to trust me."

"Well, clearly I can't," I threw back sarcastically. "You be easy." I chucked the deuces and started toward my car again.

"You need to break up with her, Owen!"

"I'll pass. And chill with that Owen shit. My girl doesn't like it."

"Rowdy, please!" I ignored her and kept walking. "Rowdy, you need to listen to me!"

"Go home, Jada."

"You're fucking your own daughter!"

THIRTY-SIX

Atlas

I WAS IN TROUBLE—EVEN MORE TROUBLE THAN MY OUTFIT CHOICE had landed me in.

I bit my lip, a nervous yet excited thrill thrumming through me as I turned my key in the lock and stepped inside the quiet, dark foyer.

Rowdy had expected me home hours ago, but I'd purposely stayed away, watching the clock until I was sure he'd be pissed enough over the late hour to fuck me into a coma.

I was so addicted to him and what he alone could do to my mind, heart, and body that, at this point, I was convinced being next to him or under him was the only way I could get a good night's sleep.

My wistful sigh was cut short when a flash of headlights chased away the dark momentarily. I heard the familiar rumble of the Hellcat as it pulled into the driveway, and then the engine shut off, and I was once again surrounded by darkness and silence as I held my breath and waited.

I was still rooted to the spot when the front door opened moments later, and Rowdy walked through it, clutching an open bottle of whisky, his face disturbingly blank even after he noticed me standing there.

"Hey," I whispered. I was nervous for a different reason now.

There was no emotion on Rowdy's face. None whatsoever. Not even the perpetual state of grumpiness that he seemed to live in and that I'd grown to love. It was like a warm blanket that I'd wrapped myself in and never wanted to leave.

"You're just getting in?" It was three in the morning, so I waited for him to ask me the same. He didn't. "Where did you go?" I gulped, unsure I even wanted to know the answer.

I was under no illusion that Rowdy would stay in on a Friday night. The city was one endless red carpet laid out for him, with doors flying open wherever he went. During the rare nights that Rowdy didn't let me tag along, he always made sure to come home at an hour that wouldn't cause my mind to wander.

Tonight was the first night he'd broken that unspoken rule.

"Went for a drive to clear my head," he answered. His tone was barren when he strode past me, taking the whisky to the head as he trudged upstairs.

A cloud of perfume that didn't belong to me followed in his wake.

My steps were slow and hesitant as I followed, my mind turning over the reasons for this sudden switch in his mood.

Had it been only hours ago that he told me he loved me?

I was starting to wonder if I'd imagined it and if the warm feeling I'd held in my belly all night had been fabricated.

I refused to believe Rowdy was *this* upset over my outfit or the late hour—especially when I purposely provoked him so that we'd end our night in a way we'd both enjoy.

Quiet as it was kept, Rowdy got off on my bratty behavior almost as much as I did when he punished me for it. He would have been bored within a week if I'd turned into his doormat.

The shower was already running by the time I reached our bedroom, so I stripped off my clothes, determined to turn this night around. Steam rose from the glass shower when I padded barefoot inside the bathroom. Rowdy stood under the spray with his head down and still holding that damn bottle as the water beat down over him.

I sucked in a deep breath and opened the shower door.

My stomach sank when I watched the muscles in his back and shoulders bunch when he realized he was no longer alone. I swallowed down the grim feeling clawing its way up my throat and forced myself forward until I could feel the familiar warmth of his skin chasing away the chill of my own.

"Owen?"

As if the sound of my voice and the question behind it caused him too much pain, his only response was to lift the bottle to his lips again and guzzle down the brown liquid in his race to reach the bottom.

I grabbed his arm and turned him around to face me before he could give himself alcohol poisoning.

A slap in the face would have been a softer, kinder blow than the sheer disgust in his eyes that knocked me back a step.

Refusing to back down, I closed the gap between us and took his face between my hands.

"What is going on? Why won't you talk to me?"

As if he wanted to hurt me, Rowdy knocked my hands away and lifted the bottle to his lips again. I snatched the bottle before he could take another swig and let it fall to the shower floor, the liquor spilling onto the clean white tile and mixing with the water before disappearing down the drain.

"Tell me what's wrong!"

He sucked in a breath. And then… "I can't."

And that was that. He kissed me… on my *forehead* before pushing me aside and stepping out of the shower.

Even though every fiber of my being wanted to, I didn't chase him.

I stayed put, feeling numbness set in as I stood under the spray until the water ran cold, forcing me from the confines of the shower.

I was on autopilot as I maneuvered through my nightly hygiene ritual before leaving the bathroom.

My eyes traveled unwillingly to the bed, expecting to see Rowdy already tucked under the sheets, but instead, I found it empty. The sheets remained undisturbed from when I'd made the bed this morning.

I slipped into a pair of sleep shorts with the matching cami, but when Rowdy still hadn't appeared, I murdered a piece of my pride and trailed from the bedroom to find him.

The house was quiet save for the sound of the dog next door barking his head off. The German shepherd had been more noisy than usual these last few days—usually at night when everyone was asleep.

I headed downstairs and into the living room, where I found Rowdy passed out on the couch, face down and snoring.

On the outside, it seemed insignificant.

A blip in our story.

A small rough patch that all couples go through every once in a while.

But inside, in my heart, it felt like the end of everything.

Today was my Saturday shift with Golden, and since Rowdy had been avoiding me all week, I knew he wouldn't come in today.

He usually did.

He usually found some excuse or reason to follow me here on his days off, but he never actually did any work. He just flirted and harassed me the whole time.

I waited the usual half-hour it took him to show up before I accepted that he wasn't coming.

Ignoring my hurt, I snuck up to the second floor of the shop and to his office. Rowdy was too arrogant to lock it, and no one except me was crazy enough to enter without his permission.

I glanced over my shoulder to make sure the coast was clear before slipping inside. I didn't exhale until the door was closed behind me. And I didn't dare turn on the light. Instead, I blindly made my way past the desk and over to the bookcase, where the teal tackle box sat on a shelf.

Digging the stolen key out of my jeans, I didn't hesitate before sticking it inside the lock.

I didn't know if Rowdy had been telling the truth and the box meant nothing to him or if it was dumb luck that he hadn't noticed the key missing in the weeks since I'd taken it.

At first, I told myself I needed to wait until his guard was down—until he'd forgotten about our argument over the box. The truth was I hadn't wanted to know what was in it. I wanted to stay in la-la land where there was no pain or loneliness.

Only Rowdy and me. Only love.

Because I'd trusted him when he said there was nothing worth knowing inside.

Now…

I blew out a breath and flipped open the lid. My throat became clogged when I saw what was inside.

A dozen or so folded sheets of yellowed notebook paper stashed inside.

With trembling hands, I plucked the top square from the pile. As if fate wanted to twist the knife a little deeper, written on the front in a familiar script were the words *For Your Eyes Only* inside a hand-drawn heart.

I backed away as if that single step could undo this path I'd started down.

But no.

The back of my leg collided with Rowdy's desk chair, and I dropped onto the cushioned seat. Unfolding the paper square, I held my breath until the last corner peeled away, revealing the secrets written inside.

Dear Owen,

This will be my last letter.

I know I say that every time because you never write back, but this time is different. This time, I know your secret. I know what you do when no one is looking. I can't believe you'd do that to him. And to me. Did you not even consider how it would make me feel?

Do you love her?

I hope not. She's not worth it. Why can't you see that?

She's nothing. I can be everything.

If only you would look past her just once. Maybe then you would finally see me.

Love,
Unrequited

A shuddering breath left me as I set the note down. I wasn't sure how much time had passed as I sat there staring at nothing. I don't remember rising from the chair and reaching for the box. I don't remember pulling out and reading the next note…and then another and another until I reached the last letter and found another photo taken twenty years ago resting on the bottom.

I set the last unread letter aside and lifted the photo from the tackle box.

The first thing I noticed was that it must have been taken the same night as the photo I possessed. Maybe even a duplicate. I looked at the factory building looming in the background, the party raging inside, and then, like a ritual, my gaze swept over each of the smiling teenagers posing in front.

Golden, Roc, Joren, Jada—

My breath hitched in my chest when my gaze landed on the short dark-skinned girl wearing large, round glasses and standing between Rowdy and Jada. She seemed out of place amongst the group. More than that, something about her seemed familiar. I just couldn't put my finger on it.

I flipped the photo over to see if her name was written on the back like before, but it was blank. I flipped it back over and stared at her image, trying to figure it out until I noticed the direction of her gaze.

She was the only one not looking at the camera. Her gaze was fixed on Rowdy.

THIRTY-SEVEN

Rowdy

ATLAS HAD LEFT ME.

Every moment since I came home two weeks ago and discovered her stuff missing had been a constant struggle to ignore my instincts—the animal prowling in my chest demanding I find his mate.

Atlas had taken only what she came into the relationship with, making her "fuck you" even clearer.

Still, I didn't go after her.

I was listening to a different set of instincts now. The ones that demanded I protect her—even from me.

So, I drank.

I drank until the river of alcohol washed away the sound of Jada screaming those fateful words at my back and taking away the one good thing it turned out I never really had.

I *couldn't* have.

I'd already had.

Jesus.

I'd looked into Jada's eyes that night and knew she wasn't lying.

Of course, there was no way for her to know from one meeting that Atlas was even her daughter, much less mine, but I knew she believed it to be true. She wasn't just telling me some wild shit out of jealousy or spite.

Jada truly believed Atlas was the daughter she'd given away twenty years ago.

I'd taken her to a bar on the other side of town in East End, where I knew there was no chance of running into anyone we knew, and I made her tell me everything.

Jada confessed to getting pregnant at fifteen and how her parents had sent her to live with her aunt—Demi's mother—before she started showing.

She'd given birth to a baby girl and had put her up for adoption while in Ossella before returning home like nothing had ever happened.

Jada and Joren's relationship had been so toxic even then that the news had reached their parents' ears, so when Jada returned to Idlewild, she simply told Joren that her parents had sent her away in hopes that the distance would make her forget about him.

Since Joren had been well aware of her parents' dislike for him, he'd bought every word, and the two had picked up where they left off.

Three years later, they were married.

It had been twenty years, but I still remembered those months she'd left to live with her aunt out of the blue, only to return less than a year later. It was the only time I'd been able to look Joren in the eye after fucking his girl behind his back.

Of course, Joren hadn't noticed because he'd been too busy screwing every girl but Jada behind *her* back.

It was heartbreak that had driven Jada to look my way in the first place. Whether for comfort or revenge, I didn't know and cared even less. I'd been no better than Joren.

Worse actually.

I was a selfish asshole willing to fuck anything thrown my way, including my best friend's girl.

And now, twenty years later, karma had finally come for me.

"Assuming the baby you gave away is even Atlas, how do you know she's mine? You were Joren's girl."

"Joren and I were barely having sex around the time I got pregnant."

"Neither were we."

"Yes, but I always made him wear a condom. I couldn't risk it after everything he'd done to me."

"So did I, Jada."

"Yes, Owen, but yours broke once, remember?"

"You're seriously expecting me to give up the only girl I've ever loved on a hunch*? Who the fuck does that?"*

"It's not a hunch," Jada snapped back.

Before I could demand that she prove it, she reached into her Birkin bag—a consolation gift from Joren no doubt—and slammed an old, worn photo on the sticky tabletop.

Peering through the darkness of the bar, I sucked in a sharp breath as I stared at the newborn in the photo.

A baby girl, no more than a few weeks old, with star-shaped markings on her face.

No, no, no, no.

My eyes frantically followed the pattern, searching for any indication—however small—that Jada was mistaken.

But when I tracked the stars and discovered the Leo at the end, my heart couldn't deny it anymore.

It was Atlas.

"Helloooo! Yo, earth to O."

The sound of my name jerked me out of that darkened bar, pushing Jada's secret that had rocked my world to the back of my mind.

I looked up from the cold lunch I'd skipped eating earlier to see Roc standing on the other side of the bar in the shop's waiting room. He was waving his hands in my face to get my attention.

"Hell nah," I said, knocking them away. "Get those dick-beaters away from me. Hands smell like you been playing with your nuts all day and got the nerve to be waving them around." My frown deepened as I stared back at my partner. "I should shoot your ass."

Rather than be offended—not that I gave a damn—Roc gave an audible sigh of relief. "Fuck all of that. I'm just glad to hear you threatening to shoot people again, even if it's me. You've been walking around here like a zombie. I thought I was going to have to call an intervention."

I said nothing and forced myself to take a bite of my burger. Food had gone from tasting nasty as fuck since Atlas left to nothing at all, but I wasn't complaining.

My gaze traveled to the bathroom door for the fifth time since she'd disappeared behind it twenty minutes ago.

Apparently, she had been staying with Tuesday of all people and not Ruen, as I'd expected when I tracked her ass down.

The shop had closed half an hour ago, and since Atlas had worked Saturday, today was her alternate Monday, meaning she only worked half the day and was responsible for closing the shop.

I'd purposely taken up a perch at the snack bar so I could watch her. I guess she'd caught on because she'd run for cover shortly after and had been hiding in the bathroom ever since.

Five more minutes and I couldn't promise I wouldn't follow her.

"Look, I know things are…weird or whatever between you and Atlas, and I never thought I'd utter these words to you, but I'm worried. It's been weeks, and you still won't tell anyone what's going on or why ya'll broke up."

My back stiffened at that. "We didn't break up," I snapped.

"You sure about that?"

"I'm *positive*." And then I thought about it. "Why?" I demanded. "You saw her with someone? Point me in his fucking direction so I can kill him."

"Chill," Roc replied. "I didn't say all of that. It's just obvious the two of y'all aren't on common ground, that's all."

I said nothing and polished off my burger before standing

and throwing the rest in the trash. My gaze traveled toward the bathroom again.

Roc must have noticed because he mumbled, "This shit is crazy."

At the edge of my vision, I noticed him storming toward the reception desk. I forced my attention away from the bathroom door when he snatched Atlas's purse off the top where she'd left it.

The only people left in the shop were the three of us. Golden's shift had ended hours ago—just in time to collect Halo from school until Roc made it home later. Joren had fucked off as soon as the shop closed, grumbling something about his wife needing him at home.

My stomach turned every time I thought about what Jada had done. And my fucked-up part in it.

"The fuck you doing?" I snapped as I rounded the bar.

"Looking for your balls," Roc's dumb ass said as he peered inside her purse. "I think Atlas keeps them in here."

"Funny. Give me this shit." I reached to take her purse from him, catching the strap at the time Roc snatched it away. The cheap strap broke in our battle for control, causing Atlas's bag to fly a few feet away.

Roc froze at the same time I did, and we watched the contents spill out of the bag and scatter all over the floor. Purse, keys, lipgloss, headphones—everything.

Fuck.

"Look what you did!" Roc screamed like a bitch—like this wasn't one-hundred-percent his fault.

I laughed as he rushed over and started frantically rescuing her stuff from the floor. I leaned against the desk to watch him throw it all into the bag with one eye while keeping the other on the bathroom door.

I was still debating storming in there after Atlas when Roc mumbled, "What the fuck?"

He lifted what looked like a photo from the ground, but he was too far away for me to see what was on it.

"What is it?" I demanded when he said nothing else. Roc continued to study the photo, his frown deepening as he slowly rose to his feet, forgetting all about Atlas's purse.

It better not have been a picture of her ex or some shit.

Roc's head turned toward me at my question, and the weird look on his face had me raising my brows. "Why does your girl have a picture of us from fucking forever ago?"

"What? What are you talking about? How do you know?"

"Because this was taken in high school. I remember this party."

Before I could walk over and see for myself, the bathroom door opened, and Atlas walked out.

She took two steps before she noticed her purse on the floor. Before she noticed us.

Her brows dipped in confusion, and then anger reared its head until she realized what Roc was holding. I watched the color swiftly drain from her face. And then her gaze, filled with fear, darted toward the exit and lingered before reluctantly trailing to me.

"I can explain," she whispered to me.

Those words were all it took for the blood in my veins to boil, for red to take over.

And then I reached behind my back and pulled my gun.

THIRTY-EIGHT

Atlas

I'D BEEN BROUGHT BEFORE THE KINGS.

The day had started off pretty ordinary, so never in a million years did I think it would end with me standing before all four Kings in the middle of their workshop.

The question was, would I walk out of here alive?

I met all four sets of glares and knew my chances didn't look good.

A month ago, I would have been confident in the irrefutable fact that Rowdy would never let anyone hurt me.

That trust had died when I'd pleaded for a chance to explain, and he pulled his gun. Roc had taken a threatening step toward me at that exact moment, and I'd braced myself to die.

But the bullet never came, and it had taken me a moment longer to realize that Roc had backed off. A moment longer still to notice Rowdy's gun trained on his friend instead of me.

"*You got me fucked up*," Rowdy had barked at his boy.

At that moment, I hadn't known what to think. And if it had been too much to hope that Rowdy had known Roc would try to hurt me and had protected me even in the face of my betrayal.

It was even harder to make sense of it when his murderous

gaze had returned to me, and he'd ordered me inside the workshop while holding his best friend at gunpoint.

Even now, he looked at me like he'd gladly empty his clip into me, so I wasn't foolish enough to think I was out of hot water yet.

After finding the photo in my purse, Roc and Rowdy called Golden and Joren back to the shop to hear what I had to say.

"All right," Rowdy began once Roc had shown Golden and Joren the photo. The reason they'd been called back here. "I'm only going to ask you this once, Atlas. How did you get this photo?"

"Someone sent it to me," I answered immediately. I knew Rowdy wasn't fucking around.

"Who?"

I lifted my chin, refusing to cower. "I'm not sure."

"You're not sure…" he repeated slowly.

"It's the truth. The sender didn't leave a name, only a letter telling me where to find you."

"Why?"

I shook my head. "I don't know that either."

It was Roc's turn to speak. "You mean to tell me someone you don't know sent you a photo of more people you don't know and told you to come here, and you just…listened?"

"I know how it sounds," I said. "It was stupid and dangerous and irrational, but being inside my head was the last place I wanted to be. My father had just died, my mother basically told me to get lost, and my—" I stopped and inhaled, not wanting to go down that road again. "Look, I needed a change, an excuse to run, so when this letter came, I saw a way out and took it." My gaze traveled to Rowdy, knowing he'd be the only one to understand. "I didn't care about this person's motives or what I might be walking into."

"And we're supposed to believe you?" Joren snapped. "Do you know how that sounds?" He took a threatening step forward, just as Roc had, but before I could react, Rowdy's head snapped in his direction.

"You must want to die today." It was all Rowdy said. All he needed to say, apparently.

Joren halted his approach, his shocked gaze flitting between Roc and Golden.

"Join the club," Roc mumbled bitterly.

I guess he was still understandably raw about his best friend of twenty years choosing me over him.

Still, he and Golden moved closer, placing themselves between Joren and me...like they, too, would protect me from him. Or maybe they were just protecting Joren from Rowdy.

Yeah, that made more sense.

Seething, Joren turned to square off with his boy. "I know we discussed you handling her yourself," he said to Rowdy, making my heart fall to my stomach, "but fuck all of that. She lied, so she needs to be dealt with. Why are we even letting this bitch explain herself? We shoot first and *never* ask questions. That's how this shit works!"

The silence that followed was so heavy that you could hear a pen drop or, more accurately, the sound of Rowdy switching the safety off his gun. "Call her a bitch again," he said through gritted teeth, "and I'm going to show you how this nine works."

My breath hitched even as my mind continued to search for a way out. I'd decided I wouldn't allow myself to hope, even fleetingly, that Rowdy still cared enough not to hurt me or let his friends hurt me. He still didn't know the worst of it yet.

"Really?" Joren spewed. "You gon' take her side when she's been lying to you—*and us*—this entire time? This ain't just about you, O. This affects all of us, so you don't get to decide alone how we deal with this."

A thousand scathing retorts rose at once, but I swallowed them all down except the one least likely to get me killed.

"Look, I can't speak to what you should do," I said in order to bring their focus back to me and keep them from killing one another. "That's for you to decide. I can only tell you the truth and pray for the best. I didn't come here with ill intentions toward any of you. I just wanted to start over without any lies."

The truth was, after falling in love with Rowdy, I hadn't cared about the reason I was sent here to find them. The truth was, even after everything, come what may, I was glad that I'd come. The truth was, I'd be worse off if I'd stayed in Ossella. If I'd stayed to watch my mom turn me away over and over and my ex and best friend start a life together with me reduced to that unpleasant footnote they both liked to pretend never happened.

"You said you weren't sure who sent this letter and photo," Golden spoke for the first time.

"Yeah?"

There was no malice in his gaze or tone when he said, "That means you have some idea."

"Not really. Only that the sender is definitely female and..." I swallowed. "Owen knows her."

"What?" His frown deepened as he stared at me.

"I—I saw the letters in your tackle box."

I saw the silent question in his green eyes at my confession. *You read them?*

Yes. Every one.

"It took me a couple of days to realize it, but..." I reached into my back pocket and pulled free one of the earliest letters I'd stolen from the box. The one where Unrequited—I still hadn't learned her name—had confessed her undying love for the love of *my* life.

I couldn't be sure the unknown girl in the photo I'd found was Unrequited, or just a coincidence, but I must have studied the youthful curves and angles of her smiling face a thousand times to force her identity from my subconscious.

I handed the letter to Rowdy, whose gaze still hadn't left mine. "The handwriting and signature are the same."

Rowdy took the note but didn't look at it as he ignored the curious looks from his boys and pocketed it immediately. I pursed my lips but said nothing.

Despite Joren being hellbent on blaming me for everything, the cracks in their friendship had started long before I entered their lives. They'd been standing on shaky ground ever since Rowdy fucked Jada.

It had taken me a couple of days to figure that out too.

That the girl Unrequited had been jealous of was Jada. And that boy Rowdy had betrayed had been Joren.

His best friend.

I sucked in a breath as the final note of Unrequited's twisted symphony slammed into me with all the intensity of a freight train.

"It was never about me," I voiced quietly.

"What wasn't?" Roc asked with a confused frown.

"The letters, sending me here…it was never about me." Unrequited's last letter suddenly made so much more sense. "It was about you…both of you…or…the three of you."

I was just the unwitting missile sent from afar to make it all collapse from underneath them.

But why?

What did I have to do with three people I'd never met and a wrong that had occurred before I was even born…

You've been lied to.

Find the Pride of Kings.

Find out who you really are.

"Three?" Roc asked as the words from Unrequited's first letter seemed to echo through me. "Who else is—" His words were cut off when the door to the workshop opened, followed by the sound of heels clicking on the polished concrete.

I kept my face blank as I watched the answer to Roc's question slowly approach. Her expensive perfume drifted toward us in a cloud, the unique scent reaching us before she did, and her beautiful face as carefully guarded as my own. My belly flip-flopped when I searched her features for any other similarities.

"Do you want to tell him?" I asked her when she finally

reached our circle and looped her arm through Joren's. "Or should I?"

I didn't bother explaining my meaning. The chances she hadn't been eavesdropping were slim to none.

Jada's painted lips spread in a practiced smile. "I'm sorry. I don't know what you mean," she lied. "I just came to collect my husband. A friend from out of town is visiting, and we have dinner plans. I'm afraid whatever this is," she said with a slow sweep of our grim faces, "will have to wait. Ciao."

Without another word, she herded Joren toward the door, and a moment later, they were gone.

"Man," Roc said, watching them go and running his hand over the waves in his close-cut in agitation. "I don't know what the fuck all of this is about, but keeping it a hundred, I'm cool on it." He looked at Rowdy. "You said you wanted to be the one to handle her, so you got it." He slapped hands with Rowdy, and they gave each other dap and a snap before Roc walked off, mumbling incoherently. "I got enough damn problems. He just gon' pull a gun on me? His boy? The fuck I look like playing detective anyway?"

I snorted and shook my head as I watched him go. I turned to Rowdy and started to speak when he cleared his throat, his green gaze sliding to Golden, who I hadn't realized was still standing there.

One moment, Golden was staring off like he was deep in thought, and the next, he was spinning on his heel and following after Roc, Joren, and Jada without a word.

Ooookay.

My gaze was slower to return to Rowdy, but when it did, I found him already watching me.

For long moments, it was all we did. We drank each other in until the silence was too heavy to stand. "Are you going to kill me now?"

I froze when he stormed toward me, driving me back until my spine pressed against the Honda Accord that Golden had been repairing earlier today.

Before I could say anything else, Rowdy's mouth was on me in a kiss so searing it melted my brain completely and loosened my tense muscles until all I could do was return his brutal kiss with just as much hunger.

Rowdy wanted control—to lead me where he wanted me—but I wasn't willing to submit just yet—not after everything he'd put me through.

I had no idea when I'd started crying, but I was vaguely aware of his hands on my tear-stained face.

Rowdy held me through it as our lips fought for dominance, tongues twisting and tangling, and teeth tearing at the skin of his lips and mine. Neither of us cared about that first taste of blood. We just kept biting at each other, wanting to make the other hurt for the pain we'd caused.

"You left me," he accused hoarsely.

I whimpered. "You left me first."

Maybe not physically, but mentally and emotionally? Rowdy had been the first to walk away. And it had hurt far worse than me packing my shit and walking.

As if my words had sparked some detail he'd forgotten, he tensed a moment before he slammed his fist on top of the Honda's roof, making me jump just before he tore away from me.

"Fuck!" I blinked as he began pacing the small space in front of me like an angry lion. "Fuck! Fuck! Fuck! Fuck! Fuck!" I stood there helpless and confused while Rowdy kicked the shit out of the Honda. His gaze flicked to me before moving away just as quickly. That same shame I'd witnessed that night three weeks ago reared its ugly head. "I shouldn't have done that. I'm sorry."

"Why? Why are you sorry? Why is it suddenly so wrong to kiss me *now* when you've been doing it for months?" I screamed back at him. Rather than answer, he shook his head, then ceased pacing to lean against the wall with his eyes closed instead. "You know what, Owen? Fine. Fuck you. I'm not going to beg you."

I walked away for the second time, hoping this time would

be the last time, and kept my gaze on the exit, refusing to look back. I knew it would only weaken my resolve if I did.

I couldn't hear much over the pounding of my heart, which was likely how he'd managed to sneak up on me. He slammed his right hand on the door, the image of a snarling lion roaring his fury as much as the hand it was tattooed into, halting my exit.

Pinned underneath Rowdy's palm was another goddamn photo. This one was a grainy polaroid of a baby that looked an awful lot like…me.

It…*was* me—unless I had a twin I didn't know about.

My parents had enough baby photos of me hanging around the house that it was impossible for me to mistake the newborn in the photo for anyone else.

It occurred to me then that the earliest photo my parents had of me was when I was maybe three or four months. I couldn't have been more than a few weeks old here.

I felt the heat of Rowdy's body pressing in as he rested his forehead on my hair. "I've been struggling with how to tell you—if I should even tell you—just how bad I fucked up." His voice was hoarse with pain.

"Why do you have this, Owen? How did you even get it?"

"Jada."

My blood went cold. "Why does Jada have a photo of me as a baby?"

"You know why, Atlas. I saw it on your face the moment you figured it out. At least half of it, anyway."

I swallowed but said nothing. I didn't have to.

Rowdy continued speaking, deciding it was time to get it all out in the open. "You found out you were adopted, and then this letter arrived telling you where to go to find out where you came from. It led you to me."

Needing to see his face, I spun around. "What are you saying, Owen?"

"I'm saying…" He swiped a hand down his face, but the pain in his eyes remained as he stared at the ground. Whatever it was he needed to tell me, once he spoke the words, it would change everything forever. "I'm saying it's possible that Jada is your birth mother."

"What does that have to do with us, Owen? Why can't you kiss me and be with me? Why can't it be like before?"

It didn't make any sense, and I wondered if Rowdy was using it as an excuse to break up with me.

But no, that didn't sound like the brash, careless Rowdy I knew. He would simply tell me if he didn't want to be with me anymore. He wouldn't care how much it hurt.

"Because…" He finally looked up. At the same time that he finally let me see the truth in his eyes, I connected the dots, remembering what I'd discovered in that tackle box.

"Because you also fucked Jada twenty years ago," I finished for him. My voice was barely a whisper, so I was surprised he'd heard.

"Yes."

"And you think you—I'm…um…"

"Yes," he croaked.

I sucked in as much air as I could after feeling like I'd been punched in the gut. I had a hard enough time coming to terms with the fact that *Joren,* of all fucking people, might be my birth father, but this…*oh, God please*…not this. How could I live with myself knowing that I—

"No," I cried and shook my head. "It's not true. Why are you doing this, Owen? You said you loved me."

"I do love you, baby. I promise that hasn't changed. Why do you think I pushed you away?"

I didn't respond. I was too busy searching for signs of myself in his features, but the details of Rowdy's face slowly blurred away as tears filled my eyes. I didn't realize I was shaking until Rowdy pulled me into his arms and held me. Slowly, my trembling faded until only my quiet sobs remained.

God couldn't be this cruel, could he? To let me love and be

loved this deeply only to take it anyway in an irrevocable way? Even in death, I would be allowed to love him. *Want* him...

But if Rowdy and I were connected in the way he feared...

Impossible.

"I want you to come home," Rowdy said as if he'd heard my thoughts and sought to defy them.

The laugh that escaped me was sad and slightly hysterical. I shook my head against his chest even as my hands tightened their hold. "That's a terrible idea, Owen."

The reasons I was forbidden to love him didn't matter. I couldn't just turn off my feelings.

Did I ever truly love him if I could?

I thought about Sutton and how I had gone numb toward him after he cheated on me. I always thought it was because my grief was too great, but maybe not. I never mourned our relationship. I don't even think I'd cried for him.

No.

Rowdy and I keeping our distance until we sorted our shit out was the best thing either of us could do.

Living with him, sharing a space, breathing his air...that would be tempting fate, and I wasn't sure I could live with the consequences.

"I know how it sounds," he told me, "but I promise it won't be like that. I know how to keep my hands to myself." If the circumstances weren't so fucked, I would have snorted at that because he absolutely did *not*. "I just want to take care of you. Be there for you. Keep you safe. No matter what ties bind us, that fact will never change."

I swallowed. "What are we going to do, Owen?"

"We're going to get to the bottom of this." His warm hand rubbed up and down my spine soothingly, and it was all I could do not to close my eyes and forget. "Whatever it takes."

Whatever it takes...

What would it take exactly?

Nothing but our souls, sanity, morals, and self-respect. And I was willing to risk anything, even my soul, not to walk this earth without this man again.

A shuddered breath left me.

This was so stupid. There was nothing concrete to suggest Rowdy and I couldn't be together.

Jada couldn't be sure that I was the daughter she'd given away any more than I could be sure the baby in the photo she'd carried around for twenty years was me—or that Rowdy was the man who'd sired me.

Conjecture.

For now, that was all it was.

I sniffed and forced myself to pull away from him—to look into his green eyes and pretend I didn't see his determination to keep me close, even if it meant damning himself. "So we just what…live in the gray until then?"

The gray.

The sliver of space between right and wrong, knowing and not knowing, salvation and damnation—between hope for a future and the calamity of us.

Because that was the gritty truth of what Rowdy was proposing.

We walk hand in hand into obscurity and hope the two sides looming over our heads don't crush us into nothing.

We hope that we wouldn't be utterly destroyed by it.

"Yes." Rowdy took my hand in his. I linked our fingers. "Together?"

I sniffed again and nodded. A lone tear for my soul trailed down my face. "Together."

Grief, after all, makes you do things.

And even though we'd agreed to hope, to be together until the truth either forced us apart or brought us closer, my heart still mourned what could have been.

THIRTY-NINE

Rowdy

I ALWAYS KNEW I WAS GOING TO HELL. I NEVER THOUGHT LOVING THE wrong woman would be the reason.

It had barely been a day since I told Atlas what Jada suspected, and so far, I'd upheld my promise. I'd kept my hands to myself. Atlas was back under my roof, which would have to be enough for now.

Last night, I'd tucked her into bed, kissed her cheek, and ignored the pain in her eyes when she realized I wasn't going to join her. I'd gone to the guest room, where I showered, avoided my reflection in the mirror, and slept alone.

It was the first time I wished Atlas hadn't made me a better man. I was still a work in progress, but nine months ago, I would have taken all I could, cut my losses on what I couldn't, and forgotten her name.

Instead, I lay awake, thinking of a plan on how to keep her. I didn't get much sleep.

From the look of her, neither did Atlas.

I was leaning against the counter, eating a bowl of cereal, when she stumbled into the kitchen the next morning. I paused mid-chew when I noticed she'd ditched the sleep shorts she'd changed into last night and now only wore one of my wifebeaters that barely covered her ass.

Was she even wearing panties? The way her ass jiggled freely under the stretched tank, it didn't look like it.

"Morning," she sleepily greeted, her eyes barely open.

I didn't return her greeting. I was too busy staring at her nipples poking through my shirt. The cotton was so thin I could see the brown areola underneath.

Atlas didn't seem to notice as she turned, opened one of the cabinets, and lifted onto the tips of her toes to reach the ceramic mugs on the middle shelf.

She liked to drink tea in the morning and sometimes before bed, so those mugs were one of the first purchases she'd made when I gave her my credit card and let her loose in here.

The bottom of my shirt rode up as she stretched, revealing the soft curve of her ass and the red string nestled where my face should have been. I didn't even realize she'd turned and caught me staring until I heard her soft voice call my name.

"Owen."

Hearing the reprimand in her tone, I tore my gaze away from her pussy hidden from me by my own damn shirt, got an eye full of her hardened nipples once more, her parted lips, and then finally, her eyes. My lips tilted when I saw the restraint in them slowly unraveling. "Yes, Atlas?"

"You can't look at me like that. You promised."

I turned away to dump my milk in the sink and collect myself. "I promised no such thing. I said I wouldn't touch you. I never said I wouldn't look. If you have a problem with me looking at you like you're a meal for me to devour, maybe you should think twice about looking so appetizing."

"What?" I paused cleaning the bowl and looked over my shoulder in time to see her look down at herself. "Oh." She flushed. "Sorry. I-I think didn't about it."

Because a T-shirt and panties were how she usually preferred to lounge around the house—to my utter fucking delight and torment.

I shrugged and went back to cleaning the bowl. "It's only a big deal if you make it one. There's no part of you I haven't already seen, touched, and tasted." I paused and inhaled, my stomach turning at the reminder of how badly I'd fucked up. "We can't take it back, Atlas. No matter how much we might want to. It's done. We can only move forward and hope for the best."

She was quiet for so long that I didn't think she'd respond—until she did. "I don't," she whispered, making me turn to face her and question if I might have misheard her. "I don't want to take it back." She looked up at me, and I could see what it cost her to admit the truth. "Not a moment of it."

I swallowed the lump in my throat and nodded. "Good. Neither do I."

Atlas closed the gap between us, and I tensed until I noticed the kettle in her hand. Another useless item she made me buy.

After she left me, it was hard to see all the changes she'd made around here and not miss her with every fiber of my being.

I shifted to the side to make room for her at the sink and watched, inhaling her oranges and vanilla scent, as she lifted the small top and filled the kettle with water.

"So, I guess we should speak to someone about a DNA test?" she asked after she was done. Her nervous gaze met mine as she chewed her lip. "I can call around after my classes this morning and book us an appointment?"

She phrased it like a question—almost like she wasn't sure I would want to since I'd already made my opinion on the matter clear during the drive home.

I didn't care what Jada said.

There was no way—*no fucking way*—Atlas came from my nuts.

I was fucked up in many ways, but wanting to fuck my own daughter was not one of them. I had to believe that if Atlas and I were truly bonded by blood, something in me would have sensed it, known it, and would have kept me from ever being attracted to her in the first place.

Even now.

It was a struggle not to nudge her thong aside and replace the string with my tongue. Instead, I gripped the edge of the sink tighter to keep from reaching out for her.

I cleared my throat and said, "That's what's up."

"Okay." She moved over to the stove and set the kettle on one of the grates before switching the burner on. "In the meantime, I guess I should put on some pants, huh?"

I smirked. "Don't bother on my account."

Smiling, Atlas left the kitchen anyway, and I watched that fat ass jiggle with each step.

Definitely not my damn kid.

And I'd give whatever DNA was necessary to prove it.

I was still standing there thinking when Atlas's tea kettle started whistling minutes later.

I moved over to the stove and turned the burner off without even thinking about it. I then grabbed the mug she set out and began making her chamomile tea the way I knew she liked—honey, milk, and a little ground cinnamon—the way I'd seen her make it a hundred times from watching her like she'd disappear if I took my eyes off of her for even a second.

Once I finished, I carried the steaming mug upstairs with me and entered the master bedroom that was now Atlas's. At least until we got this shit straightened out, and I could go back to sleeping next to her.

I set the tea down on the nightstand, then turned to leave so I could start getting ready for work when the bathroom door opened and steam poured out.

Atlas stepped into the bedroom, naked and dripping water everywhere.

"Oh." She froze in the doorway, her lips parting in shock at seeing me standing in my own bedroom. Her hands flew up to cover her breasts and pussy, even though I'd made a point to keep my focus on her face.

This was so fucking stupid.

Damn Jada and her bullshit claim.

I should have never stuck my dick in that bitch. For so many reasons. I'd always felt guilty about betraying my best friend but had never allowed myself to dwell on it—especially after they'd gotten married, and I assumed they'd live happily-ever-after.

"My fault," I said as I quickened my pace to leave.

"Wait." I'd just started to pass her when I felt her grab my hand. "Maybe you were right before," she said when I looked down at her. "You've already seen it all anyway. Stay. The shower is open."

She didn't give me a chance to argue before she let me go and disappeared inside the closet. I scrubbed my hand over my face before deciding to take her up on her offer and use the shower.

Thankfully, by the time I emerged with a towel wrapped around my waist, she was fully dressed and stuffing a textbook inside her Fendi backpack. A congratulatory gift I'd gotten her after getting her transfer into IHU accepted.

She'd gushed over that damn bag for weeks, and no matter how much I spoiled her, Atlas never stopped being grateful. It had only made me eager to give her more. Everything I had to give was hers.

"Can you give me a ride to campus?" she asked without looking up. "I forgot I left my car at the shop last night and won't have time to get it. Professor Wang gets bitchy whenever students are late."

"Yeah, I got you."

"Thanks." She kept her head down and her hands busy, and I realized she was avoiding looking at me while I wore nothing but a towel and dripping water everywhere.

I grabbed a clean uniform from the dresser before dropping the towel and stepping into my pants. My back was to her while

I faced the mirror, so I caught the quick peek she'd taken before inhaling deeply, grabbing her backpack, and fleeing the room.

I chuckled as I finished dressing before grabbing my gun from the nightstand and locking it at my waist. I followed my baby downstairs so I could take her to school, and afterward, hopefully, I could take my mind off this shit for a few hours at work.

I left the car idling at the curb as Atlas unbuckled her seat belt and turned to me. "We need to talk." I was beginning to think it was her favorite phrase. "I know we agreed on no sex until we get the results, but what about the rest of it?"

"What do you mean?"

"How does this work? With the pandemic, a DNA test could take weeks…months. Do we still go on like we're in a relationship? Do we remain exclusive, or do we see other people? I don't know about you, but the last time I checked, a platonic relationship meant friends."

I ran my tongue over my teeth as I eyed her and forced myself to remain calm. "Is that what you want?"

She shook her head. "No." Sensing she had more to say, I said nothing as I watched her tuck a curl that hadn't made it into the bushy ponytail at her crown. The faux locs she'd worn when I first met her was a distant memory, and I'd fallen in love with her natural hair. "I know it's not fair of me to demand monogamy. If Jada really is my birth mother…" She grimaced at that. "There's a fifty percent chance we'll have to break up, maybe never see each other again. But I—it's…it's what I want," she finished quickly. And then she lifted her chin to make it clear she wasn't backing down.

"All right."

"All right?" she echoed. "Just like that?"

Her words, the disbelief behind them, and the wariness in her gaze…it all felt like déjà vu. We'd come so far just to be forced back to square one where Atlas needed to be convinced I had her back no matter what.

I remembered the conversation we had eight months ago, the morning after I moved her in with me and fucked her for the first time. When I promised to kill for her.

Fuck, I'd barely known her.

That much was obvious.

I could hear my mother now. *"It's dangerous…how carelessly you young people have sex. You make babies you're not ready for. You spread diseases without regard. And I know you, son. I've known men like you. You use these women, and you barely know their names, much less where and who they come from. Could be fucking your own kin and not even know it. Take care, Owen Rashaad. Or one day, you'll find yourself in a situation you can't get out of."*

If only my mother knew how her warnings had come to pass. I knew what she and my father would say.

They'd tell me to let Atlas go.

And I had, but look where it got us? Right back to square one. I knew Atlas better than anyone. Because of her past, walking away would only do more harm than good, so I kept the promise I made to her when she agreed to be mine. I gave her what she needed, even at my own detriment.

Me.

"If I thought for one moment that the test would come back positive, I would have walked away as soon as Jada told me."

But it didn't feel entirely like the truth. Because that would imply moving on and forgetting Atlas would be easy when it would be the hardest thing I ever had to do. It felt impossible.

"But you did walk away," she accused. "You stopped talking to me, touching me…you wouldn't even look at me, Owen."

"It wasn't because I believed it was true! Okay, I'll admit at first, it fucked me up. I shut down. But once the shock wore off, and I was able to search inside myself—I mean *really* look deep, Atlas—I realized it was bullshit and decided not to tell you. I thought that would be the end of it and I could go back to normal.

Loving you, fucking you, and finding new ways to make you smile. But I...I couldn't. Without concrete proof, a small part of me still wondered, still feared that maybe it was true and what it would do to you if you found out. I *hated* Jada for planting that seed. You'd already been through so much. Lost everyone you ever cared about, and now there was a chance I'd have to walk away too and leave you to walk this earth alone again. I told myself the answer was simple. You wouldn't find out. *Ever.* I didn't want to put you through that kind of trauma. Because it was, Atlas. Living in a reality where there was even a *chance* I'd been fucking my own daughter was traumatic as fuck. I didn't want to imagine what it would do to you. Yeah, there was no way we could have known, but it didn't stop me from feeling like shit. I dragged you into this fucked-up situation with me. I pursued you, seduced you, and made you be with me. This was all on me, and I wanted it to stay that way. But now I was keeping this huge secret from you, so the guilt tripled until I was just...stuck. I did all of that to keep you from feeling any pain. I switched up, and you didn't know why. I couldn't see until too late that I was hurting you anyway by keeping you in the dark."

By the time I finished spilling my guts, there was a thoughtful furrow in her brow. "You said you hated Jada for planting that seed. You seem so sure that it's not true. Is there a reason she'd have to lie?"

"I don't know." I bit my lip and kept my gaze straight ahead, suddenly finding the IHU students walking to and from classes fascinating.

The car was silent for a while, and then, "I think you do," Atlas returned icily. I could feel her breathing fast and hard now. "When was the last time you fucked her, Owen?" I closed my eyes, not wanting to answer. Noting my hesitation and the tension in my body, Atlas let out a derisive laugh and added, "Let me guess...it wasn't twenty years ago."

"No."

"How recent?"

My hands shook, actually fucking shook, as I ran them up and down my thighs as if the friction it created would give me the strength I needed not to lie. I never had trouble giving the brutal truth before because I'd never cared about hurting anyone's feelings. Lately, I'd been wishing I could go back to the man I was before Atlas found me.

"When, Rowdy?" she snapped. Atlas using my street name was never a good sign.

"We never fucking stopped!" I finally blurted. Seeing her ebon eyes open wide in alarm, I rushed to add, "Not until you. The last time was before I even met you. Jada tried to keep it going, but I shut the shit down after we got together and told her it was never happening again."

"So…best case scenario is your *best friend's wife* has it out for me and is lying to break us up, and worst case scenario is that *my own fucking mother* has it out for me and is *telling the truth* just to break us up?" She tilted her head to the side. "Do I have that correct, Owen? Is there anyone else in my family tree you fucked? Demi, maybe?"

I'd forgotten that Demi was Jada's first cousin. That would make her Atlas's cousin too.

"Chill."

Atlas sneered. "It's a valid question."

"I've never fucked Demi, nor would I ever. Roc is my boy. I wouldn't do him dirty like that."

"And Joren isn't?"

"Joren isn't in love with his wife!" I roared. Atlas flinched, so I forced myself to calm down. "I don't think he ever was."

The only reason I hadn't come clean before was because Joren's pride ran deeper than his love for his wife. *Much* deeper. He'd never forgive me.

"How noble of you." Atlas sneered. "You want to know what I really think? I think it's rich of you to say that Joren doesn't love his wife when you don't know what love is. You're not capable of it, and I wish I'd never met you."

My nostrils flared as I stared straight ahead, pretending her words hadn't cut me deep. I knew she was angry, hurt, and just lashing out, but it didn't hurt any less. My voice was hollow when I finally spoke. "That may be, but this changes nothing between us, Atlas."

"If you say so. Look, I gotta go." Atlas quickly gathered her things, but when she reached for the door, I quickly hit the locks. Without looking back at me, she said, "Unlock the door, Rowdy."

"Chill with that Rowdy shit," I said with a snarl. Atlas said nothing, so I sighed. "Tell me you understand what I said."

"I wish I could, Owen, but it's not that simple anymore. It's too much. It's all too much. I knew you were a monster, but I fell in love with you anyway, the good, the bad, and the ugly. There was no part of you I didn't want. But for the first time since I said yes to us in that hot-air balloon, I'm wondering if I ever really knew you."

I sucked in a breath and felt the heart I'd kept on ice for her give its final death rattle. I felt her gaze on me, but I didn't allow myself to look at her. I was afraid of what she'd see if I did. She might be having regrets about us, but I wasn't. "Aight." It was all I said before I hit the locks. "You're free."

I saw her flinch from the corner of my eye, but she didn't stick around to question what I meant. She wouldn't like the answer either way.

Atlas fled, and I didn't let myself watch her go. I wasn't sure how long I sat there before I found the will to leave.

FORTY

Atlas

I'D NEVER BROKEN A HEART BEFORE, SO I DIDN'T KNOW THE SIGNS TO look for. Sign or no sign, I was pretty sure I'd broken Rowdy's. It should have been easy to detect since I've suffered it before, but heartbreak looked different in every person. Some ran from it while some wallowed in it.

And then there was Rowdy. He just pretended it never happened.

I was still living with him, but it had been a week since we'd said more than two words to each other.

It felt like we were going backward—tiptoeing around each other, sleeping in separate rooms, and being careful not to touch or let a look linger for too long.

I should have been relieved when the kit arrived in the mail, but nothing but dread filled my stomach as I stared at the multiple mouth swabs laid out before me.

None of the labs I'd called could see us before the end of the year, so I booked an appointment with the earliest availability.

Next fucking year.

In the meantime, I had the lab send us an at-home kit, and they swore that as long as we followed the directions, the results would be accurate. It was our next best option since we didn't need them to be admissible in court.

It would still take a few weeks to get answers. Every lab in the country was not only backlogged but understaffed thanks to the pandemic.

Hard to believe my sex life wasn't a priority.

I was home alone in the living room with my textbooks and notes spread all around me on the coffee table while I studied for my midterms. At the moment, I was struggling with the practice tests for my Intro to Psych II course, and Professor Saunders wasn't responding to any of my emails. She hadn't been in weeks.

Meanwhile, Rowdy was...out.

I hadn't seen him since this morning.

Since I was back in school full-time, I was only working part-time at the shop, so I didn't get to see him as much as I used to, and the rare times we were both home, we didn't talk.

When I entered a room, he left it. When I tried to talk, he ignored me.

How the hell had this turned on me?

Rowdy might have fucked Jada before my time, but it was still a hard pill to swallow. He still lied about it by trying to cover it up. He still betrayed his best friend. I knew firsthand how much that hurt.

Rowdy had listened to me cry over what Sutton and Sienna had done to me while pretending to understand when he was really no better.

How could I trust him now?

The doorbell rang, and I practically raced to it since I was getting nowhere with my studies. I ripped the door open without checking the peep hole and almost slammed it back when I saw who was standing on my porch.

"You must have a death wish," I told the two-faced bitch.

"Relax. Your boy is with my boys." She shifted nervously on her feet before asking, "Can I come in?" Ruen stepped forward like she'd do just that, but I blocked her.

"No. What do you want?"

"You haven't been answering my calls or texts, and I've missed you. I thought you might—I wanted to come clean, but I'm guessing he already told you."

"Owen didn't have to tell me you sold me out, Ruen. I figured it out all on my own."

It was something Rowdy had said after the hot-air balloon ride—about letting someone into his kingdom for me. It had taken a few days for it to click and a few more to accept the fact that Ruen must have told Rowdy where to find me that night at the club.

She'd used me as leverage to get her crew the green light from the Kings. I guess she must have had second thoughts, afraid that he might hurt me, and that was why she'd barged in on us fucking in the bathroom. Ruen had felt guilty, but it had been too late to take it back.

"I'm sorry. I have no excuse. It was a shitty thing to do."

"Thanks. Bye." I tried to close the door, but she stopped it with her boot. "Move, Ruen, before I make you move."

Her signature smirk appeared for the first time since she arrived on my doorstep. "I'm sure that would be a lot of fun, but I'm not here to fight. I'm here to make amends." She lifted the Tupperware container I hadn't noticed her holding before. "Brownies from Remedy. She misses you too." When I didn't react, she said in a sing-song voice, "I think they're still warm."

Goddamn this manipulative bitch.

She knew I couldn't resist Rem's cooking.

I tried to snatch the container, but Ruen held it out of reach, so I drove my fist into that shady bitch's stomach and snatched the brownies from her when the air whooshed out of her and she leaned over.

Feeling my mouth water, I left her there and carried the brownies into the kitchen. I was pouring a glass of cold milk when I heard the front door shut.

Ruen appeared while I was grabbing a small plate for my

brownie and made a show of looking around. "Nice crib. I see Rowdy succeeded in turning you into a house bitch."

"And I suggest you leave before he turns *you* into a dead bitch."

"I told you I had it handled, didn't I? The guys are going to text me when he leaves. I'll be out of your hair before he gets back."

I didn't bother mentioning that Rowdy had cameras all through this house. Something he had installed *after* I moved in. No doubt to keep an eye on me with his stalking ass.

"So, what do you want, Ruen? You already apologized."

"But you haven't forgiven me."

I bit off half a brownie, chewed, thought about it, and said, "If I say I forgive you, will you go away?"

"Mmmm…probably not since I won't believe you." She stared at me while I ignored her. "Are you seriously telling me you wouldn't have found your way back to him anyway?"

"I'm not telling you shit. You're the one talking."

Ruen sighed heavily as if I was the one being unreasonable. "I fucked up, Atlas, but I'm still your friend."

"Are you?"

"*Yes*. It's just that…the guys are family. Besides Rem, they were all I had for a long time. It's second nature to ride or die for them. I don't know anything else. I'm not making excuses," she rushed to add. "There's no excuse for what I did. I just—I don't want you to think it was easy for me to give you up."

She held my gaze, letting me see the sincerity in it, but since I wasn't ready to forgive the bitch, I grabbed my plate and glass before leaving the kitchen and returning to the living room.

Ruen followed me from the kitchen and sat down next to me on the couch. Giving up on psych for the time, I grabbed one of my biology textbooks. "If I thought for a second that you wouldn't be safe with him, you know I wouldn't have done it."

Still not looking at her, I flipped a page. "Is that why you stuck around to listen to us fuck?"

Ruen smiled a little. "Maybe. Mostly, I liked the way you sound when you're being fucked. And I might have been a little jealous that it wasn't me in there with you."

"Ruen," I warned.

She held up her hands in mock surrender. "I know, okay? You're not into me."

I cut my gaze at her but chose not to remark on it. Ruen had chosen her words carefully. No, I wasn't into girls, but she knew I had been into her.

I was reading the same sentence for the fifth time when she spoke again.

"What's all this?" My stomach sank when I looked up and caught her lifting the paternity kit from the table. "Trouble in paradise?"

"Would that make your day if I said yes?"

"No. I meant what I said earlier. You're my friend, Atlas, so your happiness is more important to me than anything I might want from you."

"Okay."

"Talk to me. I can tell you're hurting, and I'm guessing whatever it is, you can't talk to Rowdy about it."

I sucked in a deep breath when it felt like I might actually cave and tell her everything. I'd be a fool to after I trusted her once, and she betrayed me at the first opportunity.

Was it a coincidence that all my relationships seemed to end the same way? Sutton, Sienna, my parents—birth and actual—Ruen, and now Rowdy.

I didn't think so.

Maybe I was the problem. Maybe I expected too much of people.

"Thanks, but I'm okay," I lied without any malice or bitterness. A part of me had declined her ear because I just didn't have the energy to rehash everything. I was exhausted, and not just physically.

"There are three kits here," Ruen said, refusing to let it go.

I sighed. "Yup."

"But you haven't collected all of the samples."

"Nope."

"Mom, Dad, baby," she mused aloud.

When I didn't respond, she reached out her arm encased by a black leather jacket with silver spikes around the cuff and lifted one of the tubes.

I noticed Ruen's appearance had changed in the months since I last saw her. Her colorful wigs were nowhere to be found, and she now wore her long, natural hair in a French braid that stopped between her shoulder blades. The darkness of her hair called attention to the freckles on her light brown skin.

"Here is Dad's," she said, returning Rowdy's sample to the box on the table.

He'd collected it and left it for me to find on the table without ever saying a word. I didn't know if it meant he still wanted to be together or if he just wanted to know if he was a father.

Ruen picked up the next sample—the one with my name on it—and studied it for a long while. Long enough for the brownie and milk that I'd eaten to threaten to come back up. "I don't see a baby around, and you don't look pregnant to me, so I'm guessing you're Baby?" I gulped but didn't say a word. "That just leaves Mom," Ruen pressed on.

I could feel her assessing gaze on me, but I kept mine on my textbook, the small black words blurring together.

"Do you know who she is?" Ruen asked. I couldn't detect any judgment in her tone, but I was still on edge. I'd already told her that I was adopted shortly after we met, but I'd left out the part about coming here to find my birth parents. At the time, I hadn't known that it was the closure I'd been looking for when I came to Idlewild.

I cleared my throat before I spoke. "I have an idea."

"Do you know where she lives?"

"Yeah."

Ruen tossed my sample inside the box before grabbing the

empty tube and unopened mouth swab from inside and standing. "So let's go."

I finally looked up at her out of surprise. "What?"

"We're going to get Mama Dearest's DNA, and if she gives us any trouble, we can stick this swab up her cooch instead."

"Ruen, we can't just show up at her house."

She perked a brow. "Why not?"

"Because…" I struggled to find a reason why.

I knew Jada still hadn't come clean to Joren about her affair with Rowdy or the baby she'd hidden for twenty years, but so what? Jada had no problem showing up here and turning *my* world and relationship upside down. It had been a month since she told Rowdy, but Jada still hadn't made any attempts to reach out to me. Her true intentions couldn't have been any clearer if she'd shouted them through a megaphone.

"You know what?" I set my textbook aside, grabbed my keys from the table, and stood. "Let's go."

"Whoop!" Ruen cheered. "There's the bitch I know and love. And if your egg donor pops shit, we can always jump her ass and get it anyway."

"Really, Ruen?" I shook my head as I slipped my feet inside the fresh Jordan A1s Rowdy had bought me to match his pair. Since he wasn't talking to me, he'd left them on the bed for me to find. They had a blue and green colorway—his and my favorite colors. I'd been in love at first sight.

"Yup," Ruen said as we headed out the door, her arm slung over my shoulder. "Anything for my girl bestie."

I shoved her arm off me. "Don't push it."

This was a huge mistake.

I was glad to finally get this part over with, but I really wished I'd made Ruen stay in the car.

Ding-dong! Ding-dong! Ding-dong! Ding-dong!

"I don't think anyone is home, Ruen." She'd been ringing the doorbell nonstop for the past five minutes.

"Bullshit. I saw the curtains moving upstairs when we pulled up." Ruen pressed the doorbell harder and faster as if that would make Jada answer.

"Let's just go," I said, feeling defeated.

Who cared if Jada was my birth mom? It wouldn't change anything between us. Besides, I was already estranged from one mom. I didn't need another to *not* talk to.

"Well, she's obviously not going to answer, so unless you plan on kicking the door down, there's nothing else we can do."

Ruen sighed and finally let off on the doorbell. She glared at the door for a second before turning her head toward me. "It's a really nice house," she remarked out of the blue.

I'd been in awe of the large white modern farmhouse and immaculate front lawn that Jada probably took for granted. My parents had both earned decent wages but nothing that could have afforded them this. Still, I hadn't wanted for anything, including affection. Our humble home in our quiet neighborhood had more than kept my cup full.

"Yeah," I mumbled begrudgingly. "It really is. Whoa! *What* are you doing?"

Ruen had reached inside the backpack she'd pulled from her trunk when we arrived for some reason and produced a can of *permanent* spray paint.

She was now hard at work drawing huge rainbow dongs on the immaculate door.

"Are you crazy?" I screamed. I looked around to make sure we weren't seen and spotted some nosy Karen eyeing us from across the street as she walked her dog. "Shit!"

"No, thanks," Ruen said as she grabbed a white can from her bag and started drawing semen, to make it look like the dicks were ejaculating. "I took one before I left home."

"Will you stop before someone calls the cops?" Ruen rolled her eyes but caved and shoved the spray paint back in her bag.

"I can't believe you did that," I scolded. "If they have cameras, we're screwed."

"Relax," Ruen said as she crossed her arms and leaned against the wall. "There aren't any cameras. People move to neighborhoods like these and get too comfortable. They barely remember to lock their doors and windows."

"I guess you'd know," I shot back.

Ruen didn't respond. She was too focused on watching the opposite end of the street and the SUV turning in.

The pearl-white Benz drew closer. Ruen and I seemed to hold our breath when it slowed and turned into the driveway.

"Fuck."

"Guess she wasn't home after all," Ruen muttered.

I glared at her, but her predatory gaze was already fixed on Jada as she climbed out of the car and eyed us warily as she approached.

"Ladies," she greeted. Her gaze shifted between Ruen and me before settling on me. "How can I help you?"

"Someone vandalized your door," Ruen blurted before I could speak. "He went that way." She pointed down the street.

"I'm sorry to drop in unannounced," I said, swiftly changing the subject when Jada's focus traveled to her door full of dicks. "We need to talk."

"Do we?" Jada shot back. "I barely know you."

"You told Owen that you were my birth mother."

Jada studied her fresh acrylic set. "So."

It stung a little—the way Jada was clearly ready to discard me all over again. "Don't you think you should prove it?"

"And why would I do that?"

I took a step closer, ready to forget that I came out of her pussy and knock the bitch on her ass. "Because you ruined my relationship."

"Did I? You seemed to be doing that all on your own. Joren told me about how you purposely tracked them down. What's still unclear is why. Was it money? Did your little scheme fail, and now you're after mine? I mean, damn, little girl. I couldn't get rid of you fast enough when you were born, but you can't seem to take the hint. I *gave you up,* which means I don't owe you *shit.* Do us all a favor and go back to where I left you."

"I don't want your money, Jada, and I'm not looking for a mom. I have one. A great one. The *best* one. I'll admit that I wondered about you when I found out I was adopted. I wondered what you looked like and if I looked like you. I wondered if you were okay and if you were happy. I wondered if you ever thought about me. And then I met you, and I realized none of that mattered. You did the most motherly thing someone as poisonous as you could do. You gave me up. I'm grateful to you, Jada. I can't imagine the kind of person I'd be if you hadn't, but I know I would be no one worth knowing. I don't need or want shit from you." I paused. "Well, there is one thing."

I turned my head toward Ruen, who had been leaning against the wall quietly, watching my family drama unfold. She perked up when she saw the intent in my gaze. "The hard way?" she asked me excitedly.

"The hard way."

Ruen straightened and, without any hesitation, raised her leg and kicked out, planting her booted foot in Jada's chest. My egg donor went sprawling backward, and the moment she landed, Ruen pounced. She jumped on top of Jada and held her down with a knee in her chest and her hands locked around Jada's wrists.

"Hurry up, Twinks," Ruen said, grunting, "this frail bitch is stronger than she looks."

Jada struggled to free herself while I hurriedly removed the mouth swab from its packaging and bent to collect the sample. Jada turned her head away while keeping her lips closed firmly.

White-hot fury rushed through me, and I punched her temple. I didn't want to risk ruining the results by knocking out her teeth. "Open your fucking mouth, bitch."

Rowdy had clearly rubbed off on me. I didn't know if that was a good thing or terrible thing. Right now, it was a useful thing.

"Touch me, and I'll have my husband come and air this bitch out!" she screamed.

"Bitch, please," Ruen taunted. "Your husband is for the streets, and everyone knows it. He probably doesn't even answer the phone when you call." A truly cruel smile took over Ruen's visage. "I bet he answers the phone for his baby mama, though."

Jada and I both paused in shock. "What are you talking about?" I asked when words seemed to fail Jada. "He has a kid?"

"Yup. A cute little boy too. The baby's mother stays over in the Garden." Ruen paused to let the news sink in as her gaze scanned Jada's face. "She was definitely an upgrade."

Jada gasped, and though she didn't deserve my sympathy, my forgetful heart broke a little for her. I knew it had to be painful to hear that your husband had made a baby outside the marriage when you had given him none.

On the other hand, Ruen didn't seem the least bit sympathetic to Jada's plight and gave me a pointed look.

Oh. Right.

I took advantage of her parted lips and quickly swabbed her inner cheeks and gums before sealing the sample and standing. The moment I was on my feet, I inwardly swore when I recognized Joren's black Escalade pulling in.

Ruen noticed, too, and finally freed Jada, her hand going to the back of her waist as she rose.

Joren hopped out of the truck with a scowl and gun in hand, but what shocked me most was when three more cars appeared, burning rubber and pavement as they came to an abrupt stop at the curb.

The rest of the Kings hopped out, but I had eyes only for Rowdy. He barely made it two steps before his eyes found me and he stopped in his tracks. He seemed shocked to find me here.

"Atlas? What are you doing here?" He rudely tramped all over Joren and Jada's front lawn until he was towering over me while pointedly ignoring Ruen.

I held up the tube. "Getting Jada's sample."

"I was going to handle that," he said, seething.

"And now you don't have to."

By now, Joren had helped his wife off the ground and held her while she sobbed dramatically. I rolled my eyes at them both.

"What are *you* doing here?"

"Got a message that said Jada was getting jumped by some bitches."

"And you came to her rescue," I remarked dryly.

"I came to have my boy's back. It could have been a setup with some jack boys to get him here alone."

"What a ghetto fabulous life you lead."

"Chill," he admonished. And then he looked to my left. "Quintana."

"Wray," Ruen returned.

"I thought I told you to stay away from my pussy."

Ruen smirked and met his gaze head-on. "Then you should guard it better."

"Bet," Rowdy promised. He looked at me then and swept me closer with his arm around my waist. I was immediately surrounded by his scent and didn't know just how much I'd missed it until my knees nearly gave out. "I will." And then he bent his head and kissed me for the first time since I learned we couldn't be.

"Owen," I whined breathlessly against his lips. "We can't."

"I don't care." He pulled me closer, and I wrapped my arms around his neck. "We're in the gray, remember?"

I remembered.

It just hadn't done us any good.

We were too afraid of ruining our souls so irrevocably that there would be nothing left to intertwine or move on with when this was over.

When his tongue teased the seam of my lips, I opened for him, consequences be damned. I wasn't sure how much time had passed before someone cleared their throat and shocked us back into reality.

"I thought...I thought you didn't want me anymore. I didn't know what to do."

Rowdy squeezed my waist. "Then you should stop thinking so much and listen for once." He shook his head. "It's not your fault. I just needed a few days to get my mind right."

"Someone want to tell me what the fuck is going on?" Joren demanded.

Rowdy and I gave each other a look—a promise to finish making peace later. "I think you should tell him," I urged Rowdy. "And I think you should do it now."

He stared down at me and I could see the wheels turning. "Is that what you want?"

"Do you have feelings for her?"

"Fuck no," he said, breathing out.

"Then it's what I want. I want to put her behind us. No more secrets."

Rowdy looked over my head at his best friend and the woman who might have given birth to me. "All right."

We turned to face the angry couple together, but movement up above, in the window on the right, caught my eye.

The curtains had shifted back closed.

FORTY-ONE

Rowdy

"I FUCKED JADA THE NIGHT OF THE V-DAY PARTY," I BLURTED AS soon as we were all inside the house. Well, everyone except for Ruen, who had fucked off as soon as Joren lost his mind over all the dicks someone had left on his door. "It happened twenty years ago, but we've been fucking on and off until a few weeks before I met Atlas."

Everyone, including Atlas, sent me an appalled look at how carelessly I'd unloaded that bomb.

I didn't know why they were all shocked. That was the real tragedy. I didn't even want to do this, but since my girl insisted, I had no choice. Atlas wanted proof that I'd truly ended my chapter with Jada.

Joren's head was on a swivel, back and forth between me and Jada, who was trying her best to make herself small.

"What the fuck are you talking about, O?" I held Joren's gaze but said nothing since I'd already said it all. Well…not *all*. "Huh?" He closed the distance between us, so I swiftly moved Atlas out of harm's way and braced myself for the first swing. It was coming. Joren's fuse wasn't as short as mine, but his ego was much bigger. "Motherfucker, I think you just said you fucked my *wife*, but I'm not sure I'm hearing you right."

I shook my head and glanced at Atlas, who gave me a reassuring smile that wobbled. "You heard me, Joren, and all I can say is that I'm sorry." In my peripheral, I noticed Roc and Golden glance at each other. I was never one to apologize so hearing me do so probably shocked them more than hearing that I'd been fucking my boy's wife. "That shit was foul, but…" I glanced at Atlas again and sucked in a breath. "I wouldn't take it back even if I could." Come what may, if I hadn't betrayed my best friend, Atlas might not exist. "My mistake was the best thing that had ever happened to me."

Joren swung then.

I let the blow land, knowing it would be the only one he'd get. He'd earned that. When he swung again, I quickly maneuvered him into an arm lock before Roc and Golden could intervene. "Listen to me," I spoke into his ear. "You're my partner, my brother, my right hand. What I did was fucked up, and I don't want to lose you as my friend, but I'll understand if you can't get past this. You just need to listen to me for a little while longer. There's something else you need to know."

"Rowdy, *no*," Jada pleaded.

I ignored her.

"Get off me!" Joren roared.

I let him go, and when he swung around to face me again, I gave him a look. I knew I was in the wrong, and I was sorry like a motherfucker, but I was who I was. My understanding only reached so far.

"Did ya'll know?" Joren directed his anger at Roc and Golden.

"What? Hell nah!" Roc immediately denied it.

Golden said nothing. Only his eyes purposely gave him away when they met mine across the foyer.

He'd known.

All this time, and he'd never said a word.

Joren, however, caught the exchange, and it brought his rage to a boiling point. "Yo, say what you got to say, and then y'all can get the fuck out of my house! Including you, bitch." That last part had been directed at Jada.

"Me?" Jada shrieked. "You're going to kick me out? After everything you did to me? Ask yourself how you had no clue I've been fucking your best friend for twenty damn years! You left me alone, Joren. Ever since we were kids, your dick, mind, and heart were always elsewhere! I couldn't even creep with someone who wasn't close to home because *everyone* knows who you are! I'm your wife and always came last, so I decided to go where it cut deepest, Joren Dorsey. It was no less than what you deserved."

"Fuck all of that," Joren spat. "You—"

"She got pregnant that night," I blurted before he could spew more venom. I heard Atlas sigh next to me at my lack of tact. I didn't know if their marriage was salvageable after today, but I realized one thing while listening to Jada's rant.

She loved Joren.

His cheating had taken an emotional toll on her that she'd tried to exorcise by betraying him too. The only problem was Atlas. The baby she'd given away. Jada could never truly return the pain without revealing her most fucked-up secret.

So Jada wallowed, took it, and found ways to cope. Namely, fucking me and spending all of Joren's money.

"What do you mean she got pregnant?" Joren echoed. "She—" His head swung her way. "You got an abortion?" A waterfall of fresh tears spilled from Jada's eyes as she shook her head. "Then what is he talking about, Jada?"

"I had the baby," she cried. "I didn't know if she was yours or his, and I was so scared. My parents sent me to my Aunt Candace in Ossella to have the baby, and I..." Jada broke out into hysterical sobs.

I felt Atlas's presence draw closer to me, so I pulled her in and wrapped my arms around her. "It will be okay," I whispered to her when I felt her body shake. "I got your back."

"She told me she didn't want me," Atlas whispered back. "I

knew that already. I just...it's different when you hear it in their own words, I guess."

I was going to fucking kill Jada.

After today, Joren probably wouldn't mind, and it would give me a whole lot of satisfaction.

I was sure Jada never expected to see the daughter she'd given away again, and it must have fucked her up, but it had also been her decision to press the button that blew up all of our lives. She was equally responsible for this.

"Where is the baby?" Joren roared. "What did you do with my fucking baby, Jada?"

"I g-g-gave her awaaay!"

"I'm going to fucking kill you!" Joren lunged for her. Before any of us could react, he had his hands around her throat. "I've begged you! For seventeen years, I fucking begged you to have my baby, and all along, your hateful ass had been hiding it!"

"I'm sorry!" Jada wailed.

It took Roc and Golden to pry him off her. Jada slid down to the floor, and it was Joren's turn to cry this time. I'd only ever seen him do so when his father died our senior year.

I think losing his dad was part of the reason he'd married Jada. Grief makes you do things you know are wrong, and Joren desperately needed to refill that connection he'd lost.

"My baby." He sobbed in Golden's arms. "She gave away my seed, dawg."

"Well, if you want a baby so bad, go be with that little bastard you had on me," Jada spewed.

"What the fuck are you talking about? I don't have no fucking baby!"

Atlas tensed in my arms.

Keeping my gaze on the screaming couple, I bent my head and whispered to her, "What do you know about this?"

"Ruen," she grumbled back. It was the only answer she gave.

"That's not what I heard!"

"I don't give a fuck what you heard!" He yanked away from

Golden, but Roc swiftly moved between them when Joren pulled his gun. "Where's my fucking daughter, Jada? I swear to God, you better tell me, or you won't live to see another day."

Atlas's nails were suddenly digging into my chest, stealing my focus from the spectacle Jada and Joren made. "Please," she pleaded, her eyes brimming with agony and guilt. No doubt she blamed herself for Jada and Joren's marriage unraveling when she was far from blame. "Get me out of here, Owen. I want to leave. *Please.*"

But it was too late.

Before I could herd Atlas out of the door, Jada flung her arm out and screamed, "She's right there!"

I watched as Jada's revelation landed—as Joren's emotions shifted from anger to confusion to incredulity and then horror. Before either of them could do any more damage, I swept Atlas up in my arms and got her the fuck out of there.

We were halfway to the car when the front door burst open and Joren stormed out. Golden and Roc were hot on his heels. "Atlas," he called out. "Atlas, wait!"

A whimper escaped Atlas as she burrowed deeper against my chest. I was forced to set her on her feet when I looked over my shoulder and saw Joren gaining on us.

"Aye, back the fuck up," I barked at my boy. I pushed Atlas behind me where she clung to my back.

Joren stopped and held his hands up. "I just want to talk to her."

"That's not happening."

"What the fuck do you mean?" Joren snapped. "You owe me this!"

"And when you're ready to shoot it out, just let me know, but Atlas stays out of it. Don't come near her. Don't even speak to her. Just ignore her like you've been doing."

"I didn't know!" he roared.

"Well, now you do. If you want a second chance, it will be on *her* terms, when *she's* ready. Now go handle your marriage. I'm taking my girl home."

Not another word was said as I helped Atlas into the car.

The drive home was silent and heavy. Atlas had gone numb, staring blankly out into nothing. In our bathroom, I peeled off her clothes and then mine before carrying her into the shower.

"Talk to me, Dream. Let me know you're still in there."

She didn't so much as blink as I washed her body. I quickly cleaned us both before wrapping a towel around my waist and drying her off with another. Then I grabbed her vanilla-scented body lotion, squirted a dollop in my palm, and massaged it into her skin.

Once that was done, I moved behind her, grabbed one of her hair clips from the counter, and began pinning up her twist-out like I'd seen her do.

"Do you know why I kept those letters?" I asked as I worked. Atlas didn't respond verbally, but she blinked, and I knew she was listening. "I didn't really know why myself until you found them. I knew you took the key by the way, so when I finally figured out why I kept them, I left them there for you to read. It was proof, Atlas. Proof that I could be loved beyond reason. I know it's fucked up, but I'm not an easy man. There's no trauma or demons that made me this way. I am who I am, and the moment I accepted that, I knew what it would take. Anytime I lost hope that I would find something real, I remembered those letters. Anytime I thought about saving you from me, I remembered those letters. It was never about her. It was about you. I saved them to remind me to wait for you. I kept them as proof that there was a woman out there brave or crazy enough to love a man like me."

It took me longer than she usually took to pin her hair, but once her curls were secure, I grabbed her silk scarf she always wore to bed and tied it around her head.

"You didn't give up on me even when reason told you," I whispered while staring at our reflections in the mirror, "so I'm not giving up on you. Come back to me."

Atlas released a shuddered exhale as if whatever demon held her had been vanquished for now. "Owen."

"Let that shit go, baby. There's no one else here but me. I got you. Where am I standing?"

The reminder that I had her back broke the dam free. The tears she'd held back at Joren and Jada's now rushed down her supple cheeks. "I never should have come here." She sobbed.

My chest felt like it had caved in. "Yes, you should have. Do you know why?" She shook her head. "Because you weren't meant to find them, Dream. You were meant to find me."

Atlas's tortured gaze met mine in the mirror. "What if we were fated, Owen, but not meant to be?"

I pressed a kiss to her shoulder while never looking away. "Then I'll keep you anyway."

She sucked in a breath but didn't object this time. I knew she was feeling it too. We were already damned, so what would it matter? The world wouldn't care if we could have known. They'd judge us from inside their glass homes anyway.

"Let's hope it doesn't come to that."

We brushed our teeth and got dressed. I threw on a pair of boxers, and she stole another one of my ribbed tanks. I noticed she skipped wearing panties again but didn't remark on it. Afterward, we climbed into bed even though it was still early.

"Just for a little while," I told her when she begged me not to go. I searched underneath the covers for the remote because her ass never remembered to put it on the nightstand and always fell asleep with the TV on. Once I found it, she curled around me while I opened the Netflix app. "What do you want to watch?"

"Bridgertons."

"Man, fuck." I sucked my teeth and scrolled to find that boring-ass show. After she made me watch a couple of episodes with her last month, before Jada happened, I made it clear if she wanted to finish without me, I was more than cool with that.

"All right, fine," she said, relenting. "I finished it last week anyway since I was mad at you." I smirked at her cappin' ass and continued to browse the app. "Ooh! That one," she said when I landed on a horror movie.

"Hell, nah. So you can get scared and make me stay up to keep watch while you sleep?"

"It was one time, Owen. This one doesn't even look that scary."

"You jump one time, and I'm putting your ass out," I warned as I clicked on the movie.

Atlas said nothing and shifted closer, her leg now hooked around mine and her hot pussy pressed against my thigh. I bit my bottom lip and kept my eyes on the TV to keep from snatching her ass up and giving her this dick.

Twenty minutes into the movie, Atlas moved again, and I bit back a curse when I felt her arousal seep through my boxer shorts. I made the mistake of grabbing her hip to keep her still and looked down at her. "What are you doing?" I asked in a low tone.

"Nothing," she whispered while staring up at me. The light from the TV flickered across her face.

I shifted my hand from her hip and gripped her ass through the shirt. "It don't feel like nothing." The heat from her pussy was searing my fingertips. "Atlas…" I shook my head, catching on to what she was trying to do. "We can't."

"We already have. What's one more time?"

"We'd *know* this time."

It was her turn to shake her head. "I don't care anymore. I miss feeling you inside of me."

I slapped her ass hard enough to make her hiss. "Stop this shit, Dream."

"Why?" She whimpered. "Don't you want to?"

"Of course, I want to."

"Then fuck me."

"You'll regret it in the morning." We both would.

"I won't," she denied.

I didn't respond as I shoved up the tank and my fingers found their way between her thighs. Atlas eagerly turned onto her back and let her legs fall open. I cursed at what I found as I rubbed her swollen clit.

Atlas was *gushing*.

"Your period is coming," I mused aloud. Atlas was always horniest right before her cycle. Anything went during those few days before she bled and even sometimes during. She'd even let me fuck her ass or run a red light. The memories had me leaning down and kissing her fat pussy lips a couple of times. "Behave," I whispered to it as much as her.

"Please, Owen. Just this once. No one will know."

I was quiet as I considered my options.

Fucking her would be purely selfish. That much was clear. It didn't matter that she was begging me. I promised I would take care of her, and until we got the results back, it meant denying my baser urges.

Still, I couldn't ignore the desperation in her eyes, not just for me to fuck her but to prove that I still loved her enough to do anything for her—even to my own detriment.

I was so lost in my own thoughts I didn't notice right away when her hips stopped writhing. I looked up and the tears rolling down her cheeks from my unspoken rejection were my undoing. Her head was turned, and when she wouldn't look at me, I knew she was thinking the worst.

Yes, Atlas needed relief, but she needed a gesture of my love even more. She wanted proof that I would walk through hell for her even now.

There was only one way I could do that without destroying all that was still good and pure in her.

"Fuck."

I moved my hand from her pussy and reached across her to snatch her phone from the nightstand. I unlocked it since I knew the code and went into her text messages. I quickly found the thread I needed and typed out a quick message before I changed my mind.

SOS. I need you.

FORTY-TWO

Atlas

HE'D PROBABLY NEVER LOOK AT ME THE SAME AGAIN. I'D OFFERED him my deformed soul, and he spat it back out.

I'd never been so humiliated.

My pussy didn't get the memo, though. I was still dripping, still aching.

The door bell rang over and over like the person at the door had no home training, and Rowdy bolted from the bed and the room like he couldn't get away from me fast enough. Shame spread through my limbs like a cold frost that would never end as I curled into myself and prayed for death.

I should go home.

I thought about calling my mom but knew she wouldn't answer.

She never answered.

But I missed her voice and warm hugs.

I was reaching for my phone when I heard voices downstairs. I only recognized Rowdy's.

The other voice was softer, lower.

I couldn't hear what Rowdy was saying, but I heard the front door slam closed moments later, and then unhurried footsteps on the stairs.

I didn't realize I was holding my breath until the bedroom door pushed open, and I looked over my shoulder.

My breath rushed out of me when the shadows from the dark hallway parted, and I saw who stepped inside the dimly lit bedroom.

"Ruen?" I slowly sat up, my gaze shifting nervously to the empty doorway behind her. "What are you doing here?" I paused. "Did you sneak in?"

"It occurred to me that you still haven't forgiven me," Ruen said as she took slow steps that carried her deeper inside the room.

She'd changed clothes since I saw her earlier and now wore black leggings and a purple long-sleeved crop top that stopped just under her small breasts.

"Fine. I forgive you. Now go before Owen sees you." There was no way he'd let her in here willingly. Whoever was at the door must have distracted him.

"So, is Jada Dorsey really your mom?" Ruen asked as she ignored my warning and gave herself a tour of the bedroom.

"I don't know."

Where the hell was Rowdy?

I strained to listen but couldn't hear a sound coming from downstairs. I knew he couldn't have left because he'd only been wearing boxers when he went to answer the door.

Ruen disappeared inside the closet, so I snatched up my phone and texted Rowdy.

Where are you?

Bubbles appeared, and I waited for his response, but it never came. I threw my phone down and stood from the bed just as Ruen stepped back into the bedroom, shrugging off her leather jacket and tossing it aside.

Um...

"What's going on, Ruen? Why are you really here?"

"Rowdy asked me to come."

"He asked you?"

"Yup." Ruen plopped down on the foot of the bed and patted

the spot next to her. My heart was pounding so hard that it echoed in my ears as I obeyed. She studied my face for a while and then said, "You've been crying."

I sniffled. "I do that a lot lately."

Ruen gave me a weird look. "You're not pregnant, are you?"

"God no."

Ruen nodded and grabbed her jacket from where she'd tossed it at the end of the bed and reached inside the pocket for a little baggie containing two rolled blunts and an assortment of pills in different colors, shapes, and sizes. "Want to tell me why?"

"Not really." I couldn't relive that shame twice.

"Suit yourself," she said easily. For once, I was glad that Ruen was an asshole. She didn't push. She probably didn't even really care. "Do you smoke?"

"Not really. Rowdy lets me sometimes but only with him and blunts that he rolled himself."

Ruen nodded, and even though I could see the sarcastic reply in her eyes, she kept it to herself as she removed two of the pills. I was startled when she placed them on her tongue since I was under the impression she only sold drugs. "Do you have music?"

"Sure," I said slowly. I stood and pretended not to feel Ruen's eyes on me as I went to grab my phone. "My Little Secret" by Xscape began to play while I quickly checked my messages to see if Rowdy had responded yet.

Nothing.

I sighed and returned to Ruen. "So—"

I wasn't prepared for her kiss the moment my ass hit the mattress. I gasped, and Ruen was ready for it. She slipped her tongue inside my mouth, and I felt one of the tiny tabs on my tongue for a split second before I swallowed it down.

"Ruen!" I broke the kiss and lunged away from her. My eyes bucked as I touched my throat as if it would stop the pill she'd slipped me from working its way into my system. "What the hell? What was that?"

"Molly."

I shook my head at her. "I should fuck you up."

Ruen gave me a small smile. "You can try." She leaned back on her elbows and my gaze was drawn to her taut stomach bared despite the cool weather. "Or you can fuck me instead."

"Look, you need to go."

She stood, and I backed away when she stalked me across the room instead of leaving like I asked. My back hit the dresser, making Rowdy's and my shit roll and rattle around on the surface.

"Ruen, for real," I demanded when she stood in front of me. "I already told you I'm not—"

She kissed me again, and I was trapped with nowhere to go this time. I was vaguely aware of her reaching up and removing my head scarf and then pulling the hair clips free, one by one, until my natural curls wildly framed my face and shoulders again.

"You told me what?" she teased between kisses.

"I don't like girls, and I'm not a cheater."

"You like me, though."

"As a *friend*."

"Then why are you kissing me back?"

I had no answer for that, and when Ruen pressed her knee between my thighs, I didn't fight her. The movement of my hips as I rode her thigh was so subtle, I didn't even realize I was doing it at first. The soft cotton of her leggings provided the perfect friction for my swollen clit.

"Do you remember that night we met?" she inquired softly. "How eager you were to let me play with you?" She softly cupped one of my tits though the tank and bent to lick my nipple. The sensation kicked up the tempo of my hips while Ruen moaned and stretched the neck of the tank until both my tits were spilling over the neckline. "I remember these," she said with a sly smile. "Prettiest tits I've ever fucked on." She bent again and suckled on my bare nipple, and because she was a little cruel, she bit them too.

"Oh, fuck." *Wait. What the hell was I doing?* "Um…no. We have to stop. Rowdy—"

"Isn't *here*, Twinks. I'm here."

I blinked down at her while she continued making love to my breasts. "He called you…"

"Mm-hmm," she confirmed.

"Why?"

Ruen let my nipple go with a *pop* of her lips and kissed me hard and fast. "So you could play with *me*."

"He wouldn't."

"A lot has changed, Twinks. He can't fuck you, and judging by the way you're ruining my favorite leggings, you need to be fucked."

"It'll pass."

"Maybe. Or maybe it will get so bad you won't care what ties might bind you."

I gulped. Do I tell Ruen that it had almost happened already? Apparently, Rowdy's will was stronger than mine—or maybe I just wanted him more than he wanted me. Maybe it wouldn't be long before he sought comfort elsewhere.

The thought had me lunging forward and stealing Ruen's lips. We kissed until our lips were swollen and we were panting for breath. My hands found her waist, and I tugged on the skin-tight cotton. "Take these off," I demanded breathlessly.

Ruen didn't hesitate before stepping back and peeling them off. The puffy lips of her pussy were glistening, telling me she came ready to be fucked, and I unconsciously licked my lips before the dresser bit into my back when she returned, shoving her knee between my thighs again while she straddled mine.

"Go ahead, Twinks. Use me."

I released a broken cry when my hips began to move once more, and I rode Ruen's thigh. She did the same, her wet pussy sliding along my thigh. The dresser behind us began to rock and bang against the wall from the force of our movements as we quickly lost ourselves in the delirium.

"God, you're so fucking sexy," Ruen said, groaning. She fisted my hair and yanked my head back, baring my neck for her hot kiss while groping my tit. I was no stranger to having my hair pulled during sex. It was Rowdy's favorite pastime while hitting it from the back. "Your pussy is so hot."

The last of my restraint melted away at the rough treatment, and I heard myself whisper, "You should put it in your mouth."

Ruen laughed and nipped my shoulder once before dropping to her knees. Her tongue softly flicked my clit, and I moaned as I shifted my feet apart to make room for her. I stared down at her gorgeous face as she pressed a kiss to my pussy and then another until my head fell back.

She was eating me out in earnest now, and my cries echoed around the room and through the open door. When her focus returned to my clit, she captured it between her teeth and gave it a punishing tug.

"Oh, *fuck*, Ruen!" Lost in the forbidden pleasure, I grabbed her hair and fucked her face when her tongue teased my hole. "Oh, my God, I'm going to come."

Ruen hummed her encouragement as she gripped my ass and pulled me closer.

A strange and synthetic sense of euphoria suddenly washed over me, and I rode her face as I chased my orgasm. "You like that?" I moaned deviously. "You like my pussy in your pretty little mouth?"

Ruen's knowing gaze met mine, and she gave a wordless nod.

The Molly had kicked in.

The feeling was so, *so* good, but it couldn't make me forget. When my eyes fluttered closed, all I saw was Rowdy's face. All I did was compare them, and when my walls contracted greedily, my pussy had never felt so empty.

I didn't realize I'd shoved Ruen away until my rising orgasm suddenly dissipated, and I opened my eyes to find her wiping her mouth with a raise of her brows.

"I'm sorry." I hurriedly righted Rowdy's ruined tank top, tucking my breast back inside and covering my bottom. "I can't do this, Ruen. I like you, but I *love* him."

It didn't matter that Rowdy had sanctioned this. He'd only done it because I'd pushed him into a corner—because he didn't think there was any other way. Once again, he had found another way to take care of my needs while I selfishly took and took and took.

I rushed out of the room, bottomless and barefoot, determined to find my man and drive all night if I had to.

But I didn't have to.

Because he'd been right here all along, downstairs, in the den, nursing a glass of whisky with his head bent, arms braced on his thighs, and his heart at his feet. He was now wearing sweatpants that he must have gotten from the basket of clean clothes I'd left in laundry room.

"Owen…"

"You good now?" he asked without facing me.

"No." I rushed around the couch and threw myself onto my knees before him—where I belonged and wanted to be. "I don't want her, Owen. I want you."

Rowdy gave a dry laugh and took a sip of his drink. "It didn't sound like it. Ya'll sounded lit as fuck up there." He eyed me over his glass. "I thought you only screamed like that for me."

My lip trembled as I gave a fervent shake of my head. "It was a mistake, Owen. I love you."

The Molly had me slurring a little, and I couldn't keep still. I was still horny since I hadn't come, so I ducked my head, trying to hide it.

Rowdy gripped my chin and lifted my head. He then planted a kiss on my lips, but when I surged up for more, he dodged me. "Don't trip, pretty baby. I'm not mad."

"Then why won't you let me kiss you? You're lying. I don't believe you." I balled my hands into fists. "Why did you bring her here? To test me?"

"Because you needed it."

"I needed *you*. I was ready to throw it all away *for you*. It's not just the sex, Owen. I feel like this gray space we're in isn't keeping us together. It's pulling us *apart*. I just wanted to know that you still loved me no matter what."

Footsteps on the stairs saved him from responding. Ruen appeared, fully dressed again and typing rapidly on her phone as she made a beeline for the door. "It's been fun, love birds." She didn't look at either of us.

"Aye, where the fuck you think you going?" Rowdy barked as he scowled over his shoulder at her. "You ain't done."

I sighed. "Just let her go, Owen. I'm okay now. Really." And I was sure Ruen was already feeling some kind of way—had probably been texting another hook-up to take the edge off.

Rowdy ignored me. Ruen ignored me. *Fucking assholes.*

Ruen paused, and I could see the wheels turning before she pocketed her phone and sauntered into the den with a smirk while Rowdy tugged me into his lap. His warmth enveloped me like a blanket, and I never wanted to leave.

"Did she eat your pussy?" he questioned. I nodded. "Did you come?"

I shook my head. "I stopped it," I whispered.

"Why?"

"Because I didn't want to hurt you."

Rowdy kissed my cheek while rubbing my arms. "There was no need. I trust you like a motherfucker, Dream. I wouldn't have invited her over if I didn't."

I chewed on my lip as Ruen sat on the coffee table. I could see it in her dilated pupils. She was still hot and bothered.

I felt the moment Rowdy's focus shifted to her. "Take all that shit off," he ordered gruffly. "My girl wants to see you."

Ruen's gaze didn't so much as flicker to him as she shed her leather jacket. She then stood and tossed it aside on the recliner nearby before kicking off her shoes. Her shirt followed, and I realized she wasn't wearing a bra when her small breasts and pierced nipples came into view. She pulled down her leggings without an ounce of shyness until she was fully naked.

Beneath me, I could feel the effect she was having on Rowdy. I released a shocked gasp as I peeked at him over my shoulder. "You're hard," I teased as I wiggled my butt. "Like what you see?"

He sucked his teeth. "She's aight."

I smiled softly and patted his cheek. "Good boy."

"Chill." To Ruen, he said, "On your knees."

My friend's gaze was sharp like daggers at Rowdy ordering her around, but then she started to lower to her knees when I said, "Wait." Ruen paused and looked at me inquisitively. "Switch places with me."

I felt Rowdy tense when I started to rise. He caught my hip and kept me still. "What are you doing, Dream?"

I peered over my shoulder at him. "Whatever I want?"

Rowdy's teeth sank into his bottom lip, and I knew he was biting off his response. He let my hip go, and I stood, allowing Ruen to take my place.

She hesitated, and they both stared at each other as if they'd rather invite Dr. Heiter over for dinner. Ruen was the first to break and slid on her mask—her infamous smirk—before plopping herself on his lap. She held herself stiffly, though, and Rowdy kept his hands to himself by resting his arms along the back of the couch.

It was a comical sight because they really couldn't stand each other. They were two alphas with no interest in taming the other.

"Now what?" Ruen questioned.

"Now we have fun." I slid my sweaty palms down my thighs. The truth was I had no idea what I was doing. I'd never had a threesome before, never imagined that I would. I could only follow my instincts.

It led me to Ruen's jacket, where I removed the small Ziplock bag. There were different color pills inside, so I grabbed the yellow one. The same one she'd given me.

"The pink one," she called out. I looked over my shoulder and found her wearing a crooked grin. "If you really want to have some fun."

It must have been a stronger dose.

I debated for a few seconds before retrieving the pink pill and placing it on my tongue.

Heading back to the couch, I planted my knees on the seat

between Rowdy's spread legs and my hands on Ruen's shoulders. I could feel my man's gaze on me as I kissed my best friend.

Holy fuck, this crazy bitch really was my best friend.

I didn't allow myself to think anymore as I gently pushed Ruen until her back was against Rowdy's bare chest. "Relax," I told her before meeting Rowdy's gaze.

He lifted his chin as if daring me not to back down, and I leaned over Ruen, her naked tits pushed against my cotton-covered ones as I kissed him.

And true to Rowdy Wray, it turned nasty quickly.

When he slipped me his tongue, I responded in kind, teasing it with my own and slipping him the pill. His eyes flared with shock and then amusement when he swallowed it down and kissed me again.

"Are you sure you're okay with this?"

Rowdy reached over and slapped my ass. "Do you, beautiful."

I smiled, straightened, and lifted the ruined tank over my head before tossing it aside. Ruen and Rowdy had mirroring reactions once my body was bare for their viewing pleasure. The former reached for my tits while the latter skimmed a hand over my ass. I ran my hands up Ruen's soft thighs while she squirmed in Rowdy's lap.

It was kind of hot—Rowdy supervising while we played together.

I kissed Ruen's lips one last time before I moved down her neck and inhaled her sweet scent. Her tits were practically singing to me, so I shyly darted my tongue out, and her breath hitched when I licked her nipple. Warmth pooled in my belly from making her feel good, so I did the same to the other before trapping the dark peak between my teeth and tugging until she cried out.

"I never took you for a sadist," she said breathlessly.

My gaze shifted to Rowdy when I replied, "I learned from the best."

He smirked and then shocked us both when he cupped Ruen's

tit and brushed his thumb over the silver bar piercing the nipple. "You missed one."

I held his gaze as I repeated my actions. Ruen nearly knocked me off the couch when she arched her back and moaned, so I sat in her lap to keep her still.

I wasn't sure how long I tortured her like that before I heard, "I think you got it, baby. Her pussy is dripping."

I released Ruen's nipple with a wet smack. "Oh." I giggled. "Sorry."

"Bestie, please." Ruen moaned with her eyes closed.

A rueful grin spread my lips as I reached between us and cupped her pussy. "Oh." I guess I had gone overboard. I curved my finger and slowly slid it inside of her. Ruen's walls immediately clamped around me. "She's so tight, Owen."

"Yeah?"

Recognizing that low tone, I tempered my smile and peeked from underneath my lashes at him. "Mm-hmmm. And warm." Rowdy and I kept eye contact as I inserted a second finger inside my friend.

Ruen was snug, but I knew she could take more, so I filled her up. I had no idea what Ruen liked, so I watched her face as I fingered her pussy, easing back whenever she tensed and speeding up when she fucked me back.

The house was quiet, so there was only the wet sound of my fingers plunging deep and Ruen's little cries as I pleased her. When I felt her contracting around my fingers, I snatched them free and quickly lowered to my knees on the floor.

I didn't hesitate before I brought my mouth to her pussy. I lashed at her clit with my tongue until she grabbed my hair and came with a choked cry.

I kept going, lapping at her sweet pussy until Ruen gave a keening cry and arched away from me. Rowdy, sensing that I was far from done, held her still for me.

"Hell yeah," he said huskily. "Clean that plate, baby."

I moaned and did exactly that.

Ruen tasted like rainstorms and heartbreak. I knew I'd never have another drop. After tonight, we'd return to being platonic friends who'd had one wild night together—hopefully, with no blowback. I trusted Rowdy and Ruen and they hated each other, so the chances of this ending in bloodshed were slim to none.

Ruen came again, and I took a page out of Rowdy's book and didn't miss a drop.

Finally sated, I licked my lips and sat back on my feet, taking in the sight of Ruen slumped against Rowdy and my boyfriend watching me with a look in his eyes that said he was close to losing control.

Close wasn't good enough.

"Your turn," I said. He frowned in confusion until I reached up and tugged at his sweats. Rowdy was no help, so I said, "Ruen, lift up." She was watching me now, too, with a matching furrow in her brow, but she caught on to my meaning faster and reluctantly lifted her hips with a twist of her lips.

While Ruen wasn't thrilled about the direction this night was going, she was curious and daring enough to play along.

It didn't matter what the challenge.

Ruen Quintana would die before she backed down first.

Together, we worked his sweatpants and boxers down his ankles while he cursed us both out.

"Ignore him," I told Ruen once we got them off. I reached into his pocket, pulled out the single foil packet hiding there, and lifted the condom up for them both to see. "He's full of shit."

I tossed his sweatpants aside.

Ruen looked over her shoulder at him with a brow raised. "Relax, Wray. I'm here to save this ship, remember?"

I gestured for Ruen to climb down, and once she was kneeling beside me on the floor, I wrapped my hand around Rowdy and spat on the head. I kept my gaze locked with his as I slowly stroked him just how he liked, and once his eyes started to glaze, I lowered my head and licked the tip.

It was all it took for his head to fall back, and the moment his guard was down, I took him in my mouth.

"Fuck, Dream," he half-scolded, half-groaned.

I moaned around Rowdy's dick, and at the same time, I felt his hand in my hair, ready to pull me away and scold me for crossing that forbidden line. At the last moment, he gripped the strands with a groan and forced my head down, making me take all of him.

I greedily hummed as I bobbed my head up and down. I was distantly aware of Ruen behind me, her hands nudging my thighs apart and me obeying. Ruen laid on her back with her head between my legs, and I lowered my ass down until I felt the first swipe of her tongue through my folds.

Ruen's tongue lashed my pussy until I was riding her face without abandon, and when I felt her tongue burrowing deep, I released Rowdy's dick and cried out, my nails digging into his strong thighs as if he alone could anchor me through this storm.

"Oh, fuck! Oh, fuck! Oh, fuck!" I squealed.

Rowdy leaned down and kissed my lips. "She eating that pussy right?" My brow furrowed with pleasure, and when words failed me, I nodded. "Better than me?" he whispered.

I pressed my lips to his in answer.

No, not better than him.

Never better than him.

Rowdy kissed me one last time before shoving his dick back into my mouth. This time, he took over, holding my hair with both hands and fucking my face roughly while Ruen ate me out like she was trying to find my soul with her tongue.

With nothing to do but take it from both ends, I closed my eyes and surrendered to them until starlight burst behind my lids, and I came with a scream that was muffled by Rowdy's dick.

A moment later, Rowdy was shooting down my throat and didn't release me until he was done.

We were silent for a while, all of us catching our breath.

Ruen was the first to recover and moved to the couch, where

she sat beside Rowdy. They were both watching me now, waiting for me to tell them if I'd had enough.

Not even close.

I grabbed the condom from the floor where I'd left it, ripped the wrapper open, and removed the rubber. Ruen didn't need any direction this time when I handed it over. She took it, a silent confirmation that she was all in, and placed the condom over his leaking tip before slowly rolling it down.

Ruen and Rowdy's inebriated gazes met, and, for the first time, there was no hostility as she gave him a few teasing pumps. Something passed between them—an agreement for a temporary truce, and I almost laughed.

It was obvious they were well and truly high if they were willing to leave their territorial bullshit behind for one night.

"Sit on it," I whispered when I couldn't take the anticipation anymore.

"Are you sure this is what you want?" Ruen asked me. She was giving me another chance to back out.

To be honest, I never thought I'd see myself dripping at the thought of watching another bitch ride my man. In some twisted way, I was taking back what Sutton and Sienna had stolen from me, but there was another reason too.

Rowdy and I wouldn't be in the gray anymore in a couple of weeks, and none of this would matter. We might never have this chance again—me and Rowdy…me and Ruen. None of us.

I decided to live for tonight and worry about the fallout tomorrow.

"I'm sure."

Ruen nodded and returned to Rowdy's lap, her back to his chest so she could watch me and vice versa. There was no hesitation this time when Rowdy grabbed his dick. I could feel his gaze on me as he swiped the head through her pussy lips, lubricating himself with her arousal before bringing the tip to her wet hole.

"Slow," I reminded him when he lifted his hips at the same time Ruen bore down. Rowdy was huge, and I didn't know how much Ruen could take. I'd been fucking Rowdy for months, and I still wasn't used to him.

And then there was the other reason.

I wanted to savor every moment of watching him split her open.

Ruen was a champ, though, sinking all the way down in one go. "Fuuuuck," she whined when her pussy swallowed all of him. Her drugged gaze met mine as sweat formed on her brow. "Bitch, you didn't tell me he was this big."

Her words sent a new wave of arousal through me, and my hand found its way to my pussy. "You're not going to walk straight for a week," I warned her. And then I met Rowdy's green gaze. "Does she feel good?"

"Hell yeah." And then, "You feel better," he mouthed to me.

I smiled softly at him while I rubbed my clit slowly. I didn't want to come again yet. "Fuck her, Daddy. Please? I want to see it."

"Yeah?" I eagerly nodded, my gaze shooting down to where they were joined when he gave a testing pump. My breath caught in my chest when I watched him sink deeper and Ruen's lower lips stretch impossibly wide to accommodate him. "Play with that pretty pussy but don't come," he ordered, knowing what the order would do to me.

Ruen lifted her hips and lowered them again. Over and over, she slowly sank down on him, her eyes fluttering closed once a rhythm was set, and they truly began to fuck.

My lips parted, watching the obscene vision Rowdy's fat dick tunneling in and out of Ruen made. I moaned every time he sank deep as if it was me he was fucking.

Somehow, through the sexual frenzy, I realized how different he was when he was with me.

Rowdy didn't kiss her, touch her, or say filthy words to drive her crazy like he did while fucking me. He didn't stare into her eyes or watch her take him like he was obsessed with her.

He was detached as he chased his nut—not because he didn't enjoy it, but because he didn't have feelings for Ruen. I suddenly understood what he'd meant when he said he'd saved that part of himself for me. None of the other girls he'd screwed knew what it was really like to be with him.

The only time he truly looked into it was whenever his gaze dropped, and he fell into a trance, watching me finger my pussy to the sight of them.

Ruen was much the same.

She focused on me as she rode my boyfriend's dick...for me. They were both determined to convince me that they would do anything for me but for different reasons.

It didn't take long before Ruen drew closer to another orgasm. My fingers sped up as I watched her small tits bounce from the faster tempo. Rowdy's balls slapped her pussy as he rose to meet her, and I felt my orgasm rising as they both chased their own.

"Goddamn." He groaned, slowly losing that tight grasp on his control. He wasn't so detached anymore as his balls visibly tightened, and he fucked her in earnest now.

"Fuck, yeah, just like that." Ruen moaned with her head tossed back and her hand on her clit rubbing furiously. "Don't stop. Don't stop. Don't stop."

"Oh, my God. Oh, my God. Yes, yes, yes," I cried as I thrust my fingers deep inside and mimicked Ruen's movements. I rode my hand with my gaze fixed firmly on their union so that I didn't miss one sordid second. They were close, and so was I. "I want it. I want it."

"Don't you dare come," Rowdy barked at me.

"But—"

"What did I say, Atlas?"

My throat released a plaintive cry, and at the last minute, I pulled my fingers free of my pussy just as Ruen exploded.

Once her orgasm subsided, she collapsed with a satisfied sigh. With Rowdy still firmly lodged inside her pussy, Ruen's eyes slowly opened after she caught her breath, and she stared at me. Waiting.

Sensing what she wanted, what Rowdy had denied her because it was too intimate for him, I rose and kissed her lips. Ruen licked the seam of my lips, so I parted them, tasting myself on her tongue and sharing Rowdy's with her as we teased each other.

Rowdy cleared his throat, so I quickly ended the moment before we both got in trouble.

"Enjoy yourself?" he asked when I shyly met his gaze.

"Yes, but you didn't come," I whined. Neither did I.

"I know." He gently lifted Ruen off his dick and then, not so gently, dumped her on the couch next to him. Ruen was too spent to do more than flip him off and close her eyes. Rowdy chose to ignore it and stood. "Come here."

I didn't waste time following Rowdy's order. I stood with his help, and then he lifted me until my legs were nestled in the crook of his arms.

I didn't realize his intent until his dick was at my hole, and he plunged inside of me.

"Ah!" I cried out sharply. It had been weeks since he was last inside me, but my pussy opened up like a flower in spring as he sank deep. Without stopping to give me time to adjust, Rowdy began fucking me fast and hard. "I th-th-th-thought we c-couldn't?"

Rowdy grunted and said, "I think we're beyond that now, Dream."

I squealed, my next words stolen from me when he pummeled my pussy even harder, the sound of our wet skin slapping echoing around the room. I tossed away all thoughts of this being wrong and lost myself in the euphoria of having him inside me again.

It had been too long.

How could this be wrong when all I felt was whole again?

"I love you," I managed to say to him.

"I love you too," he echoed gruffly. "Everything will be okay."

Relieved, tears spilled free, and I held his face between my hands as he fucked me and pressed my lips to his. Somehow, we ended up on the floor with me on top of him and Rowdy flat on his back as I rode him. Unlike with Ruen, his hands were all over me as if he needed to reacquaint himself with my body.

I felt eyes on us, and through the haze of sex and drugs, I turned my head and caught Ruen watching us.

A sharp bolt of shame shot through me as the intoxicated fog cleared enough for me to remember—to worry that she might be horrified and disgusted at the line we'd crossed.

But no.

That was her hand nestled between her thighs, matching our rhythm as she watched us defy right and wrong and choose love instead.

The high must have been coming down finally because I recognized that green feeling.

That possessive feeling.

I meant it when I said this was a *one*-time thing. I didn't have to question if Rowdy felt the same. I was not about to share my dick, and he was not going to share his pussy.

I tore my gaze away from Ruen before she saw my jealousy and looked down at Rowdy. He slapped my ass when I stopped bouncing, a wordless command to keep going, and then his hands tightened around my hips in a punishing grip when I tried to rise.

"My dick is still hard, Dream. Where do you think you're going?"

"I have to tinkle," I said softly.

Rowdy paused and stared at me a moment to see if I was serious before he blew through his nose and said, "Hurry up." Annoyed, he dropped his head back to stare blankly at the ceiling.

I shrugged and let his dick fall out of me. It hit his six-pack with a wet slap and bobbed in the air a little. "Okay, Daddy."

Scooting forward until I was straddling his abs, I wrapped my hand around his neck as if that would really keep him in place.

And then I went.

FORTY-THREE

Rowdy

I WAS STARING AT THE CEILING, WAITING FOR ATLAS TO GO PEE ALREADY, when I felt something warm and wet splash onto my stomach and then temper into a steady stream.

My shocked gaze flew to Atlas, who stared down at me with a feral look in her eyes.

I was confused at first, wondering if she'd lost control of her bladder, but no.

There was a possessive gleam in her eyes that I'd never seen before. Atlas had gotten jealous before whenever girls flirted with me, but never like this.

She'd never been driven to mark her territory so ruthlessly before.

I honestly couldn't decide whether to slap the shit out of her or throw her down and fuck her into a coma. I was still deciding when the endless stream finally stopped, and she tightened her grip around my neck.

"*Mine.*"

For the first time ever, I was stunned into silence and covered in Atlas's urine. I glanced down at my stomach to see some of it pooled in my belly button and the hard ridges of my abs, and then I slowly looked up at my girl. "Yeah?"

Atlas grabbed my dick, which had gotten harder from her possessive display, and sank back down on me. Confused over my warring reactions, I let her ride me and use me, my hips rising to meet and pummel her pussy until she came with a sharp cry and flooded my dick with ejaculate. She was still squirting when I grabbed her throat and slammed her onto her back hard enough to knock the breath out of her.

Ruen jackknifed into a sitting position as if to come to her rescue, but Atlas didn't need rescuing.

What she needed only I could give her.

"Assume the fucking position," I barked as I came to my knees above her. Clearheaded now, Atlas dragged herself from the floor, blinked, and then happily flipped onto her stomach and arched her back. Her pussy was swollen and dripping, and I wanted back in that in the worst way.

Atlas had reclaimed her ownership and now it was my turn. I palmed my dick at the thought of flooding her unprotected pussy with cum and gave it a punishing tug.

Movement to my right had me turning my focus toward Ruen, who was watching us curiously now. She was no stranger to unusual relationships since it was well known around the city that Ruen had two fathers. Her parents had been in some kind of weird throuple that hadn't ended with happily-ever-after.

Two of them were dead.

It was the reason she and her twin sister had different last names—Quintana and Trevorrow—to honor both of their fathers.

"Get out," I told her.

For once, Ruen didn't challenge me. I guess the night had gotten too weird even for her. She rose from the couch, threw on her clothes, and then, with one last look at Atlas—I guess to assure herself that her friend was safe—she left.

Once she was gone, I stood and left the room to make sure Ruen got to her car safely—not because I cared but because Atlas did—and then I locked the front door before returning to the empty den.

Atlas was gone.

I wandered ino the kitchen to replenish my fluids before heading upstairs. I found Atlas upstairs in our shower, waiting for me.

She gave me a tired smile when I joined her. Coming down now from the sex and drugs, Atlas looked like she could barely keep her eyes open. "I'm sorry I peed on you," she said as I closed the gap between us. "I don't know why I did that."

I crowded her against the wall and trapped her there for my kiss. "Yes, you do, and no, you're not."

"I got jealous."

"Me too."

"So listen, that was fun, but I'm okay if it's just us from now on."

Atlas had no idea how much I needed to hear that. It was a gamble inviting Ruen here. I didn't know if I was just feeding a monster or vanquishing it once and for all.

I kissed her again, and this time, it lingered. "Bet," I agreed when I finally came up for air.

We got out once we were clean and were going through our nightly routine once again when Atlas suddenly got a second wind and yelled, "The kit!"

She rushed out of the bathroom without another word, and after I finished brushing my teeth, I threw on some boxers and basketball shorts before following her downstairs.

By the time I reached the last step, Atlas was rushing for the front door with the sealed DNA kit in her hand.

"Stop right there," I ordered.

Atlas paused and turned to face me. "What?"

"What are you doing?"

She held up the box as if it were obvious. "Mailing this?"

"At one in the morning and in a towel, Atlas?"

She looked down at herself as if forgetting she was practically naked. "Oh."

I yawned. "Come to bed. We can mail it in the morning."

"No." She clutched the box closer to her chest. "I need to

do this now." She hurriedly shook her head when my lips parted to argue. "I can't explain why. It's just a feeling, I guess, but it has to be *now*. We both know what it will say, but I want *proof.* I want this to be over so that I can be free to love you the way God called me to."

"I understand that, baby, but everything is closed."

She held up the box for me to see the top. "Prepaid label. We can just stick it in the mailbox."

I didn't point out that it still wouldn't be collected until morning and just closed the distance between us before taking the box from her. I kissed her lips. "Okay, bae."

I sighed, slid my feet into my slides, and opened the front door. When Atlas tried to follow me out, I shut that shit down and sent her ass to bed.

As I walked to the mailbox at the end of the drive, I scanned the street out of habit and noticed a car parked three houses down that didn't belong.

It could have been nothing if not for my predator instincts kicking in and recognizing another trespassing on my hunting grounds.

I played it cool.

I stuck that damn kit inside the mailbox like my girl wanted and pulled the flag up before grabbing the spare gun I had taped underneath. Why? Because I'd be damned if I let a motherfucker catch me slipping while doing something as mundane as checking the goddamn mail.

I started down the street with my heat at my side but didn't get more than three steps before the car suddenly rumbled to life. The driver turned on their bright lights, making me lift my arm and turn my head away. The driver used that opportunity to escape with the sound of squealing tires.

When the car raced by me, I took note of the make and model. A sleek, silver Tesla.

I turned and lifted my gun to shoot out the tires but thought twice about it. Instead, I memorized the license plate, which was probably fake but worth checking into anyway.

After making sure none of the neighbors had noticed the commotion, I walked back to the house, checked all the windows and doors once I was inside, then climbed the stairs to my bedroom.

Atlas was in bed and curled on her side under the covers with her back to the door. I thought she was sleeping until I climbed into bed and pulled her into me with an arm around her waist.

"Is everything okay?" she whispered. "I thought I heard something."

I didn't immediately reply, so she turned her head to blink up at me sleepily. I just stared down at her pretty ass through the dark as I questioned for the first time if I could keep her safe.

I would, or I'd die trying and take whoever wished her harm with me.

"Everything's fine. Go to sleep with your nosy ass." I kissed her neck, and she smiled softly before closing her eyes and surrendering to her exhaustion.

My thoughts kept me awake for a few more minutes, and I didn't realize I'd fallen asleep until I was startled awake a few hours later by my ringing phone.

Groaning, I reached over and snatched it off the nightstand before answering it without checking the screen.

"This better be fucking important, and if it's not, or this is some bullshit telemarketer, I'm fitting to find your rude ass and knock your block off."

Atlas whined from where she had been cuddled beside me and turned over with a sleepy frown back to her side of the bed.

"Um…hello," the woman on the other line greeted. "I'm sorry to call so late. My name is Molly. I'm a nurse here at Ossella Memorial Hospital. Can I please speak to Owen Wray?"

"You got me," I rushed to say after I'd already shot out of bed and started finding clothes to throw on. My heart was pounding out of my chest since I had only one guess why and who they were calling for.

"Good evening, Mr. Wray. I'm calling because you are listed as the emergency contact for Kareena Beck."

"Yeah, um...is she...is she all right?"

Of course, the nurse wouldn't tell me anything over the fucking phone and simply urged me to get here as soon as I could.

"Fuck."

I hung up and, for a few moments, just stared through the dark at Atlas sleeping peacefully.

Unbeknownst to her, I'd been speaking to her mom almost every day and drove down there to check on her whenever I could without raising Atlas's suspicions. I just told her there was some rare car part I needed to pick up for the custom work I did on the side or an auction that was a few hours away.

Kareena had been no better but no worse, and just as I had begun to hope, this happened.

I didn't want to—wished that I could save my baby from whatever news awaited us in Ossella—but knowing time might not be on our side, I gently woke her anyway.

Of course, she had questions and complained about being dragged out of bed at four in the morning, but I ignored her and found some clothes for her to throw on.

There was no time to pack.

Ossella was hours away, so I just grabbed her purse, my wallet, gun, and keys before locking up and rushing us both to my car.

"Where are we going, Owen?" Atlas grumbled for the umpteenth time.

"I'm taking you home," I finally replied as I entered the interstate.

"Home?" Atlas frowned. I glanced over to see her studying the signs. She'd already figured out we were heading south. "You mean Ossella," she said in a flat tone. I nodded grimly. "Why?"

I reached over and took her hand in mine. "I have something to tell you, and you won't like it. You might even hate me for keeping it from you, but before I tell you, know I love you and am here for you. I got your back. You may not want me to after you hear what I have to say, but I have it nonetheless."

"Owen, you're scaring me. Just tell me."

Fuck. "Okay, I um…a few weeks after we met, I went to Ossella to figure out what you were hiding, and I…I met your mom."

"You met my mom," Atlas echoed. There wasn't anger in her tone, only confusion. "How?"

"I broke into your parents' house."

"You did *what*?" Before I could respond, she sucked in a breath. "What did you do, Owen? Did you hurt my mom?"

"Of course not," I barked before remembering everything I still hadn't said and checking my temper. "She caught me looking around, and I told her who I was. We talked for a little bit, and then she…she went to sleep."

"She went to sleep? A man my mom didn't know was in her house in the middle of the night, and she didn't call the police. She just went back to sleep?"

"Your mom is dying, Atlas." I knew nothing except the hard truth would help her understand. "She told me she was sick when we spoke. I think she was too weak to be afraid."

Atlas snatched her hand away, and I could only spare her a quick glance before refocusing on the road. "Sick isn't dying. Why would you say that?" When I didn't respond, Atlas's breathing became rapid. "Pull over." I kept driving. "Stop the car!"

Cursing, I slowed and pulled over onto the narrow shoulder of the bridge, thankful there weren't many cars out at this time of the morning.

Before the car even fully came to a stop, Atlas had her seat belt off and the door open. She bolted from the car, and I quickly followed, rounding the hood to reach her where she was bent over the railing of the bridge, emptying her guts. I held her hair out of the way and rubbed her back.

"Why didn't she tell me?" Atlas questioned after she was done. "Why didn't *you* tell me?"

"Your mom didn't want you to know, Dream. She didn't want to hold you back from living your life."

Atlas straightened and wiped her mouth. "That's bullshit. She's my *mom*. I don't *want* a life without her."

"I know."

My girl shook her head while staring off. "I never should have left. I should have fought harder. I should have—"

"You did the right thing," I interrupted. Atlas was already hurting and frightened. She didn't need to add to it. "Your mom didn't want you around to watch her die. She wanted to protect you. You both did what you thought was best."

Atlas sniffled and looked up at me like I was her superhero and she trusted me to save her from herself. "And now?"

"Now you leave the past behind you, and we go see what's up with your mom."

A fresh wave of tears came, but she nodded anyway and let me help her back inside my Charger.

The drive to Ossella was long but quiet since Atlas had cried herself to sleep. By the time we reached the hospital, the sun was coming up, and Atlas was just stirring.

She sat up, looked around, and frowned in confusion. I knew the moment she remembered where we were and why, just before she placed her face in her hands. Silent sobs racked her body, so I undid her seat belt and mine and pulled her into my lap.

Atlas immediately wrapped her arms around my neck and hid her face in my shoulder. "I never thought I would be back here so soon. My mom was all alone," she cried.

"It was her choice."

"I *left* her."

"That was her choice too."

"The hospital…they called you and not me. What if my mom still doesn't want me here?" I could tell she was beginning to panic again, so I rubbed her back to calm her down.

I already knew Atlas had serious abandonment issues. First, finding out she was adopted, then her father dying, and her mother pushing her away before finding her birth mother, only to be rejected all over again. And now us. I might have to walk away too.

"Kareena loves you. She won't turn you away."

Atlas didn't respond as she stared in the direction of the hospital. "Okay." She sniffled. "I'm ready."

I kissed her cheek and opened the door. "Whatever happens, Atlas, I got your back, and I'm not going anywhere."

A sad smile played on my baby's lips. "I know."

But everything was not okay. When we walked into the hospital hand in hand to face this new problem head-on, we discovered Atlas's mother had suffered a blockage in the brain and slipped into a coma.

FORTY-FOUR

Atlas

MY MOM WAS STILL IN A COMA AND SHOWING NO SIGNS OF WAKING up. By day eight, the hospital walls had started to close in on me. Rowdy had left for Idlewild this morning to grab us more clothes and make arrangements since it looked like we'd be here for a while.

He promised to be back tonight.

An hour after he departed for the long drive back to Idlewild, I left the hospital for the first time in a week to check on my childhood home.

It had been exactly as Rowdy described it—a husk of what was.

The first thing I did was call the electric company and get the power back on. It was shut off after my mom was hospitalized, making the home seem even more dreary. It must have been a slow day because the lights were back on within the hour.

I sorted the mail, cleaned the house, and paid my fourteen-year-old neighbor fifty dollars to cut the grass. Afterward, I took care of the other overdue bills.

My mom had no money since she hadn't worked since my father died, and the medical bills had eaten through their savings, so I used mine. I wasn't working as many hours now that I was back in school, but Rowdy had been padding my account on the low, so it was pretty healthy, leaving me plenty to spare.

Taking care of my mom's needs seemed like a poor substitution to if I had never abandoned her in the first place, but it was all I could do while I waited for her to wake up.

By the time I finished, the sun was starting to set. My phone rang, and I smiled when my man's name and picture appeared.

"Hey," I greeted after hitting accept. "On your way back?"

Rowdy released a heavy sigh. "Yeah, some shit went down, and I'm just leaving now. Don't wait up for me, aight?"

"Is everything okay?" He sounded tired and pissed off, but that last one was nothing new. "What happened?"

"Just some shit with Joren. I'll tell you when I get there."

I ignored the sudden hollowness in my gut, knowing it had something to do with me, and swiftly changed the subject. "Oh, did you check the mail?"

"Yeah." His tone hadn't changed, so I knew what his next words would be before he uttered them. "It wasn't there."

Rowdy and I were expecting the results from the DNA test any day now. It wasn't as if either one of us had been in the mood to fuck while waiting for my mom to wake up, so we'd completely forgotten about it.

"Just a few more days then."

"Yeah."

The heavy silence that followed said what we were both thinking better than either one of us ever could. The longer we waited for absolution, the more we lost hope. It was possible we were in the dying days of our relationship and would soon face the impossible decision of doing the right thing and letting go or living in sin.

My stomach turned at both possibilities.

I never thought I'd be here—actually contemplating incest.

My throat jumped when I remembered what we did a week ago, the risk we'd taken, and suddenly, I was racing to the half bath in the short hallway that led to the backyard.

There, I emptied my guts into the toilet. There, I cried for my and Rowdy's soul. And for everything that could have been.

Rowdy was still on the line after I brushed my teeth with a spare toothbrush and dragged myself out of the bathroom.

"You all right?" he asked me flatly. By now, we were both used to my random puking spells. This was the ninth time in a week.

Rowdy presented his shame a little differently. He avoided looking at himself in the mirror.

"Just a little tired," I responded. It was a lie and a terrible one. Exhaustion didn't make you lose your lunch. "I guess I'll see you when you get here?" I didn't know why I'd posed it as a question.

Perhaps, deep down, I knew that it was best for both of us if Rowdy turned around now and forgot he ever met me.

"Yeah. Talk to you later, baby." He paused and then added, "Love you."

My heart twisted in my chest for that moment of uncertainty—not whether he loved me, but if it was right to express it.

"I love you too."

The doorbell rang as soon as we hung up, and I sighed as I walked over to it. All day, I'd been subjected to well-wishing neighbors offering their prayers for my mom and me. I opened the door without checking the peephole, and pure shock at discovering my ex standing there was all that kept me from slamming it back in his stupid face.

Handsome but stupid and conniving nonetheless. I used to think I was lucky to be Sutton Hayes's girlfriend. He was Chris Brown's doppelgänger without the talent and all of the toxicity. He'd even dyed his hair blond and wore a goatee like the singer.

"What are you doing here, Sutton?"

"Well, damn. Hello to you too," he shot back.

"You have three seconds to tell me what you want before I make you tell it to the door."

Sutton sighed. "Look, girl. I didn't come here for all that. I heard about your mom, so I came to check on you."

"Now you care?"

"I always cared, Atlas. I just…" Sutton stopped himself from saying whatever was on his mind as he thought he could dig deeper inside a hole that had been refilled and cemented over months ago.

"You just what, Sutton? Not that I care, but speak your mind so you can go. That's obviously what you really came to do since I blocked you."

And not just his number but on social media too.

I'd been content with simply ignoring him, but Rowdy wasn't having it once I moved in, and he saw just how much Sutton had been blowing me up while pretending to be couple goals with my ex-best friend around campus and on social media.

"I loved you, Atlas. I still do. I just got tired of it being all about you, all right? I had problems too, but you never seemed to notice."

"And so you buried them in Sienna's corroded pussy? What a problem solver you are."

"Sienna was a mistake."

"No, *you* were the mistake."

Sutton slammed his hand on the door jamb, but I didn't so much as flinch. "This is your problem, Atlas! You run your fucking mouth too much instead of listening! I'm trying to apologize!"

I narrowed my gaze, wondering if I needed to have my eyes checked. I didn't know what I ever saw in him. "I didn't ask you to come over here. I didn't ask for your condolences, your regrets, your so-called love, your weak stroke, or your backward-fucking apology. I've moved on, and I suggest you run back to Sienna's loose pussy because I've already forgotten that God ever made you."

I stepped back to close the door, but Sutton simply followed me, attempting to muscle his way in.

"I'm not done with you," he told me.

"No, little boy, I'm not done with *you*," a menacing voice barked from behind him. My eyes widened, seeing Rowdy appear out of nowhere. Before Sutton could react, Rowdy had him in a headlock. The veins and muscles in his strong arms bulged as he lifted my ex off his feet. "I'm just getting started."

"Get off me!" Sutton strained to say as he flailed around before turning blue.

I was torn between giddiness at seeing my ex knocked down a peg or two and saving Rowdy from going to jail. This wasn't Idlewild, so while his infamous reputation had reached all four corners of Mississippi, his sway over the police didn't.

Rowdy looked at me while I was contemplating what to do. "Why is he here, Atlas?"

With a smirk, I crossed my arms and rested my weight on one hip. "It sounds like he wants me back, but I told him to give me a day or two to think about it."

"Don't play with me," Rowdy warned. It didn't escape my notice that he'd tightened his arm around Sutton's neck. "I'll dead his ass right here."

I cocked a brow. "And go to prison?"

"As long as you bring me that pussy every weekend, fo' shit sho'. Tell his ass bye, baby."

I gave a dainty wave of my fingers. "Bye, Sutton."

"Atlas, please," Sutton choked out.

My nose wrinkled at his pitiful begging, and I rolled my eyes. What a wimp. "Let him go, Daddy. I think he's got the point."

Rowdy dropped him, and Sutton hit the ground before scrambling to his feet and scurrying to his car. Rowdy and I cracked up watching his bitch-ass run over the curb and a few trash cans trying to get away.

We went inside the house once my ex was long gone, and Rowdy followed me into the kitchen, where I unwrapped and heated the dinner I'd made for him from the little food my mom had in the house.

"Thanks, baby," he said once I served him where he sat at the small table by the window.

I walked over to the cabinet and grabbed a glass and then the bottle of Hennessy from the stash my father kept before he died.

"I thought you said you wouldn't be back until late," I asked as I poured him a glass.

"I've been parked outside for the last hour. I wanted to sneak up on your ass. I knew your ex would hear that you were back in town and come creeping around to see you sooner or later."

I frowned at that. "You don't trust me?"

"I trust you more than I trust myself. I just wanted a chance to catch his bitch-ass slipping."

"Hmm. I saw the old pictures of him and me torn up in my bedroom. Did you have anything to do with that?"

Rowdy didn't bother to look up from his food when he answered. "Of course."

I shook my head and laughed but decided to let it go. Rowdy wouldn't give a fuck how I felt about it, and Sutton's bitch-ass wasn't even worth the argument. "I was just about to head out and get some groceries." Rowdy looked at me then, and I dropped my gaze to the floor and shrugged. "I…it's just in case my mom wakes up soon. I want to have everything ready."

Rowdy nodded. "That's what's up, and she will. You just got to keep faith, baby."

I sucked in a breath. "Yeah." I swallowed when it felt like my heart was in my throat. "Do you need anything from the store?"

Rowdy shook his head as he polished off the food he'd wolfed down and stood to clean his plate. "Need me to come with you?" he offered.

"No, I shouldn't be long, and I'm sure you're tired."

"Like a motherfucker," he admitted with a sigh.

"My bed is comfortable," I offered.

"You fuck your ex on that mattress?" When I said nothing, he gave a dry chuckle. "I'm good on the couch."

"We have a guest room," I grumbled. "There are clean sheets on the bed and fresh towels in the closet if you want to shower."

"Cool."

With nothing left to say, I grabbed my mom's car keys and headed for the garage. The store was only a ten-minute drive away, so I was there in no time. I hopped out, grabbed a cart, and started throwing random shit inside since I hadn't made a list.

"Damn it," I cursed when I reached the frozen food section and realized the store was out of my favorite ice cream. I stared through the glass door of the freezer contemplating another flavor.

"You should try the pistachio," a voice over my shoulder suggested. "It will change your life."

Immediately, I wrinkled my nose at that awful idea until I turned and saw the woman lingering behind me. She was dressed in her usual fashion—wide-legged dress pants, a frilly blouse, and heels. Since it was November, she'd paired it with a long trench coat and her natural hair pulled back in a bun.

"Professor Saunders? Oh, my gosh! Hi!" I said, rushing forward to hug her. She tensed, and I chalked it up to surprise before abandoning the idea and stepping back. Maybe I'd crossed some boundary I didn't know existed between us. Oh well. "It's good to see you. How are you?"

"I'm doing as well as I can. And you? I apologize if I've been distant lately. I've had a few troubles of my own."

"I'm sorry to hear that." Remembering Sutton's hateful words, I felt a little guilty. It seemed that every time Professor Saunders and I talked, the subject had always been about me. I hadn't intended it that way but she'd always been so curious, especially about my time in Idlewild. "You've been my center for so long that I'd be happy to return the favor if you want to talk about it."

"You're sweet, Atlas, but I think I'll manage."

I blinked, a little startled at her sudden coldness. "I-I'm sorry. Have I done something?"

Professor Saunders smiled, but it didn't reach her eyes. "Of course not. I had something very important to me stolen by someone I thought was my friend, but it's not your fault. It's just… human nature."

"I…yes…that does sound bad." I was really thinking, *What*

the fuck? It almost sounded like she was accusing *me,* but that didn't make sense, so I decided I must have misunderstood her. Either way, I was ready to end this awkward encounter. "Well, I better go. Lots of shopping to do and I didn't come with a list. I could be here for *hours*."

"I hope not. I'm sure your mother will be missing you by her bedside."

This time, I couldn't keep my bewilderment from my expression. "How did you know my mother was in the hospital?" Professor Saunders and I hadn't spoken in weeks.

She blinked and then seemed to recover. "I have a friend on the nursing staff at Ossella Memorial."

"Ohh...okay." But that still didn't make any sense. How did her nurse friend know that Kareena was my mom or that I was friends with the professor?

"Welcome home, Atlas. I wish you and Owen the best. I'm sure you two will be very happy together."

Owen? I'd only ever referred to him as Rowdy in our emails.

I watched as Professor Saunders walked away, set her empty basket aside, and headed straight for the exit without purchasing anything.

I waited for a beat, and then I did the same.

Outside, I watched her climb into a silver Tesla and drive away. Feeling my heart race, I rushed to my mom's car and didn't think twice about it before deciding to tail her.

FORTY-FIVE

Simone "Sissy" Saunders

"Okay, class. That concludes our lecture for today. Don't forget to complete this week's practice exam on Canvas. You'll be automatically bumped half a letter grade on your final if you complete each one. See you next week."

It was another half hour before the last student left and another three before my last class and office hours ended.

I was packing up my materials for home when the door opened, and Susan, the department chair for the arts and sciences, walked in.

"Hello, Susan. Did you need something? I was just about to head out."

"Good afternoon, Professor. I'm sorry to delay you, but this shouldn't take long."

I released a nervous chuckle. "Sounds serious."

Susan's expression didn't soften. "Yes, I'm afraid it is. I understand that two semesters ago, you had a student by the name of Atlas Beck."

I schooled my expression as I regarded the department chair. "I may have. I've had a lot of students, Susan. It's hard to remember them all by name."

"I see." Susan sighed as if she was disappointed in my answer.

"Well, you should know that I've received a complaint from the student's mother that you've had inappropriate contact with her daughter that involved exchanged emails and disturbing letters sent by you to Miss Beck."

I frowned. "Her mother contacted you?"

"Yes. This morning."

"Well, Susan, I find that to be pretty impressive indeed, considering Kareena Beck has been in a coma for the past week."

"And how would you know that, Professor, when, as you said, you can't recall having Atlas as a student?"

My skin flushed from my careless slip and I brought myself up to full height which wasn't much even with heels. "I'm not saying anything else without a lawyer."

Susan nodded. "That is your right. It is also your right to know that a formal investigation will be launched, and if there is any truth to these allegations, your position at the university will be in serious jeopardy."

"Well, good luck with that," I mumbled as she left my classroom.

I already knew they wouldn't find anything on my work email or computer, and that this would soon become nothing more than a black mark on my reputation.

Still, someone had to pay, and I had only one guess as to who was really behind this.

That deceitful whore who'd stolen my man.

I couldn't believe my eyes the day she walked into my class a year ago. I thought perhaps it was a cruel coincidence, but no. Her face had haunted me for twenty long years.

After thoroughly abusing my teaching privileges at the university and calling in a few favors, I discovered that Atlas Beck was the baby my best friend had given away.

I was the only one outside of Jada's family who knew about the baby since her parents had wanted to keep it quiet that their sixteen-year-old daughter had gotten knocked up.

I'd only seen the picture of the baby that Jada carried around once, but I could never forget those star-shaped markings or the feeling of utter betrayal from the boy I'd loved quietly from the sidelines.

It was bad enough that he'd fucked Jada, but to give her his child?

I couldn't forgive him. I wouldn't.

Until I realized the gift fate had given me. Rowdy would never see me as long as Jada had her claws in him. She'd been the only one of his numerous fuck buddies to last so long. Twenty goddamn years. It seemed nothing would free him from her spell—except proof of her betrayal. I couldn't be the one to expose her, of course. Too messy.

So...I sent Atlas to do my dirty work for me, and with all her emotional trauma, it had been all too easy. I just hadn't expected the bitch to go and fall in love with him first.

Now, I guess that young whore had found me out and wanted to play. Following Atlas to the grocery store had been stupid, but the cat was out of the bag now, so let the real games begin.

I had already begun plans to dispose of her now that she wasn't needed anymore. Rowdy and Jada were done, and I could step in to pick up the pieces without losing the only friend I'd ever made—even if it was someone as selfish and foolish as Jada Dorsey.

She'd known back then how much I liked Rowdy. I'd been stupid enough to confide in her many times, but she'd always laugh and tell me how I didn't stand a chance. And then, to throw salt in the wound, she went and fucked him and got pregnant.

After leaving campus, I drove straight home and went into my office. I then pulled out the elegant leather gloves and stationary I kept in my desk drawer. There was no more need for anonymity, but I still had one more trick left up my sleeve.

I hadn't counted on how devious Atlas was or her poisoning Rowdy's mind so thoroughly that he would defy the laws of nature just to be with her.

This was not the man I fell in love with. A man so sick he

would fuck his own daughter. It wasn't his fault. Like Jada, he just needed to be freed from Atlas's hold.

So I penned three letters.

One to Kareena Beck for if she ever woke up, another to the Wrays, and the third to a local radio station in Idlewild.

At the moment, Rowdy and Atlas were each other's twisted secret. Let's see their love survive their friends' and families' scrutiny—the *public's* scrutiny.

By now, they will have done a DNA test, but I wanted to be sure that once the results came back, they'd have no choice but to walk away.

I was sealing the last envelope when the doorbell rang. I left my office to answer the door and my knees nearly gave out when I found *him* standing on the other side.

"Rowdy?"

"Sup, Sissy? Did I catch you at a bad time?"

"N-no. What are you doing here?"

He shrugged those shoulders I'd always admired so much. I longed to feel them under my hands as he drove into me. "You kept saying you wanted to link up, and I was in town so…"

"With her."

"With who?" he shot back smoothly. "I'm here with you."

"I…yes." I ignored the nervous flutter in my belly and said, "Do you want to come in?"

"Cool." He moved closer to come inside, and the smell of his cologne almost sent me to my knees.

I backed away and watched him shut the door behind him. "Do you want something to drink?"

"You got Hennessy?"

"No, sorry. Only wine."

"I'll take some water if that's cool."

"Great. Make yourself comfortable. I'll only be a moment."

Rowdy went into the living room, and I rushed to the bathroom to check my appearance before going to the kitchen to get his water. "So, what really brings you here?" I asked when I joined him.

"What do you mean?"

"You never seemed interested before. You always ignored me."

"I had a girl, Sissy."

"Don't you still?"

"Keeping it real?" Rowdy eyed me.

"Please."

"It's not working out with me and her. Some shit went down, and I don't know if we can get past it."

"Oh, I'm sorry to hear that."

He chuckled and scooted closer with his arm along the back of the sofa behind me. "Are you?"

I laughed as well to hide my nervousness. "Not really, no. If we're still being honest, I always thought you and I had a lot in common."

"Word? Like what?"

"Um..." Rowdy's stare was intense while I struggled for something to say. "W-we grew up together."

"I don't know about all that, baby, but I definitely like what I'm seeing."

"Thanks. I...I had a lot of work done. I know you like your women to look a certain way, and I wanted to be perfect for you."

"Hmm."

I didn't know why, but I had a feeling I'd said the worst possible thing, so I quickly changed the subject. "You probably don't remember, but I used to write you letters in high school too."

"I know," he said, killing something inside of me. I'd told myself that he never responded because he didn't know who I was. Had I been wrong?

"Y-you never wrote me back."

"I didn't know what to say."

"Oh."

"I kept them, though."

And just like that, hope flared again. "You did?"

"Yup. My girl found them and threw them away."

That little bitch. I'd teach her. I had a particularly painful death in mind for her, and once she was out of the way, Rowdy and I could move forward. My plan hadn't gone as smoothly as I had hoped, but what did it matter now when Rowdy was here, sitting next to me, finally seeing *me*.

Rowdy put his hand on my thigh, and I tensed under his strong grip before forcing myself to relax. "So listen, Sissy. I don't have a lot of time. I have to get back before my girl notices I'm gone. You gon' bust it open for a real one or what?"

I was a little startled by his forwardness, but I recovered quickly and said, "I…if you want."

"Nah, that's not good enough for me. If you know me like you say you do, you should know I don't play games. Do you want this dick or not?"

I sucked in a breath as I stared into his green eyes. "Yes, I'd like to make love."

"Fuck," he corrected.

"Yes, I'd like to fuck."

"Cool. Go upstairs and take all that shit off."

I exhaled slowly and stood on shaky legs. I made it two steps toward the stairs when I turned back to find Rowdy watching me go with a blank expression. There was no lust in his gaze, but I was sure that would change soon enough. "What about her? Atlas."

"Let's just take this one day at a time. I need to see what that pussy is like first."

"Oh. Okay."

He gave me a closed-mouth smile, and I hurried upstairs. I wished I had time to shower the day away, but I knew a man like Rowdy wouldn't like to be kept waiting, so I quickly shed my clothes and threw on a red lingerie set. I then let my hair out the chignon and refreshed my lipstick.

I had only just positioned myself on the bed when I heard footsteps on the stairs. Rowdy appeared in the doorway a moment later, and then his gaze swept me and then the room as he prowled inside.

"Is all that for me?" he asked as he approached the bed.

"Yes. I bought it in your favorite color."

"My favorite color is green, baby, but I appreciate the sentiment."

My heart fell to my stomach. "Oh." Rowdy sat on the edge of the bed and then looked in my nightstand drawer. "What are you looking for?" I asked nervously.

He wordlessly reached inside and pulled out a pair of handcuffs. "These."

I frowned since I didn't remember buying them. I figured Greg, my husband and soon-to-be ex, must have left them behind, although we'd never used them.

How had Rowdy known where to find them, though?

"What are you going to do with those?"

He peered over his shoulder at me. "You'll see." I held my breath as I watched him stand. "Give me your hand."

I hesitated for only a moment before shaking my suspicion off and extending my arm. He secured it to the bedpost and then did the other. "You're still wearing clothes," I noted breathlessly. It was an attempt at flirtation, but I only sounded nervous. It was then I noticed *what* he was wearing.

All black—like a thief in the night.

For some reason, it sent a chill down my spine, and I tugged my arms, testing the restraints. I looked at Rowdy and the cold look in his eyes had me realizing what a stupid idea this was. "I-I changed my mind. I don't want to be tied up."

Rowdy ignored me as he started for the door. I sucked in a breath when he opened it. I was afraid I'd blown it and he was leaving until another figure, also cloaked in dark clothes but much smaller than Rowdy, emerged from the shadows.

The intruder pulled back the hood covering their head, and when I saw the face underneath, I opened my mouth to scream.

Rowdy had his gun out and pointed at my head before I could make a sound.

"Hello, Professor Saunders. Or is it Todd now since your husband left you for someone less psycho?"

My initial fear faded away as anger returned at seeing *her*. "I'm not the one who's sick, father-fucker."

Atlas's smile was a little too sharp as she gazed down at me. "You got me there, teach." I watched her walk over to Rowdy, who was leaning against my dresser, letting Atlas run the show. She gripped his black hoodie in his hands and forced his head down. Rowdy, still under her evil spell, returned the kiss she demanded. It felt like it went on for hours as they licked, sucked, and bit at each other. Finally, Atlas pulled away from the obscene kiss and looked at me. "But if you ever had that dick, you'd understand."

"You disgust me."

"Don't worry, Professor. I'll be out of your hair pretty soon." Hope speared sharply in my chest that I might get out of this alive until she said, "I didn't think you deserved to die. All you did was be a little messy over a crush, but Rowdy insisted since he doesn't like loose ends. You understand since I'm sure you were planning the same for me. Nice as I am, I actually convinced him to make it quick and was prepared to just let him put a bullet in your brain and be done with it…until I found these."

She tossed something on my stomach, and I looked down to see the letter I'd written to her mom, accusing her daughter of incest. Underneath it was the letter I'd written to Rowdy's parents with the same message and another to the radio station.

She sneered down at me. "I guess all's fair in love and war, huh?"

My lips parted, and I lay frozen while Atlas lifted the gasoline can I didn't know she was holding and tipped it over. I was helpless to move as she doused me in gas, so I screamed. I cried for help as loud as I could, not caring if Rowdy shot me. It would actually be a blessing if he did.

But he didn't.

I looked into the eyes of the man I had loved my entire life, and for the first time, I found a soulless monster staring back at me. He didn't love me, didn't care for me even a little bit. If only I had realized it sooner.

"A-A-Atlas…Atlas, please! It was never my intention to hurt you! I just wanted—"

"I understand, Professor. I used to think grief made you do things, but love…" She looked back at Rowdy, and he stared back at her, his green eyes softening as they watched each other. "Love will have you follow it into the depths of hell if that's what it takes."

She tossed the can aside and lit a match while my mouth parted in horror. Our gazes met briefly over the flame, and then she said, "See you in hell, Professor."

Atlas tossed the match, and all I knew was pain.

FORTY-SIX

Atlas

I BURST THROUGH THE DOORS OF PRIDE OF KINGS, ESCAPING THE FREEZING winter rain I'd traveled through to get here. Tuesday stared after me, wide-eyed, but didn't try to stop me as I went through the blue door that led into the workshop.

It felt like déjà vu.

"Owen! Owen! Owen! Owen! Owen! Owen! Owen!"

Big Punisher's "Still not a Player" was blasting through the speakers, but my voice still carried, drawing the attention of the other mechanics as I ran past their stations until I reached Rowdy.

Hearing me, he climbed out of the black Ford F-150 he was working on and caught me when I slammed into him.

"What's up, Dream? What is it? Someone fucked with you? Let me get my gun." I caught his arm when he turned to do just that.

So crazy.

I wouldn't have him any other way.

Panting, I wordlessly held up the sealed blue envelope I'd been clutching for dear life all the way from home. "It's here," I told him when I finally caught my breath.

"It's here," he echoed slowly, still not catching on. The light went off in his head when I nodded and bounced up and down on my toes. His next breath left him in a rush. "About fucking time."

What we thought would take weeks had taken *months,* and it was finally here. The answer to if God had either blessed our union or forsaken it. We'd already had our appointment with the lab and were still waiting for those results to reconfirm the ones that were already in my hand.

"Well, what does it say? Did you open it?"

"No. I wanted to wait for you." Our eyes met, and we both seemed to ask each other the same question. Do we, or don't we? "It worked for a while," I whispered eventually. "But we can't stay, Owen. We can't live in the gray. We don't belong here. I had a father. I don't need another. I'm going to love you no matter what."

Rowdy sucked in a breath, pushed me against the truck, and laid his forehead against mine. "And I'm going to marry you someday, Dream. No matter what."

I swallowed down the pain of the happiness his promise had evoked. "So we do this."

He pecked my lips. "We do this."

"Together."

"Together."

"What's going on?" Roc's nosy ass had ambled over before I could open the envelope.

A light bulb went off in my head, and I pushed Rowdy aside and thrust the envelope out at his boy. "Open this."

Roc's ignorant ass looked me up and down. "Your hands don't look broke."

"Just open it," Rowdy snapped.

Roc snickered and snatched it from me before ripping open the envelope. I watched his gaze widen when he pulled out the papers and realized what it was, and then they frantically scanned the page.

"Out loud!" Rowdy and I yelled at the same time.

By now, Golden and Joren had wandered over too. My heart was beating out of my chest, and Rowdy must have sensed it because he pulled me into him.

"Maybe we should do this upstairs where it's private?" I said when I noticed all the prying eyes of the other mechanics.

"Aye, ya'll clear the room for a minute," Rowdy ordered. The other mechanics and technicians looked at their bosses huddled in a circle and then at each other in confusion. "Get the fuck out!" Rowdy barked when they didn't move fast enough. I covered my face with my hand and shook my head while they scrambled for the door.

He was so damn rude.

"What does it say?" I urged once we were alone. Roc met my gaze, and my heart dropped at the look in his eyes, the contrition. "No," I gasped.

"Jada's your mom," Roc blurted. I leaned back against Rowdy in order to stay on my feet. He inhaled sharply and tightened his arms around me.

"And me?" Rowdy urged. "What does it say about me?"

"In the case of twenty-year-old Atlas Beck, Owen Wray... you are *not* the father!"

I pried myself out of Rowdy's grip and grabbed Roc's work shirt. "What did you say?"

Roc smirked. "He's not your pops, little sis. Congrats and condolences."

I screamed and threw my arms around Roc's neck, holding on for dear life when he picked me up and twirled me around and around.

"You two want to get a room, or can I have my fucking girl back, bruh?"

Roc sucked his teeth and called Rowdy a hater before letting me go.

I ran back to my man and wrapped my arms and legs around him. "I knew it," I cried as I kissed his handsome face all over.

"No, *I* knew it. Your ass was keeping me up, crying every other night," Rowdy said, putting me on blast.

"Shut up, Owen."

He set me down, and we both just stared at each other for a

long while until Golden cleared his throat. "Congrats," he whispered in his raspy voice before walking away.

Roc had already fucked off back to his station, which left Joren, who was wore a haunted look as he stared off into space.

His expression was pretty much how one would expect a person to look after they'd just been told the world was ending.

"Are you okay?" I asked him.

Joren's dark gaze that was so much like mine traveled to me, and for the first time, there was no animosity there. Only devastation. Regret. His lips parted, but when words seemed to fail him, he walked off.

Joren didn't return to his station, though.

He stormed from the workshop, and I gulped. After Rowdy and I returned from Ossella, Joren had attempted to talk to me a few times, to start over, but I'd made it clear each time that I wasn't ready. I wasn't sure I'd ever be. I couldn't forget the way he'd treated me, how many times he tried to convince Rowdy to cheat on me, or how eager he'd been to dispose of me after finding that photo. But...it wasn't *impossible*. Maybe one day I could forgive him for all of it, but that day was not today.

"Someone should probably make sure he's not about to go kill his wife."

Rowdy shook his head. "I doubt it. Jada left him after that night everything came out."

"Oh." My heart gave an unexpected and perhaps guilty twist. If I had never played Sissy's—Professor Saunders's—games, Jada and Joren might still be together. They still wouldn't be happy, but together and making each other miserable nonetheless. "I'm sorry to hear that."

"It will work itself out," Rowdy returned. There was still a lot of tension between Joren and Rowdy, who hadn't spoken to each other without coming to blows since Rowdy confessed to fucking Joren's wife for their entire marriage.

"Like we did?"

"Yeah," Rowdy absently said as he looked around and then

opened the back door of the pickup truck. "Hop in for a second. I want to talk to you about something."

"Okay." I didn't think twice about it before I climbed into the back seat. Rowdy followed, slamming the door shut behind him. "So, what did you want to talk about?" I asked from the other side of the truck.

He jerked his head in his direction. "Come closer so I can tell you."

Still riding the high of knowing nothing stood in our way anymore, I was slow to recognize that look in his eyes. "Really, Owen? I'm not fucking you in some random's truck with other people around."

"That's cool, baby. We can fuck at home later with your mom down the hall listening to you ride my dick."

Shit.

I'd forgotten about my mom.

After she'd woken up from her coma and the doctor cleared her for travel, Rowdy and I packed my mom up and moved her in with us.

She had been hesitant to leave the home she'd shared with my dad, but she was also in the final stages of her life, and mine was here, hundreds of miles away. It hadn't taken much begging and pleading for her to decide it was more important to spend the time she had left with me than in that empty house alone with old memories.

The days following her waking up had been the hardest.

"You're really here," my mom whispered as soon as she regained the use of her voice.

"Yes, mommy. I'm here, and I'm so sorry that I left. I'm sorry I didn't fight harder."

"You've been fighting for so long, baby. I just wanted you to live your life."

"I only have a life worth living because of you and Dad. I was just so angry that you didn't tell me the truth, and now, all I wish is that you hadn't."

"I missed you every single day," my mom told me.

"And I'm never leaving you again. I want to be with you every single day for however long we have left."

Our relationship was still healing, but we were making progress, and I thanked God every day that He hadn't punished me for what I'd done to Sissy by taking my mom away. I knew it was only a matter of time before I had to say goodbye, but we'd been given the gift of a second chance, and I didn't want to squander it.

As for Professor Saunders, I never allowed myself to think about her. I'd known what I wanted to do the moment I followed her home, the moment I told Rowdy everything I suspected and we broke into her house and found the evidence—the emails exchanged between us on her computer, the stationary in her desk, the pictures of them from high school. Rowdy had no idea the professor I'd spoken so highly of had been Sissy, Jada's best friend.

After I killed her, Rowdy made me go to therapy—for that and for so many things—my father's death, my self-destructive behavior, the lake, my fear of abandonment, him…us.

The sessions were helping, but I didn't think I could ever go back to that innocent girl I'd once been, and I wasn't sure I wanted to. If this experience had taught me anything, it's that a little darkness was necessary to survive in this world.

And with Rowdy guarding my back, loving me in that unrelenting way of his, I never had to feel alone again.

"Okay, but make it quick." I dove into Rowdy's lap, his hands all over me, and my lips all over him as I reached for his belt buckle. My jacket and jeans were quickly shed, and my thong shoved aside as Rowdy got his dick in position.

"Goddamn, Dream." He grunted when I slowly sank down on him. "You make me want to put a baby in you when you sit on it." The sound of his palm slapping my ass echoed around the quiet truck.

"Not until I finish s-school," I reminded him.

"Yeah, yeah, yeah," Rowdy grumbled as he thrust into me. "I heard your lying ass the first nine times."

EPILOGUE

Rowdy

"ME FUCK UP."

I cracked an eye open and turned my head slightly to see a miniature version of myself, green eyes and all, standing next to the bed. His head barely crested the top of the mattress while he glared at me like he was ten feet tall. He still wore his T-rex pajamas and was holding his favorite cup in one hand and a book in the other.

"Me fuck up," Cooper said again when he saw that I was awake now.

I blinked and blinked again before sitting up and swinging my legs over the side of the bed. "The fuck? How did you get out of your crib?"

"Me fuck up."

Shaking my head, I grabbed my phone to check the time. "Shit." It was after ten in the morning, but since it was Sunday, I had the day off—at least from work. My chaotic home life, however, was a different story.

Atlas must have known I was exhausted and had let me sleep in.

After reopening Harry's, I'd gotten that itch to expand my

empire and make sure any kids Atlas and I had together would want for nothing even after I was gone.

I'd bought out the vacant properties on Temperance Street and opened a second shop specializing in customizing cars as well as a tire shop. I'd leased out the other properties, and now there was also a tattoo parlor, barbershop, nail salon, and hair depot bringing life back to that once dying corner of Idlewild.

Atlas had convinced me to partner with Demi on the latter, and I admit it had been smart as fuck since it was next door to Demi's salon, and I knew nothing about weave or selling it. To my utter fucking annoyance, those two had become thick as thieves after finding out they were second cousins, and now it was Demi this and Demi that—and vice versa.

Atlas had finished her fellowship training not too long ago and was now working for a practice in the city until she was ready to start her own.

I yawned and stared at my son as I listened to the pure chaos happening on the other side of the cracked bedroom door. "Where's Mommy, Coop?"

"Me fuck up," my son repeated louder this time.

"Aye, watch your mouth, boy."

"Me fuck up."

"You got me fucked up," I said, frowning now. "What did I tell you about repeating what Daddy says?"

"Me fuck up."

"Say it again, and no story for you."

Cooper glared but was silent as I picked him up and placed him on my lap. He handed me the book I'd just read to his ass last night and rested his head against my chest as I began to read.

I used to do the funny voices and try to make it fun like I had my other kids who had eaten that shit up at his age, but Cooper would just mean mug me until I stopped and read normally. Even now, he frowned at the page in concentration while I read as if there would be a test after, and he didn't want to fail.

Once I finished, I carried him into his room, where I gave

him a bath and put him in his play clothes. He was more settled now that he was getting what he wanted. My youngest was a bit of a control freak and didn't like to stray from his routine *at all.*

He woke up at the same time every day and liked a book before his bath, then juice, playtime, nap time, another fucking book, juice, playtime, nap time, and…you get the idea.

If we deviated from that routine even slightly, he'd get upset and tell us we had him fucked up.

His mother hadn't found that as funny as I did when we first heard him say it and would catch an attitude with me every time. Now I couldn't get his ass to stop.

I was carrying Coop out of his room to go downstairs for his juice when the door across the hall flew open. "Ooh, Dad, you're awake! Can I have twenty dollars?" my begging-ass daughter asked.

"For what, Yas? And why didn't you get Coop out of bed? You know how he gets."

My eldest shrugged and crossed her arms. "I didn't know he was awake. He wasn't even crying." Because Coop never cried. He just sat and plotted his revenge like a psychopath in the making. "I need the money because my school trip is tomorrow, remember?"

"Nope," I lied and kept walking. I had no doubt she'd already fleeced the money from her mom. Just the other day I saw her lift a hundred out of Joren's wallet when he came over to watch the game.

I swore my damn kids were some crooks.

Two more of them appeared out of nowhere as I started for the stairs.

"Hi, Daddy!" Malayah, my youngest daughter and only semi-good child, greeted me as she raced past.

"Yeah, what's good, homie?"

I stopped and spun around to regard my eldest son. "Excuse me, little boy?"

"I meant, good morning, Pops!" Sincere darted into his room and slammed the door behind him.

Coop and I went downstairs, where I sat him at the table and gave him juice and dry cereal before continuing my search. I checked the living room, where I found two more of my kids. Kyreem was standing against the wall wearing a devious grin as if there weren't three steak knives embedded in the wall next to his head, while Kashton held a fistful of knives in one hand and was frowning in concentration as he held one raised in his other hand.

I quietly backed out of the room, shooting a text to Joren as I passed by the stairs. I stopped and turned when I heard a crash and saw another one of my damn kids tumbling down them before landing at the bottom.

Zuri started crying when she noticed she had an audience, but I paid her no mind and kept going as I wandered over to the panoramic sliding door overlooking the backyard.

I scanned the huge space until I found her.

Sitting at the edge of the pool with her back to the house and her legs swishing through the water was Atlas.

After we had our second child, I packed my family up and moved us into a larger house at the edge of the city limits where I knew we'd have room to grow.

I slid the door open and stepped out while she peered over her shoulder and smiled when she noticed me.

More than a decade had passed since we met, but when she looked at me like that, I still saw that nineteen-year-old girl that gave me hell and turned my life upside now—in the best way.

"Damn, baby," I grumbled as I took a seat next to her. "This shit is getting out of hand. I think we need to send those damn kids to disciplinary camp or something. We're not the Addams."

"There is no such thing as disciplinary camp, Owen. *We* were supposed to discipline them."

I looked at her like she was crazy. "I tried to, remember? You said I couldn't threaten to shoot them motherfuckers anymore."

She giggled and laid her head on my shoulders with a wistful sigh that said she knew I would never change and loved me more for it. "Because your kids thought it would be fun to get shot and would always dare you to do it. They wanted to have bullet holes like their daddy."

"What the fuck were we thinking, bae? Seven is too fucking much. I'm fitting to drop their asses off in the middle of the hood and leave them there."

"Says the same man who whines and complains when one of them tries to spend the night elsewhere."

"I don't *whine.*"

"Remember that time Malayah had her first sleepover, and you ruined it by breaking into her friend's house in the middle of the night, scaring that little girl's parents half to death, and bringing Yah-Yah back home because you said you couldn't sleep without your daughter under your roof?"

"Stop bringing up old shit, Atlas. That was so long ago."

"That was last month, Owen."

A piercing scream rent the air from inside, and we both looked back at the house before staring at each other.

"Not it," we both said at once.

"Hmm…maybe we should call Joren to come babysit?" she suggested.

Remarkably, he was the only who could get those demons of mine to behave. They loved their G-Pop, as they called him, and I hated to think that if it hadn't been for Atlas's and Joren's capacity to forgive—each other and me—my kids wouldn't have known what it was like to have him in their lives.

"As usual, I'm already three steps ahead of you. He said he'll be here in an hour."

Atlas tapped her chin thoughtfully. "I figure we have a few more minutes before one of your kids suffers severe mutilation or death."

When I recognized the look in her eyes, my teeth sank into my bottom lip. "What should we do with that time, wife?"

Atlas slowly lowered into the water, and I spread my legs to make room for her when she reached for my shorts. "I have a pretty good idea, husband."

I caught her chin when her hand dipped inside and wrapped around me. Eyes bright with mischief, she looked up at me. "I know we met because of grief, but have I ever thanked you for finding me, Dream?"

"Yes." She blushed. "All the time."

Smiling, I leaned down and kissed her lips. "Get used to it."

AUTHOR'S NOTE

I questioned so many times if I was actually going to go through with this. It's been a journey. Two-and-a-half years since I last published. I've struggled creatively ever since. I always try to outdo myself with each book, but after the wildfire success of Lilac, it seemed impossible. I've been working on In the Gray for over a year—by far the longest I've worked on any story—and while I'll miss these characters immensely, my relief to be done is like a breath of fresh air. In the Gray has worn many faces, titles, and themes, but the only constant in this book was Rowdy. No matter how many times I switched directions (even heroines) or rewrote the beginning, he remained the same—as wild, unpredictable, and unfiltered as ever. I love him so much. I haven't been this attached to a character since Keiran. When I first sat down to write In the Gray, the trope was simply Dad's Best Friend. This was back when Ruen was the heroine (yup) and there was no Unrequited or sinister plot lurking in the background. Yes, I pulled a Fear Me and The Prince and the Pawn and changed the heroine. Ruen seemed too large for this story. I had bigger plans for her, and still do, but we'll get into all of that later. Rowdy needed someone to settle him, and Ruen would have only stoked the fire. Atlas needed someone who couldn't live without her, and Rowdy had no intentions of letting that happen. I have no regrets.

After that plot twist, I bet you're wondering, "What the fuck, BB?" Did you see it coming? Some might have, and that's okay. It means you had time to get out before you got too deep. I stepped out of my comfort zone for this one and figured if I'm going to come back, it might as well be with a bang. It's ironic how I couldn't complete Rowdy and Atlas's story until it took a darker turn. Once I set my mind on this new direction and new challenge, it was full steam ahead.

Even in the most corrupt stories, however, there is always a lesson to be learned. Love doesn't always appear in black and white. It gets messy, it gets gray, and sometimes it will even make you abandon your morals completely. I hope we're all lucky enough to find someone we're willing to let the world burn for.

Until next time, Reiders.

-BB

ALSO BY B.B. REID

Broken Love Series

Fear Me

Fear You

Fear Us

Breaking Love

Fearless

Stolen Duet

The Bandit

The Knight

When Rivals Play Series

The Peer and the Puppet

The Moth and the Flame

Evermore (novella)

The Punk and the Plaything

The Prince and the Pawn

Standalone

Lilac

The Wrong Blue Eyes (novella)

In the Gray

CONTACT THE AUTHOR

Follow me on Facebook
www.facebook.com/authorbbreid

Join Reiderville on Facebook
www.facebook.com/groups/reiderville

Follow me on TikTok
www.tiktok.com/@bbreid

Follow me on Twitter
www.twitter.com/_BBREID

Follow me on Amazon
http://bit.ly/amzbbreid

Follow me on BookBub
www.bookbub.com/authors/b-b-reid

Follow me on Instagram
www.instagram.com/_bbreid

Subscribe to my newsletter
www.bbreid.com/news

Visit my website
www.bbreid.com

ABOUT B.B. REID

B.B. Reid is the author of several novels including the hit enemies-to-lovers, Lilac. She grew up the only daughter and middle child in a small town in North Carolina. After graduating with a Bachelors in Finance, she started her career at an investment research firm while continuing to serve in the National Guard. She currently resides in Atlanta with her moody cat and enjoys traveling, period dramas, and binge-eating Häagen-Dazs chocolate-chocolate chip ice cream.